W9-BBC-556

# THE
# NOH
# FAMILY

Grace K. Shim

Kokila

KOKILA
An imprint of Penguin Random House LLC, New York

First published in the United States of America by Kokila,
an imprint of Penguin Random House LLC, 2022

Copyright © 2022 by Grace K. Shim

Penguin supports copyright. Copyright fuels creativity, encourages diverse voices,
promotes free speech, and creates a vibrant culture. Thank you for buying an authorized edition of this book and for
complying with copyright laws by not reproducing, scanning, or distributing any part of it in
any form without permission. You are supporting writers and allowing
Penguin to continue to publish books for every reader.

Kokila & colophon are registered trademarks of Penguin Random House LLC.

Visit us online at penguinrandomhouse.com.

Library of Congress Cataloging-in-Publication Data is available.

Manufactured in Canada

ISBN 9780593462737 (HARDCOVER)
1 3 5 7 9 10 8 6 4 2

ISBN 9780593532324 (INTERNATIONAL EDITION)
1 3 5 7 9 10 8 6 4 2
FRI

Design by Jasmin Rubero
Text set in Basilia Pro

This book is a work of fiction. Any references to historical events, real people, or real places are used fictitiously.
Other names, characters, places, and events are products of the author's imagination, and any resemblance
to actual events or places or persons, living or dead, is entirely coincidental.

The publisher does not have any control over and does not assume any responsibility
for author or third-party websites or their content.

*To the family I was born into:*
*Mom, Dad, Sue & David—if I had the choice,*
*I would choose you every time.*

# CHAPTER 1

Next to kimchi, Koreans have perfected one other thing: The Dramatic Pause. It's that moment right after an epic reveal that lasts only a minute but stays with you forever. After bingeing countless hours of K-dramas, I have yet to find one episode that doesn't have The Dramatic Pause. It's like the Lee Min Ho of K-dramas; it never gets old.

I have somewhat expertly (see aforementioned amount of episodes watched) broken down The Dramatic Pause into three broad categories:

(1) The good: Two star-crossed lovers finally meeting face-to-face after missing each other one too many times. Often in the rain and almost always without an umbrella. (Swoon.)

(2) The bad: The main character finding out they lost their entire family fortune in a terrible economic investment and are now destined to a life of destitution and degradation. (The shame!) Extra pause if this was orchestrated by their best friend, who secretly hates them because they are embroiled in a love triangle.

(3) The unexpected: The main character discovering that their father is not actually their father and that their

life is about to change . . . *dun. Dun. DUN!* (Like in the episode Hazel and I are watching now.)

Every Friday after school, Hazel, Seb, and I have a standing appointment to binge K-dramas at my house. Since today is graduation, I wasn't sure if they'd be able to make it. But here we are, crammed onto my twin-sized bed, watching a much-needed episode of the K-drama *My Professor, My Father* on Hazel's laptop.

Since Seb likes to pretend he isn't into K-dramas like Hazel and I are, we sent him on a very important errand that should take precisely three minutes.

"Chloe Chang! Some of us have to read the subtitles." Hazel taps me on the shoulder. "Any closer and you'll be in the screen."

I give her a pointed look. "Just because I'm one hundred percent Korean doesn't mean I don't have to read the subtitles either." Technically, not quite 100 percent Korean, but close enough.

"Okay, but . . ." She motions at the space I'm taking up, which happens to be in direct view of her screen. I scoot back, only mildly embarrassed. As my best friend since forever, Hazel knows I lose all sense of time and space when it comes to Dad discoveries.

We would've been less cramped at Hazel's, but she has five sisters (yes, five), each with very strong and very different opinions about everything. Even though she lives in a six-bedroom McMansion, Hazel claims there isn't enough space to avoid what she calls the ¡Qué quilombo!, or the shit show of personalities. Real-life drama, Hazel claims, is not as much fun as K-drama.

When I inch closer to the screen again, Hazel shoots me a dirty look.

"You're doing it again! Great, now I missed what he said!"

"He said he can't believe that all this time, his professor was his father!"

"Oh my god! Finally!" She squeals with me.

Then it comes: The Dramatic Pause.

We hold our breaths and watch as if in a trance as the camera pans from one character to the other. Cue the surprised look on their faces. Cue the single-tear trickle. Cue the original soundtrack. *Ugh.* Even when I know to expect it, it gets me. Every. Time.

Then, as we knew it would, the episode ends abruptly, leaving us completely hanging.

"Noooo!" I yell up at the ceiling.

"Arrghh! Why do they always do that?" Hazel protests with her fist in the air.

I smile at her ridiculously. Hazel and I have reached that level of obsession with K-dramas where we've started to mimic their exaggerated reactions ourselves. "How much time do you think we've wasted watching K-dramas?" Just hours after our last day of high school, and already I'm feeling nostalgic.

"Wasted? Omo!" she gasps with a hand to her chest. "You mean invested." She checks her phone and says, "And for the record, according to MyDramaList, we've watched five hundred and sixty episodes, which is roughly twenty-three days of continuous viewing. I have no regrets."

I laugh. "You're right. It was totally worth it." We lie

side by side on my bed, staring up at the popcorn ceiling. All those memories of Hazel, Seb, and I holed up in my room bingeing K-dramas will somehow have to sustain me for the next four years without them. Pretty soon, Hazel and Seb will be off to California.

While I'll still be here, in same old Oklahoma.

Seb walks in right in time with some comfort food.

"Did someone order a bowl of Shin Ramyun?" He sets down a tray with two steaming Styrofoam bowls of instant noodles on my desk.

We don't dignify his question with a response and instead grab our bowls, snapping our wooden chopsticks apart. Seb knows that when it comes to the Shin, we don't joke.

"Sebastian Elias, you are the best." Hazel gives Seb a quick peck on the lips before mixing her noodles around with her chopsticks.

How do I feel about my best friends suddenly having feelings for each other? *Psshhhh* . . . totally fine.

And, at the same time, not fine at all.

The three of us have been hanging out together since middle school, geeking out over our shared interests in fashion and TikTok dances. The summer before junior year, however, Seb grew five inches, developed muscles, and basically became objectively hot. He was the same Seb to me, though. The brother I never had. I thought Hazel felt the same way about him, until they came out to me as a couple at the beginning of our senior year. I should be used to it by now, everyone moving on while I'm standing still. Story of my life.

4

We both take turns inhaling the noodles, then coughing up the spicy soup base that somehow always goes down the wrong pipe.

"Whoa, heavy episode? You guys seem slurpier than usual today," Seb says.

"It's been a day," I manage to say while chewing the noodles. "Just glad it's over." Big events, the ones where families are expected to attend, send my nerves into hyperdrive. Maybe it's because I don't have a "normal family" like everyone else. My dad was killed in a car accident less than a year after my parents left Korea, which changed everything for my mom, who was six months pregnant with me at the time. Now, she's all the family I've got. I swear, my life sounds sadder than a K-drama when I think about it.

"Hey, I'm sure your mom will make it up to you. She always does," Hazel says, setting her chopsticks down and putting a hand on my shoulder.

"Theresa Chang may not be around to make the Shin–," Seb says, motioning to the bowls of noodles.

"Or come to graduations," I mutter loudly.

"But"—Hazel smiles with her head cocked to the side—"you know she loves you."

"Yeah, I guess." Other than my mom, Hazel and Seb know me better than anyone. They know that sometimes when Mom's at the hospital, she just plain forgets about everything, even me. Like the time she couldn't make my eighth-grade art exhibition where I showcased my first fashion designs, or the school performance where I played the role of Chip in *Beauty and the Beast*, or parent-teacher conferences—every one of them. I know it sucks now, but Hazel and Seb are right. Mom might have missed my high school graduation, but I know it doesn't mean she doesn't love me.

We're like the Korean Gilmore Girls, except without the cute boyfriends and rich grandparents. So, like, the poor, lonely reboot version.

"I was kinda hoping Ted Takahashi would show up." Hazel nudges me, snorting.

"Whatever happened to the 23andMe test we got you?" Seb asks.

"Oh, that," I say, setting the bowl of Shin Ramyun aside.

It was last year that Seb first noticed my uncanny resemblance to Ted Takahashi, the weatherman on our local newscast. Seb wasn't totally off base—I look nothing like my mom, while Ted and I have the same widow's peak hairline and almost identical low-bridge noses and full lips. Since I don't know anything about my dad, we convinced ourselves that I must be Ted's daughter. Anyway, Seb and Hazel got me one of those DNA kits for my eighteenth birthday back in March. It wouldn't exactly confirm whether Ted Takahashi is my dad, but it would at least point me in the right direction, since Mom is Korean and Ted Takahashi is proudly Japanese.

The test was supposed to be a joke, but to be honest, I wanted it to be true. Not that I dream of being the illegitimate daughter of Ted Takahashi. But lately, I've been feeling a bit, I don't know, left behind. I always felt different next to Hazel and Seb, who both have these big families with not only a mom *and* a dad, but also siblings and cousins. Over time, there were other glaring differences. Like when Seb joined a robotics club and Hazel enrolled in a film class that took up their spare time. I tried to ask my mom about taking fashion design classes, but if regular extracurriculars cost money, fashion classes cost beaucoup bucks that we don't have. Now they'll both be off to college, leaving me behind once again. So when Hazel and Seb spun a fantastical story about my parents' ill-fated romance worthy of any makjang drama, I wanted it to be true. That way, if Ted *was* my dad, I'd at least know something about him.

As it turns out, science does not take into account a person's wishful thinking, no matter how much they want it. I had to learn that the hard way.

"Got my results this morning. I'm 95.1 percent Korean. Ted is Japanese, so not my dad. Sorry to disprove your theory."

"What? No way," Hazel says at the same time Seb says, "It's gotta be wrong."

Surprisingly, they're serious. Which makes me realize it wasn't a joke to them, either.

I shake my head. "It's DNA. How can you doubt factual science? It's how murder mysteries are solved and how rapists are convicted."

Seb winces. "This conversation turned dark real fast."

"Does it at least tell you which region of Korea you're from?" Hazel asks. "Maybe that could point you in the right direction."

Seb raises a quizzical brow. "It's DNA, not GPS."

Hazel shoots him back a look. "I don't know how DNA works. I'm only trying to be helpful."

7

The snippiness in their tone with each other is unusual. The disappointment must be getting to them, too. Before things get worse, for any of us, I decide to be the first to accept my fate. A life skill I've grown accustomed to.

"Look, I appreciate it, but let's face it. My mom is right, and there are no big secrets. My dad is just some guy who died and had no other living relatives. Take it or leave it, this is who I am."

"Can I see the results?" Seb asks, and I hand him my phone with the website pulled up.

"Oh, look, it has this section about finding relatives," he says, scrolling down. "I guess if anyone you're related to also took the test, you could connect with them."

"It requires you to opt in," Hazel reads over Seb's shoulder. They both look up at me, wide-eyed.

I shrug my approval.

"Yes! I'm downloading the app and opting you in!" Seb fiddles with my phone.

"Okay, but let's not get ahead of ourselves like we did with the Ted Takahashi thing." Even though it was a far-fetched idea, I didn't realize until now how much I wanted Ted to be my dad. I don't know if I can guard myself from being sucked into the idea of yet another story about a long-lost family, and I definitely can't handle the disappointment again.

Hazel cocks her head to the side and stares at me with her big brown (technically hazel) eyes. "Another episode?"

"You read my mind." I give her a weak smile.

She pushes the mouse on her laptop to start the next episode of *My Professor, My Father*. Seb joins us in solidarity, and we cram together on my twin-sized bed. Pretty soon I forget about being alone and get sucked into the lives on-screen, proving once again that K-dramas are the perfect answer to everything.

⋇

A couple of hours later, I'm fully expecting Mom to come through the door at any minute with balloons. Or tacos. Or both. Instead, my phone buzzes.

"Ahhh, my Chloe-yah! Congratulations!" Mom's voice booms out of my phone, and I briefly check to see if I accidentally have her on speakerphone. Nope, not on speakerphone. "You're officially done with the high school!"

"Thanks, Mom," I say, chuckling. Mom left Korea precisely eighteen years and nine months ago. Besides a hint of an accent, her English is near perfect. Except she hasn't yet mastered the *and*'s and *the*'s. At this point, I'm not sure she ever will.

"How does it feel, now that you're a college student?"

"Community college, Mom," I correct her. "I feel, I dunno, the same?"

"I'm so glad you'll still be close by. Now I have you all to myself for four more years."

"Yay." The snark in my tone is unintentional. No matter how hard I try, I'm just not as thrilled as she is about going to Meadowland Community College down the street from Meadowland High School. "When are you going to be home? I'm starving."

"There's some leftovers in the fridge."

"Leftovers? You're not coming home for dinner tonight?" First she misses graduation, now dinner? This is not my idea of making it up to me. In fact, this is the exact opposite of making it up to me.

"I forgot to tell you. I took an overnight shift."

"Again?" Last time, it was for the laptop I needed for school. The time before that was because our ancient car finally went kaput and we needed a new one. Well, new to us at least. We're not destitute or anything, but Mom's single-income salary as a nurse never seems to be enough. I know it's not her fault, but it just doesn't seem fair.

"Now that you're starting the college—"

"Community college."

"I thought it would be a good idea. You know, for the tuition."

"It's just tuition, Mom. Not *the* tuition." I can't help the disappointment in my tone. Hazel's family rented a banquet hall, and Seb's family is at one of those fancy restaurants that serves bite-sized food with stuff like garnishes and sauces. Then there's me, alone at home, on the phone with Mom, hearing about the extra shifts she has to pick up since I'm going to start community college in a couple of weeks. On a day like today, I was hoping it would be a little more formal and a little less sweats-and-a-T-shirt. Maybe something where I'd finally get to wear one of the pieces I designed.

"Oh, don't worry. We're going to be just fine. It's always nice to have some cushion. You know, a 'just-in-case' fund," she says in her nurse voice.

10

Great. Now I feel guilty for making her feel guilty.

"Maybe I'll take a part-time job at Sew Fantastic. You know, that cute fabric store downtown?" Not only would I be able to help with tuition, I could snag myself a 20 percent employee discount.

"No, no, no. You'll be too busy studying for your clinicals," she says quickly.

"Don't you think you're getting ahead of yourself? Clinicals aren't for a while." Ever since I told Mom I was considering becoming a nurse like her, she treats me like I'm some sort of child prodigy.

"Don't worry about the tuition," she says. Any time I mention the idea of a part-time job, she shuts me down, like it's her responsibility alone to financially provide for us.

I sigh quietly. Growing up, I really believed that Mom could do it all. At the school's annual father/daughter dances, she'd dress up in a suit and tie, even drawing a silly mustache using eyeliner on her upper lip, and insist on taking me. On Father's Day, she'd take me to Six Flags, let me eat eleven-dollar funnel cake and ride the upside-down roller coaster as many times as I could without puking (and sometimes with puking). That was when I was younger. I'm eighteen now, and I want more than a distraction on designated Dad days that only remind me I don't have one. Mom simply cannot do it all anymore. The problem is, she won't admit it.

"By the way, I'm sorry I couldn't be there today. I had to—"

"I know. You had to work." There's a quiet lull between

11

us. Mom must've given me this excuse a million times. I thought once I graduated from high school, things would change and we'd spend more time together. But I'm realizing that, with community college tuition, nothing's going to change. Mom's going to be busier than ever.

"Mom, I . . ." My voice quivers. I'm thinking about what I really want for graduation. It isn't a big party, or an out-of-state college, or even tacos. I want to know more about my family. "Do you think you could tell me about Dad?" I never ask, especially knowing how difficult it is for Mom to talk about him. Maybe this can be her way of making it up to me for not making it to my graduation.

"Chloe-yah," she says, her voice sounding more like a sigh. She draws in another deep breath, letting it out just as slowly. Then, there it is.

A long.

Dramatic.

Pause.

As if we were in some medical drama, even the hospital machines in the background begin beeping loudly in anticipation of Mom's response. I hold my breath. This is it. The day has come. She is finally going to tell me about my dad. The real story about who he is, not some vague answer about how he died in a car crash and that was the end.

"Nurse Chang! We need you!" A sharp voice cuts through the receiver, and I deflate.

"Oh, Chloe-yah. I'm sorry, but—"

"Yeah, yeah. I know. A patient needs you." The sigh on the other end of the receiver is filled with so much remorse, it seeps into my soul and makes me regret what I said.

"I'll make it up to you. I promise," Mom says. "Okay, now I really have to go. Congratulations, Chloe-yah. I love you."

"Love you too."

After we hang up, I decide to pull out my latest design. Now that I have all night to work on it, I could probably finish it. Mom calls it a hobby, but this so-called hobby of mine started in the sixth grade when I first met Hazel and Seb and we decided to go to our first dance together. I knew Mom couldn't afford a new dress, and the ones in my closet were so basic. That's when I started making my own outfits. I even found a way to repurpose old clothes from Second Time Around, the local consignment store. I turned a muumuu into a romper, slacks into cigarette pants, and a day dress into an evening gown. Every outfit I design gives new life to an old garment. In fact, I'm quite envious of my creations. Sometimes I wouldn't mind fashioning a new life for myself.

I'm currently working on a midi day dress with a pleated pleather skirt and a ruffled top. It was supposed to be for my first day of college until I overheard Mom talking to Nurse Linda, saying that she couldn't even pay for in-state college. After that, I knew fashion school was out of the question. Now I plan on doing with this dress what I do with every one of my creations—sell it on Etsy to someone else who has a more fabulous life than I do.

My phone pings with a text notification, interrupting my thoughts, and I reach for it. Maybe it's Mom telling me she got someone to cover for her and she's coming home early to be with me. Maybe it's Hazel or Seb, ditching their families to hang out with me. I'm not usually susceptible to pity hangouts, but I'd make an exception today. No one should be spending the night of their high school graduation alone.

I check my phone and instead of an invite, it's a string of pictures from Hazel at her graduation dinner. There's a long table decorated with the University of Southern California flags and maroon-and-gold balloons tied to the chairs. On the back wall is a banner with Mylar balloons spelling out her name. Then Seb replies to the group with photos of his own family holding big cutouts of his face with different expressions; a UCLA banner hangs behind them. I smile at my phone, scrolling through photo after photo. When I think of how to respond, my smile disappears. What am I going to send them, a photo of me in my Meadowland High School sweats, eating leftovers, *alone*?

I don't reply. Instead, I do something stupid. *Really* stupid. I pull out a letter that's folded and tucked under my mattress and read it for the hundredth time.

*Dear Ms. Chang,*

*We are delighted to inform you that you have been accepted to the Fashion Design Department at the Fashion Institute of Technology. In addition, we are pleased to award you with a scholarship due to your outstanding qualifications and impressive portfolio. Kindly let us know by July 25 of your*

14

*decision. We look forward to hearing from you,*
*and congratulations on your accomplishments!*

Tears blot the paper before I finish reading it. I'd never even told my mom about it. It would be pointless. Even with the scholarship, the cost of living in Manhattan is more than ten times what it is in Tulsa. I fold the letter up again, shove it under my mattress, and try to convince myself that not attending FIT is a decision I'm making and not a decision that's being made for me by my circumstances.

I stare up at the popcorn ceiling, lying in my bed thinking about my dad, and once again I'm steeped in disappointment. Deep down, I thought that finding out who my dad was would help me know who I am. Because being a nurse and living in a small town may be what my mom wants, but it's not my dream. This can't be it for me.

Another notification lights up my phone, and I pick it up lazily, thinking it's more pictures from Hazel or Seb. When I notice it's a different kind of alert from an app I'm unfamiliar with, I jolt up. I click on the icon, opening up 23andMe.

# 23andme.com

From: Noh, Jin Young
Subject: Hello, Cousin
Friday, 11:59 PM

Dear Ms. Chloe Chang,
I am Jin Young Noh. I received a notification that our genetic tests indicate that we are a 15.5% genetic match, suggesting that we are first cousins. Hello! This is a fortuitous chance meeting.

From: Chang, Chloe
Subject: RE: Hello, Cousin
Saturday, 12:03 AM

Dear Jin Young,
Cousins? Sorry, there must be some mistake. Unfortunately, I don't have any cousins. My parents are only children. I'm afraid this must be a mistake.

Saturday, 12:04 AM

Wait. This is DNA. There aren't any mistakes with

DNA. My parents are Joon Pyo and Theresa Chang.
Are either of these names familiar to you?

From: Noh, Jin Young
Subject: RE: Hello, Cousin
Saturday, 12:20 AM

I don't know about Chang Joon Pyo, but I had
an uncle named Noh Joon Pyo. He's my father's
brother who died in America right around the time I
was born. I go to college at the Johns Hopkins and
the rest of the Noh family is in Korea.

From: Chang, Chloe
Subject: RE: Hello, Cousin
Saturday, 12:21 AM

Does this mean we *are* cousins? Am I a part of the
Noh family?

When you say "the rest of the Noh family," how
many of you are there? Not that I'm freaking out
or anything. Well, I'm partly freaking out. I've never
had a big family before—not even a small family
for that matter. This is a big deal! Okay, I need to sit
down or else I'll pass out . . .

From: Noh, Jin Young
Subject: RE: Hello, Cousin
Saturday, 12:26 AM

I completely understand this may come as a shock

to you. The family is not large, but we are very close. We live with Halmoni, our paternal grandmother, who had three sons. My father was the middle son and your father was the oldest son. There is also a younger uncle, Noh Han Pyo. He is forty-one years of age and unmarried. I have a sister, Soo Young, so now you have two cousins.

From: Chang, Chloe
Subject: RE: Hello, Cousin
Saturday, 12:27 AM

Wow, that *is* a big family! It's just me and my mom here. She's a nurse and a workaholic, so I'm alone a lot. Now that you're telling me I have family, that makes me feel like I'm not alone. Even if most of you are halfway across the world. I'm so eager to know more about you!

From: Noh, Jin Young
Subject: RE: Hello, Cousin
Saturday, 12:27 AM

I am so eager to learn about you too! What is your blood type?

From: Chang, Chloe
Subject: RE: Hello, Cousin
Saturday, 12:30 AM

My blood type? I do actually know my blood type since my mom says it's good to know it in case of an emergency situation where a blood transfusion could save your life (which is my mom in a nutshell). My blood type is B. Why do you ask?

From: Noh, Jin Young
Subject: RE: Hello, Cousin
Saturday, 12:33 AM

Oh, forgive me. In Korea, your blood type is how we know about a person's personality. B means you're creative, outgoing, and optimistic. I have a feeling we would get along really well. Along the same lines, I know this may seem rushed, but my family would like to invite you to Korea to visit us as soon as possible. Of course, we will arrange your travel and accommodations. We are so very eager to connect with you, our long-lost relative. Please let me know at your earliest convenience.

# CHAPTER 2

Of course my mom is working an overnight shift on the night that my long-lost cousin pops virtually out of nowhere and into a DNA website messaging platform. Rude.

I should be more skeptical of Jin Young's messages. I mean, what if he's a scammer? What if the next message he sends is going to ask me for my Social Security number and bank account info? Oh, and why not throw in my passwords while I'm at it. The sad part is, if Jin Young did make those super sketchy personal identity theft requests to get to know more about me, I would hesitate, just a second, before saying no. That's how desperate I am for his story to check out. I'd have a connection to my dad and a real family with cousins, aunts, uncles, and a grandma, just like everyone else.

First things first, I check my most reliable source when it comes to all things unknown—the internet. I type in the search box: Noh Jin Young. About fifty different websites pop up, each with a different Noh Jin Young, and the articles are mostly in Korean. There's no way I can Google Translate my way through that fast enough.

Remembering he said he goes to Johns Hopkins, I add

the school's name in the search box next to his name, then refresh. I click on the first page that comes up, which is the Johns Hopkins website. Under the Business Administration department, buried in a long list of student names, is the name Jin Young Noh, which confirms it's the same person—my cousin.

Goose bumps line my arms and neck. I have a cousin.

Make that *two* cousins.

I add Soo Young's name to the search, refresh the page, then click on the first link. It appears to be some kind of business trade publication. I try to make sense of the article, but it must have been translated by a badly programmed bot, because it's mostly incoherent. It isn't until I scroll down to the bottom of the article that I find what I'm looking for: a photo.

*Whoa.*

Hair immaculately styled. Makeup flawless and tasteful. And their attire? Ridiculously glamorous, dressed in head-to-toe couture. Jin Young and Soo Young are standing together with a fashionable-looking older woman. Is that their mom or grandmother? It's hard to tell. I can't be related to *these* people.

Can I?

Pacing the living room, I wait for Mom but then begin to worry about how she'll take this information. This isn't only huge for me, but for her, too. Unless . . . no, she couldn't have known about my dad's family.

Could she?

Before I jump to any conclusions (I mean, *any more*

21

conclusions), I begin to scour our tiny two-bedroom apartment for any clues or hints, starting in the most obvious place—our living room.

My mom has efficiently compartmentalized everything about my family history to one day. Every year on October 26, she prepares an annual jesa—the memorial of my dad's death. Tulsa has one Asian market. It's small, far away, and expensive, so we usually never shop there, which means Mom never makes Korean food. Dad's jesa is the one time each year that she spends the entire day making a drool-worthy spread that includes rice cake soup, steamed dumplings, and vegetable pancakes. In addition to savory foods, she also makes a wide variety of sweet rice cakes and cookies accompanied by trays of fruit. It's the only time we eat homemade Korean food; it's the only time we do anything Korean, really. More to the point, it's the only time we acknowledge my dad. We don't even talk about him. We sit there, staring at a crappy photo of him, in silence. It's so enlarged, it's too grainy and pixelated to make out any of his features. Honestly, that's how my dad is to me in real life, too. This blurred, undecipherable being.

So that's it. That's everything I have of my dad—a framed photo of him on a black lacquered table adorned with an ornate mother-of-pearl design in the far corner of the living room.

I don't find any new information about Dad in the living room, and I know for a fact there's nothing about him in my room, so that just leaves Mom's room. I slide open the door to Mom's closet, which is pretty sad. It's sparse, filled with more scrubs than regular clothes. After rummaging around, which takes approximately two minutes, I notice an unmarked shoe box on a shelf in the corner. The hairs on my arms shoot up as an eerie feeling creeps over me. Maybe there's more to this story than I know. Maybe Mom knew about Dad's family this whole time. Holding my breath, I lift the shoe box lid.

Inside the box, nestled in crumpled-up tissue paper, is a pair of unflattering black pleather shoes with an insane amount of arch support. *Nursing shoes?* I roll my eyes at no one. How easily I forget who I'm dealing with here. Of course Mom doesn't have any secrets.

As I'm putting back the shoe box, something falls from behind the shelf and slips down the back wall of the closet. When I bend to pick it up, I instantly recognize the Polaroid photo.

I run over to the corner in the living room and confirm that it's the cropped photo of my dad, the framed one we stare at during jesa every year. Except this one is the original, and it's not blurry at all. Staring at my dad's face with this level of clarity is almost as if I'm staring at him in person. I can actually see the resemblance. Not shown in the framed photo is my mom, who is next to him in this original one. She's wearing a uniform shirt with embroidery on the lapel, the letters *S* and *W* interlocked. My dad's arm is slung over hers, and they're smiling from ear to ear. In fact, I've never seen my mom look so happy before, which simultaneously tugs at my heart and tears it into tiny pieces. Behind them is a shiny gray-brick building with Korean letters on the signage. They must have been in Korea.

*Maybe Mom* does *know about the family.*

I'm still staring at the photo of my dad when I hear the key turning in the door.

"Mom!" I shoot up and practically lunge toward her.

"Well, I missed you, too! Maybe I should work weekends more often." Her hands are full of take-out boxes from Seoulful Tacos, but she still manages to open up her arms to hug me.

Instead of a hug, I pocket the Polaroid and shove my phone with the messages from Jin Young in her face. She stares at the screen with her arms still suspended in the air. After a frozen second, she slowly puts her arms down and sets the take-out boxes on the kitchen table.

"Who sent you this?" she says instead of an answer.

"This guy, Jin Young, reached out to me on 23andMe and said—"

"23andMe?" She shifts her position, folding her arms across her chest.

"It's this company that analyzes your DNA and links you to anyone with a genetic connection. Anyway, the website says that Jin Young and I share 15.5 percent of our DNA, which means we're cousins."

"Cousins?"

"I know, right? Then I told him I don't have any cousins because you and Dad are only children whose parents both passed away, right?" I carefully inspect her facial expression for any signs of preexisting knowledge of this information. She gives me none. She just stares at me blankly, unable to form words, so I continue.

"Anyway, when I told him your names, he sent me

24

these messages." I hold up my phone again. "If Dad is Noh Joon Pyo, not Chang Joon Pyo, then that means he has brothers. Which also means I have uncles and a grandma and cousins!"

She sits down slowly, digesting this information. Just when I think she's going to say something important, she starts opening the boxes. "I brought home Seoulful Tacos for breakfast, your favorite." She slides a plate over to me and puts a taco wrapped in parchment paper on it. "They don't open until eleven, but when I told the manager you were graduating the high school, he made an exception. Isn't that nice?" She glances up with a forced smile.

"Mom? Are you hearing me?" Maybe she's in shock. People act strangely when they're in shock, right? I'm pretty sure I read it in one of the pamphlets at the hospital Mom works at. "Didn't you say Dad was an only child?" I try again, this time speaking more slowly.

"I-I said your dad had no other family." She begins unwrapping a taco on her plate.

I stare at the plate, confused. "How can you think about eating at a time like this?"

Mom sighs, exasperated. "I'm trying to make things up to you, for missing your big day yesterday." She unfolds a napkin and places it on her lap.

Any other day, tacos would have done the trick to distract me. But not today.

I take her hands to stop her and look her straight in the eyes. "Mom, I know this is a lot to handle, but I need to know. What are you not telling me about Dad?"

"How come you took a DNA test?" Mom asks, completely ignoring my question.

Now it's my turn to sigh. "It was a gift from Hazel and Seb. At first it was meant as a joke, but if this is true, and this *is* Dad's family, then it's no joke."

"A joke?" She draws her head back. "What kind of joke?"

I tell her about Ted Takahashi and how we thought he was my dad.

"Well, that's just ridiculous." She balks. "Your dad doesn't look anything like Ted Takahashi."

"What's ridiculous is that you hardly ever talk about Dad," I say, getting worked up. I'm done with getting the runaround. I want to know who my dad was. So I finally ask her, "You're not surprised by any of this, so you must have known about the Nohs. Did you?"

She winces, rubbing her forehead. "Losing your father was hard enough. Nothing good can come from reopening old wounds." Her voice cracks.

"Old wounds?" I can't help but scoff. "I don't even know who my dad was. That's not an old wound. That's just a wound. It needs tending to, or else it will fester. You're a nurse, you should know."

"Haven't I been enough for you? Aren't you happy with your life?" She looks as if I've mortally wounded her, and my stomach writhes with guilt.

"It's not that you didn't do enough, but there's this whole other side to me I know nothing about. I want to know what Dad was like and what traits I inherited from him. I want to know that he's more than just a corner in our room that we think about one day out of the year.

Maybe it's time you faced the fact that you can't do it all. You can't be mom *and* dad. Not this time." My hand slides into the pocket of my sweatshirt, and I'm about to pull out the photo to ask her about it when she clears her throat.

"There's nothing in the past that can fill the void of losing your father," she warns.

"You're right. Nothing can replace losing Dad. But his family, my family, is still alive. They're inviting me to visit them in Korea—"

"*What?!*" Mom says, cutting me off. "Flying internationally to see people you never even knew existed until now?"

It should make me see how ridiculous I'm being, hearing just how drastic this decision to meet them is, but it doesn't. It makes me even more determined. "Mom, I want to go. I never got to meet my dad, and now I don't want to miss out on the chance to meet his family."

"It's not the right time to take a vacation. I can't take any time off of work," she forges on. "Besides, you'll be much too busy getting ready for college anyway." Then, ignoring me completely, she picks up the taco off her plate.

"*Community college,*" I correct her for the millionth time. Like everything, Mom is in denial. Denial about my future prospects, my interest in fashion, and now, my dad's family reaching out to me.

It's clear to me that Mom isn't going to budge. Anger replaces the guilt, and instead of pulling out the photo from my pocket, I shove it down deeper. It's up to me to find out more about my father.

"In case you haven't realized, I'm eighteen. A legal adult. If Dad's family, *my* family, is inviting me to Korea,

27

I think I should accept. I don't need your permission. As for money? I have enough to go on my own." I've never spoken to my mom in that tone before. I'm just so tired of watching opportunities pass me by. If I don't take matters into my own hands, I'll be stuck here the rest of my life.

"What?" Mom stares at me as if she's looking at me for the first time.

"I'm grateful for everything you do for me, Mom, but I need to live my life, too. While you've been spending your days *and* nights at the hospital, I've been selling my clothes on Etsy for the past year—clothes I'll never be able to wear if I follow the path you've laid out for me. Fashion is more than a hobby. Just like this trip is more than a vacation."

Unable to speak, Mom sets her limp taco down and swallows the food in her mouth. Her typical go-to response to anything Dad-related is complete silence, and I'm not expecting anything more now.

"I'm going, Mom." The words surprise me as much as they surprise her, but so did this conversation. I never met my dad, and no one can change that. But now that I have the confirmation I was looking for that I have a family, I'm not about to let that go, not even for Mom.

# 23andme.com

## MESSAGES

From: Noh, Jin Young
Subject: Transportation
Saturday, 6:23 PM

Everyone is delighted you have accepted our
offer to come to Korea, especially Halmoni. Your
electronic ticket was sent to the email address you
provided. At the airport in Incheon, I will pick you up
after you go through customs. There will be a sign
with your name on it. You will be taken directly to
meet Halmoni. I will see you soon.

From: Chang, Chloe
Subject: RE: Transportation
Saturday, 6:33 PM

Got it! I fully intend to pay you back for the flight.
Do you have Venmo? PayPal? Zelle? Also, thank you
for the neighborhood recommendations. I booked
an Airbnb in the Hongdae area in Seoul. I hope it is
close to where you live. I am super excited to meet

everyone! Please tell Halmoni I can't wait to meet her, too. I can't believe I'll be there so soon!

From: Noh, Jin Young
Subject: RE: Transportation
Saturday, 6:45 PM

We cannot wait to meet you, too! I will relay the message to Halmoni about your excitement to meet her. She is very eager to meet you. As for your accommodations, do not worry about the location and distance to where we live. We will take care of everything.

From: Chang, Chloe
Subject: RE: Transportation
Saturday, 6:48 PM

Thank you so much, Jin Young. I could not have planned this trip without you!

Wow. It just hit me. We're cousins! It's still so strange to me . . . one day I have no family and then the next, I have cousins, uncles, and a halmoni! Well, I guess that's not entirely true. I do have family, but it's just my mom. She's cool, for the most part, and she does her best, but she's always busy with her nursing job. She has a hard time ending her work when the shift is over. Which I guess I understand since you can't really tell someone who may be dying that you can't be there for them because your shift ended thirty minutes ago. By the way, what about your family? Are you close?

From: Noh, Jin Young

Subject: RE: Transportation

Saturday, 6:53 PM

> Your mom sounds pleasant. I think being a nurse
> is very admirable. You're right, it's hard to tell
> someone who may be dying that you can't be there
> for them. I am sure your mom does her best for you.
> Our family spends quite a lot of time together. We
> live together in one house. Halmoni is in charge of
> the family business. We spend a lot of time in each
> other's company.

From: Chang, Chloe

Subject: RE: Transportation

Saturday, 6:55 PM

> Are you serious? You guys live and work together?
> What kind of family business is it? My best friend
> Hazel has five sisters and I'm always jealous about
> the noise and energy of a big family. She's always
> complaining that it's not worth the drama. What is
> the Noh family like?

From: Noh, Jin Young

Subject: RE: Transportation

Saturday, 6:56 PM

> We work in the retail business. There is a fair
> amount of drama with families. Nothing that can't
> be sorted out. Halmoni takes care of everyone in
> the family.

# CHAPTER 3

The next day, I'm in the kitchen pouring myself a bowl of cereal while Mom is getting ready to go to the hospital. Even though neither of us is speaking to the other, the silence is overwhelming.

Mom grabs her keys and before she heads out the front door, she pauses. After a moment, she finally says, "Are you really going halfway across the world to meet strangers?" With her back still facing me, it seems as if she's talking to the door.

I sigh, placing the spoon down in the bowl. "Are you really not going to tell me about Dad?"

Her silence answers both of our questions, and she leaves abruptly without another word.

Later that afternoon, I invite Hazel and Seb over and fill them in on everything that has transpired since the last time I saw them.

"A week ago, if you'd have told me my best friend was living in an actual K-drama, I would've laughed in your face," Hazel muses from my bed.

"I know, right?" I smile at her. No one thought I'd have a reason to leave this town, least of all me. "It hasn't really sunk in yet."

"I mean, there hasn't really been time for it to sink in. Jin Young first messaged you on Friday, and today is only Sunday," Seb says.

"Even though things are moving at lightning speed, it's, like, not fast enough for Jin Young. As soon as I confirmed we were cousins, he started making travel arrangements." I shake my head in disbelief, placing my never-used passport in my bag. I was starting to lose hope I'd ever get a stamp in it. Until now.

"Not only was this international trip arranged at a record speed, if he was at Johns Hopkins when you messaged him, it was like one in the morning on a Saturday when he messaged you back. I'd say he's more excited to meet you than you are to meet them." Hazel's eyebrows bounce up at me.

I try in vain not to get carried away again by Hazel's flair for drama, but there's no denying it. They do seem eager to meet me. Finally, I'll have a connection to my dad I've been missing my whole life.

"How long are you going to be gone for?" Seb asks, fiddling with my phone.

"One week. It's not quite enough time to really get to know my dad's family, but it should give me enough time to find out more about this photo." I hold up the Polaroid of my parents to Hazel and Seb before tucking it back into my wallet. I've spent hours staring at it over the past couple of days. I know there's more to the story than meets the eye.

"You haven't asked your mom?" Seb raises an eyebrow at me.

"She refuses to talk about my dad. Which is why this trip means so much to me. Now I don't have to rely on her for information about my dad. I can ask Jin Young or his sister or my halmoni." The smile returns to my face, thinking about meeting them.

"Okay, but what am I going to do without my bepu?" Hazel makes the most pathetic sad face.

Hazel using the Korean slang for *best friend* makes me giggle. Even though she's 100 percent Colombian, I swear she speaks more Korean than I do.

"Don't worry," I say, noticing the torn looks on their faces. "I'll be back before you go on your Europe trip. I haven't quite figured out the long-distance rates, but I'll make sure to call you from Korea. Somehow." I scratch my head, wondering if I'll have anything left over from my Etsy fund once I pay for this trip.

"Speaking of . . ." Seb tosses me my phone. "Your update is complete," he says, sounding like a bot. When I give him a funny look, he adds, "I researched what you need to travel in Korea and downloaded the relevant apps. KakaoTalk, Naver for maps, Papago for translating. KakaoTalk is for messaging, but you can also use it to call us every day."

"By 'every day' he means multiple times a day. I mean it." Hazel points a finger at me. "We need updates in real time!"

I smile at the two of them, cataloguing this moment in my memory like I have been every moment since I found out they were leaving for college. Even though I'm the one leaving first now, I'm caught off guard by the swirl of emotions taking hold of me. The day after I come back from Korea, the two of them will be off to Europe, and then after that, it'll be Los Angeles for who knows how long. It's as if I'm saying goodbye to them forever.

"I'm surprised your mom is taking time off work to go on such short notice. She never takes time off," Seb says, jerking me back to the present.

"Oh. She's not coming," I say quietly.

"Wait. Theresa Chang is okay with you going to Korea? Alone?" Hazel asks.

"I mean, I'm an adult, legally speaking." I shrug.

"Legally an adult. Technically a toddler." Hazel snorts, pointing to the Shin Ramyun stain on my T-shirt.

I pretend to be offended, but we all know I'm hardly adult material.

"Hey, this looks nice. Is it new?" Seb holds out a hanger with my latest design on it. The darts on the skirt came out beautifully and the flutter sleeves are perfection.

"Wow. This dress is really sophisticated, Chlo. I can hardly see the invisible stitching," Hazel says, flipping over the hem of the pleated skirt.

"On pleather, no less." I beam. I can't help but show how proud I am of it.

"What's this?" She reveals an intricate stitching pattern on the inside lining.

"Oh, that? It's my brand." I bite my lower lip, second-guessing the stitching of the first letters of my first and last name, *C* and *H*, interlocked with each other.

"Your brand?" they both say at the same time.

"Yeah, lots of budding artists do that, by way of marking

their clothes. It's silly, really, but I thought it would make it feel more like an original design than a simple pattern."

"I love it. A real Chloe Chang original," Hazel says. "I think this is the best piece you've made so far."

"How much did you get for this one? I bet you can start raising your rates now that you're more established with a brand and everything." Seb nods at me.

"I'm not selling this one. I'm taking it with me." I smile at the dress, folding it neatly and placing it right on top of my bag. Hazel and Seb don't say anything. They know how much this means to me. This trip will be a trip of many firsts for me—my first time wearing one of my creations, my first time in Korea, and my first time meeting my dad's family.

"Saranghae," Hazel says—"I love you" in Korean—and pulls me in for a hug.

A second later, Seb's arms are wrapped around the two of us. "What she said."

"Saranghae," I say back to both of them.

I pack the dress in my bag and zip it up. Finally, my life is about to begin.

꙳

After I say goodbye to Hazel and Seb, I wait in front of my apartment complex for the Uber driver to arrive. Even though I went on that massive tirade about being an adult, I feel like a kid who's in over her head right now. Mom and I haven't spoken about Dad's family since I found out about them, and it feels weird leaving without saying a proper goodbye to her.

She's still at the hospital, working another overnight shift. Even with the weirdness between us, it feels so strange not to see her before I head to the airport. My eyes start to well, so I distract myself by checking my phone obsessively to confirm that the driver is en route. I hear a car approaching, so I wipe my eyes and gather my bags. When the car comes to a screeching halt, I immediately look up.

"Mom!" The tears I'd been trying in vain to keep at bay come spilling out.

With the engine still on, she jumps out of the car, leaving the door open, and throws her arms around me for a tight hug.

"What are you doing here? Aren't you supposed to be working?"

"I had someone cover for me so I could say goodbye." Her voice cracks.

"Oh, Mom," I sob.

"You're right," she whispers in my ear. "You have a right to know them. They're your family. They must love you. They must."

I'm so happy she made it in time, I forget about our argument and hug her back. There's still so much we need to talk about, but I know we'll figure it out. "Thanks, Mom. For always being there for me when it counts."

"Chloe-yah, I love you," she says, rocking me from side to side.

"I love you, too." My voice is muffled from my mouth being pressed up against her shoulder.

She pulls back and studies my face, as if to remember me. "Don't forget about me when you're with them," she says.

"I'll only be gone for a week. How could I ever forget about you?" I respond with a laugh, hoping she can hear just how ridiculous she's being.

Instead of chuckling with me, the crease between her eyes deepens. "Remember, just because you share blood, it doesn't mean they're not strangers." Her voice trembles, and a tear streams down her cheek.

It didn't occur to me until now that she might feel threatened by me meeting Dad's family. I pull her in for another hug and squeeze tight. "Saranghae," I say, hoping it'll mean more to her in her first language.

The Uber pulls up behind my mom's car, and I try to release myself from the hug when Mom's grip tightens.

"Uh, Mom? They start adding fees if I'm not on time to meet the Uber driver."

"I don't care about the fees," she says in my ear, which means a lot. Theresa Chang does not like to pay for superfluous things, not if it can be helped. "I just want to hold you one last time."

"Okay, Mom."

Seven minutes and five dollars and twenty cents later, I'm in the Uber and off to the airport. I put my hand against the window as we drive off and silently let the tears stream down my face as I watch my mom grow smaller and smaller. It would've been weird if she hadn't shown up to see me off. But she did.

At the airport, I check in at the kiosk and find my gate once I get through the security checkpoint. I have a connecting flight in Dallas, and then Seoul, here I come!

The flight from Tulsa to Dallas is so short, I barely had time to enjoy my drink before the descent. I'm still jittery with excitement when I get to my gate. As a dutiful daughter and friend, I pull out my phone and first send a quick text to my mom.

> **Me:** Arrived safely in Dallas. About to board the plane to Seoul!

> **Mom:** Call me as soon as you land. I love you!

> **Mom:** And Chloe . . . Be careful.

The next text is to Hazel and Seb.

> **Me:** Testing . . . is this thing on?

> **Seb:** 👍

> **Hazel:** Miss us already?

**Seb:** Are you messaging us from the plane?

**Me:** I landed in Dallas. About to board the plane to Seoul.

**Hazel:** I can't decide if I'm jealous or excited for you?!

**Seb:** Maybe both?

**Hazel:** Yeah, you're probably right. All I know is you're going to have an *amazing* time!

**Me:** Thanks, guys.

**Me:** Seb, since you know a lot of random facts about Korea, is it super dangerous or something?

**Seb:** My resources tell me that Seoul has a lower crime rate than the US and is relatively a safe place.

**Hazel:** ????

**Me:** Ever since I told my mom I'm going to Korea, she's always telling

me to be safe and I don't know if
it's typical mom worry or something
I should be more concerned about.

> **Hazel:** Of course it's typical
> mom worry. This is the
> first time you're traveling
> internationally. By yourself, no
> less!

> **Seb:** Knowing Theresa, this is
> more than typical. It's to be
> expected.

> **Hazel:** Plus, I refuse to believe
> a country that can produce
> a man as beautiful as Lee
> Min Ho can be anything but
> extremely pleasant.

> **Seb:** 😏

**Me:** LOL, that's a convincing
argument, Haze. OK gotta go. Love
you guys!

My pulse quickens with excitement again as I pull up
my boarding pass. There are two lines at the gate: one
for rows A–E and the other for F–J. Holy mother-of-pearl,
this is one ginormous plane! I check my boarding pass to

see which line to go in. That's when I realize my boarding pass doesn't have a seat number printed on it.

"Excuse me," I say to the gate agent standing behind the counter. "I don't have a seat number." I point nervously at my ticket.

The agent checks her computer screen, clacking away for what feels like an eternity, only to raise a quizzical eyebrow up at me.

"Is there a problem?" I say, drawing out the words. A part of me believed this was too good to be true; I just didn't *want* to believe it. "Am I not going to Seoul?" I consider emailing Jin Young on the 23andMe app when the agent motions me over to the front of the line.

She talks to another agent at the front of the line in a hushed tone, pointing back at me every now and then. I try to prepare myself for the worst-case scenario, where I'm told this has all been one big hoax. Panic rises in my chest, but before I can emotionally break down, the gate agent returns with a flight attendant from the plane. She's in a fitted cerulean skirt-suit uniform and has flawless skin, neatly tied back dark hair, and ruby-red lips.

"Apparently, the ticket was purchased via a third party with a note attached to it. This flight attendant is going to take you to your seat." The gate agent waves, smiling wide.

"So I am going to Seoul?" I look up hopefully.

The flight attendant nods and directs me to the ramp, bypassing the crowd. I try to avoid their eyes full of judgment. I get it, I'm cutting the line. "Sorry. My ticket was purchased via third party," I say as I pass the other

42

passengers. Since it's my first international flight, I don't fully know what it means, but I'm hoping they do.

When we reach the inside of the plane, the flight attendant takes me up to the front, where the business class seats are located. I wouldn't dare to even dream about sitting here.

Although, come to think of it, the photos I saw on the business website did make it seem like the Noh's retail store was doing well. Maybe even well enough to purchase a business class ticket. I hold my breath, hoping the attendant will stop at one of the seats in this section. When we pass the last row of business class seats, I release my breath and continue following her. As she opens the curtains beyond the last row of seats in business class, I laugh to myself. Of course I don't have business class seats. It's ridiculous to even think that I could sit in—

"Here we are." The flight attendant motions for me to follow her through the curtains. "First class."

The flight attendant continues down the aisle while I'm still at the threshold to what is apparently a portal to another world. She stops in the aisle, turns, and motions me to my seat . . . only it isn't a seat. It's a room.

I blink. Then blink again. "This . . . is for me?" I stare at my seat, er, room. With the light turned on above it, the entire space is illuminated, like some kind of a spotlight. When Jin Young said the family would take care of everything, I didn't realize he meant *everything*.

She nods, hiding a chuckle behind her hand. Then she offers to take my bags and stow them in the overhead compartment. "Please, make yourself comfortable," the flight attendant says when I'm still standing in the aisle.

I sink into the chair, which feels like a cloud. There's a box of chocolates and a welcome kit wrapped like a present. Inside is a fancy bag filled with name-brand toiletries, complete with a toothbrush, toothpaste, face cream, and lip balm. It's Christmas in June! There's even a set of pajamas rolled up and tied with a bow around it. The fabric is a deep navy blue and 100 percent Egyptian cotton. Is this heaven?

Another flight attendant brings me a warmed bowl with roasted nuts in it. Then she asks if I'd like anything to drink. I look around at the champagne glasses being handed out. I'm tempted to ask for one but remind myself that I have a first-class ticket, not a fake ID. Since the atmosphere here definitely calls for something bubbly, I ask for some sparkling water. The flight attendant returns right away with my sparkling water in a champagne glass.

I recline the chair back, kick off my shoes, and lift up the footrest. Before I can think to request it, a flight attendant comes by with an extra pillow and headset. It's like my every need is anticipated. If this is what being a Noh is like, I can't wait for what comes next.

# CHAPTER 4

Sixteen hours in first class feels truly magical. I watched a movie (okay, six, but who's counting?), ate caviar for the first time, practiced my Korean using the language app on my phone, and before I knew it, it was time to land. If it were any other destination, I would be sad to leave the lovely luxury cocoon of the first-class cabin. But this isn't just any destination. This is Korea, where I'm about to meet my family for the first time.

I've been up for almost twenty-four hours, but a jolt of adrenaline reinvigorates me as soon as the tires hit the tarmac. I'm the first one on my feet when the Fasten Seat Belt sign turns off. I gather my bags and feel regal as I walk out of the aircraft, but as soon as we get into the air-port terminal, I'm swept into a sea of passengers rushing to go through the immigration line. Unfortunately, there is no first-class line here. It's more of a free-for-all, which is quite jolting after spending the last sixteen hours in a private room, being waited on hand and foot.

Now that I'm here, one step closer to meeting my fam-ily, I'm nervous. What if they don't like me? What if my mom is right and I'm just a stranger to them? After all, we only found out about each other just days ago.

I already felt out of place in Tulsa. If I don't fit in with my own family, then where do I fit in?

Trying not to spiral before I even meet them, I reread my messages from Jin Young. The level of excitement in each message screams through loud and clear, setting my mind at ease. Of course they'll like me. They wouldn't have gone to such extreme lengths to get me here otherwise.

In the last exchange I had with Jin Young, he said that someone would meet me at the airport and take me to meet my halmoni. *Halmoni.* That's a word I never thought would hold any meaning for me. The stinging sensation in my nasal passages threatens tears, but I fan them away. To distract myself, I put my earbuds in and practice my Korean using the app. By the time I get through the massive immigration line and reach the exit, I've almost mastered the greetings.

"Annyeonghaseyo," I say out loud. It's the formal way of saying hello. I plan to say it the first time I meet my family. It doesn't quite roll off my tongue the right way, so I keep repeating it over and over while I look for the sign with my name on it.

Suddenly, a guy in a fitted black suit bows to me. "Annyeonghaseyo," he says, returning the greeting.

Oops. I should probably practice in my head now that I'm in Korea. It isn't until I bow apologetically that I notice the sign he's holding. It says my name, CHLOE CHANG, in large block letters.

"Um." I point to the sign, then to me. "Jin Young?" I ask, taking inventory of him. He doesn't look at all like the Jin Young I found online in the picture with him and his beautiful sister. Not that this man isn't beautiful. He's got the kind of perfect complexion K-drama heroines pine for, a pair of thick, perfectly symmetrical eyebrows, and . . . are those dimples?

His lips break into a small smile and instead of responding, he bows. Tucking the sign with my name on it under his arm, he holds out a business card to me with both hands. It reads: *Mr. Kim, Private Secretary to Noh Jin Young.*

"Oh. I mean, annyeonghaseyo." I bow again, this time with more awareness. On the way up, my eyes catch his and I quickly look away. He must be about my age, which is hardly old enough to be "Mr." anything. "Is Jin Young here? Perhaps waiting in the car?" I look around, searching for anyone who resembles the photo I found online. I could have sworn Jin Young said he was going to meet me at the airport personally, not send a personal secretary. Then again, in my excitement, it is possible I misread his message.

Mr. Kim says something in Korean.

"Neh?" I have no choice but to use my limited Korean with him, seeing as he doesn't seem to speak any English.

Instead of answering, Mr. Kim points to his earpiece. Before I have a chance to be embarrassed, he takes my bags from me and walks briskly through the swarm of people to the passenger loading area. I'm in a full jog trying to keep up with him. Once we get outside, the muggy air hits me like a wet blanket. My clothes cling to me like moist plastic wrap, which feels every bit as gross as it sounds.

Mr. Kim leads me outside of the airport, where a sleek, black sedan with dark tinted windows is parked right in front. There's a sign that reads VIP on the window. I'm giddy again, taking note of how my dad's family spared no expense to welcome me here, which helps curb the disappointment of not having any of them come meet me at the airport themselves. Mr. Kim opens the back door for me, then puts my bags in the trunk. Pretty soon, we're off to meet my family. I've waited my whole life for this.

※

The car stops abruptly and my head whips up. "I'm up!" I yell for no good reason after being startled awake. Mr. Kim looks back at me in his rearview mirror while he waits for the light to change, but he doesn't say anything. I stare out the window to try to figure out where we are. The sidewalks are shoulder-to-shoulder crowded like it's Black Friday at Best Buy. There must be hundreds of people on this block alone.

"Seoul?" I ask. I haven't yet reached the level on my language app that teaches me how to formulate a sentence in Korean.

Mr. Kim turns his head to the side and smiles, nodding.

Now fully awake, I take inventory of my current state. I breathe into the palm of my hand and almost pass out from the smell. Then I try to recover by pulling up the collar of my T-shirt around my nose, only to get a heaping whiff of BO. I cough, waving the air in front of me.

"Gwenchanayo?" Mr. Kim asks.

"Gwenchanayo," I say, lying through my morning breath. It's obvious I'm not gwenchanayo at all. The state of me is an utter and total hot mess. "My God, I stink," I mutter to myself. This is so not the way I want to meet my grandmother for the first time. If only I could shower or brush my teeth, at least.

Mr. Kim turns and hands me a small tin box. When I open it, a strong whiff of peppermint hits my nose and there are tiny white pieces of hard candy inside. When I glance back up at him, he motions for me to put one in my mouth, which does wonders for my self-confidence. As much as I'd love to pretend I don't know what he means, I know exactly what he means. Averting my eyes, I shove a handful of mints in my mouth and hand the tin back to him.

The car turns into the underground parking garage of a department store, distracting me with a series of turns that leave me dizzy and disoriented. We finally stop at an entrance with stairs that lead up to a set of glass double doors to a high-end department store. When Jin Young said I'd be taken directly to Halmoni, I just assumed it would be at her home. But this is even better. What better place to meet my family than at their family business?

Two attendants dressed in red blazers and black slacks immediately approach the car from both sides. One opens the door for me, bowing as I get out. The other takes the keys from Mr. Kim. The level of attentiveness can only mean one thing: Dad's family business must be doing *really* well. There's even a red carpet that leads us through, making me feel like some kind of celebrity.

"Gamsahamnidah," I say over and over as people open doors for me. First my car door, then the doors leading into the building, and then a second set of doors after that. An arctic gust of expensive perfumed air hits my face as I follow Mr. Kim through the last set of double doors. Bright lights bounce off the marble floor and shiny white lacquer walls, making everything in the building sparkle.

When we turn the corner, there are rows and rows of shops as far as the eye can see. I feel faint and my knees wobble, which could be an effect of traveling for sixteen hours or even jet lag, but likely it's because of the sheer and utter grandeur of this place. It's like nothing I've ever seen, definitely not in Tulsa, not on any K-drama, not even in my wildest dreams.

Mr. Kim once again has me speed-walking to keep up with him. I slow my step when I notice a flurry of staff in a roped-off area of the department store's main floor. Construction workers with vests are hauling in white lacquer blocks and drilling them together. There's a sign hanging above the area, written mostly in Korean, but some of the words are in English. It reads: FALL COLLECTION.

"Fashion show?" I must've said it out loud, because the next thing I know, Mr. Kim turns his head to acknowledge me with a closed-mouth smile. I wouldn't say it's cute, but at the same time, it's not *not* cute.

Mr. Kim continues leading me down the aisle and straight into an elevator with marble floors, white lacquer walls, and rose-gold finishes—which is easily the nicest room I've been in my whole life. The Meadowland Mall in

50

Tulsa is three stories tall, and I thought *that* was kind of a big deal. There's even an elevator attendant here, dressed neatly in a red blazer with a white dress shirt underneath. Without even asking, he recognizes Mr. Kim and pushes the button for the twelfth floor. If the staff knows who he is, then the store must be doing more than really well.

I can't help marveling at everything around me when something catches my eye. The monogram on the blazer of the elevator attendant is the same one on the lapel of the shirt my mom was wearing in the old Polaroid photograph I found of her and Dad. It's unmistakably the same: an *S* and a *W* interlocked with each other. Suddenly, the pieces start coming together. My mom must have worked at this department store. She and my dad probably met here, where his family's store also is. It's all making sense now.

And, at the same time, it doesn't make sense.

Why wouldn't Mom just tell me that's how they met? Something doesn't add up, but I'm sure I'll have the answers to my questions in mere minutes.

I watch as the illuminated light goes up in ascending order, while thinking of what type of store my dad's family owns. Accessories? Shoes? Clothing? The anticipation is reaching its max level when the doors to the elevator finally open on the twelfth floor. Finally!

I peek my head out, holding my breath. As soon as I step out of the elevator, I'm even more confused than before. There are no shops or boutiques. Instead, there's a lady sitting at a desk in front of a waiting area. Her hair is tied back in a low bun and she's wearing a black fitted skirt suit. She immediately stands up from her seat and bows to us.

If there's one thing I've learned from watching hours and hours of K-dramas (I mean, other than the culinary superiority of the Shin), it's the bowing etiquette. In Korea, there's bowing and then there's *bowing*. The first kind, which is regular bowing, is out of courtesy, like when you say hi to a neighbor, the postman, or your pharmacist. The second kind, *bowing*, is more revered, like for when you greet your elder, your boss, or the president. Essentially someone with status.

I suddenly realize that ever since we got here, people are not just bowing, they're *bowing*, as if I have status.

Mr. Kim leads me past the receptionist's desk and toward the double doors on the other end of the room.

"Mr. Kim?" I have a million things I want to ask but don't know how to. When Mr. Kim turns to me, I say the only word I do know. "Halmoni?"

Mr. Kim just points to the placard beside the ornate double door and parrots back, "Halmoni."

The placard reads, in gilded English letters:

CHAIRWOMAN

SAM WON DEPARTMENT STORE

# CHAPTER 5

Okay, there is no need to freak out.

I've only been told that the family's retail business, the one they keep referring to as "the store"—like it's a perfume stand at the mall next to the pretzel hut—is not a store at all. It's a massive multilevel luxury department store.

I knew Jin Young was being humble when he referred to it as the family business. If the business article didn't tip me off, the first-class ticket definitely should have. But nothing could have prepared me for *this*.

Before I have time to process any of it, I'm standing in my halmoni's office with my knees buckling under me. I would've been slightly more relaxed had I not just found out that my halmoni owns this entire twelve-story department store. I have no choice but to be cool. *Be cool*. Be. Cool.

As soon as the doors close, I see a woman sitting on an oversized sofa directly in front of me. She has deep lines in her face, her hair is neatly tied back in a low bun, and she's wearing a conservative cardigan set. I feel the wide smile I had on my face slowly turn down. I knew that any form of verbal communication might be a struggle, but I thought we'd be able to figure it out using body language and gestures. Instead, she doesn't move from her seat and stares me up and down. In return, I stand there awkwardly, unsure of what to do next.

Everything about this first encounter feels strange and unnatural, but that's to be expected when meeting a relative I found out about only a few days ago. I mean, it is, right?

In the silence, I take it upon myself to bow, bending the upper half of my body ninety degrees. "Annyeonghaseyo, Halmoni," I say as I reach an upright position again.

Instead of saying anything, she motions for me to step closer to her, so I do. Then she gestures for me to look to my left and then my right. Once she examines my face to a microscopic degree, she begins scrawling notes on a pad. As if she's taking into account every inch of my facial details, fact-checking that I am indeed a relative.

Without another word, she gets up and leaves the office, but not before giving me another once-over from head to toe.

As the door to the office shuts behind her, I'm beginning to doubt myself. I didn't want to believe it, but this cold reception from Halmoni is giving me no choice but to think that maybe Mom is right. Maybe I made the mistake of thinking meeting my dad's family now would make us an instant family.

The door opens again, startling me. This time, a woman draped in a woven silk A-line dress and matching three-quarter-length jacket walks in. She has a slight build, and I'm immediately taken by her tastefully airbrushed makeup. I instantly recognize her from the photo I found online of her next to Jin Young and Soo Young. Before I can guess how she's related to me, she rushes over and throws her arms around me.

"Chloe-yah. I am your Halmoni. You have no idea what it means to meet you."

"Halmoni?" A million questions race through my brain at once. But between the shock and my air passages being restricted by her death grip, I only manage to eke out one. "You speak English?"

She lets out a soft laugh. "Of course I do. I studied at Oxford University, not to mention I have been running a multinational business for decades." She releases me, holds out my hands, and takes a step back to eye me up and down. "Now, let me take a look at you."

I'm pretty sure she got a big whiff of my stench, and if she didn't pass out from that, she definitely will from the looks of me. I'm a mess.

"Ohmonah." She covers her mouth that's in the shape of an *O* and I brace myself. "You look just like my son," she says, taking me by surprise.

*She thinks I look like my dad?*

All my insecurities about not knowing who I am, not having a real dad, a real family—everything—disappears in this one crystallized moment.

"I had my doubts at first about this DNA test, but now that you're here, I know you're his daughter. You are the mirror image of Joon Pyo." She wipes her nose with a tissue. "The look he makes when he is nervous, the nose, the profile. Too many similarities." Her voice quivers, sending a chill up and down my body.

Words I've wanted to hear my whole life—*craved* to

hear my whole life—becoming a sudden reality is too much for me. The tears come instantly spilling out.

"You really think I look like my dad?" I choke out through my sobs.

She tilts her head, looks into my eyes, and says, "I bet you are as kind and generous as he was, too." Her stare is so intense that it makes me believe she knows this about me as confidently as she knew it about my dad.

Her arms wrap around me again, and this time she cries with me. I cry harder, struggling to catch my breath with each ragged inhale. My whole life, Dad has been a grainy, distorted photo. Now, he's starting to feel more real to me than ever before.

After a moment, Halmoni brings me over to the sofa, where we sit side by side, both dabbing our eyes and noses with tissues.

"Let's see now. I want to get to know all about you." She gazes at me with soft but curious eyes. "How is your health?"

"My health?" I'm thrown off by the question.

Probably noticing the puzzled expression on my face, Halmoni says, "I've missed out on your childhood. I want to know every detail about you."

"Oh. My health is fine." I smile through residual tears.

"That's so good to hear." She seems pleased.

"My mom is a nurse. She makes sure to take care of my health."

She startles. "Oh, I see."

"Did you . . . know my mother?" I ask carefully.

A frown replaces the smile she had before. "The past

can be a terribly painful subject." She pats my hand. I can see she subscribes to the same coping mechanism as my mom when it comes to grief. "Besides, there's so much I want to get to know about you. Were the accommodations on the way here suitable?"

When I remember the first-class ticket, I immediately gasp. "Oh, yes! Thank you so much, I have never been more comfortable in my entire life! That bed was as big as my bed back in—no, the whole room was almost as big as my bedroom!"

The smile returns to her face. "I hope you'll be comfortable in our guesthouse. Our main house is being renovated, so I'm afraid you can't stay with us while we are temporarily displaced."

"*Guesthouse?* I booked an Airbnb. I wouldn't want to impose—"

"We took care of that. You should find everything refunded to your account. We couldn't have you staying in that tiny studio apartment, could we?" She cocks her head to the side.

"What about you, where are you staying during the renovations?"

"Don't worry about us." She smiles reassuringly. "We have apartments nearby."

"You're staying in an apartment, and I'll be staying in a house? That doesn't make sense, surely I can—"

"No, no. I insist. You are our guest," Halmoni says to me in a way that tells me she has welcomed many high-ranking businesspeople, government officials, maybe even celebrities into her home before. "I assure you, you will be very comfortable. The house is well stocked and fully staffed. Mrs. Na is a nutritionist and a very good cook. She will take care of your meals. And Mr. Kim, who met you at the airport, is our private secretary. He is my most trusted assistant and will be with you every day. They both don't speak any English, but they are instructed to take very good care of you. If you need anything, anything at all, let me know."

I somehow manage to smile back. This is so unreal. Everything I didn't have in Tulsa is now being handed to me. On a silver platter, no less.

"When will I get to meet everyone?"

She raises an eyebrow. "What do you mean?"

"Jin Young said he had a sister and I think there's an uncle, maybe his dad?"

She adjusts her glasses. "Did he? He mentioned quite a bit to you."

"And what about that lady who was in your office before? She seemed to have a commanding presence. Is she a relative?"

"Oh, that is Lady Cha." She waves a dismissive hand. "She is my most trusted advisor. She sometimes takes my place when I am otherwise detained."

"I'm so eager to get to know everyone. Eighteen years is a long time to catch up on."

Halmoni gets up and walks over to her desk. "Soo Young is in her last year of high school, a very important year for getting into college. She is probably too busy at the moment."

"Oh?" I try but fail to hide my disappointment. "I

understand. Jin Young and I will have plenty of catching up to do, then."

"Jin Young?" She shakes her head. "He is not even back in Seoul yet. He arrives on Thursday from college."

I frown. "Really? He never mentioned that in his messages." I'm a bit taken aback. Jin Young seemed so eager to meet me. You'd think he would've mentioned that small but highly relevant detail.

"Oh, don't worry," Halmoni says, probably noticing the disappointment on my face. "He will be here soon enough, and Soo Young will have some time in between studies, I'm sure. In time you will meet everyone, I promise." She waves her hand dismissively again. "Besides, you will be quite busy yourself. I have made arrangements and your schedule is quite full as it is."

"You made arrangements for me?" I ask, simultaneously shocked and touched.

"Yes, of course. This is the first time meeting you. I want only the best for you." She leans in toward me, her face practically glowing with excitement. "Tomorrow morning, I will send over a top personal trainer. Travel can be very taxing. Exercise will help your body adjust to the change."

"Wow, I've never had a personal trainer before."

Her smile widens. "After that, I have you scheduled for a facial—but not just any facial, a very special one. Korea is very advanced in its beauty industry."

"Top-of-the-line facial?" I muse. "Halmoni, everything sounds great. I just . . ."

"What is it? You can tell me," she says, sensing my hesitation.

"I thought I'd be getting to know my family better. I will meet everyone else, right?" I was already worried one week wouldn't be enough. Now she's telling me everyone is busy, and I don't know how to interpret that.

"Oh, Chloe-yah. Is that what's troubling you?" Her eyes crinkle at the corners. "Of course you will be getting to know everyone. In due time." She squeezes my hand.

Halmoni puts my worries at ease. Maybe this is what Jin Young meant when he mentioned Halmoni takes care of everyone.

"Now, it's almost evening. I bet you're exhausted after your trip. Why don't you get settled in at the guesthouse and we'll spend more time tomorrow getting to know each other." She smiles warmly at me.

I don't disagree with her. After the day I've had, I could use a nice, long nap.

X

Mr. Kim drives me an hour outside of the bustling city to a remote area where there are more trees than people. He opens the car door for me and I step out hesitantly. Then he leads me to a metal-and-wood gate hidden among a large stone wall that wraps around the entire block. As soon as he taps his phone to the monitor by the door, the gate releases.

A gasp escapes me at the sight as Mr. Kim leads me through what can only be described as an enchanted garden. The gravel path takes us through lush greenery with different kinds of flowers and plants surrounding us.

There's even a small bridge spanning a pond full of koi. Their bug eyes stare curiously up at me as I walk across the bridge, as if they know I'm a stranger here.

"*This* is the family's guesthouse?" I stare up at the modern three-story home with floor-to-ceiling windows facing out to the garden. I can't even imagine what the main house is like.

Mr. Kim hides a smile behind his fist and watches me through the sides of his eyes. As a most trusted personal assistant to the family, he might be used to being around this type of decadence, but I certainly am not.

A woman appears at the front door. She's wearing a long beige skirt and a matching sweater with her hair neatly pulled back into a low ponytail.

"Annyeonghaseyo." I bow.

"I am Mrs. Na. I cook for you," she says in broken English.

I'm not even sure how to respond to that. Just a couple of days ago, I was heating up leftovers for myself and now I'm staying in a home more akin to an estate, with my very own cook! I respond in the only way I can.

"Gamsahamnidah." I bow deeply at her.

Mrs. Na tries to hold in a laugh and motions for me to come in. I try to remind myself of etiquette and decorum, but it goes out the door the second we walk through the threshold. I gasp at the turn of every corner as I follow Mrs. Na to my room. The floors are wall-to-wall marble with coordinating furniture, and crystal chandeliers adorn every room. The entire back wall is made entirely of windows that are somehow even more impressive from the inside, overlooking the immaculately landscaped garden.

Everything is sleek, modern, and minimalist, like a show-room from one of those ultramodern furniture stores that smell like wicker and cost a small fortune to shop at.

At the top of the stairs, Mrs. Na shows me to my room, which is as tasteful as the rest of the house. The furniture is made of reclaimed wood and the bed has a floral-print duvet with a crap-ton of pillows piled on. There's even a fancy sitting chair in the corner of the room, like I see in extravagant movies about wealthy people who have space and money for furniture that is neither practical nor functional.

Shortly after, Mr. Kim follows with my luggage and sets it in my room. I thank him and they both say their goodbyes, bowing deeply at me before closing the door. Slowly spinning on my heels, I turn, half-expecting this to be a figment of my imagination. When the four-poster bed is still there, inviting as ever, I have no other choice but to do a swan dive right onto it. The landing is as soft and plush as I'd imagined it would be, which is saying something. The reality is living up to the dream in every way imaginable.

After relishing in the decadent satin comforter for a minute, I'm reminded of Mom. I landed hours ago, so she's probably been freaking out for, you know, hours.

I rush to catch Mrs. Na to ask her about the Wi-Fi. When I open the door, she's standing right in front of me.

I gasp. "Mrs. Na!"

"Neh?" Mrs. Na's eyes jut around the room and back to me.

When Halmoni said they would be available to me at all times, I didn't think she meant it literally. "Actually, I do need something. Wi-Fi?"

She nods, smiling. "Neh," she says, holding out her hand for my phone and setting it up for me.

"Thank you—I mean, gamsahamnidah."

As soon as I connect to the Wi-Fi, a slew of messages and alerts flood my phone. I swipe them away and call my mom. The phone barely rings once before she picks up.

"Chloe-yah? Are you okay?"

"Of course I'm okay, Mom."

"Then why didn't you call me right away? You landed hours ago! I was about to come over there myself." Which is the emptiest of threats.

"Sorry, I didn't have time until now."

"Why? What did they do to you? Seriously, is everything okay?"

"Mom, I'm fine." Actually, since I got here, I've been more than fine, and she needs to know that. Otherwise, at this rate, she'll give herself an ulcer before I return next week. "In fact, I rode first class, and Halmoni put me up in their ginormous guesthouse that's the size of our entire apartment complex, and tomorrow, she arranged for a personal trainer to come work with me. Trust me, Mom. You have nothing to worry about."

"Chloe-yah. Of course I'm worried about you," Mom says, pretty much bypassing everything I said. "You're my only daughter. You're all I've got."

Guilt seizes me. It didn't occur to me until now that *I'm* all *she's* got. "Sorry, Mom. I should've called you as soon as I landed."

"Listen, I got in touch with my friend from high school.

I haven't talked to her in years, but when I reached out to her, she said she has a daughter your age. Miso Dan. She goes to the boarding school in Massachusetts but is in Seoul for the summer. I think it's good to have someone your age there to hang out with."

I'm speechless. Mom has literally never talked about her past and now she's rekindling friendships with people she hasn't spoken to in over twenty years?

"Please, do it for me. It'll give me some peace of mind, knowing you're with someone I can trust." Mom goes right for the jugular. She knows just how to guilt me, even though I'm too old for friend setups.

"Fine," I concede.

"Great, I'll send you her contact information. Call her if you need anything, Chloe-yah. Okay?"

"Yeah, sure, okay, Mom. You really have nothing to worry about. Everything has been great so far."

"What about your halmoni?" she asks. "What do you think of her?"

"Oh, Mom. She is nothing like I imagined her to be like."

She sighs again. "Chloe-yah, I told you that you might be disappointed by her, that she won't meet up to your expectations."

"But that's just it. It's better than I expected!"

"Really?" If I'm not mistaken, there's genuine surprise in her tone. As if she'd expected things to go wrong.

"Not only is she sweet and caring, she's young and fashionable. They own an entire department store!" I broach the subject strategically, reminding myself Mom doesn't know I have the Polaroid photo of her and Dad with the logo on the lapel of her shirt.

"They do?" To my disappointment, Mom feigns ignorance. I was hoping she would open up more now that I'm here with my dad's family. Instead, she's becoming increasingly secretive.

"You didn't know that about Dad?" I give Mom one last chance to open up.

"Your father said he had no family when I met him, remember?"

I let out a silent sigh when I realize Mom is doubling down on her deception. "Yeah, okay. Sure." I've known for some time now that if I want to know anything about my dad or his family, I'm going to have to find out for myself.

A commotion of monitors beeping and doctors clamoring fills the silence in our conversation. A second later, someone yells, "Nurse Chang! We need you!"

"Oh, no, Chloe. I'm so sorry, but I have to go," she says frantically.

"Yeah, sure, Mom. I understand."

"Chloe-yah?"

"Yes, Mom." I perk up.

"Don't forget to call Miso. Okay?"

"Oh. Okay."

She hangs up before saying bye, once again proving that I, Chloe Chang—her daughter—will always come second to her patients.

# 23andme.com

**MESSAGES**

From: Chang, Chloe

Subject: Long-lost Sachon

Monday, 6:03 PM

> I learned from my Korean language app that
> sachon means cousin. So, hello, Sachon! I guess
> we are crossing paths. Since your last message
> said "See you soon," I thought you'd be here by
> the time I arrived. Halmoni tells me that you'll be
> in Seoul on Thursday. That's in four days, which
> sounds like nothing, but it's more than halfway into
> my week-long trip. I'm finding that time line almost
> unbearable. Okay, I just reread that sentence and I
> cringed. Eager much? Seriously, though, have a safe
> flight and can't wait to meet you on Thursday!

From: Noh, Jin Young
Subject: RE: Long-lost Sachon
Monday, 6:15 PM

I'm sorry my last message was confusing. I forgot to mention that I am not yet in Seoul, but that I will be soon. My sincerest apologies. I am detained with schoolwork. I will be there in Seoul on Thursday. I am very much looking forward to meeting you then!

# CHAPTER 6

After a much-needed nap, I roll out of bed at ten o'clock in the evening. I guess I can forget about having a good night's sleep tonight, as I'm fully awake now.

A savory aroma lures me downstairs. On the dining room table is a colorful array of small dishes filled with vegetables and kimchi, just like the ones I've seen on K-dramas. Only now, I get to experience this for myself. Saliva instantly pools in my mouth.

Mrs. Na bows to me when she emerges from the kitchen. She takes the top off a ceramic pot in the center of the table, revealing what appears to be a whole chicken submerged in a clear broth.

"Everything looks delicious," I say, marveling at the sight. "Will you be joining me?" When I motion to the seat next to me, she shakes her head.

"No, no, no!" She seems genuinely offended.

"Then . . . this is all for me?" I can't believe Mrs. Na went to this much trouble, just for me.

Mrs. Na nods, smiling kindly. When I sit down, she ladles out some broth from the pot, along with chicken and some other things I don't recognize.

"Gamsahamnidah. Is this chicken soup?" I inhale the garlic-infused steam.

"Samgyetang. Better than chicken soup."

I take a sip. "Mmm . . . mashitdah." I hear this in K-dramas when a character eats something delicious, and that is precisely what this is. The soup is rich and flavorful and nothing like I've ever tasted before.

"Not only tasty, but very healthy. Ginseng." She points to something resembling a fleshy root submerged in the soup. "Very good for the body. These are jujubes." She points to the shriveled red balls floating around. "Also good for blood pressure."

"Wow. I didn't realize Korean food was so healthy. Actually, I didn't realize healthy food could taste so good." I take a bite of everything on the table and Mrs. Na seems pleased. In fact, she stands next to the table, watching me eat as if it's a spectator sport. By the end of the meal, Mrs. Na looks as satisfied as I am.

I try to take my empty dishes into the kitchen, when Mrs. Na yells at me in Korean. I can't fully understand her, but I'm guessing she's insisting on cleaning up after me. I feel weird about someone waiting on me like this, but at the same time, Mrs. Na is very convincing. So I thank her and go back to my room to call Hazel and Seb.

"Chloe!" Hazel shrieks, still in her pj's and lying in bed. "What took so long? You left like a billion years ago!"

"I know! It's only been a day, but it feels like so much has already happened. Hold on, let me patch Seb in."

"I'm here!" I hear Seb's voice before he steps into view.

"Hey, Seb!"

"Perfect timing! I just got here, and I have coffee." He hands Hazel a hot cup of coffee and they both take a sip, lying in her bed.

"It's almost noon there, right?" I check the time on my watch to make sure.

"Yeah, but it's the first day of summer break." Seb shrugs in a sorry, not sorry way.

"Don't judge." Hazel points a finger at me and takes another sip.

"No judgment. Glad you're enjoying summer without me." I mock pout.

"Aw, don't say that! It isn't the same without you," Hazel protests.

"It's true. Hazel has said that at least ten times since you've been gone, which is roughly . . ." Seb checks his watch. "Less than twenty-four hours."

"Tell us about Seoul. Is it living up to the K-drama hype? Don't leave out any details," Hazel says.

"I met my grandma, my halmoni, and get this: She doesn't own just any store, she owns THE store."

Hazel and Seb both stare at me over the video chat, confused.

I explain everything that's transpired in the last twenty-four hours: flying first class, Sam Won Department Store, and how much Halmoni thinks I resemble my dad. I'm about to tell them about too-handsome-to-be-my-personal-chauffeur Mr. Kim when Hazel gasps.

"Oh my God, you are a chaybowl!" Hazel says.

"Should I know that word?" My brows furrow.

"The ultra-rich, conglomerate-owning families that have hella drama?!" She stares at me with her crazy eyes.

"Oh, chaebol!" Then, a second later, after the actual meaning of the word sinks in, I say, "You think my family is chaebol? The type you described to be 'hella drama'?"

"Here's what Wikipedia says about the Nohs." Seb's got his phone out and is reading from it.

"Hold on. They have a Wikipedia page?"

"'Mr. Sung Min Noh was a thriving businessman who had many smaller retail stores. In 1975, he and his wife, Mrs. Jang Hee Lee, consolidated their smaller retail stores and began developing Sam Won Group, primarily consisting of the Sam Won Department Store, but also including subsidiaries in women's fashion and skincare. Since its grand opening in 1980, the department store has been one of the leading retail businesses in Korea, offering international luxury brands such as Prada, Hermes, and Valentino alongside high-end Korean designer brands such as Clara Sunwoo and Henri Kim.' I don't know. I'm no expert, but that's pretty convincing to me," Seb says, rubbing his chin.

"Wait, what?" I still can't believe what I'm hearing.

"My best friend is a chaebol!" Hazel screams, bringing me back to earth.

"That's—It can't be—They're not—" I start and stop so many different sentences, trying to make sense of it. My family is chaebol?

"What's wrong with being chaebol?" Seb asks.

"Well, they're so . . . complicated. At least they are in the dramas." Not only are chaebols wealthy

71

conglomerate-owning families, they're media darlings whose every move is recorded and dissected in the tabloids and they're almost always embroiled in some scandal or another. My dad's family is rich, for sure, but Jin Young seems so down-to-earth and Halmoni is as welcoming as ever. There's no way my family can be chaebol.

"Not every K-drama with chaebols is complicated," Hazel says, but even she doesn't seem convinced herself.

"Remember *Boys Over Flowers*?" I counter.

She gasps. "I'm offended by that question on all accounts. It goes without saying that as the unofficial president of the I Heart Lee Min Ho fan club, it is my civic duty to love, honor, and cherish every K-drama he stars in."

Seb rolls his eyes dramatically.

"Well, if you watched any of his dramas, you'd be Team Lee Min Ho too." Hazel nudges Seb.

"See, this is why I don't watch K-dramas with you both. There's just too much competition. I can never win against eyebrows like his."

"Guys, can we focus for a minute?" I sense that there's something deeper going on between them, but I have to get to the bottom of this first. "In *Boys Over Flowers*, those chaebol kids were so mean to each other and, well, everyone else! You're saying my family could be like that?"

Hazel takes a second to think, placing a finger on her lips. "Yeah, but Lee Min Ho ends up with the girl in the end. So love conquers all?" She shrugs.

"Okay, Ms. Lee Min Ho fan club president. What about *The Heirs*, then? Remember what happened with that family?"

"You mean the one where Lee Min Ho is the heir of the chaebol family, but then his brother gets jealous and sends him away to America, and then he's forced to choose between the money or the girl he loves?" She's holding her hands over her chest like some kind of lovesick schoolgirl.

Something about Hazel's summarized version of *The Heirs* strikes a chord in me. It's not just because it made me second-guess my family's chaebol status. "Actually, now that you mention it . . ." I pause, thinking out loud. "Okay, I don't want to have a repeat of the Ted Takahashi disaster."

"You mean when we totally let our imaginations get the better of us and thought that some random stranger was your dad?" Seb smirks.

"Yep. That one." I point a finger at him.

"But?" Hazel encourages me to continue.

"Maybe that's what happened to my mom and dad." Hazel and Seb don't seem to follow, so I continue. "I mean, think about it. She was obviously not rich, not like my dad's family. Chaebol families tend to not like that."

Hazel gasps. "Oh my God, you're right! What if your halmoni sent your mom to America and your dad followed her here? How romantic!" Hazel swoons as if she were actually watching *The Heirs* right now.

"So much for not getting carried away." Seb chortles.

"You have to admit, this is way more plausible than the Ted Takahashi thing. Right?" I ask hesitantly.

"Way more plausible," Hazel says. Seb nods, agreeing with her.

That must be what happened. My mom has been weird

about me coming here from the beginning. I bet my dad's family didn't approve of my mom and that's why they moved to a different country. It explains why they lost touch, but it doesn't explain how.

"Has your mom said anything about this?" Hazel asks.

I shake my head. "In fact, she's pretending she never worked at the department store, when I have photographic evidence of her wearing an employee uniform."

"Does that mean your mom and your halmoni have met before?" Seb asks.

"Not necessarily. After seeing how enormous the department store is, I doubt Halmoni knows everyone working here. Still doesn't explain why my mom is hiding the fact that she worked here at all."

"Maybe she's embarrassed or ashamed about the way she wasn't welcomed into the family?" Hazel offers.

"Maybe." I shrug. "Whatever it is, it must be something big for her to be this determined not to tell me anything about my dad. I'll have to ask my halmoni tomorrow. She's the only other person that knows what really happened between my mom and dad."

The crease between Hazel's eyes deepens as she taps a finger to her lips. "Is it just me, or does this sound like *My Professor, My Father?*"

"Seriously?" I roll my eyes at her playfully.

"Yes, seriously! First, there's the dad discovery, then the ultrarich family, and now, hidden secrets. You've got to admit, this has K-drama written all over it."

"I'm not sure about the K-drama stuff." Seb shakes his head. "But this does sound very dramatic."

"Maybe you'll even have your very own umbrella moment." Hazel's eyebrows bounce up and down.

"Oh my God, stop." I'm barely on board with the idea that my life resembles a K-drama. I can't even begin to entertain the idea of a romance.

"Umbrella moment?" Seb raises a quizzical brow. "What's that?"

Hazel and I exchange a look.

"Only the single most quintessential romantic prop in K-dramas," I say, practically flailing.

"It is?" Seb scratches his head.

"Think about it," I say. "It's not only a thoughtful gesture to have an umbrella on hand in case of a sudden rainstorm—"

"Which happens a fair amount of times in K-dramas," Hazel interjects.

"—it is spatially designed to guarantee an intimate moment in a short amount of time. There's no way sparks won't fly when you're that close to someone."

Seb is staring at us open-mouthed. He blinks twice before he says, "*That's* the umbrella moment?" He's not as impressed with the concept as Hazel and I are. Clearly.

"You might not think romance is so ridiculous if you cared to watch one with us," Hazel not-so-subtly adds.

Seb's brow twitches and Hazel's posture stiffens. It was funny at first, educating Seb on all things K-drama. Now it's not. Is there something going on between them? Should I say something?

Before I have a chance to decide, my stomach suddenly makes a noise. I try to cover the mic, but it's too late.

"Uh, what was that?" Seb asks.

"Do they have animals there? Was that a cat?" Hazel says.

"That was the sound of my stomach. Apparently, it still thinks it's lunchtime."

"Don't they feed you in that mansion of yours?" Hazel raises an eyebrow at me.

I roll my eyes and chuckle. "It's not *my* mansion, and they did feed me." I look over at the clock. "Oh, wow. That was almost three hours ago. How is it already two in the morning here?"

"Seriously?" Hazel checks her own clock. "It's noon here."

"You may have traveled to a different time zone, but your stomach hasn't. Clearly." Seb smirks.

"All this talk of K-dramas has me craving—" I give them both a knowing look.

"The Shin!" the three of us say in unison.

"They've got to have some stashed in this house somewhere. I'll give you a tour of the palace—I mean place—while I rummage around for it."

Hazel and Seb both *ooh* and *aah* at the turn of each corner and, after a lifetime of watching other people's lives with envy, it's thrilling to be on the other side of things for once.

In the kitchen, I open up every drawer and cabinet, only to turn up empty-handed.

"I can't believe there's no Shin in the house." Hazel's flabbergasted.

"There isn't any instant ramyun in the entire kitchen?" Seb asks.

I shake my head. If only I could ask—"Mrs. Na!" I put a hand to my chest, staring at Mrs. Na, who seemingly appeared out of nowhere.

"Neh?" she asks, staring around the kitchen curiously.

"Oh, I—sorry if I woke you. I was just looking for Shin Ramyun," I say, rolling my *r* for a more authentic pronunciation.

"Shin Ramyun?" Mrs. Na looks astonished. "No, no, no. Not healthy." She shakes her head disapprovingly. "I cook healthy." She's about to pull out an apron when I stop her.

"Gwenchanayo. It's okay. I'm not that hungry. I can wait until tomorrow." As much as I appreciate her attentiveness, this is totally unnecessary.

After finally being convinced, Mrs. Na retreats back to her room and I return to the phone.

"Is that your maid? She is intense," Seb says.

"No ramyun in the house? How dare!" Hazel appropriately freaks out.

I laugh. "I haven't been here for that long, but I gather that Mrs. Na is something of a health nut. She constantly informs me of the nutritional value of the food she cooks me."

"Are you sure Mrs. Na isn't your real grandma? She acts an awful lot like my yia-yia. Always trying to make me a home-cooked meal whenever she sees me eating Doritos."

"No, my halmoni does not look anything like Mrs. Na. She's so stylish and sophisticated, but I can tell there's a soft side to her, too. It was so great meeting her." I start to tear up, remembering how tightly she held me and how much like my dad she said I looked. "I hope it's like that when I meet the others, too."

"Well, if they really are chaebols, they probably won't want people finding out about you just yet. An extra heir always complicates things!" Hazel laughs.

"Yeah, right." I laugh with them. Me? An *heiress*? Well, that's just too ridiculous for words.

# CHAPTER 7

After my call with Hazel and Seb, I lie in bed and try to sleep a couple of hours. In the end, the jet lag gets the better of me and I spend the rest of the night staring up at the ceiling. I think about everything I want to ask Halmoni about my dad. What happened between them? How did they lose touch? Did she know about my mom? My head spins so many questions that pretty soon I'm exhausted just thinking of it. Right as my eyes are about to close, Mrs. Na tells me it's time for breakfast.

"Annyeonghi jumusyeosseoyo?" Mrs. Na bows to me when she sees me in the dining room. "Sleep okay?"

I shake my head. "Jet lag."

"Aigo," she tsks, shaking her head.

"Do you have any coffee?"

"Coffee is no good." She gasps, then goes into the kitchen and comes back with a steaming teacup. "Nok Cha—green tea. High in antioxidants." She motions for me to sit down and then ladles a scoop of thick, milky-looking porridge and hands me the bowl. "Jatjuk—pine nut porridge. Very healthy."

"Oh, okay. Thank you," I say, grabbing a spoon. It's not as appealing as a tall cup of coffee, but the taste takes me by surprise. It's creamy and nutty with a slight sweetness to it. Since I didn't get my late-night ramyun snack, I ask for a second helping. When I'm finally finished with breakfast, Mrs. Na clears the empty plates, nodding in a simultaneously shocked and approving way. I thank her for the meal and go upstairs to get ready for the personal trainer whom I was told by Halmoni is coming first thing this morning.

I didn't pack any exercise clothes, so I'll have to improvise. I rummage through my bags and the best I can find are leggings and a T-shirt. It isn't athletic wear, exactly, but it's the closest I have. As I'm about to slip off my pajamas, an idea comes to me. Before I waste any more time, I quickly pull out my sewing kit and start threading a needle.

Half an hour later, I've managed to cut and hem my leggings into a sportier mid-calf capri length and undo the stitching around the neckline and sleeves of the T-shirt to seem less tailored and more rugged. I stare at myself in the mirror in the foyer, taking in the full ensemble. Not quite lululemon, but a definite improvement. I'm admiring the clean hemlines in the pant leg in the mirror by the foyer, lifting my leg up against the wall in a weird lunge position to inspect the back of the leg, when I hear someone clear their throat.

"Oh, Mr. Kim." My face flushes hot. Immediately, I bring my leg down and pretend I wasn't practically straddling the mirror. "Annyeonghaseyo."

Mr. Kim bows to me and returns the greeting, and to his credit doesn't acknowledge the compromising, not to mention supremely awkward, position I was in. Instead, he motions for me to follow him and shows me to a set of stairs that goes down. *There's a basement here?*

When we get to the landing at the bottom of the stairs, I turn the corner and am taken aback. It's a home gym. But there's nothing homey about it. Mirrors line the back wall, the floors are padded like in a gymnasium, and the entire room is filled with state-of-the-art exercise machines—a treadmill, an elliptical machine, even a Peloton. A man in a red tracksuit is at a desk next to the treadmill. Mr. Kim leads me over to him before he bows and leaves us.

The man in the tracksuit stands up and bows to me. "I am Mr. Seo. Your personal trainer for the day."

"Annyeonghaseyo, Mr. Seo." He's so tall, my neck strains looking up at him.

"We will begin first here." Mr. Seo motions for me to join him in the center of the rubber mat. I take a few deep breaths trying to prepare myself for—Actually, I don't know what to prepare myself for.

Mr. Seo pulls out a clipboard and begins by asking me, "How often do you exercise?"

"Does walking to school count? It's about one mile to get there."

He considers my question, then scribbles something down. "How often do you eat high-fat foods?"

Feeling a little called-out here, especially after Mrs. Na lectured me on how instant noodles were so unhealthy, I'm reluctant to answer. After debating a moment, I decide to answer him truthfully. "I eat pretty healthy, but every once in a while, I eat Shin Ramyun." By once in a while, I mean every week, but he doesn't need to know that.

"How about your health? Do you have any underlying health issues?"

"Underlying health issues?" I raise an eyebrow up at him. Does he want, like, my full health history? I don't have that type of information on me.

Probably sensing my confusion, Mr. Seo says, "If you do have any health issues, I can modify the exercises today."

"Oh, that makes sense." I think hard. My mom is pretty good about educating me on my health, but even still, nothing comes to mind. "No underlying health issues," I say.

Then he points to a list of words on the backside of his paper: *shortness of breath, heart condition, diabetes, high cholesterol.* I shake my head.

"Your mother?"

I give him a funny look. "What about my mother?"

"Her health?"

"It's good?" My answer comes out more like a question.

He nods and jots down my response. "Any disease she has?"

I'm about to answer when I start to get nervous. "What kind of exercises are we doing today?"

Mr. Seo tries to answer my question but gets flustered. His face turns red and he starts and stops several times.

I have to remind myself that English isn't his first language. I definitely couldn't have asked these types of questions in another language. I can barely communicate with Mr. Kim with my limited Korean vocabulary. I apologize to Mr. Seo, but he shakes his head fervently.

"No problem. I have enough information. Let's get started." He sets his clipboard down and stands in front of the mirror wall. He starts off with a series of stretches and I follow along, mimicking his movements. So far, aside from not being able to touch my toes, I feel good.

Next, he leads me to the treadmill. I'm about to step on it when he stops me.

"First, you'll need to put these on to monitor your stress levels." He motions for me to place the sticky pads to my chest and stomach by showing me a diagram.

I do a double take. "Neh?"

"For the heart rate. Your Halmoni wants to make sure the flight did not stress you."

"She does?" I instantly melt. Halmoni cares so much about my health, she's even worried about the toll it takes on my body to travel internationally.

I place the sticky pads on me, and he flips on the monitor that the wires are connected to. Then he turns on the treadmill. It's slow at first, like a nice stroll in the park. Once I get warmed up, he increases the speed. Mr. Seo does this until I feel as if I'm sprinting up a steep hill. Right when I'm about to pass out from the lack of oxygen to my lungs and brain, he shuts off the machine.

"Great," he says, smiling at the monitor.

I'm not sure if he's talking about the workout or my heart rate, because from my stance, none of it was great. I'm still gasping for air when he motions for me to step onto the stationary bike.

Seriously? I thought he might take it easy on me. I could not have been more wrong. The bike is pretty much like the treadmill, except this time, I have a blood pressure cuff attached to my upper arm. When I'm done, I nearly collapse onto the padded floor.

Mr. Seo smiles apologetically and hands me a towel and a cold water bottle from the mini-fridge. "Gosaenghaesseoyo."

"Neh?"

"It means good job." He smiles and scribbles something down on the clipboard.

At least one of us thinks I did a good job today, because my thighs and lungs are telling me otherwise. "Gamsa-hamnidah," I say between breaths and somehow make it onto my feet to bow to him.

"I will send the results, along with an exercise plan for you, to your halmoni. She told me she will be meeting you this afternoon."

"She did? That's great."

Once Mr. Seo leaves, I take a shower and decide to wear the dress I made for this trip. I unravel it and hold it up for me to inspect. It's perfect.

When I was looking for my next project, Second Time Around was gearing up for Halloween and that's when I saw them: a black pleather Catwoman suit and a matching cape. Pleather is notoriously tricky to work with, but I do love a challenge. My approach to fashion goes beyond aesthetics. I want to fashion a new life for the garment, and what better way to transform nocturnal superhero costumes than to turn them into a flirty day dress?

I slip on the dress and look at myself in the mirror. The top is a fitted cotton blend with flutter sleeves and the bottom is pleather with pleats that fall perfectly from my waist down to my knees. It's feminine and sweet, and completely what I was going for. Pleased at the way it turned out, I smile at my reflection. I'm so ready for my first day in Seoul.

Mr. Kim is waiting for me in the foyer when I get downstairs. As soon as he sees me, he pauses, looking me up and down. He bows, greeting me in his usual polite way. As he's bowing, I catch a glimpse of him smiling, ever so slightly—only it's more like a smirk than a smile. By the time he returns to an upright position, he's back to his usual professional self. Did I just imagine that smile? I want to ask him what that was, so I rack my brain for any relevant Korean words I know. I end up taking too long to come up with a question in Korean and the moment passes. Mr. Kim is now holding the front door open for me.

As soon as we step outside, I'm assaulted by the thick, humid air. My face is damp and my dress clings to me as if its life depends on it. This is definitely not pleather weather. When we reach the car, I go to grab the door handle to the passenger side, but Mr. Kim opens the back door for me.

"Can I—" I stop myself from explaining to him that I feel weird sitting in the back seat of the car as if he were my Uber driver. When he stares at me perplexed, I gather his English is worse than Mrs. Na's, who I've been able to communicate with using basic Konglish. Granted, while most of her English vocabulary consists of the culinary kind, particularly of the nutritional variety, she at least seems to know more than Mr. Kim. Without any way to communicate with him, I reluctantly get into the back seat of the car.

From behind, I stare at Mr. Kim in the driver's seat, wondering what his story is. I'm convinced he isn't much older than me. Yet his mannerisms and professionalism are way more advanced than his years would suggest. And don't even get me started on his complexion—healthy, with a glow that screams seven-step skincare routine. If we spoke the same language, I might have gathered enough courage to strike up a friendly conversation with him about how he came to work for my halmoni at such a young age. Or at the very least, learn what type of skincare products he uses. Since we don't, we ride quietly the whole way to the department store.

※

When I'm brought inside Halmoni's office, she's standing in front of her desk, waiting for me as I enter.

"Chloe-yah." She hugs me tightly. "I hear your workout was a success." She releases me and leads me to the sofa.

"Mr. Seo is being kind. I could barely keep up with him."

"Nonsense. He gave me a glowing report. He also gave me a regimen for you to follow while you are here." She hands me a slip of paper with a list of exercises. "Please use the gym every day. We just had it newly installed, just in time for your arrival."

"Will Mr. Seo be coming here every day?"

"No, no, no. Mr. Seo is a very busy man and we are so fortunate he was available to help get you on a good plan.

Your health means a lot to me." She pinches my chin and stares deep into my eyes.

Not having a grandmother my whole life, I've dreamed of what one would be like. I imagined her to be someone who cooked for me often or knitted sweaters that were two sizes too big for me. Halmoni doesn't do either of those things, but she seems to care for me in the same way I'd always imagined a halmoni would.

"Omonah. Why are you crying?" Her eyes crinkle at the corners with concern.

"You are everything and more that I could've ever wished for in a halmoni." I sob quietly, sitting next to her.

"It's the same for me, too. You are turning out to be everything I hoped for, Chloe-yah." She wipes a stray tear from my cheek.

"I don't know if I've said this before but thank you so much for taking such good care of me while I'm here."

"Nonsense. Nothing but the best for our special guest. Now I get to know all about you. So. Tell. Me." She pats my hand with each syllable. "What is it that Chloe Chang wants most in life?" she asks with raised eyebrows.

I don't have to think long to answer this question; it's what I've wanted my whole life. "I want to know about my dad. My appa." I stare so deep into her eyes, I'm sure she can see just how desperate I am to know him. After a lifetime of questions, I'm finally going to get some answers.

"Your appa?" The crease between her brows deepens. "You don't know anything about him?"

"No. My mom hardly talks about him. What can you tell me?"

I'm about to pull out the Polaroid photo of my parents when she says, "Your father was very bright. Top of his class." She sits up, puffing her chest out proudly.

"He was?" I whisper. Finally, I'm getting the details I craved to know about my dad my whole life.

She nods. "Oh, yes. He went to the Seoul National University—the Harvard of Korea. He had such a promising future ahead of him, if it wasn't for . . ." She blinks back tears.

"The accident," I say, finishing her sentence with tears in my own eyes.

She startles, as if she'd forgotten I was in the room. "What about you? Are you smart like your appa?" she asks in a completely different tone.

"Smart?" I shake my head, confused by the sudden change of topic.

"What kind of education background do you have? You must be in college now, eighteen?" Suddenly, she is studying me as if I'm some kind of a candidate applying for a job at the department store. My knee-pits begin sweating and the pleather material sticks to me, squeaking as I shift uncomfortably in my seat.

"I-I'm into fashion," I stammer clumsily.

The warmth returns to her face. "Like your father, I see." She gazes at me like she did yesterday, simultaneously intrigued and sentimental.

Like I'm chasing a high, I crave for that look to never end. I can't help myself when I tell her, "I got into the Fashion Institute of Technology." I'm surprised at how easily the words flow out, as if I have no qualms about lying.

Though technically—*technically*—it's not a lie. I did get accepted; I'm just not going. A simple distinction that I don't feel is important to clarify. It's just that the look on her face, the one she's giving me now, is confirmation that I am, as I suspected, like my dad.

"FIT? My, my, that *is* impressive. Your father always had a flair for designing items."

*He did?* The tears instantly begin welling in my eyes. "I design clothes, too," I say, barely in a whisper.

"Turns out you are more your father's daughter than you knew."

"In fact, I made this dress myself." I stand up for her to see it in all its splendor.

She puts her glasses back on her nose and studies the fabric up close. "What is this?" She rubs the fabric at the hem of the skirt.

"It's pleather. It was the only fabric they had big enough at the thrift store."

"Pleather? Thrift store?" She draws out the syllables, like it's the first time she's speaking these foreign words. This is so not impressing her the way I hoped it would.

"Materials can be expensive, so . . ."

She peers up, with her glasses hanging at the edge of her nose, as if she can't believe what she's hearing.

That look, the one where she gazes at me as if I'm her son who has come back to life, is gone again and I panic. I'm about to make up some excuse about why I shop at a thrift store, when she says, "What's this?" Halmoni's attention is now on the inner lining of the hemline.

89

"Oh, that's my brand. I heard some designers put their mark on their clothes."

She's silent, staring at the stitching. Her fingers rub it over and over, as if she's memorizing the pattern. I begin to wonder: If my dad was interested in fashion design, like me, maybe others in the family are too. Like some kind of family trait.

"Is Jin Young studying fashion design? I think Johns Hopkins is a school that specializes in the medical field. Although I could be mistaken."

As if I'd said something to break the spell, she startles. "Jin Young studying fashion design?"

"Or Soo Young? Is she planning on applying to design schools next year?"

Her posture stiffens like it did when she was talking about my father a minute ago. "Yes, yes. Jin Young and Soo Young are very smart. Top of their class."

"Wow, that's impressive. I can't wait to meet them—"

"Chloe. An idea just came to me." She puts a hand on my knee, stopping me. "Come, follow me."

# CHAPTER 8

Halmoni takes me to the third floor of the department store. Behind one of the displays is a door leading to a storeroom. There are two levels of racks against the wall that are filled with clothes and there are desks in the middle of the room. A woman with bright pink lips and dressed in a black skirt suit is staring at a rack of clothes when we walk in. She fumbles with a ruffled blouse and hanger at the sight of Halmoni and bows immediately.

Halmoni nods at her. "This is the head buyer for our ready-to-wear fashion, Ms. Song." I bow back awkwardly. "Ms. Song, this is my special guest, Chloe. She is very interested in women's fashion and has a great deal of potential."

"You think I have potential?" I say in disbelief. From the way she reacted earlier, I was sure I'd disappointed her in some way.

Halmoni smiles endearingly at me. "In fact, she is going to FIT in the fall."

I shift at the lie, but less so when I see Ms. Song nod at me, impressed.

"I thought Chloe could benefit from your expertise.

Maybe show her how we do things here?" She winks at me in a way that makes me feel special, and my stomach does a flip. "When you're finished, send her back to my office."

"Neh, Hwejangnim." She bows to Halmoni before she leaves.

Ms. Song takes me to another section of the back room and says in perfect English, "This fall season, the trends in women's fashion are monochromatic styles in warm tones. For example . . ." She motions to a young man who is dressed in a black suit and tie in the back of the room, checking inventory. He rolls over a rack of clothes. "This is one of the suits in a fall line we purchased from our local designer. The blazer, shirt, and pants are the same color, made in the same matte material."

I let the fabric slip through my fingers. I'm used to working with faded, threadbare, and sometimes even ripped secondhand fabrics. This luxurious piece of cloth feels smooth and is easily the fanciest piece of clothing I have ever touched. Peering up at her through wide eyes, I urge her to continue. I want to absorb as much information as I can.

"Last year, prints were the big trend. Animal, geometric, and floral—to name a few examples. As a result, this year women's fashion is responding by doing something very different, using mostly monochromatic color schemes."

"The fashion is responding?" I'm not quite sure whether I misheard her or something got lost in translation there.

"Yes, absolutely. Fashion is very much fluid and continuous. When a year sways one way, the following year responds by swaying the other—a yin to its yang. A trend is a response to the year before, and like many things in this world, it's all about finding a balance."

Suddenly I feel very small and out of my element. Sewing home designs by hand is one thing; finding the yin and yang in fashion is on a whole other level.

"This is a shift dress with a long vest in the same matte blush color. One way in which women's clothing differs from men's this season is in the fit. The men's clothing line is slim and form-fitting, whereas the women's line this fall is loose and baggy." Then she looks around before she leans in and says in a quieter voice, "There is a rumor that the women designers are changing the fashion to suit women for comfort and make men feel the constraints of tighter, more fitted clothes." She puts a hand over her mouth and covers a giggle.

A soft laugh escapes my lips. I wouldn't mind wearing something looser now. I'm realizing, too late I'm afraid, that pleather has zero give and my body is so bloated by the humidity here that the waistline of my outfit is cutting off circulation around my midsection.

Ms. Song takes me to the next floor, which has a sign for the fifth floor. It makes me do a double take. "Ms. Song?" I ask as we step off the escalator. "We were on the third floor before and now we're on the fifth. What happened to the fourth floor?" Hearing the question out loud makes it sound stranger than in my head.

"The number four in Korea is considered unlucky. In many establishments, it is custom to omit the number," she says almost robotically.

"Just because it's labeled differently, it doesn't mean it's not still the fourth floor," I say.

Ms. Song smiles politely and shrugs as if that's an explanation. I'm still thinking about the weirdness of the skipped floor, but Ms. Song has moved on with the tour.

"On the fifth floor is our mid- to high-level clothing lines. It's where our young generation, like yourself, would shop."

"Is this the last floor of women's wear?" I ask, feeling sad our tour is almost over.

She nods. "Except for the top floor, the secret floor above the twelfth floor. There is a button on the elevator that doesn't have a number on it."

"I wonder what it looks like up there," I say, thinking out loud.

"That is for our executive-level clientele. Invites only."

"People like the Noh family?"

"Oh, no. Chairwoman Lee does not even let her own family shop on the top floor."

What? Her own family isn't even considered VIP at their own store? It begs a follow-up question for sure. "Ms. Song?" When we turn the corner, I get distracted by the sight and forget about the question I was going to ask. The whole floor is sectioned off into different designers and each section has its own mini display with backdrops and mannequins.

I take my time weaving in and out of sections, touching the fabrics and inspecting hemlines. It's sensory overload. On impulse, I boldly take a fitted leather jacket off the rack and put it against me in front of the mirror. The material is soft and buttery, and as much as I love the pleather creation I'm wearing, the superiority in the quality of the material is undeniable.

"Why don't you try it on?" Ms. Song comes to help me with the hanger stuck inside the sleeves of the jacket.

I catch a glimpse of the price tag that reads 1,250,000 won, which is intimidating with all those zeros. After a quick calculation, it comes out to over $1,000.00, which is even more intimidating. I could never justify buying it, no matter how many outfits I sold on Etsy. "Oh, no. It's okay. I was . . ." I don't want to seem uncultured. Clearly, Ms. Song thinks I'm the type of person who can afford this type of clothing. I don't want to correct her, so instead of finishing my sentence, I smile and bow. "Thank you for everything."

"My pleasure. I'll bring you to Chairwoman Lee now."

X

"How was your tour with Ms. Song?" Halmoni gets up from behind her desk to meet me.

"It was unreal." I sit down next to her on the couch in her office, in a daze. "I still can't believe you own all this." I motion around me.

"I pride myself on my accomplishments, something that certainly did not happen overnight. When we first started this business, my husband, your harabuji, had the eye for fashion and I had the business strategy, but we had no money. No capital." She tilts her head at me. "Our story could have ended there, but it didn't. Because I had the secret to success."

I lean in, filled with curiosity. "What was it?"

"Determination."

*That's* the secret to their success?

"Without it, you might succeed. But with it, you will surely succeed."

Her words make me think about my own determination. I've been able to design clothes, despite not having proper training, and I even managed to get accepted into a prestigious fashion school. Things that once made me feel different are now starting to make sense to me. Maybe I have the same determination she's talking about. Maybe I inherited that part from her.

"I've seen that sparkle in your eye before. You are definitely a Noh; I can tell."

A lump forms in my throat hearing Halmoni refer to me as a Noh. This is what I've always wanted, to be a part of a big family. I can't wait to learn more about them. "When can I meet everyone else? Today?"

"Oh no, no, no," she tuts. "Lady Cha said not today."

The lump in my throat disappears. "Lady Cha?" I raise an eyebrow.

"My most trusted advisor. You met her yesterday, remember?"

"Oh." Now I remember. The lady I initially mistook for Halmoni.

"She said Thursday is a lucky day for meeting everyone else. Which is good news because Jin Young will arrive on Thursday too."

"Lucky? What does that have to do with meeting each other?" I think out loud.

"When you are a family like ours, you take no chances. Lady Cha is never wrong."

I decide I don't like Lady Cha. "I'm only here until Sunday," I remind her.

"Don't worry," she says. "You'll meet everyone. In due time."

Before I can protest, the intercom buzzes. Halmoni stands up and walks over to pick up the phone. She holds the receiver up to her ear and then a second later, the blood drains from her face.

As soon as Halmoni hangs up, she yells something in Korean in the direction of the anteroom outside her office doors. Immediately, her secretary rushes in and out of her office, speaking in rapid Korean. I follow Halmoni out of her office, where her secretary is holding out her bag while simultaneously helping her put on a silk embroidered jacket.

"Halmoni, is everything okay?" I stand helplessly in front of her.

"Oh, Chloe-yah. I'm sorry, but I must go. Now." There's panic in her voice.

"Go? Where?"

She hesitates, with an arm halfway through her jacket. "I wasn't going to mention anything to you . . . but my son is very sick. He has liver disease." She finishes slipping her jacket on slowly.

"Your son?" That would make him my uncle. Jin Young never mentioned this to me. "I never knew he was sick."

"I didn't want to trouble you, so I didn't tell you, but his illness has unexpectedly taken a turn for the worse. Now he is in the hospital." She grabs her handbag and meets her secretary by the elevator door.

"Oh, Halmoni. I am so sorry." I sigh, suddenly feeling like a nuisance. As if she didn't have enough on her mind, she's been busy taking care of me. "Can I at least come with you?"

"Absolutely not," she says without a moment of consideration. "He's too sick to take visitors. Now, I must go to my son. Mr. Kim will take you home and I'll call you later." She pushes the illuminated elevator button again.

Even though I don't know my uncle, not personally, I'm related to him. I want desperately for that to mean something. "Please, let me know if there's anything I can do to help."

The elevator door opens at that moment, and she stares at me intensely. Her secretary holds the elevator door open for her. Halmoni grabs the tip of my chin and looks like she's going to say something, but when the elevator beeps, warning the door is about to close, she hops in. The door closes right away, and she disappears without another word.

# CHAPTER 9

Although I recently learned my halmoni is chairwoman of the Sam Won Department Store, the literal head of a conglomerate empire, I've discovered there is one person who seems to have authority over her. That person is Lady Cha.

I have no idea what Lady Cha's exact position or title is within the company, but it's clear her area of expertise is scheduling, as she is busy dictating when we can and cannot meet. With Halmoni detained at the hospital, I find myself in a position I never thought I'd be in here: alone.

I decide to reach out to my mom's friend's daughter, Miso Dan. Mostly because I now have an entire day to fill but also because my mom wouldn't stop pestering me about it, texting me relentlessly: Did you call Miso yet?, Miso is waiting. Last, but not least, my favorite: It'll be rude if you don't call her. It's not even worth mentioning to Mom that it wasn't my idea to call her in the first place, so technically it wouldn't be *me* that's being rude. I may not know much about how family dynamics work, but I know mom-guilt when I see it.

Anyway, now that I have the rest of the day to myself, it might be a good distraction to meet another local. Plus,

I am in Seoul. There is so much I want to see.

I texted Miso as soon as I got home from the department store and instantly regretted it. I mean, she's technically a stranger to me. What if she's a complete psycho? But then, when Miso suggested we go shopping, I knew right away we'd get along. Besides, after the tour of the department store with Ms. Song, I am dying to see more of the fashion trends in Korea.

When I agreed to meet Miso at Myeong-dong Market, I naively expected it to be similar to a strip mall. The second we arrive, I know that this is no ordinary market. The streets are lined with shops practically stacked on top of each other, and hordes of people fill every square inch between them. It's like shopping on steroids. Even if I had a photo of Miso (which in hindsight, I probably should've asked for), it'd be like trying to find Waldo on a six-foot wall scroll. Impossible.

*It's fine,* I tell myself. *I am a competent eighteen-year-old who can figure out how to seamlessly sew a hidden cross-stitch pattern on a silk garment. I can do this. Just look for a Korean girl who is about my age with short hair and glasses.* When I scan the crowds and see that roughly 60 percent of the population on this street fits that bill, I realize I'm screwed.

"Chloe?" a girl taps me on the shoulder and asks, just as I'm about to spiral.

"Miso?" She's much shorter than me, with a round face, baggy retro-'90s pants, and round glasses sitting close to the edge of her nose.

She nods with a smile that takes up half of her face.

"Oh, good! I was afraid I'd have to call my mom and tell her I couldn't find you. Then I'd really be in trouble."

"Me too!" I smile, relieved.

"Sorry about suggesting this place, but I just got back from the States last week and I missed it here." She looks around. "Problem is, with K-dramas becoming so popular these days, I keep forgetting how much of a tourist attraction this place is now. I've become a visitor in my own country. *Wah!*" she mock sobs.

I laugh, instantly feeling at ease with her. "How did you find me?" I ask. "This place is wall-to-wall packed."

"It wasn't too hard, actually. You stand out like a gyopo thumb."

"Gyopo? What's that?"

"That's what we call Koreans who aren't from Korea."

"You can tell that I'm not from here? How?"

"It's not anything big. Your style—your makeup, hair, and clothes—is pretty different than everyone else's around here." She looks around dramatically for effect.

"Oh." I'm used to hearing that I easily stand out in my small town, where there are few Asians and even fewer Koreans. Scanning the crowd, I can see that Miso's right, which makes me wonder if I fit in anywhere.

"Are you hungry?" she asks, saying the magical three words that trump my thoughts at any given time.

"Always."

"Follow me."

Miso takes me through the bustling shopping area to another closed-off street filled with people. Instead of shops lining the streets, there are food vendors as far as the eyes can see. A cacophony of spicy, sweet, and savory scents fills my nose at once, making it hard to decipher what everything is. Crowds form around the food stalls, some watching, some waiting, and others eating.

She spins on her heels to face me. "What do you feel like?"

"I don't know. This is overwhelming."

"Oh, good." When I give her a funny look, she follows it up with, "I mean, it just reminds me that I'm still a local and not a complete traitor to my country."

I smile, relieved. "What do you recommend?"

"Hmm. Everything?" When I laugh, she laughs too. "I guess it depends on what you're looking for." She stops at a stall. "Most of these vendors have been here for decades. There's the classics, like tteokbokki and uhmook." She points to a steaming pan of cylindrical rice cakes slathered in an almost-neon shade of red-pepper sauce being stirred around by the vendor. Next to it is a pot of broth with skewered fish cakes bathing in it. "Then, if you like mandoo, there's a ton of places that have different kinds—kimchi, meat, veggies." She points to a vendor with a bunch of dumplings on trays.

"What's that?" I point to a stand that has plastic corn dogs on display on the metal ledge hanging over the food cart. "That doesn't look very traditional. In fact, it looks very American."

"Yeah, this isn't just any corn dog. Inside this one is a layer of cheese rolled around a hot dog. And this one is fried with an outer layer of crinkle-cut french fries. It's delicious."

"You're right. Doesn't sound like any corn dog I've heard of."

"Koreans are good at doing that."

"Making corn dogs?" My brows furrow.

"Taking a simple idea, like the corn dog, and taking it somewhere unexpected. I mean, look at this." She points to a stall with a single potato spiraling around a foot-long skewer. "This is a crazy take on curly fries, don't you think?"

I laugh. "Wow, that's pretty unexpected."

"What about the desserts, you say, Chloe?" I laugh as she holds a fake mic to her mouth and does her best imitation of an announcer. "Well, here's an example." She points to a vendor filling a cone with green-colored soft serve from a machine. When it looks like an adequate amount of ice cream, he doesn't stop. He keeps going and going and going . . . until the frozen green treat reaches about a foot tall!

I catch myself drooling at the towering matcha creamy goodness.

"Let's get one," Miso says, dropping her faux announcement voice and returning to her normal one.

"Yes, let's."

A minute later (technically eleven minutes because of the line ahead of us) we are both holding our own matcha ice-cream cones. I practically have mine down to my waist in order to take my first lick.

"God, I missed this." Miso savors her first taste.

"The flavor is more intense than anything I've ever had before."

"It is," Miso says, walking beside me. "It's a skill Koreans value. Take an idea and improve on it."

"Huh." I stop walking.

"What is it?" She licks the side of her cone that's starting to drip onto her thumb.

"I guess that's where I get it from." My mouth turns to a slight frown.

"Get what from?"

"I design clothes, but not just any clothes. I repurpose outfits, updating old ones to newer styles or even changing them completely, like turning a dress into shorts and a top."

"Oh, that is so cool! And yes, very Korean."

"Thanks." I smile into my ice cream that's melting faster than I can eat it. I take a big sweeping lick, then continue. "Anyway, I guess until you said that, I thought, or rather I was hoping, that I got that skill from my dad's side of the family. Now it sounds like maybe that's just the Korean in me?" It's reassuring news either way.

"Can't it be both?" Miso says simply. "I mean, your dad is Korean, no?" I nod. "He's into fashion too?" I nod again, this time more hesitantly since I don't know this information firsthand. "Then it could be both. You're Korean and you're your father's daughter."

By now, I've decided I definitely like Miso. No, it's not because she suggested dessert before dinner. It's not even that she insisted on paying for the ice cream, since I'm a visitor and this is her hometown. I like Miso because she is the first person I can talk openly to about my Koreanness without feeling any judgment.

"Let's go shopping," she suggests after we finish our cones. And now I like her even more.

If the food in Korea blew my mind, then the shopping is totally obliterating it.

Not only do they have exponentially more stores in this outdoor market than any mall I've been to, each one has its own specialty, Miso explains. There are shops that sell suits, shops that sell dresses, even shops that just sell pants (no tops!). It's shopping magnified. Miso even helped me get a good deal on a long, flowy skirt. She was able to haggle with the storeowner to drop the price by a few won, which is also a totally new experience for me.

"I must have passed like five skincare boutiques." I count, looking at the row of shops behind us.

"That's nothing. Wait until we go down the next block. There are at least a dozen more."

"At the Meadowland Mall, we have a Sephora and a MAC, and I thought that was a lot."

"What can I say. Korean culture has become image-obsessed."

"Has it?" I tug on my clingy top self-consciously.

She nods. "Which is why I've decided to rebel against the unrealistic beauty standards here."

"You are? How?"

"Hell yeah! I mean, why do you think I dress like a '90s wannabe rapper?" She motions up and down herself.

"To be retro?" I draw out the words, not wanting to offend her. If anyone understands how fashion is a form of artistic expression, it's me.

"No, because it's baggy. I've got a dozen Hammer pants in my closet and it isn't just because they're comfy. It's because it goes against this notion of an ideal body type people are brainwashed to think is beautiful." She points to a poster for an advertisement on the side of a building, displaying a tall, thin model with voluminous shiny hair and glowing skin. "It's no wonder so many people have such an unhealthy obsession with image."

"I feel the same way. I mean, how can this be the standard of what beauty is when there's nothing normal about it?" I motion to the billboard. "That's why I started creating my own designs—to tailor them to fit real people and not some idea of what a person should look like."

Miso draws her head back, staring sidelong at me. "Okay, Beyoncé. I see you," she says, making us both laugh. "You know, I have to admit, when my Mom told me about you, I was skeptical. But I'm glad you reached out."

"Same." My mouth stretches out in an awkward smile. "So, Hammer pants, huh? I suddenly have a newfound respect for them."

"I know, right?" Miso displays her pants leg. "Plus, I am a sucker for animal-print fabric in bold colors."

I laugh into my fist. Okay, now I am loving this girl. She is totally refreshing and 100 percent different from anyone I've ever met.

"I mean it! Give me a purple zebra-patterned outfit and I'm hopeless. I'm working on bringing them back in style."

"Well, you've convinced me. I'm a definite fan of them now." I wipe my brow for the hundredth time while Miso seems adequately sweat free. "I don't know how you keep cool in this humidity. I'm melting."

She smiles broadly again. "I'm used to it. Local, remember?" She points her thumbs to her face. "But we can go to a café if you want."

"Oh, I've always wanted to go here." I show her on my phone.

# CHAPTER 10

After a ten-minute trek, we're basking in an air-conditioned café, sitting across from each other on leather couches, waiting for our beverages. The price of the drinks is highway robbery, priced at almost quadruple the amount of what they should cost, but considering the immersive experience the café has promised, it's totally worth it. Miso, however, does not agree.

"Um, what are we doing here?" She shoots a dirty look at the llama (yes, *llama*) breathing down her neck.

"Because! It's a llama!" I squeal, snapping a photo. I've read about these animal cafés and I knew I had to experience one in real life.

"Let me guess, you saw it on a K-drama or on a vlog." She rolls her eyes.

"Both. Although I wanted to go to the hedgehog café, but I read that one closed down."

"For good reason, too! Cafés are in no way, shape, or form a suitable habitat for animals. It's hardly suitable for humans." She points to a couple sitting on one side of a booth together, attached at the hips and staring dreamily into each other's eyes. "Get a room!" she says loudly.

"Shhh!" I sink farther into my seat, even though the

couple doesn't flinch or even know we exist for that matter.

"Most everyone understands English here, but they don't always get nuance." She winks at me.

The waiter comes and drops off two drinks. A pineapple smoothie for her and a grape soda for me.

"Speaking of nuance . . . how come you can speak English with an American accent?"

"I've gone to boarding school in Massachusetts since I was fourteen, so I've been there for four years now."

"At fourteen, I don't know if I could have gone to another state, let alone another country. In fact, this is my first time overseas."

"What? No way!"

I nod. "How come you decided to go to boarding school?"

She shrugs. "I guess I just never felt like I fit in here with the others. My parents and I decided that maybe it might be a good opportunity to go abroad."

I can't hide my surprise. I always thought if I'd been born in a place with more people that looked like me, then I wouldn't feel so different from everyone. Now I'm not so sure.

Reading my reaction, Miso says, "I mean, look at me. I'm weird!" She puts a preemptive hand up to me. "And before you embarrass us by trying to come up with compliments we both know are a stretch, I just want to say I'm okay with it. It's a choice to dress this way, and standing out is part of the greater purpose to normalize different body types."

"Wow. I have never met someone so self-assured as you. Sorry if I'm fangirling."

"Pshhh, fangirling." She swats a hand at me. "I'm more confident now, but it was only six years ago I wanted to cut my nose off and shave my chin and cheeks with a cheese grater."

"Whoa. A cheese grater?"

"Apparently, your face is only beautiful if you have a narrow jaw line and a tiny button nose." She scoffs loudly.

"Oh my God. That's terrible," I say, appalled.

"My parents were sick of seeing me so sad, so they decided to send me to boarding school to have a fresh start. Plus, it gave them mad bragging rights to their friends to send me *to the boarding school* in America," she says, mocking her parents. She takes a sip of her pineapple smoothie and spits something out into her napkin. "Gross, I think that's a hair. I mean, it could be a pineapple fiber, but now it doesn't matter because I'm surrounded by llamas and all I can think about is their hair in my mouth." She shudders and pushes away her drink.

I laugh, but then check my own drink. Hair free, thank God. "My mom likes to say that, too, but instead of 'the boarding school,' she says 'the high school.' *Chloe-yah, I can't believe you graduated from* the *high school.*" We both laugh.

"My mom was so desperate to see me happy, she even took me to a fortune-teller, changed my name."

"*What?*" I ask, not sure if I heard her correctly.

"I know, right?" Miso continues. "My real name is Dan Sarang, which literally translates to Sweet Love. The fortune-teller said that was part of the problem. I was looking for love, but I needed to seduce them with my smile. She was the one who told me to change my name from Sweet Love to Sweet Smile."

"Are you serious?"

"Unfortunately, I am." She shakes her head shamefully. "But you know what? I kind of think Miso suits me better, so I'm cool with it." She smiles really wide, tilting her head and pointing to her mouth.

I nod. "That is one killer smile." I'm envious of Miso for being able to say the things she wants and not worry about what other people think.

"Plus, I didn't want to hurt my mom's feelings after everything she'd done to try and make things better for me," she adds.

"You sound really tight with your mom."

"Are you and your mom not close?" She raises an eyebrow up at me.

"No, actually. We're really close. Since it's just the two of us, I feel an overwhelming sense of guilt if I let her down. I'd never be able to tell her my real problems."

"What about your dad? You said he was interested in fashion, like you. Are you close to him?" She takes another sip of her drink, then makes a face. "God, take this away from me. I keep forgetting it's contaminated with llama hair." She pushes the cup away. I laugh. A beat later she asks, "What does your dad do?"

"Actually, my dad is dead."

"Oh, I'm sorry." She puts a hand over her mouth, as if she'd just put her foot in it.

"He died before I was born, so I never met him."

"Oh, I see," she says.

111

"Now I'm here meeting his side of the family for the first time."

She raises an eyebrow. "You're meeting your dad's side of the family? After eighteen years? Sounds like there's a story there." She scoots her chair closer and leans in. "I'm listening."

I laugh lightly, but then gear myself up to tell her the story, the short version. "I took a DNA test and it linked me to this guy, Jin Young, and he messaged me last week, saying that the test suggested we were cousins. Apparently the story checks out and our fathers were brothers. Then the next thing I know, they're inviting me to Korea to meet the rest of the family, so now I'm here."

"Get out!" she says, her mouth in an *O* shape. "You found this out last week and now you're here?" Then, after a second, her face becomes pensive. "If you're here to meet them, then . . . why are you here with me?" She's about to take another sip of her drink when I stop her.

"Don't!"

"Oh, right. Thanks, Chloe. Good looking out." She juts her chin at me.

"I met my halmoni on Monday when I arrived in Seoul and it was a dream come true. She hugged me so tight, as if she was making up for all the missed hugs in my eighteen years." I put my hand to my chest, reliving the moment with tears in my eyes.

"Oh, you're going to make me cry." We both start fanning our eyes and then laugh at the state of us. "So how come you're not hanging out with this awesome halmoni

112

of yours? I mean, I'm fun, but I don't claim to have Halmoni status." She snorts.

"Well, that's the weird part. I came here expecting to meet everyone, but I've been here for three days and so far I've only met my halmoni. Don't get me wrong, meeting her was everything I'd hoped for and more. But now that I've been here for a few days, I've spent more time with her employees than I have with my family."

"Employees? What kind of employees are we talking about?" She looks at me skeptically.

"There's Mrs. Na, who cooks for me at the guesthouse; Mr. Kim, who's their personal secretary and drives me around; and Mr. Seo, the personal trainer."

"Wait, wait, wait—guesthouse, driver, *personal trainer*? What does your family do again?"

"My halmoni owns a department store."

"What?!" She shrieks so loud the three llamas in different areas of the room all flinch in unison. "You're telling me I've been hanging out with a chaebol this whole time without knowing it?!" I'm startled by my family being referred to as chaebol. Even after Hazel, Seb, and I made the connection, it's still not something I'm used to hearing. "Which department store? Shinsegae? Lotte? Galleria?"

"Sam Won."

"No! My God, you're kidding me! Your cousin Jin Young is *Noh* Jin Young? The heir to one of the biggest fashion conglomerates in Korea?" She has her hands over her mouth and is hyperventilating into it.

"You know them?"

"When you're chaebol, *everyone* knows about you."

"Seriously? You probably know more about my family than I do, then."

"We just passed like five stores your family owns while we were walking around. Shinae Beauty, Star Boutique, Haneul Hanboks—and not only that, a lot of those clothing stalls sell knockoffs of the brands your family makes. God, Chloe! I didn't know I was sitting here with a bona fide chaebol! Here, take a selfie with me. With the llama." She makes kissing noises to try to lure the llamas she was hating on just a second ago.

"Wait, wait, wait." I push her phone down. "Are you telling me that chaebols in real life are like the ones in K-dramas?" I think back to the ridiculous plots of squabbling heirs, arranged marriages for the benefit of business mergers, and too many scandals to list.

She narrows her eyes at me. "Stick with Unni, I'll tell you what's what."

We push the drinks aside and lean in closer. I even forget about the llamas and focus only on what Miso is going to say.

"Chaebols are considered royalty for two reasons. The first, because of the extravagant lifestyles they live. *Multiple* multilevel homes in the city, which is a big deal in Seoul thanks to our population density. Jet-setting across the world on a whim, Paris shopping sprees, relaxing in the Maldives, galas in Geneva, et cetera, et cetera. The world is their playground. And their toys . . ." She whistles, shaking her head. "The best of everything money can buy, on a scale that doesn't seem possible.

They wear watches that cost more than most people's homes."

"So far, this all tracks. I mean, the personal trainer alone oversaw my health to a biological level. They even have a brand-new state-of-the-art home gym."

She gasps as if she's remembered something. "Are you staying at their home in Seongbuk-dong? I heard it's like the Pentagon. Like, no one knows what it actually looks like, hidden behind so many barriers and so much security."

"Uh, that's not exactly what the house I'm staying at looks like . . ." I pull out my phone and connect to the free Wi-Fi in the café, then pull up the house on Maps, where I have it pinned. "Here, I'm staying at their guesthouse."

She tilts her head, and a crease forms between her eyes. "That's Seocho-dong. That's south of the Han River."

"What's wrong with that place?" Something about her expression makes me uneasy.

"Oh, nothing. I could've sworn that's their winter home." She shakes her head. "But what do I know, I'm just a commoner. I get my information from the tabloids. From now on, I'll have to go straight to the source." When I give her a blank stare, she says, "That's you!"

"Oh, right. Heh-heh." Even though the Nohs are chaebol, I'm having a harder time convincing myself that I am. "That doesn't necessarily make me a chaebol." The more we talk about them, the bigger deal they are, and that makes me feel insecure.

"You took a DNA test, right?"

I nod.

"They have the results, too?"

I nod again.

"*Ppffftttt!* Then you're in their inner circle! You have nothing to worry about!"

Her line of reasoning seems to make sense, and it does make me feel slightly less insecure.

"So how is it? How do the rich live?" She stares at me wide-eyed.

"It's like you say, a multilevel home made almost entirely of glass with no expense spared."

"I knew it!" She squeals, reminding me of Hazel's reaction yesterday. "Everything about them is larger-than-life, right down to their temper tantrums. I'm talking giant, Godzilla-sized ones."

I think about Hazel and the way she describes her big family being full of drama. If everything Miso is saying about Koreans and chaebols is true, then the Noh family drama is no ordinary drama. It's next-level K-drama.

"I'm afraid to ask, especially since you compared it to a destructive sea monster the size of a skyscraper, but what type of drama do the Nohs have?"

"Well, the biggest thing the Nohs are known for lately is your cousin. He has all the makings of a heartthrob— he's single, good-looking, and most of all, the heir to the Noh fashion and beauty empire."

"Wow, I didn't realize how big of a deal Jin Young is. He's so down-to-earth in his messages."

"Seriously? Good looks, money, *and* a soul?" She glances sideways at me. "That's something you don't see every day."

I beam with sudden pride about my cousin, whom I've never even met in person. It's a delayed reaction, but witnessing Miso's instant recognition of my dad's family is making the reality that my family is chaebol finally feel real.

"Oh! Now I remember." She jumps. "She's known to be really superstitious, your halmoni. I remember this because she sometimes doesn't make it to fashion week depending on what day of the year it falls on."

"What?"

"I know, right? A leading retailer not making it to fashion week? It's definitely something tabloid-worthy."

"Why would she do such a thing?"

"She's got one of those highly sought-after fortune-tellers on her staff . . . I'm forgetting her name right now." Miso turns her attention back to her phone.

I don't wait for her to find it online, because I already know. "Lady Cha," I say.

"Yes, that's right. Have you met her yet?" She looks up from her phone.

"I did."

"What's she like? Did she tell you your fortune? Is she going to try to set you up with someone?" Miso's line of questioning, plus the fact that she mentioned she had been to a fortune-teller herself when she was younger, is making me think that maybe this isn't as strange as it sounds.

"So this isn't weird?" I raise an eyebrow.

"What's not weird?"

"Lady Cha? The fortune-teller?"

"No, lots of people are superstitious here." She swats

a hand at me. "I mean, your halmoni does seem a bit extreme, but it's not unusual to seek the advice of fortune-tellers."

My shoulders relax. Knowing that Lady Cha, Halmoni's most trusted advisor, is a fortune-teller, is pretty out there, but at least I know not being able to meet everyone else in the family is nothing personal.

"What else do the blogs say about my family?" I realize how ridiculous it is, that I'm googling gossip pages about my own family. But now that I'm becoming increasingly aware of who they are, I can't help it.

She gasps, putting a hand up to her mouth.

"What is it? Is it about my dad?" My body tenses up, wondering if she knows how my dad lost touch with his family.

"No. Jin Young's dad. He died about two years ago of a heart attack. How did I not know about this?"

"Oh, no. He did?" Inexplicably, I feel an intense wave of sadness over an uncle I never knew and a cousin I haven't met yet.

"Did he say anything about it when he told you about the family?"

I shake my head slowly. "He never mentioned anything about it." I stare pensively at the wall, thinking about how loss is an extremely personal thing. Talking about the absence of my dad isn't always easy, and I never even met him. I can't even begin to imagine what Jin Young is feeling. "Then again, it's not something someone mentions over emails."

"No, it's not. In fact, it's not something that was really

mentioned in the news articles either," she says, turning her attention back to her phone. After another minute, she sets her phone down on the table. "Maybe they wanted privacy over the matter and told the press to back off."

Miso's response makes me wonder what other privileges chaebols have. "You said there were two things that chaebols were known for. What's the second?" I ask.

"Companies get passed down, usually from father to son, but now it can be from husband to wife or daughter. When there's a lot of people in the family, it can be a real shit show." After she sees me biting my nails, she says, "Uh-oh. Did I scare you?"

"Well, it's just . . . My best friends, Hazel and Seb, have these really loud and colorful families, and I've always wanted to be in one too. Now that I'm a part of a family, a big one, I really want them to like me. Hearing how important they are makes me nervous they might not easily welcome me. They might think I'm here for the wrong reasons."

"Look, you said Jin Young contacted you first, not the other way around. And your halmoni hugged you, right?" I nod. "That's like a Korean urban legend—halmonis don't do that. They nag as their way of showing affection. If your halmoni already embraced you with open arms, then you're golden."

"Really?"

"Yep. Korea may still be a patriarchal society—fathers and sons and all that. But everyone knows it's the matriarchs who hold all the power."

"They do?"

She nods. "If your halmoni accepts you, then the family has no say in the matter."

Miso was right about everything today—the food, the shopping—and now I hope she's right about the rest of my family.

# CHAPTER 11

Wednesday morning, I wake up and do my exercises. By the time I shower and come down, Mrs. Na has a breakfast of abalone porridge and pickled cucumbers waiting for me. As usual, it's not only extremely satisfying, it's also "very healthy." I've learned in a short time that Mrs. Na's limited vocabulary includes three short phrases, all involving food: *You hungry?, very healthy,* and *very unhealthy.*

After only two days here, I'm feeling well-rested and full of energy. I can see why rich people—and by rich, I mean my halmoni—would hire a personal trainer. If I start every day like this, I'm sure I'll live to be a hundred.

After I shower and change, Mr. Kim is waiting for me in the foyer to take me to my facial appointment.

He bows deeply at me. "Annyeonghaseyo." As he bows, I notice something different about him. Today, nestled in his underarm, is a compact, and very intimate, umbrella.

"Annyeonghaseyo, Mr. Kim," I somehow manage to say without blushing.

Maybe Hazel isn't too far-off in thinking I could have my very own umbrella moment here.

I follow him to the car, staring at the back of him. His suits are always so impeccably tailored, and his neatly styled hair hits the collar of his shirt just so. The umbrella peeking out under his arm is making the heat rise to my cheeks, and my mind begins to race with questions I have no business asking, even if I could speak the same language as him. Does he use pomade or gel? Does he have a stylist? Does he have a girlfriend? *Girlfriends* (plural)?

The thing about Mr. Kim that I'm drawn to is that for all his put-togetherness, there isn't an ounce of pretension. Almost as if he carefully curates his looks not out of vanity, but duty. Which makes him all the more intriguing.

Lost in my thoughts, I don't realize when we reach the car. Mr. Kim abruptly turns around, inadvertently catching me ogling his neck. Flustered, I reach for the passenger-side door. He stops me, gently, then reaches to open the door to the back seat.

"Oh, right," I say, still burning with shame as I slip into the car. Sitting in the back seat is a stark reminder that Mr. Kim is my driver, employed by my halmoni and therefore off-limits.

I distract myself by thinking about the facial I'm about to get. Having seen countless spa scenes in K-dramas, excitement takes me over. Though I doubt Halmoni arranged for me to go to that kind of spa; they're probably a bit too lowbrow for her taste. But maybe I'll still be able to get one of those body scrubs that Korean spas are notorious for or gorge myself on snacks and the hard-boiled eggs that K-dramas somehow always make look so tasty when I don't even like them. Maybe there'll even be Shin

Ramyun. My mouth is salivating just thinking about it. I can't believe I've been in Korea for three whole days and I haven't had the Shin yet. I get that wealthy people hire nutritionists and personal trainers and, to be clear, I'm not complaining, but . . . I just want a bowl of spicy and supremely satisfying, albeit not exactly healthy, instant noodles. Is that so bad?

I'm still dreaming of Shin Ramyun when the car stops in front of a plaza with buildings and restaurants. I exit the car and follow Mr. Kim inside a building to an elevator that takes us up to the fifth floor. Next to the elevator button is a sign that reads: MEDICAL SPA.

*Medical spa?*

The pairing of those words throws me off. I've seen enough spas on-screen to know what they're like in Korea. After countless hours of waiting for Mom at St. Francis Hospital, I *definitely* know what medical facilities are like. When the elevator dings and the doors open, I'm wondering, *What kind of facial is this?*

Mr. Kim peers over at me and I smile at him nervously. The expression on his face is hard to read, but he's not his usual stoic self. A crease that wasn't there before forms between his brow, which is confusing and doesn't calm my nerves. When my feet don't move, I notice he hesitates as well. Just as the elevator door is about to close on us, his hand reaches out to push it back open, startling him just as much as it startles me. Quickly, he recovers and motions for me to step out.

What was that all about?

In the short time I've known Mr. Kim, I've never seen

him off his game, which is why this moment strikes me as odd. Then again, I could be imagining it, since he seems to be back to his usual self by the time we reach the spa door.

As soon as we step into the waiting room behind the glass double doors, I know instantly this place is more medical than spa. There are no trickling water fountains, no soothing ethereal music being played on surround sound, no bathrobes being handed out. Instead, there's a sterile waiting room with a receptionist wearing pink scrubs.

"Chang, Chloe," the receptionist calls, right as I'm about to sit down in a chair.

On reflex, I raise my hand, then quickly put it down by my side. Mr. Kim speaks softly to the receptionist and she nods eagerly, seeming to understand everything, while I merely stand there and watch.

The lady in the scrubs motions me over and I follow her into a room that is a cross between a dentist's office and an exam room. There's a reclining leather chair with a moveable light fixture above it and on the counter there's a sink and gauze and bandages. Lots of them.

"Ms. Chang?" A different lady holding a clipboard walks in. She, too, is wearing scrubs. When I nod, she sits down in a chair next to me. "Is everything correct?" She hands me the clipboard and on it is a sheet of paper with *Patient Information* written at the top. To my surprise, it's filled out pretty thoroughly, with my name, height, weight, and some other general health information. Even my eating habits are listed. An eerie feeling creeps over me, like my personal information has been leaked somewhere. Then I quickly remember that I filled out this information yesterday with Mr. Seo, the personal trainer. Halmoni now has that information, which makes sense since she's the one arranging everything for me. When I realize I'm being paranoid for no reason, I give the clipboard back to her and confirm that everything is correct.

She hands the clipboard to her assistant, then proceeds to put on rubber gloves, which reminds me of my mom. All of a sudden I'm thinking of Mom and wondering what she's been up to in her spare time. It's funny because I can't think of my mom doing anything other than working or spending time with me. Which makes me sad. So sad that it takes me a full second to register that the lady is tying a rubber tourniquet around my upper arm. By the time she reaches for the needle, I snap out of it.

Sitting up, I ask, "This is for a facial, correct?" I even point to my face for added measure. Maybe there's been some sort of mix-up with my appointment. What possible reason could they have to draw my blood?

The aesthetician nods, undeterred. "This is for the PRP facial—platelet-rich plasma—or vampire facial. We use your own blood platelets and plasma to regenerate collagen and stay youthful. It's very popular and very natural and very expensive." She raises an eyebrow as if to congratulate me for being so lucky to receive such a treatment.

I refrain from reminding the aesthetician that I'm at an age where I don't want to look younger. It seems impertinent and rude, especially to Halmoni, who so clearly went to such great lengths to arrange for this extravagant facial. So I lean back and let the aesthetician draw blood.

"Wow, that's a lot of vials," I say when she's finally done.

"We must spin the blood in a centrifuge to separate the blood cells from the platelets. We want to make sure we have enough." She smiles, placing a hand on my arm. "My assistant will put numbing cream on your face, and you can rest while we spin your blood."

"Numbing cream?" I thought the worst was over, but apparently not.

"In order for the platelet-rich plasma to yield the best results, we will use a microneedling technique—"

"Microneedling? What's that?"

"Small needles that will poke holes in the surface of your skin, allowing you to absorb as much as your platelet-rich plasma as possible."

I was hoping it meant something else, but unfortunately, the term *microneedling* means exactly what it sounds like.

"Oh, don't worry," she says, probably noticing the fear in my eyes. "You won't feel a thing after the numbing cream takes effect." With a polite nod, the aesthetician leaves, and her assistant begins slathering numbing cream on my face.

X

When I leave the "spa," a term I use very loosely, I can't feel my face, but I know it's sticky and slathered in my own plasma. Now that I'm back at the guesthouse, I inspect my face in a handheld mirror in my room.

Halmoni didn't schedule anything for me after the facial. She insisted that I stay at the house to rest my skin. At the time, I had no idea what that meant, but now I do. The numbing cream is starting to wear off, and my skin looks and feels as if it's been sunburned. How is this supposed to look good, I wonder?

My phone rings while I'm angling the mirror at my face, and I press the Accept button without realizing it's a video call. But it's too late.

"Chloe-yah, is that you?! What happened?" Mom's voice shrieks. "What's wrong with your face? It's red, like kimchi!"

"Mom, I'm fine," I say, smiling through the pain. I think it's safe to say that the numbing cream has completely worn off.

"You're not fine. Your skin looks burned. Tell me everything."

"Really. It looks worse than it is. This is a highly sophisticated high-tech facial using my own plasma—"

"You got the PRP facial?" Instead of easing Mom's anxiety, I've somehow managed to worsen it.

"You know about this?" Of course she knows about this. She's dedicated her life to the medical profession. "Apparently, it's all the rage here. Halmoni arranged for me to get one. Isn't that cool?" Though I have yet to witness the benefits of this so-called facial, I try my best to sound convincing.

The thing is, I know Mom doesn't quite trust Halmoni. Until she's ready to tell me why, I'll never understand. The only thing I can do is try to make Mom understand that Halmoni is not the enemy.

"I can't believe they took your blood." She shakes her head in disbelief.

"I got it back. Well, most of it." I lightly pat my face, suppressing a wince. "Anyway, in a couple of days, my skin will look youthful and firm."

"It already is youthful and firm," she says, calling me out.

"Well, it's a nice gesture, don't you think?"

Mom is not convinced. In fact, she seems determined as ever. "I don't like it. What kind of a person inflicts that kind of invasive beauty treatment on a child?"

"Relax, Mom. It didn't hurt." *Much.*

"Of all the things to do in Korea, I can't believe she—"

I can tell Mom isn't going to let this go, so I change the subject. "What kind of things did you used to do in Korea?"

Catching her off-guard, Mom hesitates. "What?"

"I know you haven't been back since I was born, which is at least eighteen years. Don't you miss the place where you grew up? I know I would." A montage of still frames flicks through my memory, of me, Seb, and Hazel crammed on my bed, watching endless hours of K-dramas. A sudden pang of homesickness hits me.

"When I came here, I had nothing left for me in Korea. My father left when I was five and my mom died of a heart attack when I was in college. Since I didn't have any other relatives, I had to support myself somehow. I had no choice but to take a year off of college and get a job to save up to go back the following year."

"Oh, Mom. I had no idea," I say, tearing up. Hearing Mom open up for the first time takes me by surprise. For as long as I can remember, she's never talked about hardship. A single tear trickles down my cheek, stinging my skin. I react without thinking and wince at the pain, quickly wiping away the tear.

My sudden reaction wakes Mom up from her trance, and her brows clench together. "Are you sure you're okay?"

I understand Mom a little better now that I've heard her story. Halmoni probably disapproved of her poor background, but that's in the past. If I ever want a relationship with both her and my halmoni, Mom needs to know that I'm doing fine.

"Mom." I tilt my head to her. "I have a fitness instructor who created a workout regimen for me, a cook that makes me healthy, homemade meals, and a driver to take me anywhere I want. I'd say Halmoni is taking good care of me, don't you think?"

She pretends to be distracted by a loose thread on the sofa. She picks at it for a moment and then eventually turns her attention back to me. "You're right. It sounds like she's taking good care of you," she finally lets herself admit. "I still think it's irresponsible to subject children to such an invasive facial."

"I'm an adult, remember?" I smile gently at her, mostly because the numbing cream has definitely worn off by now and stretching my mouth to a full smile is too much.

But also because I want Mom to really believe me. "Trust me. Everything is going great."

After we hang up, I can't stop thinking about how different our views are about Halmoni. Without my dad around, I know that I'm the only thing keeping them tied to one another. If I want to be close to both of them, I have to find a way to repair their relationship. Somehow.

# <u>23andme.com</u>

**MESSAGES**

From: Noh, Jin Young
Subject: Dinner tonight
Thursday, 7:00 AM

> Halmoni apologizes for being detained so long. She said she mentioned her son, our samchon, is not well. She has made dinner reservations tonight for 7:00 p.m. Mr. Kim will take you to the restaurant. Tonight you will meet the others in the family. I hope you were not too inconvenienced with the time alone.

From: Chang, Chloe
Subject: RE: Dinner tonight
Thursday, 7:08 AM

> Of course I would have liked to have spent more time with everyone, but I completely understand. Halmoni's son is sick and she seems very dedicated to the family. The time spent alone wasn't too bad for me, either. I met a family friend who ended up being really fun and she showed me around to

some really great places around the city. Still, even with the tantalizing sights and scenes of Seoul, I have to admit the only thing I'm interested in is meeting you all tonight. To be honest, I think I may be nervous. Are there any tips you want to give me?

From: Noh, Jin Young
Subject: RE: Dinner tonight
Thursday, 7:13 AM

Just be your charming self. I am sure they will like you.

# CHAPTER 12

Thursday morning, I wake up and do the workout routine Mr. Seo planned for me. After, Mrs. Na has bibimbap waiting for me, which is a large bowl filled with rice, sauce, and a variety of sautéed vegetables. When I try to eat it right away, Mrs. Na admonishes me.

"Aigo." She takes my spoon from me and mixes the ingredients together before handing me back the spoon. The mixture is a deep red from the chili paste, and the sweet-and-spicy scent tickles my nose as I take my first bite.

"Mmmmm!" I manage to say with my mouth full. The burst of bold flavors mixed together takes me by surprise.

She nods as if to say *I told you so.* "Also very good for you—high in fiber," she adds.

I stifle a chuckle. It's only been a few days, but I've already settled into a comfortable routine here.

After breakfast I'm about to go upstairs when I notice Mr. Kim in the foyer. He has a large white box that requires him to hold it with both hands.

"Annyeonghaseyo." I bow to him.

"Annyeonghaseyo." He bows deeply to me, then hands me the box.

"For me?" I stare at the large box. It's wrapped with an expensive-looking ribbon in the same crimson and gold colors I noticed at the department store.

He nods, smiling at me.

I tear open the box in front of him. As I remove the tissue paper, it reveals the same leather jacket I was looking at during the tour in the department store with Ms. Song. I lift it up in front of me, admiring it. When I remember the price, I gasp, dropping it back in the box.

I carefully try to put it into the box in the same way it was presented to me, with no luck. "Gamsahamnidah, but no. Too bissah," I say, hoping Mr. Kim can understand Konglish.

Mr. Kim presses his lips together, probably trying to suppress a laugh, and pushes the box back to me, handing me an envelope.

Curiously, I take it from him and open it. It reads:

*My dear Chloe,*

*I am detained all day and will not be able to meet you again until dinner tonight. Please accept this gift as my apology. I will see you tonight at Ginza Sushi, 7:00 p.m.*

*—Lee Jang Hee*
  *CEO & Chairwoman of Sam Won Group*

Feeling like I can't refuse the gift, I reluctantly accept the expensive name-brand leather jacket. Mr. Kim leaves and I rush back upstairs. An idea pops into my head and I pull out the skirt I bought with Miso at Myeong-dong. I start ripping apart the fabric, then cutting out the patterns and pinning them together with pins from my sewing kit. With the leather jacket, the dress I've envisioned will be perfect for tonight's occasion. Determined as ever, I gather my sewing kit and get to work.

Right before dinner, I pull the needle through the fabric one last time, securing the stitch in place. The dress is complete just in time.

My fingers graze the blue and red pieces of cloth that are stitched together like a mosaic. I even incorporated something I remembered Ms. Song saying about the fashion for women being less conforming and more loose-fitting and created a shift dress. Most people think the shift dress got its name because of its undefined shape, making it easier to shift around in. What's lesser known is that the term also signifies a shift in culture, changing it from one thing to another. Meeting my dad's family for the first time tonight is definitely going to change things for me.

After slipping on the dress, I take one last look at myself in the mirror before going downstairs. A sudden wave of emotions hits me. Like the stitches in the fabric, it feels like I'm stitching together pieces of my life.

In the foyer, I find Mr. Kim waiting for me and I greet him. As he returns the greeting, I notice he's doing it again. That thing where he eyes me up and down before one side of his lips curls up, ever so slightly, as he bows to me. Does he actually think I can't see him doing that?

And what is that little smirk? It's definitely not a compliment. It's the look of silent judgment. Not being able to communicate with him in either English or Korean, or even body language for that matter, is beyond frustrating.

In the car ride to the restaurant, I grow increasingly insecure about my dress. It's irritating that Mr. Kim's reaction is making me feel that way. It doesn't help that the last time he did his smirk-thing was when I wore another one of my designs. I would blame his rude gesture on his lack of fashion sense if I could, but if the past three days of being driven around by him have taught me anything, it's that he lacks nothing when it comes to fashion.

As soon as we pull up to the restaurant, the adrenaline kicks in and I forget about everything else. Mr. Kim speaks to the hostess and a waiter takes me right through the waiting area and straight to a private room in the back of the restaurant. When the doors open, I hold my breath. This is it. I'm finally meeting the rest of my dad's family.

Halmoni is sitting at the head of an oval dining table, looking elegant as ever in head-to-toe Chanel. I look for Jin Young, but he's not here yet. Instead, there are two women sitting at the table.

The young woman sitting directly next to Halmoni is about my mom's age; she's dressed in an ivory linen gown so shapeless, she appears to be drowning in it. Her makeup is nonexistent, and her hair is tied back in a low ponytail. The girl next to her must be Soo Young, but she's nothing like the glamorous photos of her I saw online. She's plain looking, sporting a uniform plaid skirt and crested blazer, her hair styled in a simple blunt cut. After what Miso said about the chaebol lifestyles, neither of them give me any crazy rich Korean vibes. I suddenly feel way overdressed and out of place.

"Ah, Chloe-yah. I see you received the present I sent you," Halmoni says, inspecting me.

"Yes, thank you so much." As soon as I slip off the jacket, a waiter appears and takes it to the coat check for me. "It's way too expensive. You shouldn't have."

"When Ms. Song said you were admiring it, I knew I had to get it for you." She smiles wide, showing off a gold-capped molar.

I'm touched by her kindness and begin to tear up. "Halmoni, you're too generous." Feeling their eyes boring into me, I glance at the other two women. Instantly, my tear ducts dry up. Where Halmoni's gaze is kind and comforting, theirs is the exact opposite.

"Chloe, this is my granddaughter, Soo Young, and her mom, my daughter-in-law." Halmoni gestures to the two women next to her.

"Annyeong, Soo Young!" I wave to her, admittedly much too enthusiastically, as I sit in the seat across from her.

Soo Young doesn't return the greeting. Instead, she eyes me up and down and snorts. "What is she wearing?" she mutters loudly to her mom.

"A trash bag apparently," her mom retorts, and they both snicker.

Shocked by the fact that they speak perfect, albeit rude, English, I blurt out, "Everyone speaks such good English here, I'm so impressed."

"Soo Young and Jin Young speak English *well* because

they attended the Dae Han International School and the best hagwon since they were five years old. They learn four different languages to one day work in the family business." Soo Young's mom puffs up her chest proudly.

"That's impressive. I can barely speak one language." I laugh, attempting to lighten the mood. The sudden tension is making me sweat in this overly air-conditioned room.

"You don't speak *any* Korean?" Soo Young asks, flabbergasted.

"Well, no, but—"

"What kind of Korean mother doesn't teach Korean to her daughter?" Soo Young's mom sneers at me.

I wipe a film of sweat off my brow. Within minutes after meeting Soo Young and her mom, I'm getting the sense that the disapproval of my mom is a sentiment shared by both Soo Young and her mom.

Trying to show my sincerest interest in the family, I remember something Miso and I discovered.

I tilt my head and turn to Soo Young. "I am so sorry about your father, Soo Young. I heard he passed away two years ago. I wish I could have met him." Saying the words out loud makes me think of my own dad. Emotions begin rising in my chest, when a collective gasp from the three women takes me by surprise.

"Omo!" Soo Young's mom covers her mouth with a hand.

"What did you say?" Soo Young practically snarls.

Even Halmoni's eyes narrow at me ever so slightly.

Well, this is not the reaction I was hoping for. *At all.*

Eventually, Halmoni raises a silencing hand at them

with her eyes still locked on me. "Chloe is only trying to be polite," she says calmly. Which does little to ease the tension in the room.

"I'm sorry if I said anything out of turn. I wanted to give my condolences. You know, since my own father—"

"How long are you staying for and when are you leaving?" Soo Young says abruptly.

"Soo Young-ah," Halmoni admonishes her. "That is not nice."

"Omonim, she is wondering because with Samchon being sick, we don't have time to entertain guests right now," Soo Young's mom interjects.

"Chloe is no ordinary guest," Halmoni says.

"How is Samchon?" I ask hesitantly. Since Soo Young's mom mentioned him first, I'm sure it's okay to ask about him. Besides, I've been wondering about him ever since Halmoni left abruptly the other day.

Her face immediately darkens. "He's not doing well. Unfortunately, it looks like finding a donor will be his only chance at surviving. In fact, I'm glad you're all here, because everyone in the family should be tested to see if anyone is a match." As she says this, she takes turns looking at the three of us.

At first, I react in the same way as Soo Young and her mom, our heads hung low and our faces solemn. Then a second later, it clicks that I, like them, am family, too. My head cocks to the side. Is Halmoni talking *to* me or *about* me?

"Lady Cha says she is sure we will be able to resolve this issue by September. I was hoping it would be sooner, of course, but some things are too important to rush," Halmoni says with grave determination.

I shiver involuntarily at the mention of Lady Cha. Now that I know who she is, or rather *what* she is, Lady Cha's role in this family affair is more confusing than ever. Of course, I'm not, like, a complete skeptic. I have been known to read my horoscope in the fashion magazines at Barnes & Noble from time to time, but this is a little too woo-woo even for me. Surely Halmoni isn't relying on Lady Cha, a fortune-teller, when dealing with matters of life and death, is she?

A waiter comes barging in and the loud restaurant noise from outside interrupts my thoughts. As soon as he sets down the platter in front of me, I suddenly become distracted.

"I hope you like Japanese food." Holding her chopsticks in her hand, Halmoni signals everyone to eat.

I blink and blink again, staring at the plate. Yep, just what I thought. The food is moving.

"Um . . . do they have any rolls here? Like California roll?" I ask timidly.

My aunt stares with her mouth slightly ajar, and Soo Young laughs hard, then quickly covers her mouth, apologizing to Halmoni for the sudden, and very embarrassing (for me, not her), outburst.

"You don't like octopus?" Halmoni asks, probably noticing the fear in my eyes. The tentacles wriggle around in a pile; one even almost falls off the plate, trying to escape. I suppress a cringe.

I might feel inclined to be more adventurous if the food

weren't actually still alive. It's a lot to ask of someone whose only experience with raw foods is eating raw carrots, and even those have to be slathered in ranch for me to get them down.

"Probably your mother never taught you how to eat such delicacies," Soo Young's mom sniggers, dipping a moving tentacle in red pepper sauce and popping it in her mouth. This is now the second jab at my mom. I'm not sure how much longer I can stand it.

"Not at all. I love sashimi," I say, determined not to prove them right. I go to pick up my chopsticks and they slip through my fingers and fall to the floor with a clang. Everyone stares at me. My face, I'm sure, is kimchi red, as my mom would say. Halmoni pushes a button by her side of the table and a waiter instantly comes bursting through the doors. Quickly, he hands me a new pair while scooping up the soiled one off the floor.

I bow apologetically.

"You don't know how to use chopsticks?" Soo Young says, more like an accusation. They stare at me like I'm some kind of caged animal feeding myself for the first time.

"I can use chopsticks, but I haven't used the metal kind before." These flat silver ones are heavier and harder to keep in place than the wooden ones we have at home.

Before they can say another word, I stab a piece of nonmoving, very dead white fish and pop it in my mouth. I barely chew before gulping it down.

"Who taught you to use chopsticks like that?" Soo Young's mom asks, flabbergasted. "The ends are too close together; you'll never find a good husband like that."

I almost laugh, but a quick glance at their faces tells me it's not a joke. Apparently, my chopstick skills, or lack thereof, are going to be the reason why I will be alone, forever.

"Never mind that," Halmoni admonishes Soo Young's mother. "There's still time for you to learn how to use chopsticks properly." When she waves her hand dismissively at them, her napkin falls to the ground.

Noticing the napkin holder right in front of me, I get up and take one to her to replace the one that fell. All three women gasp collectively.

"What?" I jump, reflexively.

"Two hands!" Soo Young's mom shouts at me. "Never present your elders anything with one hand. You must always use two hands. Like this." She then shows me how to hand Halmoni the napkin, one hand supporting the other.

The social etiquette for showing one's respect for elders is something I'm very familiar with. I've seen this type of thing before, many times . . . *on-screen*. But this—*this* is real life. And as much as I'm a fan of watching K-dramas, I'm making a total disaster of living one.

"What kind of a mother doesn't teach their child how to respect elders?" Soo Young's mom spits the words out venomously.

My stomach is gurgling and it's not from the raw fish. This is now the third jab at my mom. Offending me is one thing; at least I can speak up for myself. My mom, however, isn't here to defend herself. So I take it upon myself to speak up for her.

I narrow my eyes at Soo Young's mom. "I guess she had more important things to worry about, like how to manage work while raising a child as a single mom." I know it's rude in any culture to talk back to an adult, but I can't help it. That insult was the last straw.

Soo Young's mom exchanges a look of mutual shock with her daughter. "Omonim—"

Halmoni cuts Soo Young's mom a sharp side-eye, causing her to forcefully close her mouth. The glare, however, remains plastered on her face.

"Chloe is new to our ways, so it is up to us to show her how things are done here," Halmoni says to them, then turns to me. "You have to understand, Chloe, that we do things here quite differently than you're used to." She motions to the seat next to her. "Soo Young's mom is spending an entire year at the temple, praying for our family. She came here tonight just to meet you."

Ah, temple. That would explain the monk-garb. It doesn't, however, explain her hostility toward me and my mom. Aren't monks supposed to embody inner peace?

"Jin Young and Soo Young both sacrifice their youth for the best education, for the sake of the family business," Halmoni continues. "So, you see, Chloe, we sacrifice a great deal for each other. Sacrifice is the true measure of a family's strength. It's something you can learn in time." She finishes with a neutral smile.

I nod, staring at my hands in my lap. Suddenly I feel as if I'm being chastised and the worst part about it is, I have no idea why. I didn't understand, *didn't want to believe*, that Mom could be right, but now that I'm here, I wonder why I ever assumed I'd automatically be welcomed into the family with open arms.

"Is Jin Young coming tonight?" I stare longingly at the empty seat next to me.

"Jin Young?" Soo Young's mom pipes up again at the mention of her son. "He has no time for this."

Halmoni puts a hand up as if to shush her. "Of course Jin Young will meet you. Just not today. Lady Cha thinks it's better if you meet only the women tonight. Saturday is better for Jin Young."

I frown at my plate. Why had Jin Young been so eager for me to fly out to Korea if he wasn't even going to be here? Now I'll only see him the day before my flight home?

"Do not worry, you will meet him soon enough," Halmoni says in a cheerful tone. "I have plenty for you to get to know us better."

I peer up at her. "You do?"

"Yes, of course." She nods confidently. "That is why I arranged for you to go shopping at the department store tomorrow. After that, Soo Young will meet you for lunch."

"Halmoni!" Soo Young protests at the same time her mom says, "Omonim!"

"Ttuk!" Halmoni says, slamming her fist on the table. Immediately the two other women recoil.

Miso was right. As long as I have Halmoni's support, the rest of the family will have no choice but to follow. It doesn't make me feel any better, though. I don't want them to welcome me with open arms because they have to. I want them to do it because they *want* to.

On the way home, I'm in the back seat of the car while Mr. Kim drives us home, and for once I'm thankful for being alone in the dark. Tonight was such a jarring reminder that not every family member loves you solely based on the fact that you're related. After the way this spectacular whirlwind of a trip had been going, I didn't want to admit the possibility that today would go any differently.

I catch Mr. Kim's eyes in the rearview mirror every now and then. I'm trying not to show him I'm upset, but it's hard. Thinking back to how cold Soo Young and her mom were to me, the tears come spilling out without warning. I begin to search the car for a tissue but there isn't one.

"Gwenchanayo?" Mr. Kim hands me a handkerchief while we're stopped at a red light.

I bow my head in thanks and take it from him. "I'm not gwenchanayo. I'm not gwenchanayo at all." I blow my nose on the handkerchief and realize, too late, that there's no way I can return it to him tonight. Not after that.

The light turns green, but Mr. Kim stares at me deeply in the rearview mirror, only looking away in brief spurts as we drive on. Feeling vulnerable and somewhat touched by his kind gesture, I decide to tell him something I can't seem to share with anyone else. I tell him how I really feel.

"If I feel like I don't fit in at home and I don't fit in with my family here, will I fit in anywhere?"

When I arrive at the guesthouse, I'm not feeling sorry for myself anymore, but I am feeling something else. Anger. *I* was the one being lectured on etiquette and respect, but *my* behavior wasn't the one that was disrespectful. As soon as I get to my room, I can't hold it in any longer and I call Hazel right away.

"Hey, hold on a sec while I patch Seb in," I say when she picks up.

"No, wait." She stops me. "We don't have to do *everything* together. I mean, right?" she says, as if she's trying to convince herself.

"Uh-oh. Did you guys have a fight or something?" I'd been noticing a disconnect between them the past couple of calls. I thought it seemed that way because I'm so far away. Guess my initial instincts were right.

"Not a fight, really." She bites her lower lip, hesitating to continue. "I'm beginning to wonder if we have what it takes to make it work long-distance," she says eventually.

I wrinkle my nose. "Long-distance? You're both going to be in Los Angeles."

"I know it sounds silly." She rolls her eyes at herself. "But we'll be in different schools for the first time. Do I really want to tie myself down with a boyfriend? Does he want to tie himself down with *me*?" She shakes her head. "It just seems like right now would be a natural time for us to break up."

My ears are numb. Did I hear her right? "But you're so—and he's so—How can you—?" I finally got used to the idea of my two best friends as a couple, I don't know how I'll cope if they break up.

"I haven't made a decision yet. I'm just thinking out loud. Now that I'm hearing myself, I'm more confused than ever."

"Does Seb know?"

"Sort of." She shrugs. "I need time to process before I talk to him." She's silent again. After a moment, she does a head-shake and says, "Anyway, let's not talk about me anymore. I want to hear how dinner went."

"Are you sure?" I scrunch my eyebrows together. "I hate seeing you so down."

"Positive. Just tell me how things were with Jin Young. That'll make me feel better."

"I doubt it." I bury my head in my hands just thinking about it. "Dinner was a total disaster," I whine.

"What? Why?" Hazel asks.

I recount the details of tonight's dinner, including every last jab at me and my mom.

"This is classic jealousy, just like in the K-dramas!" Hazel says in a complete mood shift as soon as I finish.

"It is?" I say, not as convinced as her. "In K-dramas, the family drama is so intense, in a sitting-on-the-edge-of-your-seat way. In real life, it's just intense. I'm going to have to spend the rest of the night trying to untwist my bowels."

"Okay, well, let me help you jog your memory of every K-drama where the ordinary girl tries to fit in with the chaebol family and gets hated on out of pure, unfiltered jealousy: *Beautiful Gong Shim, Boys Over Flowers, Star in My Heart, The Heirs* . . . I could go on."

I consider her argument. "If we're sticking with the idea that my life is a real-life K-drama, then I guess it tracks. It's just . . . why does it feel worse than it looks on-screen?"

"I'm sure it does, but this is the necessary part of the plot where the ordinary person needs to prove to the chaebols that they can't be intimidated. Don't worry. You'll end up fine, they always do."

"They?" I raise an eyebrow up at her.

"The lead character. And in case you haven't figured it out yet, that's you!"

I guffaw in disbelief. "Am I?" Hazel has way too much faith in me. I've never been the lead, not in my life or anyone else's.

"You have single-handedly lived out so many K-drama themes, how can you even question it?" She flails her arms at me.

I think about it a second. "Chaebol families are definitely a K-drama theme, as proven by your aforementioned list of stellar, yet painfully realistic, list of dramas."

"There's also Halmoni, the powerful matriarch, discovering long-lost relatives, and definitely a family secret around how your dad became disconnected from everyone," Hazel says, counting on her fingers.

"Oh, fortune-teller!" I scream-talk excitedly, once again getting carried away with Hazel into the land of K-dramas.

"Lady Cha!" Her eyes grow two sizes bigger. "Also, after tonight, we know there's a fair amount of jealousy."

"Also their disapproval of my mom because of her poor background." I frown, reliving tonight's dinner. "No wonder Mom doesn't want to talk about it."

"It couldn't have been that bad."

I give her a pointed look. "It was. In fact, I might have confessed to the non-English-speaking Mr. Kim just how sad I was. Even though he didn't understand a word I said, he seemed very concerned. He gave me this handkerchief." I hold it up to show her.

It somehow makes her squeal with delight. "Now we can add my all-time favorite K-drama theme: the heiress and the distractingly hot hired help. A love story."

My lips pinch together, unamused. "Did I say distractingly hot?"

"I'm improvising. Don't rule it out." She points to me.

"Whatever." I laugh it off. "Unless we perfect the art of miming, I'm not sure we'd get very far in our *relationship*," I say, using air quotes. "Although . . . he does carry an umbrella around at all times."

"He does?!" Hazel practically screams, and we both fall into a fit of laughter.

"It hasn't rained yet, but it feels like it might any day." Great. Now Hazel's got me believing in this nonsense.

"You never know." Hazel shrugs with a gleam in her eye I've seen before. "Anything can happen in K-dramas. That's the beauty of them."

Hazel's right about one thing. Anything can happen in K-dramas.

# 23andme.com

**MESSAGES**

From: Noh, Jin Young
Subject: Apologies about tonight
Thursday, 11:59 PM

> Dear Chloe, I am so very sorry that I did not show up tonight. It was Lady Cha's advice that it would not be a good day for me to meet you. Please know that I wanted to, very much. I hope you are not too offended by me or anyone else in the family.

From: Chang, Chloe
Subject: RE: Apologies about tonight
Friday, 12:01 AM

> I have to admit I was sad not seeing you tonight. I wished you could make it, but I understand it's not your fault. Your sister and mother, however, did not like me very much. Can you help me understand why? My friend Hazel thinks it's jealousy, but I'm having trouble believing they could be jealous of me. What could they be jealous about?

**From: Noh, Jin Young**

**Subject: RE: Apologies about tonight**

**Friday, 12:03 AM**

Your friend Hazel is very astute. Soo Young and her mother are jealous of you because you compete with them for Halmoni's attention. She is a busy, powerful woman, and right now they see you as competition. Do not worry. In some time, they will accept you. I am sure they will.

**From: Chang, Chloe**

**Subject: RE: Apologies about tonight**

**Friday, 12:05 AM**

Thanks for your vote of confidence and your explanation. It makes sense how they can see me as a threat, even though I want nothing but to have a close relationship with everyone. I hope you're right and that they'll accept me. I'm only worried that we won't have much time to get to know each other. Lady Cha apparently has many opinions about our meeting and says Saturday is a better day to meet. It's strange that you're the first person I connected with from the Noh family, but the last one I'll be meeting. Anyway, I guess it's better than not meeting at all.

From: Noh, Jin Young

Subject: RE: Apologies about tonight

Friday, 12:06 AM

Chloe, I am sorry. Lady Cha is quite skilled, and Halmoni is dependent on her predictions. We must abide by them. I will make sure we meet before you leave. I am, like you said before, very interested in meeting you too.

# CHAPTER 13

By Friday morning in the gym, I start seeing the benefits of having a personal trainer. I can now run on the treadmill a whole mile without passing out. A feat I didn't think was possible in a matter of days. Next, I go upstairs to find a healthy and delicious meal Mrs. Na laid out for me. Chaebol or not, I could totally get used to this kind of life.

While I'm in the shower, I reflect on my time here so far. In a span of four days, I've learned more than I've ever known about my dad. Yet I still feel like I have more questions than answers. I'm not sure how our family dynamics are going to change after this trip or what type of relationship we'll have. Maybe we'll be the type of family that visits each other during the holidays and summers. Maybe we'll even take vacations together. Or maybe we'll be the kind of family that only sends each other postcards every once in a while. With little certainty of the future, there's a sense of urgency burning in me to get to know as much information as possible during my short stay here.

On the other hand, Halmoni assured me that there'll be plenty of time for us to get to know one another. With only three days left of my stay, that must mean she plans on many more visits in the future. Plus, I still haven't met Jin Young, and Halmoni is taking me shopping today. There's still so much to look forward to here.

It isn't until I find Mr. Kim waiting for me in the foyer that I remember what Hazel said about him. He's not distractingly hot. *Is he?* As I walk toward him in the foyer, I slow my step, taking inventory of him. I mean, sure. He's objectively good-looking, with a fashion sense that is undeniably tasteful. I haven't seen him wear a jacket that wasn't tailored to fit him perfectly. And don't get me started on his complexion. His dewy glow is as flattering as it is enviable.

That's not to say he doesn't have great nonphysical qualities too. He's punctual, always waiting for me in the foyer at eight o'clock on the dot every morning. He's also kind, holding doors open for me and *always* carrying an umbrella around with him. Plus, he's generous. He lent me his extremely fashionable handkerchief. Which reminds me . . . I tried to wash the snot out of it, but that ended up warping the fabric and it looked terribly shabby. As an apology slash thanks, I made him a new one with the leftover fabric I had from the dress I made. I reach in my pocket to pull it out and think of the words to convey my thanks to him.

"Gamsahamnidah." I present him the handkerchief with both my hands. *"Uh-jeh . . . man-hee . . . sul-puh . . ."* I say clumsily, stringing together the few Korean words I know. Except the way I'm saying them, it sounds more like: Yesterday. Very. Sad.

"It's okay," Mr. Kim says, politely hiding a chuckle

behind his fist. "I hope you're feeling better this morning."

"I am, thank—" My eyes practically bulge out of their sockets. "You . . . speak English?" Not only that, but it's near perfect, with only a hint of an accent.

One side of his lip curves up into a half smile. "Sorry I didn't tell you before."

"Halmoni said you didn't speak any English, I'm sure she did." I rack my brain, thinking back to my first meeting with her.

Mr. Kim shifts his stance. "Conversing with the members of the family is outside of my station as a personal secretary."

"Oh," I say. That makes sense. I guess. But then a second later, it doesn't. "Then why are you speaking to me now? You still work for Halmoni, right?"

He chuckles. "Yes, I do. But after seeing you so sad yesterday, I wanted to be a friend to you."

My head hangs down and I'm staring at my feet. "Oh. You heard about last night, huh?" How embarrassing that Halmoni was talking to Mr. Kim about how badly dinner went last night.

His cheeks and neck turn blotchy red.

"It's okay," I say. "Halmoni must trust you if she's talking about such personal details with you."

"Let's just say it's part of my job to know personal details about the family." He checks his watch. "Speaking of your halmoni, I don't want to keep her waiting."

When we get to the car, Mr. Kim opens the back-seat door to the sedan and I stop myself from getting in.

"Do I have to sit in the back? Can't I sit up in front, next to you?" Warmth creeps up my neck. Did I really just ask if I could sit next to him?

"Oh, I . . ." He hesitates. "I don't think it would be very professional." He looks away as if he's embarrassed, which now makes me feel embarrassed.

"Oh, okay." I quickly slide into the back seat, heat flooding my face. Despite his reasoning, I still can't help feeling the slight sting of rejection.

He starts driving to the department store and in the silence, we catch each other's eyes in the rearview mirror, then look away awkwardly.

"If it were up to me, I would definitely not mind you sitting next to me," he says.

"Uh-huh," I mumble, looking out the window. I know he's trying to make me feel better, but it's doing the opposite.

"This job, it's very . . ." he pauses, searching for the right word. "Demanding."

This is the second time he's mentioned the importance of his job. I might be naive, but being in the car with him is the most relaxing part of my days here. "I didn't realize this job was so stressful."

"Oh, yes. Working for your halmoni—that is, any big family like the Nohs—is a coveted role, and not an easy job to get in Korea. Not one toe can be out of line."

Of course he's intimidated by her. She's chaebol. I keep forgetting that seemingly large detail about my dad's family. Probably because Halmoni is so kind and soft-spoken, unlike the terrifyingly intimidating conglomerate heads that are often portrayed on K-dramas. I'm sure that part is dramatized for plot purposes, but it helps me understand why Mr. Kim wouldn't want to cross her.

"I understand. I'm sorry I put you in an uncomfortable situation. I'm not used to sitting in the back seat while someone's driving me around. It makes me feel like I'm in a taxi and you and I are strangers."

He stares at me through the rearview mirror, revealing a smile. "I'm glad you understand. I mean it when I say if it were up to me, I would definitely not mind you sitting beside me." His eyes dart back to the road, so I can't read his expression anymore.

It isn't his words that convince me he's telling me the truth. It isn't even the reminder that his boss, my hal-moni, is a powerful and influential public figure. It's the red blotchiness on his neck creeping up to his face that shows me his sincerity. So I don't press him about it any further, and we spend the rest of the ride in comfortable silence.

When I get to the department store, I'm told that Halmoni is on the main floor, where the fashion show is being set up. The area is decorated from top to bottom in preparation for the event—there are fake trees with monochrome leaves in shades of maroon and pink, plush mushrooms big enough to sit on scattered against the back wall, and butterflies suspended in midair with invisible strings to appear as if they're fluttering around. The entire space has been magically transformed into a fairy-tale forest. It's utterly breathtaking.

The runway is nearly finished, with an elevated T-shaped stage complete with champagne-colored velvet curtains hanging along the back wall. There are men setting up chairs in the audience portion of the area who are setting place cards on each chair. Halmoni walks over to a chair in the front row on the right side of the runway. She rips the sign off and mutters something under her breath.

"Mr. Kim!" she yells, and instantly he rushes from behind me and up to her. He bows deeply, with his arms by his side. She begins berating him in Korean, then balls up the paper and chucks it at him.

Mr. Kim bends over to pick up the wadded paper while simultaneously apologizing. He rushes past me, but I stop him.

"What was that about?"

"They must have put your samchon's name on one of the seats." He wipes his brow, staring back at the seat.

"Samchon? The one that's sick?"

As soon as he nods, Halmoni's voice interrupts our conversation "Mr. Kim! I am not paying you to flirt."

He blushes feverishly and bows at a ninety-degree angle toward my halmoni and then a shorter bow to me before scampering off. For the first time, I can see why he's intimidated by Halmoni.

"I'm sorry you had to witness that," Halmoni says in a softer voice. "My son is not going to make it to the fashion show and every time I see his name here, I'm reminded of his illness." Her face is ashen and looks as if it's aged since the last time I saw her. I'm torn between empathizing with Halmoni and feeling sorry for Mr. Kim.

"Let's get out of this mess," she says. Visibly irritated, her heels clack against the stone floor with notable force.

When we get to her office and the door shuts behind us, she sits down at her desk, pinching the bridge of her nose with her eyes shut.

"Is everything okay?" I sit down carefully in the love seat facing her desk.

She sighs a deep throaty sigh. "This department store . . . means a great deal to me." She stares at a black-and-white photo of a construction site hanging on the wall. "My husband and I worked in a factory growing up. We studied hard and saved everything to go to the best schools. We sacrificed everything for our first store." She points to another photo of the early model of the store. "This department store is more than a business, it's my legacy. When my time is up, it will be passed down to the next generation, and so on. With my youngest son's illness, I'm terrified for the future of Sam Won Group."

I study the photos of blueprints and construction sites, searching for any personal details. But there are none.

"Halmoni? What about my dad? How did you guys lose touch all those years ago?" I ask. Witnessing her so distraught over Samchon's illness, I wonder how it was possible that Halmoni wouldn't have moved heaven and earth to stay connected to her son.

"Your father moved to America. One day he's alive, the next, he's dead," she says, as if it were that simple.

Without any follow-up, I pull out the Polaroid from my pocket. "Halmoni, I have this photo of my parents—"

"Aigo . . . No, no, no." She shakes her head and forces my hand back in my pocket. "Lady Cha says pictures of the dead bring bad luck."

"Are you serious?" In the moment, I forget my place, and the words come out more impertinent than I'd intended.

Halmoni stills, her eyes boring into me with such intensity. "Chloe," she says, placing a hand on my shoulder and squeezing it tightly as if to convey the seriousness of her message. "Even I do not display any photographs of my own husband after he died. It is a sacrifice we must make. For the family."

I get that sacrifice is a big deal in this family. It's a big deal in my family too. My mom sacrificed her life to raise me as a single mom. I sacrifice my happiness for the sake of my mom's. It's a never-ending vicious cycle of sacrifice that Halmoni does not even know.

"I understand what it means to sacrifice yourself for your family. I've been doing it my whole life. I only want to know more about my dad." Without realizing it, my fists are clenched.

"Oh, Chloe-yah," she says in a completely different tone. "I don't mean to be harsh. It must be the news about my son that is troubling me." Her posture softens along with her tone. "You see, it became clear some time ago that my youngest son would be the chosen one to carry on my legacy. Since then, he obediently listened to Lady Cha's recommendation to live a certain life, unmarried and unattached. And now, I'm being told that a liver transplant is his only chance to survive this disease. It seems so unfair." Halmoni sobs into her hands.

"Oh, Halmoni." Now it's my turn to have a sudden mood shift. I allowed my own disappointment to cloud my judgment. "I'm so sorry. After last night, I think I'm feeling a bit insecure."

"Last night?" She sniffs, dabbing her eyes with a tissue.

"I get the feeling that Soo Young and her mom don't like me."

"Nonsense. After the lunch that I have arranged for you and Soo Young, she will love you the way I do."

Halmoni seems to have way more confidence than I do. I don't want to be rude, so I smile and say, "Thank you for setting up the lunch. I hope you're right about Soo Young."

"I am never wrong," she says, placing a hand on my arm and grazing the sleeve of my shirt. "What is this material?" she asks, suddenly becoming distracted by the mesh cutout.

"Oh, that." I glance over. "I used the fabric from a fishnet stocking and stitched it onto the sleeves of the shirt. It's great for ventilation and also looks kind of cool . . . don't you think?" By the time I finish describing my ensemble, I can tell Halmoni isn't listening anymore.

"That reminds me." She checks her watch. "We have something very important to attend to right now."

"We do?"

"Let's get you some new clothes." She abruptly opens the door to her office.

In the elevator, Halmoni presses the numberless button above the twelfth-floor button.

"The top floor?" I say, suddenly remembering what Ms. Song told me during the tour.

"You know about the top floor?"

"Ms. Song mentioned it. I heard it's exclusive."

161

"Which is what you are." Halmoni taps me gently on the nose.

"What? Are you serious?" My mouth hangs open. Halmoni is allowing me to shop in an area reserved for elite clientele only? Ms. Song said Halmoni doesn't even allow her own family up here. Which is confusing.

"Halmoni, I thought you didn't allow family members to shop here."

She cocks her head to the side. "Who told you that? The staff?" She waves a dismissive hand and laughs. "You can't believe everything you hear, Chloe. What good is being the owner of a department store if you can't take liberties once in a while? Especially for someone like you." She pinches my chin endearingly.

Tears prickle the backs of my eyes, but when the doors open, I immediately become distracted.

There's a set of shimmering floor-to-ceiling curtains in rose gold hanging in front of us. Halmoni peels back one side of a curtain and I gasp at the sight. Plush chairs, shiny mirrors, and a miniature runway carpet—all for me. Hazel is right. No matter how much I try to fight it, I can't deny it anymore. I am living a real-life K-drama. Even the music playing in surround sound is like my very own OST.

As soon as they see us, a flurry of staff snaps to attention. Halmoni goes straight to one of the two oversized tufted chairs in a blush color with brushed gold legs and motions for me to sit down. Immediately, two attendants come out, each holding a tray with a champagne glass filled with a sparkly lilac-colored drink. As they hold out the trays to us, Halmoni and I take our glasses. I sniff mine and the bubbles tickle my nose with a fruity scent.

"Plum wine champagne for me, and plum-flavored soda for you." She tilts her glass toward me before putting it to her lips.

I take a sip of my drink and it tastes as sweet as this experience. Just when I think it can't get any better than this, a string of women come out, one by one, wearing this season's latest collection. The first lady is wearing pleated red shorts with a black-and-white silk blouse, great for daytime wear. She sashays toward us, then stops, turning in a slow manner and then making her way back. Another lady follows behind her, wearing a sheer day dress in a light pink color. The lady after her comes out in a tailored black dress with sharp lines and angular shoulders and studded booties that are to die for. It's like my own private runway show. I can see why Halmoni doesn't allow just anyone here. The amount of effort put into just one show is astounding.

"What do you think?" she asks, leaning back in her chair.

I can't seem to peel my eyes off the clothes, staring at the hemlines, the draping, and the way the fabrics move with each movement. It's breathtaking. "I love the asymmetrical lines on that dress. It makes the dress stand out against the plain monochromatic color scheme. And the darts on the bustline of that blouse. They're noticeable, but not obtuse," I think out loud, staring at the models strutting toward me, one after the other. Everything Ms. Song said is coming together. With the monochromatic backdrop of these pieces, it's all about the details.

"My, my. You certainly have an eye for detail." Halmoni nods, impressed. "Most people think fashion is just about pretty clothes, but you can see the fine lines and color pal-ates and how they work together. Only the truly talented people can do that. I can see why you got accepted to FIT."

My smile instantly disappears as I gnaw on my lower lip. It hasn't been sitting well with me these past couple of days, misrepresenting myself to Halmoni. "About that . . . I'm not sure I'm going to FIT."

"Really?" She stares down her nose at me.

"I got accepted. I-I just haven't made my decision about going yet." I had every intention of coming clean, but in the moment, it feels as if I'd be letting her down if she knew the truth.

"I hope you reconsider. You have quite the eye for fash-ion." Halmoni's eyes glow with pride, a look that makes me desperately want to reconsider my options. Except I remember I don't have any options. I only have one, which is to turn down FIT and attend Meadowland Community College in the fall.

"This dress reminds me of the one you were wearing the other day." Halmoni nudges me, snapping me out of my pity party. "It is from the new collection line of Clara Sunwoo. Their liquid leather is breathable. It's casual, yet classy. More importantly, it does not make any noises." She smiles knowingly at me.

"It's beautiful," I manage to say, despite my embar-rassment. Having only worked with used, secondhand materials, I had no idea about these other types of high-end fabrics. Pleather may look nice on a hanger, but I now know that in intense moisture due to humidity or overactive sweat glands, it does not wear well.

After the last model leaves, Halmoni leans over to me. "So tell me. Which ones did you like?"

"Um, all of them?" I say truthfully. It's not every day I'm taken on a shopping spree.

She nods, then says something to the main attendant. "Done," she says to me.

"Wait, what? Are you serious?"

On the way out, Halmoni and I are followed by two attendants holding an obscenely large amount of boxes and bags. The whole way down the elevator and to the car, I'm in a daze. I'm having my very own *Pretty Woman* moment. Minus the whole prostitution thing, of course.

# CHAPTER 14

After the whirlwind shopping spree, I'm off to meet Soo Young for lunch, but not before changing into the breathable liquid leather dress Halmoni just bought me. The neutral-colored, belted day dress with micro pleats on the skirt is sophisticated, feminine, and more to the point, nothing like the dress I wore when I met Soo Young for the first time. Hopefully she won't have any negative comments to say about my outfit when we meet this time.

When I get into the back seat of the car, Mr. Kim takes notice, as usual, and does his usual smirk-smile. *As usual.*

It isn't until he closes the driver's-side door and it's just the two of us that I can't hold it in any longer. "Now that I know you can understand what I'm saying, I need to know. What is up with that look you're giving me?"

"Pardon?" Mr. Kim looks at me through the rearview mirror with eyes the size of two large buttons.

"You know, *this* look." I do my best imitation of him, turning my head and smile-smirking. "I can't tell if you're laughing at me or mocking me."

Instead of responding, he turns his attention to the road and remains silent. Which is increasingly irritating. He pulls over in front of an Italian restaurant with grape leaves adorning the trellis at the entrance. By the time he puts the car in park, he still hasn't answered my question.

"Is it because I look funny to you? I know I don't quite fit in here, but I'm trying." I realize it's unfair to unleash my insecurities on him, but I've been feeling out of place since I got here.

He turns sideways, glancing down and not at me. "You misunderstand me." His skin is red and blotchy again. "I think you look very nice. However, it's not part of the job to let you know what I'm thinking. If you saw me hiding a smile, it means I'm not doing my job well. I hope you accept my sincerest apologies." He bows.

Is he telling me that his smile-smirk is a *compliment*?

Having just been made aware of how self-involved I'm being (not *everything* is about me), I take it upon myself to apologize.

"Actually, I'm the one that's sorry since I misunderstood you. You're only trying to be nice."

"Not at all. Thank you for reminding me I need to be more professional when I'm on duty." He faces forward in the driver's seat and becomes silent and serious, which makes me feel worse.

"No, no. It's fine. You shouldn't have to hold back anything when you're with me."

Mr. Kim shifts uncomfortably in the front seat before saying, "Actually, there's a great deal I have to hold back when I'm around you. It would be highly unprofessional if I were to be overly friendly with my employer's granddaughter."

While I'm trying to decipher what exactly Mr. Kim

167

meant by "overly friendly," I can tell he's feeling increasingly awkward.

"I should take you in the restaurant. Soo Young is waiting," he says, switching back to professional mode. He gets out of the car and comes around to open my door for me. When we get to the front door of the restaurant, I pause before stepping in.

"Is something wrong?" Mr. Kim asks.

"No, it's nothing. I just hope Soo Young likes me."

"Remember what I said. Don't take it personally. And for what it's worth . . ." He pauses, shifting his stance. "I think you look very nice today."

Not quite the pep talk I was looking for, but it does help to relax me. The hostess shows me to the reserved seat in the private room where Soo Young is already sitting. She doesn't look up from her phone as I approach her.

"Hi, Soo Young," I say, this time with the appropriate amount of enthusiasm.

Instead of returning the greeting, she eyes me up and down. "What are you wearing?"

Taken aback, I begin to ramble. "The material is lightweight . . . you know, with the weather being so humid . . . it's perfect for the day . . . and the color—"

"No, I mean how did *you* get the latest Clara Sunwoo?" She glares at me.

"Oh, that." I finally catch her meaning. "Halmoni bought it for me when she took me to the top floor—"

"She took *you*? To the top floor?"

Halmoni said not to believe everything I hear about the family, but I'm beginning to think the rumors are correct. Halmoni has never allowed Soo Young to shop there before.

"Anyway, this place looks great." I quickly sit down and hold up the menu to cover my face. A poor attempt at changing the subject, but I've clearly made the wrong impression with Soo Young. Again.

Luckily, Soo Young doesn't press me any further and resumes thumb-typing on her phone.

"Hm . . . I can't decide what to get. Do you have any recommendations?"

"Nope," she quips.

I stare at her, desperately hoping she'll look up from her phone. She's so different than I imagined. So different than Jin Young.

"Are you and Jin Young very close?"

She stirs, eventually setting down her phone. "We're okay."

"Oh. I'm an only child."

"Uh-huh," she says in a way that tells me she's not even listening to me.

Staring at her profile, I take inventory of her physical characteristics. While she is a spitting image of her mom, Jin Young must look more like his father. Since I look like my father, Jin Young and I look more closely related than he does with his sister.

"You and Jin Young are so different from each other," I muse out loud.

"Yeah." She snorts. "I'm the nice one."

I do a double take. In what universe is Soo Young "the nice one"?

Not to seem rude, I smile and say, "I guess there's a lot about the family I don't know yet. What can you tell me about them?"

"Excuse me. I have to go to the bathroom." She abruptly gets up.

"Oh, okay. I'll be . . . here." Without looking back, she bolts out, leaving me alone in the room with a basket of bread.

Twenty minutes and an entire basket of bread later, Soo Young has not returned. I get up to go to the bathroom to check on her, when I realize she took her bag with her. As I open the bathroom door, my sneaking suspicion is confirmed. The bathroom is empty. Which means Soo Young ditched me.

Standing in the doorway of the restroom, I have two choices. I can go back to the table, eat by myself, and then go back to the empty guesthouse. Or . . . I can start doing the things I want.

✕

A minute later, I'm out on the street level looking for the car. Mr. Kim is leaning up against it, staring at his phone, when he notices me. Startled, he fumbles with his cell before straightening out his jacket and bowing to me.

"Lunch is finished already?" He checks his watch.

"Uh, yeah. Apparently, Soo Young has more important things to do than to hang out with her long-lost cousin."

Disappointment shrouds his face, which makes me feel slightly better. "I'm so sorry. Should I take you home?"

170

"Home?" I repeat. An empty house with hired help catering to my every need? That's not what home is. Hazel's right. This is the point in the K-drama where I, the lead character, need to take charge and do something for myself. If I'm not getting the answers I want, then I should do something about it. But what?

Then I remember something Halmoni told me about my dad. The only thing about his life I've learned since I've been here: the name of his school.

"No. Can you take me to Seoul National University?"

Mr. Kim seems troubled, like he's at war with himself.

"Is it far from here?" I ask when he doesn't respond.

"It's not that. Your halmoni, she would want you to do as she planned."

"It's not my fault Soo Young ditched me," I remind him.

Mr. Kim thinks about it a minute longer before he concedes. "I guess you're right." He opens the door for me hesitantly. Although he's going along with it, I can tell he's not completely convinced.

"Don't worry. I won't tell if you won't." I zip my lips and smile at him closemouthed. His face relaxes and I seem to have put him at ease, for now.

On the way, while we sit in stop-and-go traffic, I begin to wonder what it is that makes him feel conflicted about taking me to my dad's school. It's hardly a place one would be concerned about. Is he really that scared of Halmoni, the powerful matriarch of a chaebol family? Or is there more to the story I don't know? All I know is that after the past couple of conversations, I know better than to assume anything with him.

171

"Can I ask you something?" When he nods, I continue. "How did you come to be Jin Young's private secretary?" At the mention of his job title, he sits up straighter.

He hesitates before saying, "I guess there's no harm telling you. My mother works at the department store."

"Really? Have I met her?"

He shakes his head. "She works as an in-house seamstress in menswear. She alters clothes purchased in-store and therefore works in a back room."

"Wow, I bet she could teach me a thing or two. I'm pretty good for a self-taught sewer, but I'm always hungry to learn more."

"She's not only good at sewing, she can design, too." He tugs on the collar of his suit jacket.

"You mean . . . *she made that*?" I stare, flabbergasted. I've been admiring his suits for days and I was sure they were a designer label. "I must insist on meeting her now. Anyone who can create something as impeccable as that—by hand no less—has a fan in me."

"I'm sure she'd like that." He smiles gently at me through the rearview mirror.

I'm smiling back at him when my eye catches the sign for Seoul National University. Not wanting to miss a second of this experience, I practically plant my face against the window as we turn into the campus.

The university is unlike any I've seen in the US. There are no wrought iron arches welcoming us to the school or rows of fraternity and sorority houses lining the neighboring streets. Instead, there are a series of business-like buildings sprawled out over a vast, hilly campus with roads driving throughout. Mr. Kim pulls up to the first building and puts the car in park before turning around to face me.

"This is the entrance to the university. Where would you like to go?"

I admit, as determined as I was, I didn't have a plan beyond getting here. "Halmoni said my dad had an eye for fashion design. Maybe they know about him in the arts department?"

Mr. Kim nods, enters an address into the car navigation, and drives to another part of the campus. "This is the fine arts building, where the departments of textiles, merchandising, and fashion design are."

"My dad had to have studied here, then." I don't wait for Mr. Kim to open the door for me before I get out of the car and make my way into the building, prompting him to jog to catch up to me. I slow my step when we get to a guard in a booth right outside the building. "Can you ask them where I can find information about an alumnus from here?"

Mr. Kim asks the old man with weathered skin in the blue security guard uniform. They exchange a few words before Mr. Kim nods and bows to thank him.

"He said we can use the computers in the library around the corner."

I follow Mr. Kim into the library, and he motions for me to sit down at the first available computer. "Actually," I say, turning to him before sitting down. "I don't know how to read Korean. I wouldn't know how to type it either."

Catching my meaning, he nods. "I can help." Then he

sits down and begins typing. "Noh Joon Pyo." After pushing the Return button, he pauses, brows furrowed.

"What? What does it say?"

"It says there is no record of him in the arts department."

"What?" I briefly wonder if there could be some mistake. Maybe there's another school with a similar name? No, it can't be. I clearly remember Halmoni saying how prestigious a school it was. This is definitely the right school. "That doesn't make sense."

Mr. Kim is too busy typing on the keyboard to hear me. "Ah," he eventually says. "Here he is."

I sigh, relieved.

"He graduated from the business department. Would you like to go there?"

I nod eagerly.

A few minutes later, we're at a different part of the campus, walking around the halls of the business department building. It's sterile and not particularly grand, but I am completely enamored by it.

"Wow, my dad actually roamed these halls." I gaze aimlessly around. Being on the same college campus my dad attended makes me feel close to him in a way I never have before.

Mr. Kim stares sidelong, with an amused and bewildered expression. It reminds me of the time I watched my very first episode of a K-drama.

I stop and turn to him. "Thank you so much for bringing me here." My voice cracks and tears instantly flood my eyes.

Mr. Kim goes right for his handkerchief, the one I made

him, and is about to pull it out when I stop him.

"No, it's okay. I don't want to ruin another one of your handkerchiefs." I sniff hard. "Besides, these aren't tears of sadness. They're happy tears." I swipe away a stray tear on my cheek.

Something changes in Mr. Kim and he's no longer watching me. Instead, he's looking at me. "This . . . really means a lot to you, doesn't it?" The smile disappears; he seems deep in thought.

"It really does." I nod.

We walk the halls a little longer. Looking around, I catch Mr. Kim's gaze lingering on me. I can't tell if it's the humidity or being at my dad's school or something else entirely, but I'm feeling light-headed and I lean against the wall to catch my breath.

"Are you okay?" Concern lines sweep across Mr. Kim's forehead.

"Yeah, I'm probably just overheated." I fan my face.

He looks around and spots a vending machine. "I'll be right back."

Watching him as he jogs over to get me a cold bottle of water, my pulse quickens. I know Hazel and I were joking, but maybe she's right. Maybe there is room for romance.

# CHAPTER 15

Later, Mr. Kim drops me off to meet Miso for lunch at the address she sent me. I cross the street and look around for a sign that says Chi-Maek, but I don't see one.

After walking up and down the block once, Miso comes running up to me. She's wearing leopard-print Hammer pants and platform high-tops that make me smile.

"There you are!" she cries. Then a beat later, "What happened to your face?"

I draw my head back dramatically.

"I mean, it's glowing! What did you do?" She points right at my nose.

"You mean, it worked?" I tap my face. "Halmoni got me this weird facial using my own blood—"

She gasps at my face. "You got a vampire facial!"

"You know about this?" I motion to my face.

Instead of an answer, she leans her head back, dramatically eyeing me up and down. "Who are you?"

"Oh, this?" I fan out the dress and do a twirl. So much has happened since I went shopping this morning, I almost forgot. "Halmoni took me on a shopping spree."

She's at a loss for words, flabbergasted. "I-I can't—"

She starts and stops so many times until she finally says, "I need to sit down to get all the deets. Come on." She hooks her arm around my neck and leads me down to the spot where I was dropped off.

"Sorry I'm late. I couldn't find Chi-Maek anywhere."

She stops in her tracks and busts up. "Chi-maek isn't a restaurant name. It's a meal. Specifically, two items: fried chicken and maekju. Chi-maek." When I furrow my brows, she clarifies. "Maekju is beer." She points to a store with a sign depicting a cartoon chicken with a beer mug in its hand-wing.

"Oh. Fried chicken and beer?"

"Precisely. You sounded so down on the phone about Soo Young ditching you, I thought we could use some good old KFC."

I look again at the sign. "KF—"

"Korean Fried Chicken," Miso clarifies.

She leads me by the shoulders into the small casual dining place bursting with the robust scent of fried yummy goodness. Miso orders half a chicken and two beers, and I find us an open seat for two people in the corner. The room is filled with young people, who each have *at least* one glass of beer in front of them. A second later, Miso sits down with our order.

"What's so special about fried chicken and beer?" I ask with a raised eyebrow. Unlike the street food, this looks like regular fried chicken.

"What's not special about it? It's perfect for almost any occasion. Watching a big soccer match? You want some chi-maek. Just finished a big exam at school? You need chi-maek. It's a Wednesday? Chi-maek. It is never *not* a good time for chi-maek."

"Okay, I get it. Why are we still talking about chi-maek and not eating it?" I look for a drumstick and take a bite. It's crispy and juicy and the savory flavor hits my palate instantly. "Oh my God."

"Told you. It's double fried for double the flavor," she says with her mouth full. "Eat it with the pickled radish. It'll blow your mind."

White cubes float in a bowl with clear liquid. I pick one up with a wooden chopstick and pop it in my mouth. "Oh my God," I say again.

"You're welcome. Now top it off with a nice swig of beer." She puts the glass mug to her lips and takes a big gulp, then makes a sound from her mouth that resembles ice crackling.

"Okay, what the heck was that sound?"

"That's the sound of the most supreme palatable experience. You must try." She pushes the frosted mug of beer toward me.

I pick up the mug and am about to take a sip, but I find that I can't. "Sorry, I just don't like the taste of beer."

"What? You don't drink beer?" She stares at me like I have two heads.

I'm suddenly embarrassed, feeling as if I'm some sheltered dweeb defending myself in front of the coolest kid on campus. "My friends and I, we never really partied . . ."

"Wow."

"Does that make me seem as uncool as I sound?"

"No, not at all. A lot of people feel pressured to drink at a young age here. It's one of those cultural expectations to drink socially, not just at a party."

"People start drinking this early? Everyone's liver must be made of steel." I finish off my drumstick and look for a wing next.

"It's actually quite a problem."

"Drinking?"

"Liver damage." Miso takes a sip of beer, then smiles sheepishly. "Don't get the wrong idea, I don't drink that much. But there's enough people suffering from liver-related diseases that the Korean government is worried about organ trafficking. Unless you're related, first cousins or closer, then you have to go on the long donor list and some people don't have that long."

"Halmoni mentioned she's getting tested to see if she's a match for her son. In fact, I think everyone in the family is getting tested."

"Oh, wow. It's that serious?"

"Yeah." I toss the chicken bone onto the basket. "What if the patient doesn't have a big family?" I frown. Before I found out about the Nohs, the only family I had was just my mom.

"I know." She shrugs, licking the grease and crumbs off of her fingers. "But rules are rules."

"The government should just make an effort to educate the people about the damaging effects of long-term drinking. It seems like it would be a more sustainable way of living."

She stares at me like I just spoke an alien language.

"Tell Koreans not to drink? That's like telling Americans to stop making new seasons of *The Bachelor*. It's impossible!" I laugh, seeing her point. "Drinking is just too ingrained in our culture to change." She tosses a bare bone into the basket and wipes her fingers on a napkin. "Wow, I'm stuffed."

"Me too." I pat my stomach. I couldn't eat another bite. Except if it was—

"Dessert?" Miso raises an eyebrow up at me.

"Definitely," I reply without skipping a beat. We both laugh.

We decide to balance out the grease with something sweet, so she takes me to a bingsu place around the corner. We're sitting on sofa seats with tall backs made of smooth velvet in a cool and blessedly air-conditioned café. Miso orders us a red-bean Korean shaved ice to share and I stare at the picture on the menu for way too long.

"It comes with red bean *and* mochi?" Talk about a dream team.

"You've never had patbingsu?"

"This will be my first time."

"I'm honored." She puts a hand to her chest.

A few minutes later the waiter drops off a fancy glass bowl with a heaping mound of frozen decadence. Miso crams a spoonful in her mouth, then immediately puts a hand to her forehead. "Brain freeze! God, I'm so impatient."

I laugh. "Relatable." I take a bite, much smaller than Miso's, and savor the mix of flavors. "*Mm-mmm.* So yummy."

"Right?" She takes another bite and wipes her mouth

180

with a napkin. "So, have you met Jin Young yet?"

I shake my head. "I'm meeting him tomorrow night."

"Eeeeee!" She screeches. "That is exciting!"

"I don't think he has a girlfriend." I set my spoon down to pick up my phone and google my own cousin's love life. "I could put in a good word for you." I nudge her.

"Ha! Right. He could have anybody he wants. Besides, he's not really my type."

My lips twist, staring at her. "You mean, rich and handsome isn't your type?"

"Unfortunately, he has one too many Y chromosomes for my taste. If you know what I mean." She points the end of her spoon at me.

I know exactly what she means. "You're—"

"Into girls? Yep."

"Oh." I nod. Then a beat later, I ask, "If you're not into him, then why the heart-eyes?"

"Because! This is the celebrity IT guy, Noh Jin Young—Tabloid Legend. The Perpetual Bachelor. Mr. Clean!"

I wrinkle my nose. "Mr. Clean?"

She snorts. "It means he has a clean image. No scandals."

"Oh, I get it. Mr. Clean." I chuckle.

"In fact, I don't hear any scandals about any of the Nohs. You would know better." She nudges me with a wink.

"I don't know them much more than you, or anyone else in Korea." I think back to my short time with them. It's barely enough time to get to know them, let alone learn about any scandals. "Hey, can I get your opinion about something? I just found out that my halmoni's personal

181

secretary, the one that's been driving me around every day, can speak perfect English. And not only that, he's been told by my halmoni to not let me know."

Miso raises her eyebrows.

"Yeah, that's what I thought. It's not normal, right?"

"Well, normal and chaebol don't really go in the same sentence. How'd you find out?"

"Mr. Kim confessed. He also told me not to tell Halmoni I know. He's afraid of losing his job. Over *this*."

"Well, getting a job in a big conglomerate like Sam Won Group is no joke. I'm sure he doesn't want to do anything to jeopardize it."

"Yeah. I guess that makes sense. I thought it was strange at first."

"What's strange is that he was told not to reveal his knowledge of the English language, but he did. What do you think that's about?" Her eyebrows bounce up and down suggestively.

I roll my eyes. "It's not what you think it is. After he saw me upset about dinner last night, he wanted to make sure I was okay. Then he took me to my dad's school, where I got to roam the halls of the building where he attended classes."

"Look who's got the heart-eyes now," Miso singsongs.

"Excuse me?"

"I'm just calling it as I see it." She motions to my face.

"What you're seeing"—I motion to my face—"is my expression of joy over getting to know more about my dad. I thought he was a fashion design major, but it turns out he was a business major. I know it doesn't mean much, but when you know nothing about your dad, the slightest bit of information means a lot."

Her smile disappears. Something I said must have struck a nerve. "Everything okay?"

"Hearing you talk about your dad makes me think about my relationship with my dad. Ever since I went to boarding school, we've drifted apart. Now we hardly talk when we're in the same room. The hard part is, I can't tell if it's because I came out last year to my parents or if it's just the way our relationship is."

"Oh, Miso. I'm so sorry." She swats a hand at me like it's no big deal, but I know it's a big deal. I feel shame for monopolizing our conversations with my family drama. Obviously, Miso has a lot going on, too. "How about your mom? Are you two close?"

"My mom has been supportive, but even she doesn't know what's going on with my dad these days. I guess a part of me is worried my coming out has complicated our already fractured relationship. Korea is still pretty conservative, so I didn't always feel like I fit in here, but I'm not even trying to fit in anymore and it's freeing. Besides, there's a growing queer community in Seoul, something I wouldn't have imagined even a few years ago. They even include gay couples in K-dramas now."

"I remember. *Record of Youth*, *Prison Playbook*, *Reply 1997*, *Romance Is a Bonus Book*, *Love with Flaws* . . ." Thinking about those dramas reminds me that fitting in is a challenge anywhere.

"Still, we've never had an outright conversation about it. Until then, it's this big question mark looming over us.

At this rate, we may not talk about it all until I bring home a girlfriend."

"Are you seeing anyone now?" I ask.

"Not at the moment. I can't even begin to think about meeting someone I want to be with when I'm still trying to figure out who I am. You know?"

"Sort of. Not about dating, but about figuring out who I am. My mom thinks fashion is just a hobby and that I want to be a nurse, like her."

"You don't?"

"Honestly, I don't even know if I legitimately don't want to be a nurse or if I'm resisting it because I don't want to become her."

"Whoa. That's harsh. Is that why you can't tell her the truth?"

"I went along with the idea to be a nurse because I didn't think I had any other options. It's practical and respectable and most importantly, my mom can afford the tuition."

"What about now? Do you have another option?" Miso raises her eyebrows up at me.

The short answer to her question is no. Meeting the Nohs didn't change anything about my options, but it certainly changed my views on them.

"Before I knew anything about my dad, making clothes was something I was always passionate about. Now that I know my dad's family is one of the leaders in fashion merchandising, it's liberating, almost like it's giving me permission to be myself. I get excited being around clothes in a way that makes me feel a special connection to him.

184

I can't help but feel that I owe it to him to pursue my passion—*our* passion—for fashion. The thing is, my mom can't afford to send me to New York and I don't know if I can tell her how I actually feel." I bury my face in my hands, frustrated. "What do you think I should do?"

Miso raises an eyebrow. "Why don't you ask Lady Cha?"

When I look over at her, unamused, she can't hold it in any longer and busts up laughing. I end up laughing with her too. "Thanks for nothing." I roll my eyes playfully at her.

"You're welcome. Seriously, though, if there's anything else I can help you with, I mean, future careers notwithstanding, let me know."

"Actually, there is. I need to do something about this." I point to my hair.

"Oh, that? I thought that was your style." She grimaces.

"What, like the shipwrecked-without-a-brush style?"

"Hey, who am I to judge. '90s rapper much?" She motions to herself up and down. "Like I said, Unni's got you. What time are you meeting Jin Young tomorrow?"

"Not until evening."

"Good. That gives us time to tackle that beast." She motions to my hair. "I'll make an appointment and send you the address."

"Thanks, you're the best Unni."

# CHAPTER 16

Saturday morning, I wake up with a mix of emotions. On the one hand, it's the day before I leave Seoul. On the other, I get to meet Jin Young today. *Finally.*

My emotions decide to concentrate on the latter for now.

Filled with excitement, I head down to the basement where the gym is, when Mrs. Na stops to tell me my halmoni is on her way to the guesthouse.

"Halmoni is coming here, right now?" When she nods, I spin on my heels to go back upstairs to get ready, but Mrs. Na stops me.

"Exercise first." As rigid as her command is, she eyes me encouragingly to let me know she's coming from a good place. Still, she blocks my path to go back upstairs, determined as ever, so I have no choice but to obediently head down to the gym in the basement. I do my exercises quickly—not too quickly, or else Mrs. Na might think I've cut corners—and after I've completed my workout, I head back upstairs. Mrs. Na smiles, pleased by my sweaty state.

After I shower, I've just finished changing in my room when I hear wailing from downstairs. The kind that makes your blood curdle.

I rush to open my door. "Mrs. Na?" I call out while running down the stairs. When I get to the landing, I'm taken by surprise.

Halmoni is on the floor, like a wilted flower, clutching her phone to her chest.

"Halmoni?" I rush over to her and bend down and put my hands on her shoulders, taking a quick assessment of her physical state. "Are you okay?"

"I'm . . . not okay. I just had a call."

"Is it . . . Samchon?"

She shakes her head. "None of us are a match. Now the doctors tell me he has to be put on a general donor waiting list. That could take years! He barely has months." Her petite frame shrivels, and suddenly she looks no bigger than a child. Tears stream down her cheeks and I search for a tissue.

"Oh, Halmoni. I'm so sorry." I hand her a tissue, presenting it to her with both hands. "What can be done?" Tears prickle my own eyes.

"Nothing, it appears," she wails, crying harder. Dabbing her eyes, she peers up. "This family is my whole life."

Every time she mentions the word *family*, there's a tug at my heart. After almost a week with my dad's family, I don't feel any closer to them than I did when I first found out about them. With only one day left of my visit here, I want to leave with some assurance that we are a family.

"In fact, I must go see Lady Cha. She will know what to do. I'm sorry, Chloe, but I won't be able to spend time with you this morning." Halmoni gathers herself up off the floor and is about to put her shoes on when I stop her.

The mood shifts and I wipe the tears away as I sit down on the couch facing her. Every time I hear the mention of Lady Cha, I don't know how to react.

"Halmoni, I've been meaning to ask. Lady Cha, is she a fortune-teller?" I can barely get the words out without hearing how ridiculous I sound.

Halmoni doesn't share my level of skepticism. "Lady Cha is very talented. With the specific information about your birthplace and exact time of birth, she can predict your fortune with a precise accuracy that makes her high in demand. As you can imagine, she is *very* expensive. But when family is concerned, money does not matter." She tilts her head and pinches my chin with her fingers. "In fact, Lady Cha says you will bring good luck and fortune to the family."

"What?" Something doesn't sit right with me about her answer, and it's not just because Halmoni confirmed that Lady Cha, her most trusted advisor, is a fortune-teller.

"How does Lady Cha know that about me?"

Halmoni takes her glasses off, sets them on her lap, and stares down her nose at me. "She really never told you anything about me, huh?"

"Who?"

"Your mother."

"*My* mother?" I draw my head back.

"The last time we saw each other, we both agreed to never talk about each other again. I never knew she would keep her word all these years." She tuts and shakes her head in disbelief.

"You . . . and my mom?" Surely, I can't be hearing her correctly.

"Twenty years ago, Lady Cha warned us that the marriage between my son and your mother would be doomed. I told them, but your mother ran away to America. Not only that, but she took my Joon Pyo with her. That was the last time I saw him." She dabs her eyes with the tissue I gave her. I feel the emotions swelling in my chest, but they never fully rise. Not this time. Nothing seems to be making sense.

"I think you might be mistaken. My mom, she couldn't have known about any of this." I knew it was likely my mom wasn't easily accepted by Halmoni, but I could never imagine her going head-to-head with her.

"Your name, Chloe . . . Chang?" She raises an eyebrow up at me.

I nod.

"That is your mom's last name. Not your father's."

I open my mouth to protest but close it, realizing she's right. How did I not think about that before? Why did Mom do that?

"It's because of the curse," Halmoni says as if she can read my mind. "Shortly after they got married, like Lady Cha warned us, your father died. One month later, my husband died. Then later, my second son. The men are cursed in our family now, you see?"

I don't even know how to respond to that. I mean, the fortune-teller was hard enough to wrap my head around, but a curse?

"My youngest son is now sick too. It never ends." She dabs her eyes with a tissue again. "All because your mother took my Joon Pyo away. Your mother knows this, that's why she changed your name and never spoke of us before to you."

"I-I . . ." I stammer, trying to defend my mom. This time, it's much harder to do given that she never told me about my dad, Halmoni, the curse—any of this.

Halmoni puts up a hand to shush me. "You're like your father. I can see that now. Lady Cha thinks highly of you. She thinks you might even end this curse once and for all."

I want to believe everything she's saying about my dad, but that would mean that my mom has been lying to me.

I thought getting to know my dad would give me more clarity about who I am, but now what Halmoni is saying is making me question everything I thought I knew.

✕

As soon as Halmoni leaves for the hospital, I call my mom.

"Chloe-yah, what is it? Are you okay?" Her hushed tone tells me she's at the hospital.

"Halmoni told me everything," I blurt out.

"Everything?" Her voice is soft and unchallenging, which is just as good as admitting she's been lying to me all these years.

"And it's time you told me everything too. About knowing Dad's family all along. About working at Sam Won Department Store. About the curse!"

The line goes flat. I check the phone to see if we've lost the connection, but she's still there. "Mom?" I say after a good minute.

"I can't believe she told you." She sighs a deep and breathy sigh into the receiver. Almost like she's relieved. "The last time we saw each other, she made me promise never to speak of each other again. I kept them from you, not because of her. I thought it was best to stay away from people who only saw us as bad luck. It was killing me keeping that kind of secret to myself."

"It . . . it was killing *you*?" I can barely say the words through my rage. All these years she's been lying to me and *she's* the victim?

"Chloe-yah, I thought about telling you a thousand times. I-I had to keep my word." Her voice trembles. "You're not mad, are you?"

"I can't even begin to answer that question, Mom. I mean, how would you feel if you just found out your whole life was a lie?!" I'm screaming at the top of my lungs and flailing my hands in frustration.

"Your life isn't a lie." Her voice cracks, and she whimpers, softly. "Chloe-yah, I did what I thought was best for you. I'm not perfect, but I love you. Please come home now so we can sort this out."

"There's no way I'm coming home early, not after this."

"Please, no," she pleads desperately. "You can't stay another day with them. You can't trust anything they say—"

"I can't trust anything *they* say?" I balk dramatically through the receiver. "That's rich, coming from you. Halmoni tells me things, things about my dad, about my past. She's not the one I need to worry about lying to me."

She sobs so quietly, I can hear the monitors beeping

191

in the background. "You don't mean that." I'm not sure if she's saying this to me or trying to convince herself of it. "This is a lot to process, I know you're upset. You have every right to be. I'm sure if you knew everything, I mean *everything*, you'd understand." She sniffs.

"How can I be sure I know everything? You never tell me anything." I release another exasperated sigh. All those years of getting the runaround about Dad come to mind and it reignites my anger.

"I promise, from now on I won't keep any secrets from you. All you have to do is ask. Please. Chloe-yah, please," she begs.

The sincerity in her plea gets to me and I draw in a deep breath and try to calm myself down. I'm just so utterly confused by how someone so loving, so caring, could lie to me about something like this. She must've had a good reason. She must. Or else how could she deny me the right to know my own family?

"Start at the beginning. Tell me how you and Dad met," I say firmly but calmly.

"Your father and I met at the department store."

"Where you worked," I say now that we're being honest with each other.

"Where I worked," she admits. "Your father was in line to take over the company, as the heir to the Noh family. He was doing his rounds in my department and that's how we got to know each other."

"Halmoni disapproved?"

"Lady Cha said I would cause the family to lose their fortune."

"You didn't believe in it, did you?"

"Of course not. Still, your halmoni was so adamantly against the marriage. I tried to break it off with your father, but he didn't listen."

"Is that why you left Seoul? To try to break it off with Dad?"

"We left to get a fresh start. Before we left, your father, he tried to—"

"Theresa! This patient is unconscious." Nurse Linda's voice calls out from my mom's end.

"Oh, no . . . Chloe, I—"

"I know, Mom. You have to go."

"I-I'm sorry. I'll call you back, and I'll tell you everything. I promise."

"Why bother, Mom."

"What's that supposed to mean?" I can hear the panic in her voice over the clamor of the background hospital noise.

I'm so tired of trying to explain my disappointment to her. If she doesn't understand me by now, I'm beginning to wonder if she ever will.

"Maybe Halmoni's right. Maybe we are cursed," I say instead of an answer.

# CHAPTER 17

After the call with Mom, I crawl back in bed and under my comforter, where I plan on spending the rest of the day. That is, until I remember I have to meet Miso at the hair salon. Which then reminds me that I'm supposed to meet Jin Young tonight.

A part of me considers canceling everything on account of me finding out my life, up until now, has been one big hoax. The other part of me rationalizes that by not meeting Jin Young, I would be accomplishing the very thing Mom had set out to do by deceiving me in the first place— which is to not meet anyone in the family. That would be reason enough to get out of bed and go on with my day, but something else urges me to move. A longing for a friend in the family. Halmoni, as nice as she's been, is somewhat intimidating, and Soo Young and her mom are clearly not interested. But Jin Young . . . he's different. Since the beginning, Jin Young has been kind and dependable, like a friend. The truth is, I wouldn't give up meeting him for anything. Not for Lady Cha, not for a curse, and definitely not for my mom.

Later that day, I'm with Miso on a bustling street near Hongik University, where she swears the most stylish hair salons are—at least, they were the last time she was here the previous summer.

The streets are swarming with a crowd full of people around our age. Stores have their doors open with mannequins in the latest fashions on display and music blasting on speakers that clash with one another, but not in an unpleasant way. And the smells, ugh. I almost suggest changing course and taking a detour to the stall on the corner of the street selling fried pancakes filled with sesame and honey.

"Focus, Chloe. Hair first, stomach later," Miso says, reading my mind.

When she finally coaxes me back on course, she leads me to a salon on the second floor above a retail shop. An automatic glass door slides open and a burst of arctic air hits me in the face. Just in time, too. I've only been outside for five minutes, but my face is melting off.

I'm not one to frequent fancy hair salons in Tulsa, but if I did, I hardly think they would look anything like this one. Between the upbeat music blasting in surround sound and the trendy young women sporting styled and dyed hairdos, I swear it feels like I've stepped right onto the set of a K-pop music video. The air reeks of perfume and chemicals, and I can't hear anything the hairdresser says over the loud music and blow-dryers when she takes my hand and drags me to a chair in the corner of the busy salon.

The main hairdresser has a sleek bob in an ombre red that shines under the fluorescent lights, and her assistant has long locks that are curled to perfection. Before I can open my mouth to ask a question, they both descend on me with their brushes and combs.

"How do they know what to do? I didn't even tell them what kind of hairstyle I want," I say to Miso, who is sitting on a stool next to me.

"Oh, girl. You've never been to a Korean salon?" When I shake my head, she says, "Then you're in for a shock. This is the only place where the customer is *not* right. Oh, and try not to be offended. They know what they're doing," she warns ominously.

"Too tangled and frizzy," the hairdresser says to me through the mirror.

Her assistant nods. "And dry," she adds.

Miso gives me an "I told you so" look and I try to heed her warning, but it's near impossible.

After pulling my hair in every direction, they douse it in a solution that stings my eyes and nose. Then they section it out and brush it onto plastic sheets that extend out of my head like I'm some kind of electrocuted person.

I peer over at Miso skeptically. "This is going to look good, right?"

"Have I ever steered you wrong?" When I shake my head, ever so delicately, she says, "Listen to Unni, you are going to look just like a Noh when I'm finished with you."

"After the past few days, I wonder if I'll ever fit in with them."

"This is classic K-drama stuff. I mean, where do you think they get their material anyway?"

"You sound just like Hazel."

Miso snorts. "Do you have a picture of Hazel? Because

she sounds just like my type." When I show her a picture on my cracked-screen phone, she says, "Long hair, dark complexion? Yep, definitely my type."

"She's also definitely not gay. She's dating my best friend, well, *our* best friend, Seb, short for Sebastian."

"Uh-oh, love triangle? This definitely sounds like a K-drama."

I don't know if it's quite a love triangle, but it's definitely along the lines of being a third wheel. "You ever feel like you don't fit in, even on your best days?" I say, thinking out loud. Here I am with everything I've ever wanted, only instead of feeling more complete, I feel more unsure about myself than ever.

Miso gapes. *"Hello?!"* She motions to herself up and down. "Have you not been listening—have you not been *looking* at me?"

I laugh, embarrassed by being so clueless. "Right, sorry. I just got lost in my thoughts."

After the laugh dies down to a lull, she says, "So, uh, this straight perm takes two hours, so we've got time. If you want to unload anything, I'm listening."

I laugh lightly. "I don't even think I cared about Seb, not in that way. I think it was more the feeling of rejection that hurt. Like, why not me? Now, with the Nohs, I'm afraid of that type of rejection again. If I don't fit in with my own family, where am I supposed to fit in?"

"I don't know about being in a family like the Nohs. I'm not a chaebol, not by a long shot. But I do know a lot about rejection, particularly rejection from your own family." She leans her head against the wall with a heavy sigh.

"Things still weird between you and your dad?" I say in a quiet voice.

She sighs. "Yup. Still weird."

"Jeez, I'm sorry, Miso. I guess I've been a little more than self-involved to notice."

"Ah, it's okay. You have a lot going on right now." She swipes a hand at me. "By the way, I completely understand your fears about the Nohs rejecting you. I really do."

"Thanks," I say. It's been a long time since I've felt anyone really understood what I was going through. Especially now that I know my mom has been lying to me this whole time, I don't know who to talk to.

After a while, the hairdresser comes in, cutting our conversation short. She and her attendant get right to peeling off the plastic boards and take me to the sink area to wash my hair. When I come back, the hairdresser is armed with a pair of scissors and does a major Edward Scissorhands on my hair. My eyes are clamped shut the entire time, too scared to look, but I can hear Miso making gasping noises, which is not at all reassuring.

Next, the hairdresser blow-dries my hair, tugging it this way and that with her heavily bristled brush. She spritzes a solution on me that smells like floral perfume, then she and her assistant stare at me intensely. After consulting with each other in Korean, they allow a small satisfied smile to grace their lips before they spin me around to face the mirror.

"Whoa!" I touch my hair, which doesn't actually feel like my hair. The silky strands slip through my fingertips, so smooth and straight. She even cut these banging layers that totally give me edge. I've never had edge in my life! The hairdresser and her attendant smile triumphantly through the mirror as if they have achieved the impossible.

"Much better," the hairdresser says.

"No more messy," her attendant adds.

"Just remember, bluntness is a form of endearment here," Miso says as we make our way out of the salon.

"Yeah, right." I smile.

On the street level, everything smells so good we have to stop in our tracks to strategize our meal.

"Okay, now. The age-old conundrum: sweet or savory?" she asks.

I stand there a minute, legitimately torn. "Both?"

"You read my mind." We both laugh. Then something catches Miso's eye behind me, and she snickers.

I turn back to see what she's looking at, but all I see is a boy and girl about our age walking out of a building, holding hands.

"What? What's so funny?" I turn around and ask.

"That right there is what they call a love motel." She points to the three-story brick building.

"Love motel?"

"You know, where you rent the rooms by the hour."

"Eww!"

"It's not that bad. I mean, most Koreans live in tiny apartments with their families until they get married. It doesn't leave people with much choice. I laughed because it's like two in the afternoon on a Friday. I assumed people frequented them in the evenings. You know, when people can't actually recognize you walking out of one."

"Okay, why are we talking about love motels when we can be stuffing our faces with fried foods? This is a carnie's dream right now. What should we eat?"

We decide unanimously on crinkle-cut encrusted corn dogs and hotteok—sesame-and-honey filled pancakes.

"Why don't you stay here for the hotteok and I'll go get the corn dogs?"

"Got it," I say.

At the front of the line, I tell the vendor, "Doogae, joo-sayo." When he hands me two fresh-out-of-the-frying-pan pancakes, I'm astonished. I successfully ordered something in Korean by myself. Pretty soon I won't have to mime my way through this country anymore.

On my way back to meet Miso, I'm carrying very warm, and very tempting, sweet pancakes in my hand. It takes every bit of my concentration not to take a bite that when a couple turns onto the path, cutting me off, I don't stop in time. We collide and the hot sticky pancakes are smooshed against my shirt. When we peel ourselves off each other, I begin apologizing.

I bow. "Jesonghay—Soo Young!" I blurt out as soon as I'm standing upright. She is the last person I'd expect to run into here.

She panics and pushes the guy out of her way. He takes off running. "What are you doing here?" The scowl on her face returns.

"I got my hair done. What are *you* doing here?" I look up at the building she walked out of, recognizing it as the love motel Miso pointed out to me earlier.

"I-I . . ." Soo Young starts the sentence, sounding unsure of herself.

It's unfamiliar to see her so frazzled. I think about putting her at ease by saying I'm not going to tell Halmoni, when she regains her composure.

"You never saw me, *okay*?" she says with narrowed eyes.

"Was that your boyfriend?"

"Look, no one will believe you anyway. You'll upset Halmoni and Lady Cha, so you better think twice before you say anything to anyone. Understand?"

I pause, not because of the harsh tone, but because everyone in the family seems to be under the whim of Lady Cha. It makes me wonder how much truth there is to her predictions.

Soo Young takes my silence as a yes and storms off without saying goodbye.

$$\text{X}$$

Miso returns with two giant corn dogs in her hand and a smile that can be seen for miles. I apologize to her for the squished pancakes and tell her about my run-in with Soo Young.

"You're shitting me!" She gapes.

"I wish you'd been there to witness it, because I'm not doing it justice."

"Aw, man! Stupid, delicious corn dogs." She tears off a huge bite, then hands me my corn dog. "Well, do you feel better? I mean, you have the upper hand now."

I take the corn dog and exchange it for the hotteok. "The thought did cross my mind, but . . . the last thing I want is to blackmail my cousin into liking me. I want her to like me for me, not because she is forced to."

"You, Chloe Chang, are a better person than I ever could be."

"I doubt that," I say. "But thanks for your vote of confidence."

※

After I get home from hanging out with Miso, I pick up my phone to make a call. This time, instead of calling Hazel, I decide to call Seb.

"Chloe?" Seb answers.

"Hey, Seb." There's a shelf full of sports trophies and a Fortnite poster on the wall behind him. "Where are you?"

"I'm at my cousin Tony's house."

"Is this a bad time? I can call back if it is," I say, sitting on the chair next to my bed.

"Nah, it's cool. He's been in the 'bathroom' for fifteen minutes now," he says, using air quotes. "Last time this happened, he was at his neighbor's house playing Xbox. He's fine."

"Oh, okay. If you're sure."

"Hazel's, uh, busy, so I don't know if you want to call back later."

"I know. I wanted to talk to you and see how you're doing."

His head dips knowingly. "Oh. Hazel told you." He

sighs, raking a hand through his hair. "She's supposedly at the spa for some *alone time*," he says, rolling his eyes. "I don't know if you can technically call it that if you're with your sisters."

"Aw, Seb." Even though I wasn't so thrilled to hear they'd become a couple, I'm overcome with emotions at the prospect of my best friends breaking up.

"I can't say I didn't see it coming. She's been pulling away from me ever since graduation."

"If it makes you feel any better, she's having a tough time with it, too."

"I guess. It's not always easy for me either. I mean, don't take this the wrong way, but when the three of us are together, I feel like I'm some kind of a third wheel."

My head whips up. "*You* feel like the third wheel?" I'm pretty sure if anyone should feel like a third wheel in this scenario, it should be me—the one that's *not* in the relationship.

"Didn't you notice? She's always pulling you aside to talk to you about Lee Min Ho, or K-dramas, or Lee Min Ho."

A snort escapes me, and I quickly cover my mouth. "I'm sorry. That was insensitive."

"Even when it's just the two of us, now that you're not here, it's like she'd rather be talking with you."

For so long, I'd felt like the odd man out in our group. It's surprising to hear Seb say he's the one feeling left out. "I'm sorry, Seb, if you ever felt that way. I had no idea. I may have been too consumed with thinking I was being left out to notice."

"Of course." He rolls his eyes at himself. "What am I talking about? You must have felt this way when we told you about our relationship."

"Sort of." I pick a loose thread on my jeans. Even though this is what prompted me to call him, it's not easy to talk about it to his face. "I tried to pretend everything was okay, so that's probably why it never came up. If I'm being honest, I did feel left out."

"Chloe." He sighs deeply. "I. Am. So. Sorry," he says. "Why didn't you say something?"

"I thought I was the only one that ever felt like I didn't fit in. Which, I realize, sounds ridiculous now that I've said it out loud."

"Of course you're not the only one, and I'm sad you didn't think you could share your feelings with either of us."

"Yeah. I'm sad I didn't think I could come to you, either." I give him a weak smile. "No matter what happens between you and Hazel, let's promise to never keep our feelings from each other again."

"Agreed."

Even though there's no guarantee Hazel and Seb will make it as a couple, I hang up with Seb feeling better knowing that no matter what happens, we're going to be okay.

# <u>23andme.com</u>

**MESSAGES**

From: Chang, Chloe
Subject: Tonight!
Saturday, 2:50 PM

Hey, Sachon! It's finally Saturday! Is it me, or was that the longest five days ever? Wow, did that make me seem as pathetic as I sounded? Halmoni planned a lot for me, so I had a jam-packed week that helped the time fly by. I didn't get to eat Shin Ramyun (boo) but I did get to know more about my dad and fashion here in Korea. Even though my flight leaves tomorrow, today couldn't come fast enough for me. I feel like I've known you for so long and we're only now meeting in person. How weird is that? Anyway, what are we going to do tonight? How should I dress? Can't wait.

From: Jin Young Noh
Subject: RE: Tonight!
Saturday, 3:20 PM

Dear Chloe,

No, you don't sound weird, and yes, I've been looking forward to meeting you, too. As for tonight, we'll be going somewhere nice, so please dress accordingly. When you get to my apartment building, take the elevator to the top floor.

# CHAPTER 18

It's my last night in Seoul and I'm on my way to meet Jin Young. I'm not sure exactly where we're going, but if it's like any of the restaurants we've been going to, it'll be high-end. Thankfully I have the perfect outfit, thanks to Halmoni—a sleek black dress with a leather jacket and black studded booties. Plus, with my skin healing quicker than I thought and my new hairstyle that frames my face with silky strands of jet-black hair, I look and feel like a brand-new person.

I keep checking and rechecking my makeup in the car. I'm not, like, trying to impress him or anything, but everyone in the Noh family is so impeccably put together. I want to fit in. Or at the very least, I want to look like I belong. I have Halmoni's approval and I even think I understand Soo Young a little better now. With Jin Young, though, I have this feeling that we could be really close, like Seb and his cousins, who are as close to each other as siblings. I have such a short time here and there's so much ground to cover—like what kind of music does he like? And does he eat the crust off his pizza? Can he roll his r's? I'm so eager to start getting to know him in real life.

Mr. Kim watches me from the mirror, like usual. Only this time, I notice his stare linger longer.

"What? Do I look funny? You'd tell me if I was making a fool of myself, wouldn't you?"

"No, you look good." His eyes dart back to the road, but I can see the skin on his forehead turning pink.

"Thanks," I say, more like a question. Even though his words suggest otherwise, it doesn't necessarily sound like a compliment. "Tell me, what kind of relationship do you have with Jin Young? Are you close?"

"It's both close and not close at the same time."

"Okay, that's super helpful."

He chuckles. "What I mean is, I know a lot about him, and he depends on me for many things, both personal and business related. You could say I'm his right-hand man." A beat later, he adds, "But I wouldn't say we're close."

"I'm just so excited to meet Jin Young finally. I tend to let my imagination get carried away. Well, I blame my best friend Hazel for that, but to be fair, I go along with it, so I'm just as guilty. It's just that I feel like Jin Young and I would get along really well and I hope it's not something I'm over-dramatizing in my head." It must be my nerves that have me rattling on about my insecurities.

Mr. Kim doesn't say anything. Instead, he stares intensely at the road, his jaw clenching from time to time.

When we stop at a tall apartment building that towers above the other buildings around it, Mr. Kim gets out of the car and comes around to open my door. As soon as I step out, Mr. Kim stops me from walking away.

"You shouldn't get too worked up about meeting Jin Young," he says, surprising me.

"What do you mean?" My brow furrows.

He clears his throat. "I-I mean, he's just a guy," he stammers. "He may not be perfect."

If I didn't know any better, I would think that Mr. Kim is jealous. Which is weird.

"He's my cousin, remember?" I remind him in case he forgot.

He doesn't seem as amused as I am; an expression of worry crosses his face, but eventually he says, "You're right. He's your cousin. I'm sure everything will go well with him tonight." He bows, then disappears back into the car.

I haven't seen him behave this oddly since that day at the spa when he almost didn't get out of the elevator. That was when I didn't think he spoke English. I guess I could ask him a follow-up question, but as soon as I check the time on my watch, I realize I'm running a few minutes late, so I head off to the building instead.

Inside the apartment building, the floors and walls are dark and sleek and there's pop music playing in the lobby. In the emails, Jin Young told me his apartment is on the top floor. When I get in the elevator, I notice the top floor is not a number. It's two letters: PH, which stands for Penthouse. Because of course.

Suddenly, I'm feeling nervous and insecure again. I check my reflection on the inside of the elevator door so many times, it's starting to feel like a funhouse mirror. I'm second-guessing everything Miso said, wondering if I made myself look more like a clown and less like a Noh. The elevator bell dings and the butterflies in my stomach do flips. I take a calming breath and push the doorbell to the only door on the floor. After a few seconds, it opens.

Jin Young looks just like the photos I've seen of him online, except less formal and more casual-cool, dressed in slim-cut jeans and a dress shirt under a sports coat. Instantly, I identify our similarities. The low bridge of our nose, the fullness of our lips. It's familiar and at the same time, eerie.

"Hi. Nice to finally meet you," I say clumsily.

"Sure," he says, barely looking up at me from his phone. Instead of letting me in, he comes out and pushes the button for the elevator. Not quite the greeting I was expecting. He seemed equally excited to see me when we were messaging. Then again, it's quite possible I've built this moment up to be bigger than it is. I have been known to get carried away from time to time.

"Oh, okay. I guess we should get going then." We stand at opposite corners from each other in the elevator and I'm feeling awkward. For all his ease over email, something isn't translating to real life. I think about bringing up the emails, the nice things he said, but the elevator door opens up and I feel like I've missed my window.

In the parking garage below, I follow him to his car, which isn't far. It's no surprise that living in the penthouse affords him the best parking spot in the entire garage. Jin Young pushes the Unlock button and a sleek white sports car with black tinted windows beeps. When he opens the door for me and it glides up and not out, I gasp. It's like the car from *Back to the Future*, only way nicer. I slip into the passenger side and look around, amazed.

With my mom's unpredictable work hours, I mostly relied on Hazel and Seb. I've had my fair share of being driven around in shiny new cars, since they both got one for their sixteenth birthdays, but this is so not the same thing. If we're comparing cars to airplane seats, Hazel and Seb's cars are economy and Jin Young's is first-class.

Jin Young revs the car and maneuvers it like he's playing a video game, moving around the leather knob on his shift gear and weaving in and out of traffic seamlessly. The ride is smooth, but nevertheless I find myself gripping the leather seat. I feel like I'm on some amusement park ride and I'm about to go upside down at any minute.

"Where . . . are we going?" I manage to say. Between the driving and the stale air, I'm surprised I could say anything coherent.

"Night," he says, keeping his eyes glued to the road. Except he says it with a Korean accent, somehow making the one-syllable word into three.

"Na-ee-t?" I carefully try to repeat what I heard. "What's that?"

"Nightclub" is all he says.

"Ah." I nod in acknowledgment. I want to ask a follow-up question or make reference to our emails, but I'm getting the sense that Jin Young isn't much of a conversationalist. I try not to overthink it. Some people are better over email than IRL. Besides, his driving is more than enough to keep me distracted during the silent ride.

When we get to a district where the buildings have

neon signs and the streets are packed with young people dressed for an evening out on the town, he stops in front of a door with a roped-off entrance. Immediately a group of big guys with thick necks wearing security earpieces swarm the car. I'm about to panic, thinking we're being car-jacked, but I quickly realize they're opening the door for us. One guy takes the car keys from Jin Young and drives off with a roar of the engine, while another guy ushers us past the roped entrance while bowing constantly.

Jin Young points back to me and says something to the guy at the front door in Korean. The guy looks me up and down and nods, allowing me beyond the roped-off area to the front door.

As soon as the door opens, a loud burst of pop music hits my eardrums. Inside is shockingly bigger than I'd expected from the outside, resembling something of a stadium. I've never been to a nightclub before, but this isn't like any of the clubs I've seen on shows or in movies. There's no bar where people order drinks or get hit on by guys who've had one too many. In fact, other than the dance floor, there's no mingling. It seems very organized, like dinner theater, except with strobe lights flashing around us and music that is the type of loud you can feel in your chest.

A waiter ushers us upstairs, away from the dance floor and into a quiet hallway. Then he opens a door to a private room with a table and two couches and a karaoke machine to the side. Behind one couch are windows facing the dance floor and DJ who is situated directly below us.

"Sit." Jin Young points to one side of the couch while he sits on the one adjacent.

"You must be jet-lagged. I know I was when I first got here." I give him an awkward smile. In fact, everything is awkward right now, even the mood.

He shrugs, then pulls out a cigarette and offers me one. I politely refuse and he lights up.

Even though we're in a public nightclub, we're at least by ourselves right now. I take this moment to pull out the photo of my parents from my bag. It's getting wrinkled from all the times I've brought it out to share with people, but it's still recognizable. "In case you're curious, I brought a photo of my mom and dad. It looks like they were in Korea here. Do you recognize this place?"

He reluctantly takes the photo from me, exhaling smoke over it. Before the smoke clears, he hands the photo back to me, shaking his head. "Sorry, can't help you."

"Oh. It's okay." I inconspicuously wipe down the photo before returning it to my bag, not that Jin Young would notice. The door opens, breaking our silence, and a group of guys and girls enter boisterously. They look like they come from wealthy families, wearing fancy tailored suits and designer dresses and handbags. Jin Young butts his cigarette, then stands up and greets them in a mix of English and Korean with bro hugs. Then their attention focuses on me.

"Oh, this is Chloe," Jin Young says with little fanfare.

A skinny guy with overly gelled hair eyes me up and down with a smirk on his face.

"No, it's nothing like that, byung shin." Jin Young laughs

213

it off, playfully shoving him, and I can't help reading too much into his response. Why doesn't he just tell them who I am?

We sit and I finally get the courage to ask, "Are they your friends from school?"

"Sort of. Most of us went to Dae Han International School; the others went to boarding schools in the States. We're mainly connected with each other because we run in the same circle."

"Do they all work at the department store?"

Jin Young shakes his head with a smirk. "They have their own family businesses." He points to the girl on the very edge of the couch and says, "Ae Jung over there, her family owns the largest Korean skincare brand. Jung Hwan, the guy hanging on her, is the heir to the global food chain. Pinkie's dad is a producer of K-pop bands. Everyone here belongs to big-name families."

*Whoa.* It's one thing being in the same room as one chaebol. It's quite another being in a room full of them. Everyone's got that same airbrushed, glossy-magazine look, and even with my skincare and hair makeover, it's no comparison. They're Bergdorf Goodman and I'm Hobby Lobby. It makes me sink deeper into the corner of the couch.

A couple of waiters come in with trays of fruit cut up in a fancy presentation, dried roasted snacks, and alcohol. Lots of alcohol. For the next thirty minutes, the guys and girl drink and eat and banter back and forth. I might as well be invisible, as no one is acknowledging my presence, not even Jin Young.

I'm about to excuse myself to get some fresh air when the door bursts open and a heavyset guy with too-tight clothes and a mop of curly hair stumbles in. Despite having just arrived at the nightclub, he's already glassy-eyed and his cheeks are flushed.

"Jin Young-ah!" He opens his arms out and motions for Jin Young to come greet him by the door.

Jin Young's demeanor immediately changes, and a particular smile appears, as if he is putting on an act. He obediently goes to hug him. The guy ruffles his hair and jokes around with him in front of everyone in the room before sitting down beside him. He's about to pour drinks when he notices me. I gulp.

"Girlfriend?" He leans over, getting into my space. The way his eyes scan me up and down makes my skin crawl.

"Nah, it ain't like that." Jin Young playfully shoves the guy but looks visibly uncomfortable, wiping his brow. "This is Chloe. She's visiting from the US. She's . . . a family friend," he says, and my heart sinks to my stomach.

I bow and say hi, but barely. I'm trying so hard to keep it together. We're not family friends. We're *family*. I get that we found out about each other exactly one week ago, but is it really that hard for Jin Young to acknowledge it?

"Chloe, this is Bum Soo," Jin Young says, and I bow again. "He's my cousin."

My jaw literally hangs open. His cousin? Does that mean—

"On my mom's side," Jin Young is quick to say, as if reading my mind.

"Oh" is all I can say. I want to ask more questions. Like

how come nobody ever talks about his dad? How many other cousins does he have? Why can't he introduce *me* as his cousin? But as much as they're burning at the tip of my tongue, the words never make it out.

A girl squeals about the song the DJ is playing and points to the dance floor. The group decides to go dance and tries to convince Jin Young, but his eyes flicker back at me and he declines. I'm about to tell him he should go and not worry about me. It's not like he's paying any attention to me anyway. But Bum Soo says he's staying behind, too, and as soon as the others leave, it's just the three of us.

"How old are you, Chloe?" Bum Soo asks, heavily groping me with his eyes.

"Eighteen," I say.

"Are you in college?"

I shake my head. "Not yet."

"She's going to FIT in the fall," Jin Young says in a way that I want to say resembles pride, but then again, I'm not sure since he's not even willing to admit I'm his relative.

Bum Soo nods with an expression like it's no big deal. "FIT, Parsons, RISD . . . they're all the same, aren't they?" He sniffs. "It's the real work experience, though. Isn't that right, Jin-yah?" He wraps his arm around Jin Young's neck and fake wrestles him. "People like us have more important things to do than fashion school."

"Yeah, right." Jin Young smiles tensely. "How's the job going? Working hard?" he asks Bum Soo.

Bum Soo nudges Jin Young, smirking. "You know how it is, more like hardly working."

Jin Young laughs politely. "Yeah." He catches me eyeing the fruit plate, then discreetly hands me a piece of fruit on a toothpick.

I take it from him and say, "Thanks." It's probably the nicest thing he's done for me this entire night. How epically sad. I'd confront him if it weren't for Bum Soo's presence. I mean, what is up with the complete one-eighty he's giving me right now? It's as if our email conversations meant nothing to him.

Bum Soo's expression changes as he watches me take the cantaloupe from Jin Young, and he suddenly zeroes in on me.

"Chloe. Why don't you pour us a drink?" He says it with a level of authority that makes me do what he's asking, even though I wonder why he can't pour the drinks himself.

With the speared cantaloupe still in my hand, I scan the table for two clean shot glasses, then pick up the bottle with my free hand and start pouring.

"Huh-huh!" Bum Soo admonishes me, making me jump. "How dare you pour me a drink like that." He tsks and stares down at me with hardened eyes.

"Hyung," Jin Young tries to intervene, but Bum Soo waves him off.

"Didn't anyone teach you proper respect? I am your elder. Use two hands."

My hands are trembling, but I do what he says. I set the fruit down and pour the whiskey holding the bottle with two hands. I'm about to pour the second shot glass when Jin Young puts a hand over it.

"None for me, thanks."

Bum Soo tuts again and says, "You're not going to let me drink alone, are you?"

Jin Young shrugs. "Sorry, Hyung. I drove."

Bum Soo swears in Korean, then looks at me. "Yah. You drink for him, then."

"Huh?" I look up.

"Oh, you must be a goody-goody back in the States. It's okay! You can drink here, so be a good girl and listen to your oppa." He pours whiskey into the other shot glass, this time with one hand, signifying the distinction between him and me. Then he slides the shot glass in front of me.

I glance over to Jin Young with pleading eyes, but he looks as helpless and as uncomfortable as I am, so I see I have no choice. I pick up the shot glass and put my lips to the rim. Before I taste the alcohol, Bum Soo is yelling at me again.

"Yah, who does this girl think she is?" He turns to Jin Young and scoffs. "Take the glass with two hands, turn your face away from me when you drink it, and show me some goddamn respect!"

I swallow the lump in my throat. I'm not sure what's worse, being verbally abused by this total stranger or Jin Young standing by and letting it happen to me. My brain goes on autopilot and I pick up the drink, with two goddamn hands, and turn my body away from him so my back is facing him. Then, as I'm about to down the shot of whiskey, Jin Young grabs my arm to stop me.

"I'll drink with you." Jin Young takes the shot glass from my hand and clinks it with Bum Soo.

Relieved, I sigh. "Wait, what about your car—"

"I'm fine." Jin Young cuts me a sharp look that shuts me up.

I sit back while the two of them throw back their shots of whiskey. Then the door opens and a waiter comes in with two girls that don't look familiar. Bum Soo sits up animatedly and gestures for the girls to sit next to him.

"Yah! We need more alcohol!" Bum Soo yells, holding up a credit card. He holds it up long enough for the girls to see it's an American Express Black Card. Once they *ooh* and *aah* at it, he throws it in the waiter's face. The waiter fumbles to catch it and leaves as soon as he does, bowing the whole way to the door.

Bum Soo's mood changes completely, chatting with the girls in the most pleasant manner.

"Who are these girls?" I discreetly ask Jin Young.

Jin Young glances over at Bum Soo, making sure he isn't listening. Seeing Bum Soo preoccupied by the girls who are fawning over him, taking turns feeding him different kinds of dried fruit and alcohol, he turns back to me. "It's called booking. The waiter brings girls to different rooms or tables to 'introduce' them to each other."

"Really? The waiters take girls to random rooms?"

"Sometimes random. Sometimes not." He glances over at Bum Soo, who doesn't seem to realize we're in the same room with him anymore.

"What do you mean?"

"When you have families like ours, you get preferential treatment."

"Is Bum Soo in the family business, too?"

He nods, with his lips pressed firmly together. I want to ask more questions, but loud music comes over the speakers, grabbing everyone's attention. It's the karaoke machine. The girls are in front of the room, singing for Bum Soo. One of them starts making eyes at Jin Young.

My stomach feels sour and the room is filled with too much cigarette smoke. I feel the need for fresh air, so I excuse myself to go to the bathroom. While I'm washing my hands at the bathroom sink, a couple of girls stumble in laughing. They reapply their makeup and talk animatedly. I watch them through the mirror, missing Hazel and Seb. We wouldn't be in the bathroom of a nightclub, reapplying makeup and talking about boys, but we'd be laughing comfortably with each other for sure. The loneliness from the past week overwhelms me and suddenly I miss them so much it physically hurts. Next thing I know, I'm locking myself in a bathroom stall and crying into my hands.

I already knew I wouldn't understand most of the people in this country with my limited Korean vocabulary, but I'm realizing that I don't even understand the people who speak English. Why is Bum Soo giving me such a hard time? And why was Jin Young being so cold to me? Tonight is going so differently than I imagined, and now that I'm leaving tomorrow, I'm overwhelmed with disappointment.

After a string of girls comes and goes, the bathroom is finally empty again, making me feel brave enough to emerge from the stall. I dab my face with a paper towel and blow out a deep breath. The night isn't over yet, I remind myself.

In the hallway, on my way back to the room, I bump into Bum Soo coming at me from the other direction. I try to turn the corner so that he doesn't see me, but it's too late.

# CHAPTER 19

"Where did you run off to? Booking?" Bum Soo has a lazy smile on his lips that makes my skin crawl.

"Nope." I shake my head and try to move past him. Everything about the guy screams sleazy.

He puts an arm up to block my way. I flash him a fake smile, but he stares back with a cold, hard expression.

"Tell me something, Chloe. Why are you interested in the Noh family? Is it money? A job?"

"What? No!" I blurt out. His presumptuousness is bad enough, but accusing me of being a grubby little gold digger is too much. I feel the tears rising again, but I fight them back hard. Something tells me that tears would only egg him on.

"Okay, sure. That's what you say." He flashes his own fake smile. "But if you want a way in, Bum Soo oppa can help you."

My head whips up. "What?"

He leans in as if to tell me a secret.

"I can give you what you want, if you give me what I want. Be good to Jin Young's oppa. I hear the girls in America are *very* willing."

My shocked and disgusted expression seems to irritate

Bum Soo more. His face turns kimchi red and his jaw clenches. He's about to say something, but he gets distracted by something behind me.

"Hyung!" Jin Young yells, pointing at me. "Leave her alone." He walks over to us.

"Jin Young-ah, I'm kidding. You know me. I like to give people a hard time." He throws his hands up by his sides, like he's been joking around this whole time. Only it's not a joke, not to me.

"Go home, hyung. You've had too much to drink," Jin Young says tersely.

Bum Soo seems appalled by being spoken to in such an informal manner by Jin Young. "I see what's going on." His eyes bounce back and forth between me and Jin Young. "I'll let this slide once, because you're with her. Make sure you get home safely, dongsang-ah. Okay?" He swaggers off, intentionally bumping into Jin Young's shoulder on his way back to the room.

We stand there a second, wordlessly, the faint music of the club thumping in the background. I'm not sure if I should thank Jin Young or yell at him for bringing me to this place.

"Let's go," he says before I can decide.

I follow him to the same back entrance we came in through. Upon seeing him, the bouncers immediately scramble, talking into their security radios. A minute later Jin Young's white sports car comes roaring up and he gets in.

I slide into the passenger seat and hold back the urge to say something about Bum Soo. Jin Young revs the engine and drives off just as fast as he did on the way here, if not faster. There are fewer cars on the street than before, but there is still a fair number of pedestrians. My fingers grip tightly to the seat as we go zipping down the alleyway.

"Watch out!" I point to a couple holding hands who are about to cross the street. They jump back in time and I glance over at Jin Young, who is unfazed by the close encounter. He finally slows down at a red light and I'm able to breathe again.

"Thank you," I decide to say. "For helping me earlier with Bum Soo."

He stays focused on the red light and an indecipherable crease forms between his eyes. It must be a sensitive topic, the way he tenses up every time Bum Soo is near or even mentioned. I'm about to ask him about it when the light turns green. Jin Young's foot hits the accelerator, and the car is thrust forward. I see a car ahead making a left turn. We're about to hit it.

"Stop!" I scream.

Jin Young swerves the car to the right, hard, but it's too late. We crash into something and my body lurches forward. The seat belt jerks me back. My head nearly misses crashing into the dashboard, but I'm disoriented nevertheless. A mix of vertigo and seasickness hits me like a ton of bricks. I blink hard a few times, trying to get my bearings straight. When my vision clears, I turn my head to Jin Young, who is slumped over the steering wheel.

"Jin Young!" I shake him gently. "Are you okay?!"

His limp body makes me break into a cold sweat. I

keep shaking him. "Please wake up!" I'm about to check his pulse when he coughs. I audibly sigh. "Are you okay?" I scan his face. Other than a slight bruise on his head, he seems fine.

It takes a minute for him to realize what happened, but then he jolts to attention as if he's had a shot of adrenaline. "No, no, no, no, no! This can't happen!" He looks panicked.

"It's going to be okay," I try reassuring him. "Let me check your—"

"Halmoni's going to kill me!"

"Look, maybe you hit your head harder than I thought. You only had one drink tonight and that was a long time ago. This is an accident. She would just be thankful that no one got seriously hurt."

"No, you don't understand. This isn't just a car accident. I may have only had one drink, but how would this look? I've left a nightclub with someone like you—everyone is going to assume the worst. I can't have a scandal! Halmoni will never forgive me." He looks around, raking a hand through his hair frantically.

"Hey, you need to calm down," I say sternly.

Instead of calming down, he takes it a notch higher. He grabs my arms and looks me straight in the eye. "You don't understand. She'll cut me off . . . of everything! You have to help me."

I'm not sure I fully understand, but I hear sirens approaching and I know we're running out of time. "Okay, I'll help you. Please, promise me you'll calm down."

As if I'd said some magical word, Jin Young's face

dramatically changes. "This is perfect. No one knows who you are." He takes his seat belt off and opens his side of the door.

"Excuse me, what?" I can barely keep up, but it sounds like he's asking me to take the blame for the accident.

"Just tell them you're not from here and that you're confused." He gets out of the car. The sound of the sirens grows louder by the second. "I need to get out of here before they see me," he says right before he closes the door.

I roll down my window and yell out at him, *"You're leaving?* Are you serious? How do I even explain how I got the keys to your car?" I gape at him. Jin Young asking me to cover for him is more shocking than the accident itself.

"Just be creative. You'll be fine." Without another word, he disappears into the dark, holding his phone to his ear. Can this really be the same Jin Young I've been messaging with the past couple weeks? I know people can seem one way online and another in real life, but how could he be this different? How could he abandon me here?

For a split second, I think about leaving, too. If I flee the scene, like Jin Young did, then the accident will be traced back to him. If I stay, however, they wouldn't be able to trace me back to the Nohs and I could save everyone a lot of trouble. Maybe this is what Halmoni means about sacrificing yourself for the sake of the family.

I decide to slide over to the driver's seat, just in time. A second later, the blaring sirens pierce my ears and the flashing lights are disorienting.

A commotion of muffled sounds grows nearer and

eventually someone knocks on my window. When I roll it down, I hear a man's voice speaking rapid Korean.

Shielding my eyes with a hand, I don't say anything. Instead, I pull out my Oklahoma driver's license and hope that will take care of everything.

The police officer takes the license, inspects it, and motions for me to get out of the vehicle.

Tears well up in my eyes, not because of the thought of going to jail, but because it was Jin Young, my own family member, who suggested I take the blame in the first place. Right when I'm about to break down in a pleading cry, a car comes to a screeching halt and someone quickly comes running out toward us. My vision is blurred from the tears and I wipe them, blinking rapidly. By the time the figure approaches, I'm able to see clearly who it is.

"Mr. Kim!" I'm so happy to see him that I begin to sob.

"Are you okay? Are you hurt anywhere?" he asks in a panicked voice. When I shake my head no, he sighs in relief. "What happened?"

"Jin Young . . . he crashed . . . and then left . . ." Thinking back to how I was abandoned by my own cousin, I bury my head in his chest and cry. I'm too vulnerable to care that I'm making a snotty mess on his fitted silk-blend suit jacket.

I can't see his facial expression, but I feel his chest exhale in an exasperated sigh. "Let me take care of it for you." He slips off his jacket and places it over my shoulders, ushering me to his car.

While I sit there, trying to calm myself down, I watch him explain my predicament to the policemen. He hands them his business card, which seems to give them pause. Then after a few more minutes of conversation, they shake hands and leave.

"What did you tell them?" I ask when he returns.

"Don't worry about it. It's nothing to trouble you with." He pulls out his phone and dials a number, speaking in Korean into the receiver. When he finishes, he sits in the driver's seat next to me but doesn't turn the engine on.

"Who was that? Not Halmoni, was it?" Now that I've decided to take the blame for the accident, Halmoni will be livid with me, not Jin Young.

He shakes his head. "I called a tow company to come get the car."

"Then I'm . . . not in trouble?"

"No. Not in trouble." He tucks a rogue strand of my disheveled hair behind my ear.

The warmth of his finger grazing my ear sends an unexpected tingle through me, and my eyes flick up to meet his. For a moment, staring deep into his dark eyes, I almost forget where we are. Mr. Kim must've felt something, too, because he quickly pulls his hand away and averts his eyes.

I clear my throat, looking out the window. "What about Jin Young?" I ask.

A flash of annoyance crosses Mr. Kim's face but quickly disappears. "Don't worry. He'll be fine." The look in his eyes and his demeanor tell me this sort of thing has happened before.

I bury my face in my hands. "This is a disaster." I don't

mean tonight, I mean this whole trip. I'm supposed to leave tomorrow, and I'll be leaving with more questions than I came here with.

"Everything's going to be fine, I promise you."

I know Mr. Kim is talking about tonight and the accident has been taken care of, no thanks to Jin Young. But what about everything else? I don't feel like I know anything more about my dad or his side of the family since I got here. And instead of bringing me closer to them, I feel farther apart than ever. Tears begin streaming down my face again.

"Hey, no. Don't cry." Mr. Kim opens up the arm compartment in the car and pulls out some tissues. "Are you sure you're not hurt anywhere?"

"Just my heart." I cringe at the corniness of my reply, but it's true. There's an ache in my chest that won't leave me.

"What? Your heart? We should get it checked out—"

"No, no. That's not what I meant." I bust out in a laugh.

"If your heart is hurting, it isn't a laughing matter."

"It's an expression . . ." I can't finish my sentence without being overcome by a fit of laughter.

"Then . . . you're not in pain?" Mr. Kim scratches his head, puzzled.

"No." I sigh. "Just really, *really* sad." The frown returns to my face.

"Oh," he says. A second later, the side of his lip curls up. "I know what will make you feel better."

I draw my head back, raising an eyebrow up at him.

A few minutes later, we're staring at the microwave count down to zero under the fluorescent lights of a twenty-four-hour convenience store.

"How did you know this would make me feel better?" Aside from getting to know more about my dad, eating convenience store food was a top priority. Almost every K-drama Hazel and I have watched together has an eating scene from one of these places. It's as recognizable as any other landmark here.

A wry smile spreads across Mr. Kim's lips and he hesitates before he says, "I had a hunch."

I smile to myself. His hunch was spot-on.

When the microwave dings, we take out our steaming bowls of Shin Ramyun and sit on the counter stools against the street-facing window.

"Can I ask you a question?" When he nods, I continue. "How old are you?" I snap the chopsticks and rub them together.

"I'm twenty-three. Why?" Mr. Kim tears off the lid to the bowl and begins mixing around his noodles.

"Is it customary here to call people less than five years older than you Mr. and Mrs.?" I stare at him with the chopsticks in my hand. Having been berated by Bum Soo about my ignorance in the presence of an elder, I'm more conscientious about the cultural differences.

"Ah," he says, catching my meaning. "It's not customary, but it's more because of my role with the family and our professional relationship."

Well, that's one way of using the term that takes the excitement out of the word *relationship*. "Professional, huh? Is that what this is? Part of your job?" I motion to the steaming bowls of uneaten noodles in front of us. Surely this goes well beyond his job description? I'm not sure what to think anymore, since the cultural whiplash has me second-guessing everything. "I mean, what were you doing there anyway? How did you get to the scene of the accident so quickly? How did you even know about it?" Suddenly my mind races with so many questions.

He sets down his chopsticks on the bowl and fidgets with his hands. "You're right. I'm not being professional. I'm sorry, you must forgive me." He stands up and bows, startling me. "I'll wait in the car." Before he can leave, I grab his arm.

"Wait. You're misunderstanding me. I'm not offended. I like hanging out with you," I blurt out before I have a chance to run any of that through my filter. It at least gets him to pause and glance sideways at me.

"You do?" His perfectly groomed, trustworthy eyebrows arch up.

"Yes, I do." I nod reassuringly. "Anyway, you can't leave now. Not with two bowls of instant ramyun. I mean, real talk, I won't have any problems eating them both, but I probably shouldn't. The sodium in one of these alone is enough to give someone a heart attack." I accidentally let out a snort, which makes Mr. Kim laugh.

"If you're sure." He sits down after I nod. "And to answer your question," he says, talking to his bowl of noodles, "I don't consider this to be part of my job." His skin turns a pretty dark shade of pink, like the summer sun right at dusk.

We take turns slurping up the noodles, catching each other's gaze from time to time. My face feels flushed. I'd blame it on the spiciness of the soup base, but I doubt Mr. Kim would believe me.

"If this isn't considered work to you, do I still have to call you Mr. Kim?" I dab my mouth with a paper napkin.

He looks up thoughtfully, wiping his own mouth. "I guess not?"

"Do you have a first name? Please don't tell me it's Mister." I laugh.

He covers his laugh with a fist, shaking his head. "My name is Bong Suk."

"Bong Suk," I repeat. "Is it okay if I call you by your name rather than Mr. Kim?"

"Sure." He nods at his Styrofoam bowl. Then his brows, the ones that make my stomach do flips, scrunch together. "Maybe not while I'm on duty?"

"You're on duty, like, one hundred percent of the time I see you!"

He hides a chuckle behind his fist. "You're right. Then maybe you should keep calling me Mr. Kim. Your halmoni would disapprove." He slurps up the last of his noodles.

"Halmoni really doesn't want us to get to know each other, does she?" He's mentioned it more than once now.

He sets his chopsticks down and pushes the bowl away from him. "It's a great honor to be working for your halmoni."

"You said your mother works at the department store. Did her connections help you get the job?"

"Sort of. Jobs are frequently advertised internally, but since I lack the proper upbringing to be considered, my mother never paid much attention to them. This job, however, didn't have many requirements. In fact, the ones they did specify were more personality based, like being discreet, resourceful, and dependable—all things that accurately describe me."

"That's all they required for the job? You'd think being the personal secretary to the heir of a fashion empire would have more of a screening process. No offense."

He laughs lightly. "They did have a lot of applicants, but I had something they all didn't."

"An amazing sense of style?"

He laughs again, shaking his head. "With Jin Young studying in America, they needed someone to follow him around, watch over him, and to protect his image. They needed someone who could easily understand both cultures. Since I lived in the US for ten years, I decided to apply for the job. Turns out, my experience abroad is more valuable to your halmoni than any fancy diploma."

"Really? I guess that would explain why you speak English so well." I shake my head at myself for not realizing it sooner.

He nods. "My family immigrated to LA when I was eight. They had a dry-cleaning business, and my mom did alterations. It was doing well until one of the machines malfunctioned and sparked a fire. The entire store went down along with the one next to it."

"Oh my God." I put a hand to my mouth. "Did anyone get hurt?"

"No, but it did irreparable damage. It never occurred to my parents that they would need special insurance for business owners. As a result, the fire not only destroyed their business, it also took their dream of living in America. After I graduated high school, we came back to Korea with less than what we had when we left. They couldn't afford to send me to college in the US, and I couldn't compete with the applicants in Korea. With no future prospects and a considerable family debt, I was stuck. My family and I never dreamed I would have an opportunity at a company like Sam Won. But now I do."

"Wow. I can't believe you went through all that." You would never be able to tell judging from his appearance.

"Your halmoni took a chance hiring me despite my lack of wealth and education. I depend on this job—my *family* depends on this job."

"Now I get why this is so important to you. I'm sorry if I ever made your job difficult for you."

"No, don't be sorry. I blame myself for compromising my career by choosing to engage in conversation with you. I've never disobeyed her before. I could lose my job if your halmoni ever found out, since it would be entirely inappropriate and disrespectful if we ever formed . . . an attachment." He flushes hot as he says it.

I almost let a laugh escape. With Mr. Kim telling me that he, the hired help, is forbidden to date me, the *heiress* (for lack of a better word), my K-drama life is complete.

"People really don't like the rich person/poor person relationship. By poor, I mean not wealthy. I see it in K-dramas all the time," I say, thinking out loud.

He laughs lightly. "It's not an ideal situation."

I'm no longer thinking about Mr. Kim and me. "Like how it must have been for my parents," I say. Suddenly, I'm not amused anymore. I'm upset.

Seeming to understand, Mr. Kim's posture relaxes a bit. "It's complicated. It's not just because rich people look down on those who don't have as much as they do. Many Korean people like to know what a person's salary is, how old they are, where they're from . . . and it's not because they are nosy. It is to discern their status in comparison to the other person to avoid offense. Because here, status matters. We have an honorific and plain way of speaking, bowing, and overall etiquette."

"So I've been told," I say, thinking back to the way Bum Soo scolded me. I set my chopsticks down and run a hand through my hair.

"When two classes mix, it's confusing. And people are often afraid of what they do not understand."

"You know, watching Korean dramas made me believe I know a lot about this culture. Now that I'm here, it's made me realize that seeing it on-screen is different than experiencing it in real life." I shake my head at myself. "Sounds obvious, doesn't it?"

"No, it doesn't. I love Korean dramas, too. For many of us, it's an escape from reality, not reality itself."

"I'm starting to feel the same way." Mr. Kim's words ring truer than any K-drama I've seen.

He clears his throat and checks his phone. "It's late. I should get you home." He stands up, takes our bowls, and throws them in the garbage receptacle. When I check the time on the wall clock, I'm shocked to see that it's almost two in the morning.

The rest of the ride, we take turns catching each other staring through the rearview mirror. Like some kind of version of tag, but with stolen glances. When we get to the house, he hesitates as if he doesn't want the night to end. He eventually gets out of the car when I open the door and get out.

"Good night, then." I bow, smiling.

"Good night," he says, bowing to me.

"Good night," I say, just as I realize I've already said that. I roll my eyes at myself. "I mean, I'm going."

He tries to hide it, but even in the dark I can see his face is a deep shade of red.

It isn't until I get in bed that I'm reminded of the car accident. I sit up against my pillow, deciding between worrying about Jin Young and being annoyed with him. How could he abandon me like that?

Then again, it wasn't just the accident that was a disaster. It was the whole night.

I click on my phone and pull up the 23andMe site. When I read back the messages, I'm reminded that I definitely wasn't imagining the connection Jin Young and I had. He was really interested in meeting me. With the 23andMe site still on my screen, I decide to message him.

# 23andme.com

From: Chang, Chloe
Subject: Are you okay?
Sunday, 2:59 AM

> Hey. I'm just checking in to see if you're okay. So, are you okay?

From: Noh, Jin Young
Subject: RE: Are you okay?
Sunday, 3:01 AM

> Chloe, I am sorry for running away like that. I was in a panic and didn't know what to do. I was afraid of letting Halmoni down, but I see now that I have put you in the middle of things and I feel terrible. Also, I hate myself for leaving you behind to deal with the police by yourself. You are a much braver person than I am. I am indebted to you. Can you ever forgive me?

From: Chang, Chloe

Subject: RE: Are you okay?

Sunday, 3:09 AM

I admit I'm bothered by the fact that you left me like that. However, I also believe you are sorry and I accept your apology. Could Halmoni really be that scary? She cares a lot for the family. I'm sure she will understand.

From: Noh, Jin Young

Subject: RE: Are you okay?

Sunday, 3:11 AM

You're right. Halmoni cares a lot about the family.

# CHAPTER 20

"Your halmoni is here."

"Hm?" I say groggily, rubbing the sleep out of my eyes. When Mrs. Na becomes clearer to me, I see the expression on her face. The sharp angle of her eyebrows sends a shot of adrenaline through my body.

"I'm up!" I jolt awake.

"Ppalli, ppalli," Mrs. Na says sternly, looking at the clothes she laid out for me on my bed. I don't need to ask what that means. Halmoni shouldn't be left waiting.

After I change, I rush to the bathroom, cram my toothbrush in my mouth, and splash some water on my face. At the foot of the stairs, I take a moment to steady my breathing before I walk down as casually as possible.

As I get closer to the first floor, I see Halmoni sitting on the couch with her back toward me. Her back is stiff as a board and she doesn't move a muscle as I approach her. When I turn the corner of the couch to face her, I bow deeply.

"Annyeonghaseyo, Halmoni." On my way up to standing, I steal a glimpse at her. She's poised, with an unreadable, neutral expression.

"Sit," she says, pointing to the seat behind me. As soon

239

as I settle in, she says, "I heard you came home quite late last night."

"You did?" My posture tenses.

"Yes, you must be very tired." She leans in and inspects my eyes.

"A little, but I can sleep on the plane. It leaves in the evening." As soon as I say the words, I realize this is my last chance to ask Halmoni for the answers I've been looking for. I'm sure we'll keep in touch, but who knows when the next time I'll see her face-to-face is. I clear my throat and say, "Halmoni—"

"You said you wanted to know more about your father, so I searched through our old things and found this."

She opens up her bag and pulls out a rectangular pouch made of pink and blue silk in different designs. It resembles a quilt, but much smaller and with two different fabric swatches.

She holds it out for me to see the inside lining. "Your father made this for me when he was about your age."

I pull it closer, rubbing my fingers over the stitching. I was going to ask her for something that belonged to my father, something I could take with me, but she had already been thinking about sending me off with this. The emotions are overpowering my senses and tears well in my eyes.

"That day, when I saw your dress, the patchwork seemed very familiar. Then I happened to notice the stitching on the inside of the pouch. I knew I'd seen it before, and I was right. You see here?" As soon as she points to the inner lining, the hairs on my neck and arms shoot straight up.

"Joon Pyo always had a way of personalizing each item he made. A simple stitch of his initials interlocking with each other. He called it his brand. In fact, he was the one who designed the Sam Won Department Store logo. After he died, I never saw this brand again. Until I saw your dress."

My vision blurs as tears come pouring out of me uncontrollably. Without asking for it, Halmoni handed me the connection to my dad I'd been hoping for during this visit. This stitching, his brand, not only confirms that I look like him, but I *am* like him.

Halmoni hovers over me, staring down at the pouch I'm cradling. "You see," she says quietly. "These two fabrics, very different in texture and quality. One is refined and solid and strong. The other is thin, worn, and faded. But this stitch, right here. It connects the two different fabrics. That stitch is you."

"Oh, Halmoni." I can't stop sobbing. "Do you mean it?" This whole time I've been secretly wanting to repair the fractured relationship between my mom and my dad's family. To hear Halmoni's been feeling the same way too is overwhelming.

"Of course I mean it. Lady Cha says you are the answer to this wretched curse, and she is never wrong."

"Oh, that's what you mean." I deflate. When it's clear to me that she's referring to the curse and not my mom, my tears dry up. "I do hope we can keep in touch, in the future. Maybe we can meet in Baltimore when Jin Young is back in school at Johns Hopkins?"

"I cannot think that far ahead. My son's prognosis worsens and it's the thing that troubles me every hour of every day." She shakes her head. "Which reminds me why I came here in the first place. Chloe, I need to ask you for a favor." She places a hand on mine.

"*You* want to ask *me* for a favor?" Is it possible that I could have misheard her?

"Now, you can refuse if you want. I know it's a lot to ask of you." She stares me square in the eyes with deep intensity.

Perspiration lines my upper lip. What could I possibly give her that she doesn't already have?

"I was wondering, since my son is gravely ill . . . would you like to attend the fashion show in his place?"

Caught completely off-guard, I cough, choking on my spit. "What?" I say after recovering. "Yes! You don't even have to ask!" I answer without the slightest bit of hesitation.

"Good." A wide smile takes over her face. "I'll have Mr. Kim reschedule your return flight." She begins typing on her phone.

"Reschedule?"

She peers up at me above the rim of her glasses, holding her phone in her hand. "Yes. The fashion show is next week. Unless . . . do you want to go back?"

Next week, Hazel and Seb will be gone and my mom will be working late, as usual. I have nothing waiting for me. So I answer her truthfully.

"No, I don't want to go back," I say definitively.

The smile returns to her face and she continues typing. "Done," she says, clicking off her phone and bending down to place it in her Hermès handbag. When she sits back up, Halmoni has a box in her hand. She places it on the coffee table between us and pushes it with an index finger toward me.

"What's this?" I ask, carefully picking up the box. When the lid slips off, it reveals a shiny, sleek new phone. It looks like the one Soo Young has. "For me?" I stare up at Halmoni, open-mouthed.

"Now that you'll be staying here longer, you'll need a way to communicate with us. I had Mr. Kim input everyone's number in there." She pinches my chin. "Make sure to take it with you everywhere you go."

"Gamsahamnidah, Halmoni," I say, even though I think it's a waste to have a brand-new, right-out-of-the-box phone for the short period of time I'll be here. Still, I'm not going to argue with her about the impracticality of her gift. I'm sure money isn't an issue here and I'm extremely touched by her gesture.

After she leaves, I'm in my room, inspecting my new phone. Just as she'd mentioned, all the Nohs' numbers have already been put in. Halmoni, Soo Young, Jin Young. Even Mr. Kim's number. Of course, my mom's number isn't in there, so I pull out my old phone and give her a call. This time, she doesn't pick up, so I send her a text.

**Me:** Mom, I'm going to stay a little longer. Halmoni needs me.

As soon as I send the message, it occurs to me that Halmoni didn't say when I'd be flying back home. I'm sure it was an oversight and I'll find out later. I don't want to worry Mom, so I add another message.

243

> **Me:** I'll send you the new flight
> itinerary when I get it.

I toss my old phone aside and look back at my new one, admiring the rose-gold finish and the shiny black screen, sans crack. My finger hovers over Jin Young's contact before I eventually click on it and type a message to him.

> **Me:** Hi. This is Chloe. Halmoni
> bought me a new phone and I
> wanted you to have my number.

I wait for him to respond, but he doesn't. Instead, my old phone pings with an alert.

# 23andme.com

**MESSAGES**

From: Noh, Jin Young
Subject: Hey
Sunday, 8:59 AM

Hello, Chloe. I received your message on my phone, but I think this way is easier to respond. I feel like we made a connection on this app and am more comfortable communicating with you here. Anyway, I am happy you are staying longer. It gives me a chance to make it up to you, like I said I would. How about we meet later at a café and I can try to make it up to you?

From: Chang, Chloe
Subject: RE: Hey
Sunday, 9:01 AM

Is it weird to say that I feel the same way about communicating on this app? I know it's not a conventional way of messaging each other, but each time I receive a message, I feel like it's a reminder that this isn't a dream and that discovering my family on 23andMe really did happen.

As for your offer, I would love to meet at a café. I have a special affinity for Korean cafés and would love to hear more about the family.

From: Noh, Jin Young
Subject: RE: Hey
Sunday, 9:05 AM

My heart warms at the thought you feel the same way. You said it best: meeting you in person is not a dream. It's better than a dream. I will have Mr. Kim pick you up at noon and I will take you to a café, where I will be happy to tell you more about the family. It's the least I can do to make up for last night.

# CHAPTER 21

Like clockwork, Mr. Kim is waiting for me right in time to take me to meet Jin Young.

"Is everything okay?" By now, I've spent enough time with him to know something's off. "Haven't you heard? I get to stay longer." I smile obnoxiously in his face, which gets him to crack a smile.

"Yes. I heard."

"Well, don't hold back. Tell me how you really feel about me, Mr. Kim." I tap him sarcastically.

"Pardon?" Mr. Kim flinches.

"Sorry, it was a joke. A bad one. I only meant that it seems like you're not happy about me staying longer." Insecurity unravels my confidence and I begin fidgeting.

"No, you misunderstand—" He cuts himself off, changing colors again, like a pink chameleon. "As long as you're happy, then that's what matters." He nods politely.

Relieved, I smile. "I am. I'll be able to get to know the family better, and Halmoni even invited me to a fashion show!"

Mr. Kim covers his laugh with a fist. "You have a new phone now, too."

"I do." I beam up at him.

"With my number in it."

"Yep."

"You can call me if you need anything. You know, work related. Or not."

"Thanks." Then a second later, when I catch his meaning, I say, *"Oh."* My face flashes hot.

"For the record, I am really glad you're staying."

"Me too." I stare at my feet.

He clears his throat. "We should get going. Jin Young will be waiting for you." On the way out, Mr. Kim dutifully grabs an umbrella.

I smile to myself, staring at the umbrella tucked under Mr. Kim's arm. Though the thick air teases us with rain, it never comes. Maybe now that I'm staying longer, we'll have an opportunity to use the umbrella, Mr. Kim and I. Yet another thing to look forward to during my extended stay here.

After Mr. Kim drops me off at the entrance to a hotel, I stand there a few minutes, in a daze. I was supposed to be packing to go back home tonight and now I'm staying in Korea, spending more time with my family, going to a fashion show, and getting to know Mr. Kim better. There are so many plot twists in my life, I'm beginning to think Hazel's right. My life really is a K-drama.

I'm still standing there when a Mercedes sedan with dark tinted windows pulls up. The attendant opens the door and it's Jin Young. He approaches me right away.

"Chloe. Hi." He seems softer and more unsure of himself than yesterday. "Thanks for meeting me here."

I nod. "Thank you for your messages. They were very kind."

"It was the least I could do. After everything you did for me." His mouth stretches into a closemouthed smile. "Shall we?" He motions inside the building.

"Is this where we're getting coffee? The Sheraton?"

"What? You don't like the Sheraton?" He rubs the back of his head, looking up at the sign.

"No—I mean, I thought we were going to a café."

"Yes, we are." He seems puzzled. "The café here has the best desserts."

"They do?" I perk up. Well, that changes everything.

The hotel staff instantly treat us the same as if we were in the department store. Everyone knows who Jin Young is and their eyes are focused on him, even mine.

From the side profile, his features are eerily similar to mine. Even if I didn't have the genetic confirmation, I'd swear we were related. From the downward sloped eyes to the heart-shaped mouth our lips make when our faces are resting in a neutral expression, like now, the similarities are uncanny. Even the single freckle above the right side of our mouths is the same.

Everyone, from the staff to the locals, who are staring at Jin Young are now also staring at me. Based on their reactions, they're probably drawing the same conclusions as I am about us—that we are undoubtedly, indisputably related.

When we get to the café, which is just past the lobby, I ask, "Is it always like that?"

"Like what?" he asks, oblivious.

"The people, staring." I motion a finger around us.

"That?" He waves a dismissive hand. "You get used to it."

I nod like I know what he means, even though I don't

remotely know what he means. I could live here a hundred years and I don't know if I'd ever get used to that. But for a split second, I got a sense of what it would've been like if I'd grown up here as a Noh. It's exciting for sure, but also intense, with an extreme amount of pressure riding on your every move. I'm not condoning Jin Young's behavior last night, but I'm starting to understand better why he panicked when he crashed the car.

The café is elegant and ostentatiously decorated with crystal chandeliers and black onyx marble floors and walls. There's a grand piano off to the side, with a pretty pianist in a flowy pink gown playing classical music. The entire back wall is floor-to-ceiling glass with a waterfall flowing from a rock wall on the other side of it.

We get shown to a table in a prime spot, right between the piano player and the waterfall, and the waiter hands us our menus. Jin Young waves his away and orders himself an Americano. I take my menu and glance at it.

"Is this, like, an American menu?" When he wrinkles his forehead at me, I go on to explain, "I mean, everything on this menu is typical American food. Ham and cheese sandwiches, cheesecake, and . . ." I squint my eyes to make sure I'm reading it right. "Churros?"

"These hotels cater to a lot of foreigners. You forget that American food is typical to you. It's not typical to us," he says.

"Oh, right." I feel sheepish for thinking all of Korea should be just like the vlogs. It reminds me how much of an outsider I am here. I order the churros since you can't ever go wrong with churros.

When the waiter leaves, Jin Young leans in. "Thank you again for covering for me last night," he says in a low voice.

"It's okay. I guess I can understand your reaction now that I know what you're up against." I glance around the room, noticing how almost every table is gawking at us. "I just didn't expect you could leave me like that so easily. I thought we were friends." I finally say the words I've been wanting to say since we first met face-to-face.

"I wasn't thinking clearly last night, and we are friends. How can I make it up to you? Is there anything you want while you're here? Looks like Halmoni already took you on a shopping spree, but there are plenty of other high-end shops in Gangnam."

My brows twitch. I hope he didn't forget about what he promised me. "No, that's not necessary. I would be okay with learning more about the family. Like you mentioned in your last message, remember?"

"Right. *I* said that," he says, seemingly jogging his memory. "What is it you want to know?" A flash of annoyance crosses his face, as if he regrets offering information about the family to me in the first place.

"Well, what about you?"

"Me?" He puts a hand to his chest.

"Other than our messages on the 23andMe app, we don't really know much about each other. Are you into fashion design too?"

He wrinkles his nose. "Fashion design is a trade skill akin to laborers."

"But Halmoni said my dad had a flair for fashion design."

"Don't get me wrong, fashion design is a partnership we

rely on as a leading retailer, but it's beneath us. We are in the business of fashion, which means we are businessmen above all things."

"And business*women*," I clarify.

"What?" He startles, his posture tensing.

"Did you forget that Halmoni is a woman?"

Jin Young's face is red in an instant and he fumbles for his cigarette case. "Yes. Of course she is."

I feel bad for making him flustered, but I couldn't listen to him talk down about fashion design anymore. It was insulting, and not just to me. To my dad, too.

Right when the lull in our conversation is about to turn into an uncomfortable silence, the waiter comes over holding a tray and places a coffee cup in front of Jin Young and two mini churros with a caramel dipping sauce for me. I wait for the waiter to bow, then walk away.

"Sorry, I didn't mean to sound harsh," I say in a gentler tone. "I never knew my dad and I may be unnecessarily overprotective of him. No one seems to talk about him, and maybe that's just the way it is when someone dies, but I miss him so much. You probably understand what it's like, since your father passed away, too." I tilt my head with a sympathetic smile.

He draws his head back quickly. "No, it's not like that. What happened to my dad is not the same thing as what happened to your dad." His voice is tepid and void of emotion.

"What happened?"

"I guess I should tell you. I mean, after everything

you've done for me." He picks out a cigarette from his case, but after tapping it around a few times, he places it back inside. Eventually he continues. "My father was a gambler. He'd made some bad investments, almost ruining the department store. Lady Cha told Halmoni that cutting him out of the family business was the only way to survive the scandal, so she did. The next day, my dad killed himself."

Stunned, I put my hands over my mouth to cover a gasp. "Oh my God. I'm so, so sorry. Online it says—" I stop myself from admitting I've been reading up on the family, but it's too late.

He leans in, speaking in a quieter voice. "If the investors heard about the scandal, it would have caused unnecessary fallout. We had no choice but to hide the details of his death. Besides, it's a completely private matter. The press doesn't need to know everything that goes on in our family. Just what we tell them."

Though it feels misleading, I can't say I blame him or anyone in the family for wanting to keep it a secret from the press when my own mother doesn't share her grief with me.

"How have you been handling everything since your father—well, you know."

"Soo Young and I are doing fine, but my mother probably has it the worst."

"Your mother?"

He nods. "Halmoni tell you about the curse?"

"Yeah . . ."

"Well, Lady Cha thinks that if my mother does a

mourning ritual for one year at the temple, it will lift the curse."

I'm trying to wrap my head around what Jin Young is saying, but something about his explanation doesn't make sense to me. If Halmoni is the head of her company *and* her family, why is Lady Cha the one always calling the shots?

"How did Halmoni meet Lady Cha?"

"The story is that when Halmoni and Harabuji were about to break ground for the department store, Lady Cha approached Halmoni and warned her not to use the construction company. That it would lead to their ruin. Something about her warning must have struck a chord in Halmoni because she ended up canceling their contract, losing much of their investment. The construction company went on to build another department store and a few years later, it collapsed, killing more than five hundred people."

"Oh my God. All those people." It comes out like a whisper.

"So you can see why Halmoni depends on her. For everything."

"I see." I understand why Halmoni might feel indebted to Lady Cha. But surely the family can't believe in everything she says. Can they? "Do you believe in Lady Cha's predictions?" I ask hesitantly.

He shrugs. "Some of the stuff she says is right, some of it is vaguer."

"What about the way your dad died? Doesn't that make you think Lady Cha made a mistake? Don't you think it's dangerous to put all your hope in this one person? That maybe, just maybe, she *can't* predict the future?"

"Halmoni cut my dad off as Lady Cha instructed and the business was saved. Revenues are better than before, by threefold. My dad's death was unrelated. As far as Halmoni is concerned, she blames the curse for his death." He sighs, as if he's bored with the conversation. "Anyway, what does it matter? If Halmoni believes it, the family has to believe it," he says matter-of-factly. "It's his replacement that's making things difficult."

"His replacement?"

"Remember my cousin, Bum Soo?"

"He replaced your dad's position in the family business?" I shudder, recalling my encounter with him last night.

He shakes his head. "It's his dad, my mom's brother, who replaced my dad. Bum Soo is the spitting image of his father, in looks and personality."

"No wonder he acted like he was so superior to you."

He rolls his eyes. "It's all for show. Bum Soo does stuff like that because he's got a big chip on his shoulder."

"What kind of chip?"

"My uncle considers himself part of the Noh family, since he stepped in to take over my dad's position. Halmoni will never see him as a Noh and that's the problem."

"Bum Soo seems like he has a good life—a family, money, and opportunities. Sorry, but I'm having a hard time understanding why he would be so petty." Plus, I don't like the guy.

"It's more than just money, it's status," he says plainly. "In Sam Won Group, there are the Nohs and there's everyone else. There's no in-between. Bum Soo doesn't feel like everyone else, but he's definitely not a Noh."

"Oh, right. He's from your mom's side. He's definitely not a Noh, then."

"Even if he did have the last name, he wouldn't have the same dollimja." He must've noticed the deer-in-headlights expression on my face, which makes him continue. "See, every generation in each family has their own syllable that signifies which generational line they are from. In ours, my and Soo Young's second syllable is Young. It's small things like that that make Bum Soo feel like he's on a different level than us. That's why I tolerate his behavior. Because I know he'll never have what he wants, and I can't change that."

I frown, staring at my uneaten plate of churros. Not only is my last name different than theirs, I don't have a Korean name. If I did, I wonder whether it would have the same last syllable as the others in the Noh family.

Jin Young checks the time on his watch, then looks up at me. "So. Are we good? Is that explanation good enough for you?" He leans in with a raised eyebrow.

It's not quite the quality time I was hoping for with him, but I did learn more about the family. I nod and say, "Sorry about your dad."

He shrugs and flags the waiter over for the check for the untouched churros and half-drunk cup of Americano.

While we're waiting for Mr. Kim to bring around our car, I study Jin Young's profile. He's once again cool and reserved, but this time I understand him better. Jin Young grew up knowing everything about his dad, so it makes sense that he's trying to move on with his life, looking to the future. I, on the other hand, know nothing of my dad, which is why I can't let go of the past. We're both, in different ways, suffering from losing our fathers.

Ж

Mr. Kim rolls up in the car and the attendants open the doors for us. When we get in, Mr. Kim takes us back to the department store, where we've been summoned by Halmoni.

Soo Young arrives at the VIP entrance to the department store the same time we do, and she stares at the bags in the front seat.

"You two behave while I go talk to Mr. Kim," Jin Young says, eyeing Soo Young before leaving us.

The second he steps away, Soo Young wastes no time. "Why did Halmoni extend your stay?" She eyes me up and down suspiciously.

"I think she wanted to spend more time with me," I say carefully.

"Why would she want to spend more time with you?" By the strained look on her face, I wonder if she's worried I told anyone about the other day when I caught her in front of the motel.

"Don't worry. I didn't say anything to Halmoni about you and . . . you know, the other day."

Her head jerks back and her nose scrunches up. "What? Why did you do that?"

Her reaction catches me totally off guard. "I-I just thought maybe you didn't want Halmoni to know about that." I didn't want anything in return for covering up for her, but I thought she'd at least be grateful.

"You can keep your favors. It won't do you any good. Halmoni would never believe you over me." Her jet-black hair whips around as she spins on her heels and marches up the steps of the entrance.

I'm just standing there with my mouth hanging open, watching her walk away, when Jin Young returns from his conversation with Mr. Kim.

"Is Soo Young giving you shit?" He shakes his head, watching her storm off.

"I . . ." I debate telling him about the conversation, but think better of it since I'd have to tell him about the love motel. Even though she says she doesn't mind, I'm pretty sure Soo Young wouldn't want her brother to know that information about her. I mean, I'm hardly comfortable knowing this type of information myself. Instead I say, "She's probably going through a lot, you know, with your father gone."

He snorts. "She's not grieving. She's jealous."

"'Scuse me?" I can't have heard him right. I slow my step at the foot of the staircase. Wait until Hazel hears that she was right about Soo Young all along.

"She's never been allowed to get her hair done or go shopping on the top floor of the department store."

"What? Are you serious?"

"Halmoni is strict and education is very important here. It was like that for me, too. Until you get into college, it's nothing but study."

"Oh," I say. Education must *really* be important here.

Which naturally reminds me of my own educational background.

"Don't worry about it. You're going to FIT in the fall, right? You've earned it."

"About that . . ." I feel the urge to come clean to him. If I can be honest with anyone, it's him. Knowing that I embellished this part of my life isn't sitting well with me. "I'm not actually enrolled at FIT."

"You're not?" When I shake my head, he asks, "Did you even get in?"

"I did and I would go, except for the fact that my mom and I can't afford the tuition."

"You didn't notify the school yet?"

I shake my head. I knew the minute I notified FIT that I wouldn't be going there in the fall, it would be final. I guess I wanted to hold on to the dream just a little longer. It sounds ridiculous, so I don't say it out loud.

"Jin Young!" Jin Young's mom comes rushing out of the store building, followed by Soo Young. "We must go to the hospital, now! Your samchon's condition is getting worse."

Jin Young rushes out behind them and I'm standing at the doorway, wondering if I should stay or go when he turns back to me. "Are you coming?" He waves me to follow them and I do.

# CHAPTER 22

We're at the hospital and Soo Young, Jin Young, and their mom are greeted by everyone in the VIP ward. I try to follow behind them when someone stops me. She looks like a nurse, about my mom's age, in scrubs. When she continues to speak to me in Korean, I just stare at her, wordless. Thankfully, Jin Young steps in and talks to her in rapid Korean. He seems frustrated.

"What's the problem?" I ask.

"Only the family members of patients are allowed in this ward. She needs your family ID to get past this point."

"I don't—"

"Yeah, I explained your situation. I said you're a relative and it just hasn't been documented, but she still can't admit you."

Soo Young and her mom are already in the hospital room and I can tell Jin Young is getting anxious. "Don't worry about me, I'll just sit here," I say, but I doubt he heard me. He's already halfway down the hallway.

As I sit in the waiting room, the nurses at the counter whisper, pointing at me. I know there's a Family Members Only rule at the hospital where Mom works. But there are no stupid proof of relationship cards that family members need to present before entering them. I feel so useless sitting here by myself when the rest of the family is by Samchon's side, even if I've never met him before.

Thirty minutes go by before Jin Young emerges with his sister and mom. They look like they've been crying. He tells me to wait while he walks them out to their car. A minute later he returns.

"Is Samchon okay?" I ask him.

"It's not looking good, since none of us passed the first round of tests. His blood type is B, and Soo Young and I are As. Halmoni is the only other B in the family, but she's too old. In fact, she's arguing with them right now."

I look at him funny. "*I'm* a B, remember?" I could've sworn we had this conversation.

"You are?" Then a split second later, he opens his mouth as if he just remembered something. "That's right. You should definitely test to be liver donor for Samchon, then."

"Yes, yes I should. Because I'm family." It irks me that Jin Young said everyone in the family got tested, because *I* didn't. I'm genetically a part of this family as much as Jin Young and Soo Young are since birth. Yet I'm not even allowed in the hospital room to visit my own samchon?

"How could we let them know if you're not on the registry?" Jin Young says, more as if he's thinking out loud than talking to me.

"What about the DNA match from the 23andMe app? Isn't that sufficient evidence that I'm family?" I blurt out in frustration.

He scratches his head. "I don't know. It's worth a try."

Before he finishes answering, I'm logging into my account on my new phone. When it pops up, it shows the link, clear as day, proving that Jin Young and I are a 15.5 percent genetic match. I hand the phone over to him.

"Here. I don't think anyone can dispute this; it's DNA."

He takes the phone from my hand, and before he goes to show the administrator, he does a double take. "Whoa, that's wild. They even somehow know we're linked by our dads."

My brows furrow. "I know. It's right there when you click on the tree icon. Is this your first time seeing this?" His expression makes me think he's never set eyes on the results before.

"Oh, no. I mean, I've never clicked on this icon before, so I didn't see this visual. Anyway, I just hope this is enough to convince them."

As he's speaking with the attendant, I'm trying to convince myself that it's not that big of a deal that Jin Young didn't browse through the results and study them as if they weren't life-altering. Like discovering our genetic connection doesn't mean as much to him, to any of them, as it does to me. But when Jin Young returns with a smile on his face, my anger subsides.

"It worked! They'll let you take the tests. I set up an appointment for tomorrow."

"Great! Then can I meet Samchon now, too?" I stand up to start walking down the hall when a commotion coming from the other end of the hall stops me.

A group of doctors and nurses are huddled around

someone, each trying to talk over the others. When they get closer, I see Halmoni at the center. She somehow looks as if she's aged ten years in the past few hours, with more wrinkles and dark puffy circles around her eyes. I rush over to meet her.

"Halmoni. Are you okay?" I ask.

She looks up in a daze, startled to see me standing in front of her. "You came?"

"Halmoni, Chloe is—" Jin Young starts to say, but I cut him off.

"Going to catch a ride with Jin Young." When Jin Young shoots me a questioning look, I subtly shake my head, eyeing Halmoni. She's far too distracted to notice. Instead she barely nods in response.

The staff clamor around her, offering their assistance as she walks out. One nurse even rolls over a cushioned wheelchair. Upon noticing it, something must snap in Halmoni, because the next thing I know, her posture stiffens and she's waving them off. "Dwaesseo!" she yells, then proceeds to march out of the hospital.

"How come you didn't tell her the news? About getting tested?" Jin Young asks as soon as Halmoni's out of sight.

"What if I don't pass the initial tests? Until then, I don't want to say anything to her. I don't want to disappoint her."

❌

The next day, Jin Young has arranged for the initial testing without alerting Halmoni. He asks Mr. Kim to take me to the hospital where he'll help me fill out the paperwork. When I arrive in the foyer, Mr. Kim is waiting for me. Instead of his relaxed self, today he's pacing.

"Is something wrong?" I ask, startling him.

"I've been instructed to take you to the hospital, without Halmoni's knowledge. I don't know if that's such a good idea. Your halmoni—"

"You don't have to worry about her. If you get in trouble, I'll be sure to explain everything to her. She'll understand, I'm sure of it." I plead with my hands, rubbing them together. As touched as I am by his overprotectiveness, I don't want to tell Halmoni about my plan before I know it can actually work. She'd be devastated if we later found out I wasn't even a viable match for Samchon.

Mr. Kim seems to be wrestling with the idea, eyebrows squished together tightly. "Okay, fine." Eventually he relents, but I can tell he's not completely convinced.

"Even Jin Young is involved in this, so I'm sure that between the two of us we can convince Halmoni that none of this is your fault." I ramble the whole way to the car. Mr. Kim is nodding along, but he seems distracted.

I slip into the back seat and before he closes the door, Mr. Kim pops his head down.

"I forgot something in the house. An umbrella. I'll be right back."

"Of course," I say, smiling. "I'll be here." Every day, the moisture grows thicker and thicker in the air. I keep waiting for the first fall of rain, knowing that Mr. Kim is always prepared with an umbrella. Then, my K-drama experience will be complete.

About five minutes later, which is a pretty long time to fetch an umbrella, Mr. Kim returns.

"My apologies. Mrs. Na misplaced the umbrella. We're ready to go now."

"Great," I say, looking at the time on my new shiny phone. "KakaoMap says it's only thirty minutes away from here, and my appointment isn't for another hour, so we have plenty of time."

He nods through the rearview mirror and turns the engine on. When he hits the gas pedal, immediately a loud pop startles us both.

"What was that?" I shriek. "Was that a firecracker?"

"Let me see what the issue is." He steps out of the car and stares at the tires. When his face appears distressed, I get out and join him.

"What is it? What's wrong?"

"The front tire, it's been punctured by something. It needs to be replaced."

"Okay. Can you do it? Or do we need to call someone? Can I help?" Desperate to find a solution, I fire away suggestion after suggestion.

"No, I'm afraid there is no spare tire. We'll have to call a tow company." Mr. Kim is already on the phone when he tells me this. After a brief conversation, he pockets the phone and shakes his head. "They can't come for another hour."

"An hour?!" I check the phone again. "I'll miss my appointment." Frustrated, I run a hand through my hair and look around. My eye catches a cab parked down at the end of the street. Without thinking, I run over to it.

"Wait, stop!" Mr. Kim calls, running after me. Before he reaches me, I'm in the cab. I push the map in front of the cab driver and while he studies my phone, Mr. Kim knocks on the car window.

"Wait until the car is fixed. I'll take you," he insists.

"I'm sorry, but I can't wait for the car. I'll miss my appointment. I have to go."

The driver hands me back my phone, then yells something to Mr. Kim in Korean. Mr. Kim is reluctant at first but eventually has no choice but to back away when the car starts moving.

※

I make it to the hospital just five minutes after my appointment time. Jin Young is waiting for me in front of the hospital, staring at me with his hands in his pockets.

"What took you so long? I've been waiting for twenty minutes." He has the slightest bit of annoyance in his tone.

"There was an incident with the car. Mr. Kim got a flat tire. I had to catch a taxi and try to explain to him using my broken Korean which hospital I needed to get to. Then my phone died so I couldn't call you to let you know. I'm so sorry I'm late."

He considers my words and softens. "Oh. I thought maybe you'd forgotten."

"I couldn't forget about this."

"Let's go get you signed in then."

We rush over to the VIP section of the hospital wing and he checks in for me at the receptionist desk. The two women behind the desk giggle after he leaves, whispering and pointing.

"Here," he says, handing me the clipboard. "Fill this out. This top part is your name and address, which I can fill in later. The bottom part is asking about your family history."

I take it from him and fill out as much as I can, then flip it over to the backside.

"What does this part say?" I point to the next section.

"It asks for your paperwork from the registry, but you can skip it."

"Oh." My face falls, remembering how much he argued with the staff just to get my initial testing. I hope this isn't another obstacle standing in our way. "Will it be a problem later?"

"I already took care of it." He waves dismissively.

"You did?"

"I showed them the 23andMe results, but I also reminded the hospital chief of staff that the VIP ward was built largely in part due to my family's generous contributions in the past, and that seemed to be enough for him." He nudges me and smirks.

So many things about his explanation bother me. Why can't they just get me on the official family registry? Why do they have to make low-key threats like I'm not a real family member? I don't know if I'm becoming overly sensitive to everything since the blowout with my mom, but suddenly I don't know where I stand with the family.

However improper Jin Young's actions were, it must have worked because the next thing I know, a nurse is ushering me into a doctor's office in the VIP ward. Jin Young follows me inside and does most of the talking while a nurse does regular triage stuff, like checking my temperature, blood pressure, and heart rate. Then we're shown into another office, where the doctor sits behind a desk and reviews my chart. He eyes me up and down before I sit on the sofa seat in front of him.

"You are big," the doctor says to me with a heavy accent.

Jesus, I didn't realize getting an examination here meant getting body shamed.

"It's good." He nods.

I blush hard, turning kimchi red. It's bad enough he's pointing out my problem areas to me, but Jin Young sitting right next to me doesn't help.

"Means you have good chance for the liver match."

"It does?"

"Yes. This means you probably have the large liver, which is ideal to be the candidate."

"That *is* great news," I say once I realize his comment is not a superficial one.

"The patient is slight of figure for a male. This is good." He looks at Jin Young, full of hope.

Jin Young sighs with a smile. The doctor then tells him to leave so that I can change into a gown for the rest of the exam. After I change, a nurse comes in to escort me somewhere else.

"Oh!" She covers her mouth as if she's surprised to see me, and bows instantly. "Annyeonghaseyo." She looks vaguely familiar, but I don't know many people in Korea.

We must have seen each other in the waiting room when I was with Jin Young. This must be what it's like being related to who Miso refers to as a tabloid legend. I don't want to be rude, so I give her a polite nod in return.

After she recovers, the nurse takes me down the corridor and into a room. Inside, it's spacious and frigid, with a large tube-shaped contraption in the center. She instructs me to lie on the table, so I do. When the scan whirs alive, it hits me that I'm trapped. Panic begins to take hold of me.

I start counting to ten slowly, but instead of stabilizing my heartbeat, it intensifies. I know I'm the one that asked to be tested, but as the machine moves around my body, I'm beginning to question my decision. A lot has happened in a short amount of time, and I can't tell whether I'm acting out of good will or reacting to fill a void. Is this about Samchon, or is it about my insecurities and how I fit in with the family? Am I doing the right thing?

By the time I count to one hundred and eighty, the whirring stops, and the exam is over. I change out of the gown and return to the waiting room. Jin Young is sitting on the couch. When he sees me coming, he stands up.

"How did it go?" Concern lines frame his eyes.

I shrug. "They did a CT scan, but I don't know if they can tell whether I'm a match or not."

Just then, the doctor comes out and says something in Korean to me, and I look to Jin Young for translation. Whatever he said, it must be good news.

"The doctor says everything looks good today and that you passed the initial tests. We'll know for sure in two days when they have the results," Jin Young says.

269

The doctor says something to me in Korean, patting my shoulder.

"What did he say?" I ask.

"He said you worked hard," Jin Young says.

Hard? I didn't do anything but lie there. The nurses did everything.

Suddenly, there's a jab in my side as I think about my mom. Being a patient makes me feel vulnerable and isolated, like I'm in this on my own. I know that's not the case, with Jin Young here with me right now. Still, I miss my mom. She would know exactly how to comfort me, as a nurse and as a mother.

Regardless of whether or not I go through with it, it occurs to me that Mom should know I'm getting tested to be a liver donor for Samchon. I haven't spoken to her since I found out about her betrayal, but time has cooled my anger.

When I get home from the hospital, I call her, but it goes straight to voice mail. That's strange. She doesn't always answer her phone, but it at least rings. Wondering if she's screening her calls, I pull out my old phone on top of my dresser. I'm about to call her on it when I see a voice mail notification. I hit play and listen to the message.

"Chloe-yah . . . I'm . . . to talk to you . . . I'm sorry for not telling you everything about your father. When . . . there . . . I'll . . . you everything."

I replay Mom's message over and over, but the choppiness must be poor reception on her end. Still trying to decipher her message, the phone rings in my hand, startling me. It's Hazel.

"Hello?" I answer.

"Where have you been? I've been calling you for hours. Is this because I didn't pick up your last call? The spa had one of those heinous No Phone signs. The lady actually made me put my phone in a basket, can you believe it?" Hazel is flailing.

"I'm not mad. A lot's been going on. In fact, I'm not coming home today, like I planned." I sit down on my bed and swing my feet up, but the tension doesn't leave my body.

"What?!" She shrieks so loudly my ears are ringing. "Tell me everything."

So I do. Right up to the point where I pass the initial testing to be a donor.

"Wow." Hazel shakes her head, still in shock. Then a second later, she gasps. "Oh my God! It's like that episode of *Hospital Playlist*. You know, where the daughter donated part of her liver for her dad. It saved her dad and their family, too. That could be you! By donating part of your liver, your uncle will be saved, and the curse will end!"

As much as I'd like to believe Hazel, I don't. Not this time.

"This isn't a K-drama, Hazel. It's real life. This is a major surgery for not just me, but my uncle, too. There's so much at stake and there are no guarantees I'll have my happily ever after." Saying my fears out loud for the first time forms a rock in the pit of my stomach.

The color almost instantly drains from her face. "Oh, God, Chlo. I've been a terrible friend."

I exhale a regretful sigh. "No, you haven't, and I'm not mad at you. It's just that this is all happening so fast, I'm processing it out loud in real time."

Concern lines sweep across her forehead. "I'm sorry for getting us carried away. I seem to have a problem with that." She bites her lower lip.

"It's not your fault. I wanted everything you said to be true so badly that I let myself believe I would have my happily ever after."

"What can I do?"

"I don't actually know and that's what scares me."

"In case you need to hear it, you don't have to do anything you're not comfortable with. You know that, right? I'll be there for you, no matter what you decide to do."

As grateful as I am for Hazel's support, it's way more complex than that. If I'm a viable candidate to be a donor for Samchon and I go through with the transplant, then I put my life at risk for a man I've never met before. If I don't, then he could die. It's a lot to process and I don't have the emotional bandwidth to even talk about it with Hazel right now.

"Can we talk about something else? Please?"

"Are you sure?"

"I can say with absolute certainty that it's the only thing I've been sure about today. So please. Tell me about USC, or your itinerary once you get to Greece. Tell me about all the carbs you're going to gorge on in Europe—baguettes, pasta, pita—don't hold back."

"Oh." She shrugs. "I don't know if I'm going to go."

"Things still weird between you and Seb?"

"Yeah. It's still the same." She whines into a pillow. "I want him to do something that makes my heart skip a beat—like publicly declaring his love in the middle of a crowded mall, or surprising me with a back hug every now and then, or—"

"Show up with an umbrella when you're caught in a sudden rainstorm?" I smirk at her.

"Exactly! My point is, why can't he be more like Lee Min Ho?" She whines again.

We both sound miserable. Which leads me to think, there's only one thing that would cheer us up. "Do you want to watch a K-drama?"

"Always." She manages to smile.

For the next hour, we escape reality by watching a K-drama about a time traveler who falls in love with a modern-day girl. Swoon.

And for the moment, everything seems right in the world.

# CHAPTER 23

On the day of the fashion show, I slip on the fitted black dress I got from the shopping spree, the one with the capped sleeves and intricate darting on the front. Somehow, despite the street food Miso has been supplying me with, it fits me like a glove. When I try to bend down to slip on my studded booties, however, the dress simply won't let me. I twist every which way but can't get them on my feet. Even sitting is a challenge.

"Here, let me help," Mr. Kim says, startling me. How long has he been watching me struggle?

"No, that's okay . . . I got it . . ." My tongue sticks out as I try to toe the opening of the bootie, only to fail. The shoe topples onto its side, beyond my reach. "Okay, I don't got it."

Mr. Kim smiles kindly, kneeling down in front of me. He holds his hand out for my foot and I lift it up. His hands are warm and soft to the touch.

"I know what it's like not to be able to fit into something. Sometimes you just need a little help." He somehow manages to get my foot into the bootie with a firm but gentle push. He even zips up the side of the shoe in one swift, effortless movement. When he gets to the other foot, the air is thick with tension. I've never had someone touch me in such an intimate way. The tingly sensation that started with his touch is now taking over my entire body. It's hot in the room and I can't tell if it's me or him. Or both of us.

"Gamsahamnidah," I whisper.

"Any time," he says softly, staring at my feet.

This moment with Mr. Kim didn't involve an umbrella, but I'm feeling definite sparks. And even though I was the one that told Hazel not to get too carried away, I'm finding it hard to heed my own warning.

X

At the department store, the nervous energy is on over-drive.

I timidly step into the staging area, where I spot Jin Young next to a makeup table, talking to a girl who looks like a model. When he sees me approaching, he waves her away and eyes me up and down. He gives me an approving nod.

"Not bad yourself," I say, gesturing to his impeccably tailored three-piece suit in heather gray.

"Good. 'Cause I can barely breathe in this." He adjusts his waistline.

I cover a laugh, remembering how Ms. Song mentioned this year's menswear trend being payback for all the years women had to wear binding clothes.

"What? I don't look bad or anything," he says, seeing my amused expression.

"I know, it's not that. I'm just really enjoying this." I smile, gesturing around me.

"Wait until the show starts. It's a completely immersive experience with the fog machine and the lighting. The room will come alive."

My eyes light up. "I can't wait!"

Soo Young sashays across the staging area wearing a one-shoulder draped ball gown with a giant bow on the shoulder. I gasp. Jin Young just rolls his eyes. "Soo Young always goes oba at these events—which is Korean slang for 'overboard.' "

I laugh but can't say I don't understand her. Everything I'm experiencing right now I'd only ever dreamed about. I try to soak it in, not knowing when and if there will ever be a next time. Dressing tables with mirrors for hair and makeup line one side of the staging area and racks of clothes, shoes, and accessories line the other half of the stage. It's like I'm flipping through the pages of *Vogue*.

Pretty soon, the models start trickling in and they look just as I'd imagined they would. Tall, rail-thin, with angular faces and moody expressions. Jin Young gets easily distracted by them and abandons me again, which I don't mind. I'm a little distracted myself. I watch from the curtain, trying to stay out of everyone's way.

Henri Kim walks in, to loud fanfare. Like him, his outfit is over-the-top, pretentious, and colorful. He gestures, animatedly air-kissing each model and pointing a finger at every detail he particularly likes. His enigmatic, boisterous energy permeates the entire room, bringing it to life. I'm getting even more excited about the fashion show, which I didn't think was possible. This whole experience so far is entirely surreal.

Halmoni approaches me, almost glowing. "You look amazing, Halmoni!" I gawk at her. The dark circles and concern lines from the other day are completely erased from her face.

"I should hope so. This makeup team is not only the best, they are costing me a fortune. Speaking of . . . Soo Young-ah!" Halmoni shakes her head disapprovingly at Soo Young sitting at a makeup table. "That silly girl, making such a fuss. What are people going to think?" She waves Soo Young over, and a second later, she and Jin Young are standing next to me.

Halmoni takes turns inspecting the three of us. When she gets to me, her lips purse, staring closer at my dress. "This is not the outfit I had picked out for you." She looks around. "Ms. Song!" She barks loudly and within a second, Ms. Song comes jogging up to us.

After a scathing exchange, Ms. Song bows apologetically.

When she turns to me, the smile returns to her face. "Ms. Song made a mistake. She will now take you to the dressing room."

Ms. Song ushers me to a black-curtained makeshift dressing room where a garment bag hangs on the hook inside.

Once I'm inside the room and after closing the curtain, I unzip the garment bag with my heart racing out of my chest. This dress was hand-picked by Halmoni for me, so it must be special. I smile at the black fabric peeking through as I reveal the outfit and pull it out from the hanger to see it under the light. When I step back and inspect it, my smile fades. A black skirt suit?

I search the bottom of the bag, turning it inside out, wondering if there isn't a shawl, a petticoat, or a completely different gown in there. Because this simple pencil skirt and black blazer look eerily similar to the one Ms. Song is wearing right now.

Nevertheless, I slip off my slim-fitted gown and put on the skirt suit with the white button-down blouse. It's a perfect fit, which makes me think this isn't a mistake. I was meant to wear this outfit. The one that looks like the staff uniform. Not exactly thrilled with my wardrobe change, I step out of the dressing room self-consciously. Ms. Song just smiles, giving me the thumbs-up, unaware of the insecurity swirling through my head.

When I return, Halmoni is talking to Soo Young and Jin Young.

"Jah, the guests will be entering soon. You know who the investors are. Be charming, smile constantly, and be liberal with your compliments. And above all, modesty!" She points to Soo Young and Jin Young. When I approach them, they stop and stare at me. Jin Young and Soo Young exchange glances and Soo Young snickers.

"Ah, a perfect fit." Halmoni nods approvingly at me.

There's my confirmation. This definitely wasn't a mistake. "Halmoni, why am I wearing this?" I can't help staring longingly at Soo Young's ball gown that is over-the-top gorgeous.

"You are our special guest." She smiles, tapping my nose. "We don't expect you to do any work, of course.

Since you are so interested in fashion, I thought you could spend this time watching and learning from Ms. Song." She points to Ms. Song, who is sporting a headset and walking around to each model with a clipboard. "This will help her distinguish you as someone allowed backstage. It is a great privilege to be back there," she assures me.

"Neh, Halmoni." I bow.

She's right. It's everything I dreamed of, to be backstage at a fashion show. But Halmoni singling me out like that makes it feel like some sort of punishment.

I do as Halmoni requested and stay behind with Ms. Song, watching her meticulously check off each item on her list. Everything is written in Korean on her clipboard and she's constantly speaking into her headset rapidly. I feel like I'm in her way, so I end up watching from behind the curtain.

Like Jin Young promised, the room has been completely transformed into a forest. The smoke machine creates a dream-like state with trees and woodland creatures, even butterflies and leaves that look as if they're suspended in midair. It's magic.

When the seats begin to fill up, I watch Halmoni regally greet guests and investors. Soo Young is next to her, bowing and covering her laugh modestly as people compliment her looks. Jin Young is also playing his part well, laughing with men and women more than twice his age wearing couture and stiff suits. I know Halmoni is right. I don't belong out there with them. I could never be as comfortable and sophisticated in this type of crowd as Soo Young and Jin Young are. But being here while the rest of the family is out there makes me feel *other*, feeding into my growing insecurities. Will I ever really be a part of this family?

Just then, I hear a noise that makes me spin around.

Henri Kim threw a lint brush on the floor, which caused the loud cracking noise, and a swarm of attendants now surround him. I watch with curiosity, trying to piece it together. When Ms. Song comes toward me, I quickly ask, "What's wrong?"

"The model is sick, and they sent a replacement, but she is a different size and the clothes don't fit right. I have to tell Hwejangnim." She's trembling, but there's more than just worry in her eyes—there's fear. The panic is quickly spreading backstage like a disease and I steal a quick glance at Halmoni, whose face is the essence of zen, as if working the crowd is soothing to her. If Ms. Song goes to her, it will surely change that, and she's already had a rough week at the hospital. This may send her over the edge.

"Ms. Song, I can help," I quickly say.

I don't wait for her approval to get started. I pull out my sewing kit from my bag and begin threading the needle. The adrenaline must be making me forget about where I am and who's around me because the next thing I know, I'm barking orders: telling the model to put the dress back on and asking the attendant next to her to bring me something for her to stand on. Even more surprising, everyone listens to me. Even Henri Kim.

"Ppalli, ppalli!" Henri Kim shouts, clapping his hands at everyone when I give direction. He reminds me of a parrot, flapping the sleeves of his multicolored silk top.

With the dress on the model now, I can see where her proportions are different than those of the model the dress was originally fitted for. This model is fuller in the chest with a longer torso, creating a slight raise in the fabric. It adds to the difference of where the dress is supposed to hit her waist and hips. It's only a matter of centimeters, but when you're talking about clothes, a few centimeters can make all the difference. Especially when you're revealing your new collection for the first time in front of a crowd of investors and buyers. I can understand why Henri Kim is so upset. But this is fixable. I can do this.

After pinning the first dress, I tell the model to put on the next one. "Ppalli! Ppalli!" I imitate Henri Kim, motioning to the model to move faster. There are five outfits in total, some needing more alterations than others. Everyone is working as a team, with me at the head. I tell Ms. Song what I need, she translates, and the rest of the workers scatter like minions, procuring things from different colored threads, to sewing scissors, to steamers. I finish the first dress by the time I hear the announcer kick off the fashion show. I can alter the others between outfit changes, but that will mean I have to stay in the back and miss the entire show. I don't mind, though, not when I'm totally in my element. Plus, I wanted an immersive experience with fashion, and you can't get more immersed than where I'm at now.

The model bows profusely, thanking me in Korean each time. Henri Kim is by the curtains doing final checks on each model going down the runway, but he makes a point to bow to me every time the outfit I just altered passes his inspection. I don't have time to even acknowledge him, with the clock ticking before the model returns for her next outfit. By the time she's out for her last outfit change, I release a breath I didn't know I was holding in. I feel like I ran a marathon—no, two!—but there's a sense of total and utter satisfaction. What a rush.

I finish just in time to watch them all walk their final time down the runway together. Henri Kim walks down with them, and on his way back, he puts his hands up in front of him with his thumb and pointer finger crossing to make finger hearts. When I look up at his eyes, he's staring right at me.

Oh em gee, Henri Kim is flashing me the finger hearts! *Me!*

As soon as the whole show is over, Henri Kim runs up to me and hugs me. When he sees my shocked expression, he asks, "Gwenchanayo?"

I nod. For the first time in a long while, I am more than gwenchanayo.

He smiles wide at my reaction, then continues going on in rapid Korean. Ms. Song comes rushing over with a smile, translating for him.

"He cannot thank you enough for what you did. You have not only saved his clothes, but his reputation as well."

I'm at a complete loss for words when Halmoni shows up. There's a look of concern mixed with uncertainty. "What is going on?" she says sternly to me.

I recoil. I've seen Halmoni speak that way to others,

282

but never to me. I'm about to explain when Ms. Song steps in and recounts what happened in Korean. I watch Halmoni's reactions, most of which are reaction-less. When she's about to finally say something, she's pulled away by Mr. Kim. I don't have time to dissect what just happened because Ms. Song is calling me over to the model I helped. She wants to thank me, and Ms. Song translates.

"She says you saved her career. Like many people in the fashion industry, her career hangs on the line of a very fine silk thread. She didn't make the initial cut to be a model for Henri Kim, but when she was called in at the last minute as a replacement, she had a rare second chance. However, when the clothes didn't fit right and Henri Kim was upset with her, then it could have meant the end of her career, over before it even started." The model starts to tear up, and Ms. Song hands her a tissue.

"The success of the model is due to the success of their showing. If she didn't show well, then they blame the model. Today, when you fixed the clothes, you not only saved the show, you made her the star. Now Henri Kim has asked her to be his runway model at every one of his shows this year."

"Oh my God, really?" I shriek, my eyes bouncing from Ms. Song to the model.

"Neh!" the model squeals with me and embraces me. I didn't get to actually see the show, but it was a win for me, for so many reasons. For saving her career, for saving Henri Kim's reputation, for saving Halmoni's fashion show.

After the fashion show is over, Jin Young and Soo Young

are long gone and I'm waiting for Halmoni at the runway by myself. I watch the workers sweep up the streamers and confetti littering the floor and gather up the empty champagne glasses scattered on the counters. When Halmoni returns, she approaches me with a triumphant smile.

"The show was a huge success. Because of you." She's looking at me like she looks at Jin Young or Soo Young, and the feeling of being hidden away like some shameful family secret disappears. "Today you made me proud to be your grandmother."

Her words catch me off guard and tears prickle at the back of my eyes. Hearing Halmoni say the words that she's proud of me makes me realize how much I've been needing her to validate my existence. That I really am part of the family. That I belong.

"Halmoni, I want to tell you something," I say, smiling through the tears. "Jin Young explained to the doctors how I'm related to the family with the DNA results and they let me test to see if I would be a good candidate for Samchon's liver donor."

She seems surprised, mouth ajar and eyes wider than I've ever seen them.

"I wanted you to hear it from me first. I got the news that I passed the initial test."

"How did you—When did—?"

"We asked Mr. Kim to take me and to keep it a secret from you. Please, Halmoni, don't be mad at him. I begged him." I plead with my eyes.

"You . . . did all this, for me?"

I nod.

Her eyes glisten with moisture as she slowly approaches me. I hold my arms out, expecting an emotional embrace, but it never happens. "Come with me," she says in a serious manner. "I want to show you something."

# CHAPTER 24

Mr. Kim drives me and Halmoni about an hour outside of Seoul to a quiet suburb. When we get out of the car, I look around. It's a pretty isolated street, other than the big white stand-alone building that nearly takes up the whole block. I want to ask where we are, but the mood is tense with an unknown energy, so it doesn't seem appropriate.

Halmoni leads me through the glass double doors. The cool air is inviting but there's a quiet calmness in the building that is unsettling. The floors and ceiling are made entirely out of granite and our heels clack loudly, echoing as we walk. Along the sides of the walls are doors leading to other rooms. Halmoni takes me to the second door on the right-hand side. The room is empty, and much of the same gray granite on the floors is on the walls, except for one of them, which is lined with rectangular drawers with bronze plaques on them.

"In this room is where the bodies of many generations of Noh men are buried."

The hairs stick up on my neck and arms. I didn't realize we were in a mausoleum.

"Each drawer is filled with their ashes. This one is your father's." She opens the drawer in front of us and I peek in, my heart racing a million miles per second. "As you can see, it's empty. When your father died, he was in America. I never even got to bury him."

I look down at my feet, solemnly. "Mom scattered his ashes—"

She puts up a hand to shush me. "I don't want to know what your mother did with him. The important thing is that he's not here, where he belongs." Her tone is icy. "Lady Cha said that by not burying him here with everyone else in the Noh family, we are disrupting the order of the natural laws. The ancestors are angry and that is why the men in the family are cursed."

I'm not sure if I understand or even believe in the curse, so I don't say anything. In the silence, Halmoni continues.

"The only way to end the curse is to bring him back. Which we know is not possible." She stares down her nose at me. "Until now. Now I see why Lady Cha said that you are so important to us. You bring us a solution that is going to save my son, but also save the family from this wretched curse."

"I-I just don't know if I believe in that," I finally say out loud. "I don't know if I can do what Lady Cha predicted and end this curse."

"Nonsense. You already have."

"I have? How?"

"I didn't understand her reading at first either. Now that you tell me your liver is a match, I see how you will bring him back, just like Lady Cha said. You carry half of his blood in you. Sharing your liver with your uncle will save his life, make us whole again, and break the curse." She turns to face me, grabs my hands in hers, and squeezes tight. "Chloe, *you* can bring peace to our family once and for all."

I'm too overwhelmed by what I'm hearing to say anything. Ever since I met the Nohs I've wanted them to want me as much as I want them—to need me the way I need them. The way Halmoni is looking at me, with that same intensity and desperation, I should be elated.

Except that I'm not.

This curse, it's changed everything. Being a liver donor is no longer just a family affair. It's a matter of belief, and I'm not sure we're all on the same page. How is it possible for someone who doesn't know about the curse—doesn't *believe* in the curse—to be part of the solution?

※

I'm still thinking about what Halmoni said as I'm getting ready to go to the hospital the next morning. Since I'm a candidate for the liver match, I have some more tests to take. Only now I'm more nervous knowing that not only does Samchon's life depend on me, but so does everything Halmoni believes in.

When I offered to be a donor for Samchon, I wanted to help. To do my part as a member of this family. But ending curses and restoring peace? That's a lot to ask of an eighteen-year-old. What if it doesn't work? What will the family think of me then? I can't help but see my worth in the family tied to the outcome of the procedure. The mounting pressure is too unbearable to even think about.

I put on a pair of tapered skinny pants and a sleeveless silk top I got at the department store. By the time I finish getting ready, I've convinced myself it's all in my head. My fear of not being valued in this family is just the effect of bingeing one too many K-dramas. Yes, that's right. I'm just suffering from a bit of K-drama-itis. That's totally a thing. When I get to the foot of the stairs, I smile when I see Mr. Kim waiting for me, like clockwork. Except this time, he's pacing. My smile disappears.

"Your halmoni is requesting you come to the store. Right now," he says with an urgency that makes me scramble to find my shoes.

I rush out the door, pulling on the straps to my new studded Valentino sling-backs. By the time we get to the car, I'm fighting to catch my breath.

"Is everything okay?" I ask.

He shakes his head but gives me no other details for why I'm being rushed.

"Is it Samchon?" I try again. "Am I too late?"

"I cannot say. I've only been instructed to take you to the department store, and quickly."

Mr. Kim helps me into the car and when he's in the driver's seat, he accelerates through the traffic, weaving in and out of lanes. When we get to the VIP entrance of the department store, I don't even wait for the attendant to open the door for me. I fly out of the car and race up the steps to the elevator.

On the ride up, I draw in a few deep breaths, stabilizing my heartbeat. *Everything is going to be fine*, I tell myself. It's not like liver failure happens overnight. At least, that's not what I've read on the internet. It's a long and arduous process that can take time. I don't know why I'm getting myself worked up.

The elevator door dings, and I won't have to wonder about it for too much longer. I'll find out in a matter of seconds what the emergency situation is. Halmoni's secretary stands up immediately, rushing to the entrance of Halmoni's office door. She knocks and waits to hear a response. While we wait, I overhear part of Halmoni's conversation with someone; whoever is in there is clearly angry. Whoever it is, she's speaking in Korean, so I don't understand what's being said, but her voice is unmistakably familiar. The secretary knocks again, louder. This time Halmoni tells us to enter. When she pushes open the door, I see Halmoni standing behind her desk and a woman with her back to us. She turns around to face me.

*"Mom?"*

# CHAPTER 25

"Chloe-yah!" She runs over and throws her arms around me. With my blood circulation cut off at my chest, I'm definitely not imagining this. "I've been worried sick!"

My arms stay by my side, partly because of her death grip and partly because I don't know how I feel about seeing my mom . . . *here*. In the very same room as Halmoni.

Halmoni sits back in her chair, arms folded across her chest, staring with narrowed eyes.

Mom eventually pulls away from me. Dark bags hang under her eyes and her hair is frizzy, like mine was when I first got here.

"How have you been? Have they been treating you well?" She scans my body, putting her cold, clammy hands on my forehead and cheeks. A second later, she pulls back and stares at me from head to toe. "What have they done to you? You look—"

"What . . . are you doing here?" I'm still trying to understand what's going on. Mom is here. In Korea.

"When you didn't call or answer my phone calls, I was worried about you."

"Oh, right. I forgot to tell you I got a new phone. A lot's

291

happened in the past couple of days. I just got busy."

Her brows twitch and she stares at me like I'm a stranger. "Chloe. I've flown halfway across the world to see you. Is that all you have to say to me?"

"It's not like I haven't been on my own before. I haven't made a definitive decision about being a liver donor yet, I'm trying to understand . . ."

"You were on your own when I was at the hospital. *Working.*" She grips a chair next to her as if she's been hit with a sudden episode of vertigo. "I always checked on you, one way or another."

"You relied on other people. Strangers, Mom." I think of the times neighbors and co-workers would stop by, checking in on me when she wasn't around. They seemed like permanent fixtures in my life, sometimes more consistent than my own mom.

"They were not strangers. These people are—" She holds her hand out toward Halmoni.

"They're my family, Mom! And if you had clued me in on them, I could've had a different life." There it is. The truth that's been eating me up for too long. The opportunities I've missed out on, feeling like half a person without any family history most my life. If she had only told me the truth from the beginning, I could've had a different life, a better life.

The hurt slashes across her face, and she looks as if she's about to fall over. "What's wrong with the life you have? I thought you were happy, you're going to the college—"

*"Community college."*

"Community college." She nods, wiping her nose. "Soon you'll be a nurse, what's wrong with that?" she whispers, almost as if she's talking to herself.

My insides feel as if they're being torn into two. Part of me wants to run to her and apologize for hurting her, and another part of me is relieved to finally say the things I've felt my whole life.

"A nurse?" Halmoni scoffs. "That's typical of you, forcing your dreams on someone else. You did it to my son and now you are doing it to your own daughter. What good is getting accepted to FIT if she's going to be a nurse?"

Mom's face turns from distraught to confused. "FIT?"

I might as well tell her everything, since we're being honest with each other for once. "Yes, Mom. I got into the Fashion Institute of Technology."

"When did you . . . Why didn't you . . ." She stops and starts so many times, not knowing what question to ask first. I take it upon myself to answer them for her.

"I never told you because I knew you would tell me you couldn't afford it."

"You see? She will never let you follow your dreams," Halmoni says sharply.

Mom's knuckles are white from gripping the chair. She holds her head up and glares straight at Halmoni. "You can't have her liver."

I wince. Halmoni must have told her about me being a liver donor. I'd hoped to tell her in my time, but what's done is done. She's a nurse. If anyone can understand the circumstances of Samchon's dire situation, it's her. I open my mouth to explain but Mom cuts me off.

"I won't let her risk her life for you; you can't use her like that. I'll never give my permission."

Mom speaking on behalf of me, as if my voice has no say in the matter, makes me snap. For too long I've had to watch my life choices be dictated by my circumstances—I will never really know who my dad was and what parts of him are in me. I can't afford to go to fashion school, and I can't ever leave the town I grew up in.

But not anymore. Not now. I have a choice.

"I don't need your permission." Both of their heads whip over to me simultaneously. "I'm eighteen, Mom. A legal adult. I can do what I want."

After a second, Mom's body deflates and her face falls in defeat. She knows she's lost this hand and she has no other cards left to play with.

"I think you should leave," Halmoni says, pushing the button on her desk. Within seconds, the door opens, and the secretary is told to escort Mom out of the building. There are two security guards who come out of the elevator at the same time, armed with batons. I don't disagree with Halmoni; Mom should leave. But as the guards draw nearer, the thought of watching my mom being manhandled is too much for me, so I act fast.

"I'll take her," I say to Halmoni. "I'll show her to the front door and come right back." After a second, she nods.

✕

"How come you never told me about FIT?" Mom says once we're on the sidewalk in front of the department store.

The streets are crowded, and people are dodging us from left to right. I grab Mom by the arm and move to the side of the building. Even if the humidity wasn't creating a thin film of moisture on my face, it'd be damp with sweat anyway. Why did Mom have to come here and ruin everything?

"What would be the point, Mom? We both know we couldn't afford it, even with the scholarship."

"Scholarship?" Her face crumples. "You used to tell me everything."

I sigh, running a hand through my hair. She has kept so much from me that I can't believe she can even utter those words. "It doesn't matter, don't you get it? Now I have a chance to do something, something good. I could save a man's life. You should be happy for me."

"I don't think you've thought this through. Being a liver donor, there's a huge risk, and I'm not sure you know what you're signing up for."

"Nothing's going to happen to me. Halmoni said—"

"Chloe-yah! You could die!" She's almost shouting at this point. "I've seen it happen a number of times!"

I jump back in shock. I don't think I've ever heard Mom's voice so loud, so tense. But I'm not going to let that deter me from my decision.

"Don't you get it, Mom? This is what it means to be in a family. You make sacrifices for each other, risk your life for them if you have to. Halmoni even hired the top specialists in the country. They have the means and resources to make sure everything goes smoothly."

"Money can't solve everything." She scoffs.

"It can solve a lot of things, Mom. You just don't know because we've never had it."

She grabs her gut like I've just inserted a knife in it.

"I'm not trying to hurt you. I finally have a connection to Dad, a connection to this big dynamic family who is also passionate about fashion the way I am—everything I'd felt I've been missing out on my whole life. Can't you just be happy for me?"

Something in her snaps and she straightens up and grabs me by the shoulders. "Listen to me. No matter what you think of me, just listen to me this one time. Doing this for them, being a liver donor, it's not going to change anything. This family, the Nohs, they're different from other people. If you're part of their family, you think you'll have your own life?" A guttural laugh comes out; it's almost maniacal. "They will *own* your life. Tell you what to do, how to live. That's not any kind of life."

"Mom, I get that you were never fully accepted into the family. I know Halmoni didn't think you were a good match for her son."

Her head whips up, her face a cross between shock and sadness.

"But you can't let your resentment toward them prevent me from getting to know my own family. I am not you." I look deep into her pupils, trying to get my message across once and for all. "Whatever happened between you and Halmoni was years ago. Maybe you need to realize that this has nothing to do with you and everything to do with me. The Nohs, they're *my* family, connected by blood. You can't expect me to cut them out of my life the way you cut them out of yours."

She's shaking her head in disbelief, alternating in bursts of laughs and cries. I wonder whether she's jet-lagged or just plain losing it. And then she wipes her eyes and puts her hand on my shoulders, staring straight at me, and says, "I didn't want to have to tell you this, but she knew about you from the beginning. Your halmoni knew about you but she didn't want to have anything to do with you, with us."

I place my hand over my mom's and remove it from my shoulder. "Mom, you need to stop. Otherwise, we're going to say things we'll really regret. I believe you when you say you did your best. That's why I didn't want to burden you with how I really felt."

"How you *really* felt?"

"Yes, Mom. I don't want to go to MCC and become a nurse like you. I don't want to live at home with my mom during what are supposed to be the best years of my life. And I don't want to sit around, wondering if you're going to make it home for dinner or if I'm going to have to eat alone for the millionth time. I'm tired of waiting for my life to finally start!" I'm fuming, hands clenched into tight fists and my face throbbing with pent-up anger. I hate to do this to her, but it's been a long time coming. I've been holding back my true feelings for so long, trying to protect her when I know she's trying her best. As much as it's destroying me, she needs to know.

"Look, Mom. I'm sorry. I didn't mean it to be like this. I was going to tell you, but then everything happened so quickly."

"Chloe, honey, please. You can give them everything

and they still won't accept you the way you think. They'll never see you as part of their family."

"You know what, Mom? I really didn't want to say it, but you're jealous. Admit it."

"*Jealous? Of them?*" She scoffs, pointing to the building.

"Yes, them! They can give me the opportunities you can't, and it kills you. I'm not going to stay and live by your side so I can be your companion for the rest of your life. I need to live my life, too, and now that I have the option to leave you, you're scared."

She winces as if I've hurled a physical bomb at her, not just a verbal one. Looking around while drawing in deep breaths, her eyes rest on the department store sign above us. She stares at it, eerily calm, as if she's not even here anymore. "I can't believe this is happening again. I tried so hard to prevent this, but it's still happening." It's as if she's talking to someone who's not here.

"It didn't have to be this way. If you had just shown your support for me, we could've made this work. It's like Halmoni said, I'm going to have to choose for myself, and for once I'm going to do what I want." When she looks as if she's going to plead with me again, I don't have the emotional strength to go on, so I say, "Please go home, Mom. I'll call you later, but I need to do this for myself." I begin to step away.

"Chloe, wait!" She calls out for me, but I'm already in the revolving doors to go into the store.

My face pulses with rage as I make my way to the elevator, drawing in deep breaths to calm myself down. When the elevator door shuts, it closes out the white noise, leaving me alone with just my thoughts. I've imagined the conversation in my head a hundred times. The one where I tell my mom how uncertain I feel about my future as a nurse. About wanting to know more about my father, the other half of my genetic makeup. I've thought about even telling her how lonely and abandoned I feel with her working all the time. I knew it wasn't ever going to be an easy conversation, painful even. I never in a million years thought it would've gone down the way it did.

This is the first time I've ever spoken to my mom like that, so angry and bitter. Even when I wanted to yell at her for not being there in the past, there was always an excuse that made my anger feel unjustified. A patient needing a life-saving procedure. A co-worker asking her to cover a shift. An extra shift for an unexpected but necessary expense. How could I bring up my own selfish desires for her to be around when someone or something else needed her more? And it's not like she was never there for me. She tried her best. She always managed to make it for the big moments.

By the time I reach Halmoni's office again, I'm more confused than ever. Am I so desperate for my family's acceptance that I can't see I'm being used? Could it be that Mom is right and I'm wrong?

"Did she leave?" Halmoni asks while looking over the papers in her hand.

"Yes." I nod. "But I'm wondering if I made a mistake. Shouldn't I at least try to help her understand? She is my mom . . ." Tears sting the backs of my eyes.

Instead of an answer, Halmoni pushes the paper in her hand toward me. It's written in Korean.

"What is this?"

"Your contract."

"Contract?" I ask skeptically.

Halmoni leans forward and steeples her hands. "For your enrollment at FIT. All you have to do is send your letter of acceptance. We'll take care of the rest. After you graduate, we will talk about your future at Sam Won Department Store."

"What?" I can't believe what I'm hearing. When I look closer, something doesn't add up. "Who is Noh Eun Young?"

"You didn't have a Korean name, you said. So I gave you one. *Eun* means *grace*, which is what you are."

She picked out a Korean name for me? And it has the same second syllable as Jin Young and Soo Young.

"Oh, Halmoni." I tear up.

"You proved your talent at the fashion show and now you've shown me how much you're willing to do for the family. We need loyal people like you in the family business. There are not that many people I can trust."

And there it is. The validation I needed. They *do* see me as family.

# CHAPTER 26

Later that day, I'm back in my room, still in a daze. Did that just happen? Did Mom fly halfway across the world for me?

The phone rings, startling me, and I nearly jump off the bed. I fumble with my cell and see that it's Seb.

"What are you doing up so early? It's six in the morning there." For as long as I've known him, never once has he been a morning person.

"I'm at the airport, about to leave for Europe." He gives me a half smile.

"Ohhhhh." I try desperately not to make it sound like a pity *oh*. Good for him for going on the trip, even if Hazel was having second thoughts. "Are you excited to see your family?"

"Definitely. We're just not sure how the sleeping situation is going to work out."

"*We?*" I blink twice.

Seb's brows scrunch together. "Uh, me and Hazel?"

"Did someone call my name?" Hazel appears on-screen and hands Seb a steaming cup of coffee.

"Aww, you two made up!" Tears well in my eyes, seeing my two best friends back together. "I don't know what I would've done if you guys weren't on speaking terms."

"Apparently we have you to thank." Seb smiles wide and points a finger at me.

"Me?"

Hazel nods. "You reminded me why I love watching K-dramas. Because it's an escape from real life. I made the mistake of putting such unrealistic expectations on Seb, and that wasn't fair." She squeezes his cheeks while baby-talking the last part.

"If I wasn't so thrilled about you two making up, I'd be barfing in a bag right now."

"After our talk," Seb says to me, "I realized that even though I didn't like being compared to Lee Min Ho"—he gives a subtle eye roll and Hazel nudges him playfully—"I wasn't really helping the situation by being so closed-minded. In fact, it was pushing us farther away from each other. And hearing how much you worked so hard at your relationship with your family inspired me to try harder at our relationship. We owe so much to you."

"You have no idea." Hazel nods in agreement. "Once I explained to him how much I missed having someone to share the K-drama experience with, Seb's even agreed to start watching them with me. We've got ten hours to kill on this flight, so what better time than now."

Seb's raised eyebrows say otherwise. "Look, I'm all for watching K-dramas with you, but you have to admit, watching a drama called *Crash Landing on You* on a ten-hour flight is in poor taste, no?" We burst into laughter and the baby strapped to its dad standing next to them nearly jumps out of the carrier.

"Aw, man. You're making me wish I was there with you right now." Nostalgia kicks in and FOMO hits me like a ton of bricks.

Hazel pauses. "Uh-oh. What's wrong?"

"Who says anything is wrong?" I cock my head to the side.

"Chloe. I've been your best friend—"

"*We've* been your best friends," Seb interjects, giving Hazel a pointed look.

She nods. "*We've* been your best friends since the sixth grade."

"We know your disappointed face by now," Seb says.

I chew on my bottom lip.

"Is it about being a liver donor? Hazel told me yesterday."

"I hope that's okay," Hazel says.

"Of course it's okay. Except my halmoni told me yesterday that if I am a match, not only could I save my Samchon, I could also break the family curse."

"What?" Seb says at the same time Hazel cries, "No way!"

"Yeah, but what if Lady Cha is wrong?" I shake my head in disbelief. "I mean, I want to help them, but I don't even believe in any of that. Not even a little bit. What if Samchon dies and I don't end the curse, whose fault is it then?"

"Well, it's not yours. And if they're your family, then they won't blame you," Hazel says.

"I know, but somehow it doesn't seem that simple." I sigh again.

"What about your mom? What does she have to say about this?" Seb asks.

I cringe, thinking about my argument with Mom. "She's

upset about it and every time I try to see it from her point of view, I can only see her lies. She kept me from knowing my dad's family. My family. I don't know if I can trust her anymore." I groan loudly. "What should I do?"

Hazel and Seb are silent. For a moment, all I can hear is the white noise of an airport. The fuzzy haze of the scattered conversations, the occasional announcement over the airport intercom, and luggage being rolled across the walkways. Hazel and Seb are the ones with big family drama experience, and this is one that's stumping even them.

"As much as we want to help, we're not the ones that can make that decision for you," Seb says.

"For what it's worth," Hazel says after a minute, "you know, I was the one that got us carried away, but you're the one who made me realize that K-dramas aren't reality. Once I separated the two, it helped me to see what's real and make the right decision." She interlaces her fingers with Seb's and leans into his chest.

Seb hugs her back. "Whatever happens, we know you'll make the right decision too, Chlo."

There's an announcement on the speaker cutting our conversation short. It's time for Hazel and Seb to board the plane.

"I can't believe you guys are leaving." I give in to the sad face I've been holding back. After they return from Europe, they'll be off to LA, and who knows what drama will be going on in my life by then.

"Technically, you left first." Hazel smirks.

"Yeah, you're right. Now that you're leaving too, it feels so final." I blink back tears.

"As soon as we get to my family's house in Greece, we'll call you." Seb points to me through the phone.

"And, Chloe," Hazel says, giving me the heart fingers. "Saranghae."

"Saranghae, guys." I return the same heart fingers.

After we hang up, I stare as my phone's screen dims and eventually turns black. I'm so happy that Hazel and Seb have found their way back to each other. I want to believe them, but Hazel comparing Seb to Lee Min Ho isn't quite the same thing as what I'm going through. Am I making the right choice by offering to be a liver donor for Samchon?

⚹

The next day, Miso says she needs to give me something, so I give her my address and ask her to come to the family guesthouse.

"Shut the front door!" Purely by coincidence, the door behind her shuts just as she says this.

I hide my laugh behind my hand.

She walks around with her mouth in the shape of an O. "I did not know there were houses this big in Seoul!"

"Can I get you a drink?" I say, opening the fridge and handing her a bottle of water.

"Daaaaang!" she says, following me into the kitchen. "It's like one of those mini-fridges at the fancy hotels, except there's nothing mini about this place!"

I laugh, but she's not wrong. I'm still not used to the size of this guest home. "Do you want a tour?" I ask.

"Maybe later. After you catch me up on your medical drama."

"Even though the doctor told me the answer I wanted to hear, that I passed the initial tests, I'm still feeling unsure."

"You passed the initial tests?" She checks her phone. "It's only been a few days since I last saw you! That happened so quickly!"

"Yeah. Tell me about it."

"What did you have to do to get tested?"

"It happened so fast, it was over before I knew it. I got a CT scan and then that was it. They didn't even take my blood or anything. It's weird."

"Just because you passed the initial tests doesn't mean you're a match. Even still, you haven't agreed to anything," Miso says, practically reading my mind. "Definitely sleep on it. It's a huge deal, being a live organ donor."

"Yeah, you're right," I say, but I'm not really convinced myself. Something about this feels like maybe I'm already too far into the process and have already reached the point of no return.

"I can't believe I'm Samchon's only possible candidate. You'd think a family like mine would have more options than just me."

"Oh, no. I believe it. Families like the Nohs have to be extra careful. They can't ask just anyone to be a donor for them. Only family members. Or else it will look suspicious to the public."

"Suspicious? How?"

"Remember what I said about organ trafficking? It's illegal here. Everyone knows that if it wasn't, chaebol families would be the first people to pay for something like that. For people like the Nohs, family members being a live donor is the only option. The gossip blogs would have a field day with that sort of thing."

"They're really afraid of the tabloids, aren't they?"

"Yep." Miso nods. "I told you chaebols were like royalty, and this is one of those things. Even though they control most of the money and power in Korea, they make up only, like, one percent of the population. Ninety-nine percent is everybody else. And that's power, too. They know they can do whatever they want, as long as the people—AKA lowly plebs like myself—don't turn on them. Actually, I thought I saw a reporter hanging outside the gate to the guesthouse. No camera, but the telltale all-black outfit and black baseball hat."

"Outside the house? Right now?"

"Yeah, I saw them from the taxi I took. Or . . . maybe your life is going full K-drama and you've got a stalker!" Seeing my horrified expression, she quickly relents. "That was a joke, by the way. I did see someone outside checking out the house from the street, but they probably were just gawking at how the rich live, like any normal person would."

"Now I'm starting to get curious . . ." I debate a while, wondering if I want to go there. Because once I know, I can't unknow this kind of information. Eventually, curiosity gets the better of me and I ask, "What do your gossip blogs say about my dad?"

Miso has her phone out. "You said your dad is the eldest Noh son?" After a second, a wave of confusion sweeps across her face that makes me nervous.

"What does it say?"

"Noh Im Pyo?" she asks. "He died like two years ago."

"No, my dad is Joon Pyo. He died before I was born."

"Joon Pyo? I don't think I've heard of him." She does another search. "Yeah, it says there are two sons in the Noh family dynasty. Im Pyo and Han Pyo, but no Joon Pyo." Suddenly she chuckles. "Heh-heh. Get it? *No* Joon Pyo, like Noh and No? Homonyms?" When she sees I'm too preoccupied with my thoughts to laugh, she says, "Sorry, that was totally insensitive."

"Do you think . . . ?" I can't even finish my question. I don't want to believe Halmoni would be capable of erasing my dad, her own son, out of the family. The one she was so tearfully remembering with me. Instead I ask, "Well, we know the story about Jin Young's dad isn't true. You don't think they could do that about my dad, too? Could they?"

"Hey, all the chaebols do it. Your family isn't, like, worse than anyone else's," she says, as if that's reassuring news.

"It's still wrong, chaebol or not. If I don't fit in with them, will they want to cut me out of the family, too?" I say, thinking out loud. Peering through my fingers covering my face, I catch a glimpse of Miso chewing on her bottom lip. A reminder that I'm not the only one feeling left out of my family. "Hey, what about you? Are things better with your dad?"

"Actually, that's what I came here for." She lifts up the purple bag in her hand and plops it on the kitchen island. "A parting gift. For you." She smiles her big Miso smile.

"A parting gift? Are you going somewhere?" I take the bag from her.

"Yeah, I'm leaving tomorrow for a trip. After that I'm going to visit some relatives in California before I start at UPenn in the fall. So . . . this is it."

"Hey, at least we'll be on the same continent. I'm sure we can figure something out."

"You're right! This isn't really a farewell, it's just goodbye for now." She gives me a sentimental smile, then pushes the bag toward me. "Open it up!"

"Aw, you shouldn't have. I didn't get you anything." I start taking the tissue paper out of the bag.

"You did. You gave me a huge gift."

I pause from unwrapping the gift. "What do you mean?"

"My relationship with my dad has been drifting since I left for boarding school. Things were so distant between us already that when I came out, I didn't feel like I could talk to him about it. We kept drifting farther apart and until I met you, I just thought that was the way things were going to be from now on. Our new normal." She sighs, downcast.

"I'm so sorry." I sit down on a barstool and lean my head against my hand. "I wish I could help you get closer to him."

"But that's just it. Seeing how far you came to find a connection to your dad made me realize there's still time to do something about it. I may barely have a relationship with him, but he's alive at least. So I put my big girl pants on—literally—then told my dad how I've been feeling. And guess what? He said he's been feeling the same way!

That he may not know how to communicate with me, but he's committed to working on it because he loves me. Now he's planned a father-daughter bonding trip to Busan!"

"Oh, Miso." I start bawling. "This is so amazing!"

"I know!" Miso fans her eyes, which makes me fan mine. Pretty soon we look like two flightless birds, flapping our hands ridiculously.

"So you see, you inspired me, and I wanted to give you something as a token of my appreciation."

I finish unwrapping the gift and find a stack of clothing in loud prints and colors. I pull out an item and let it unfold.

"Hammer pants?" I raise an eyebrow at Miso and laugh.

"I feel like I had a pretty big breakthrough with my dad, thanks to you. It reminded me of what you said about creating something new out of old fabrics, so I thought it would be symbolic to leave you with these beauties."

"Aw, Miso." I choke up.

She snorts. "I mean, not gonna lie, it'll be hard to make these into anything superior to what they already are." She puts a hand on my shoulder. "But if anyone can do it, it's you."

"I love it," I say, hugging the pants to my chest. I already have a dozen different ideas for how to use these quirky patterns."

We smile at each other, teary-eyed. We've only known each other for a short time, but I feel deeply connected to her.

"Look at us. Getting closer to our families." Miso smiles with her hand to her chest.

Something about her words hitches my breathing.

"Yeah. Right." Two weeks ago, I was feeling stuck in Tulsa with no life and no future. Now I'm going to fashion shows with my halmoni and securing my future working at a global fashion company. It's like I've died and gone to K-drama heaven, where every dream I've ever had is coming true.

And yet . . . something is bothering me.

"What is it? Why are you smelling the fart?" Miso asks.

"Hey, are you, like, on the Dan family registry?"

"Yeah, of course." Then she gives me a funny look. "What brought that on?"

"Well, it's probably nothing, just being oversensitive about it since we don't have it in the US, but they asked for my family registry at the hospital and I didn't have it."

"Oh, shoot. The law. You're probably not on the family registry since they just found out about you."

"Right." I point a finger at her.

"How'd you bypass—"

"Money." I cut to the chase.

"Right." She points her finger to me. "Crazy rich chaebols." She chuckles.

"Yeah, right." I force a smile. Miso's reaction makes me think it's not that big of a deal not to be on the registry. "How hard is it to get on the registry?"

"Not hard. You just have to file some paperwork along with proof of your relationship, whether it's a birth certificate or a—"

"DNA test?"

"Yeah, which you already have." Then a beat later, she says, "What, are you thinking about making it official?"

"You think it's too forward to ask?"

She jerks her head back and gives me a funny look. "You're asking if it's too forward to ask your own family to add you to their family registry? Do you have to even ask? They've already accepted you into the family."

"Yeah, but . . ." I hesitate. Suspicion has been needling me for too long. Any longer and my insides will be stitched into a quilt. If I can tell anyone, it would be Miso.

"What?" Miso asks encouragingly.

"What if my acceptance in the family is dependent on my ability to save Samchon's life?" I swallow thickly, almost instantly regretting giving voice to my fears.

"Hey." She places a hand on mine. "Remember, if you're a match, you still have the ultimate say, don't forget that. I'd still respect you if you decided not to donate part of your liver. Man, that shit is scary, and saying no takes guts. Regardless, no matter what your choice is, asking to be put on the family registry is a completely unrelated topic."

She's right, I know she is. But why am I getting the feeling that it's not that simple?

# 23andme.com

**MESSAGES**

From: Chang, Chloe
Subject: Sachon to Sachon
Thursday, 8:29 PM

Hi. I hope you're still checking these messages. It still feels comforting to reach out to you here, and right now I could use a friend. I'm feeling alone, which is weird because I'm surrounded by more family than ever. You know how I said I'd always dreamed about being a part of a big family? I'm wondering if I could get added to the family registry. How do you think Halmoni will receive the news?

From: Noh, Jin Young
Subject: RE: Sachon to Sachon
Thursday, 9:10 PM

I'm so sorry you're feeling alone. Know that I am always here for you. I don't think right now is the best time to approach Halmoni with such matters. Believe me when I say that things are difficult for her right now. She doesn't respond well during times of crisis. It will be better to wait until after the surgery to see how things go. Then wait for the right time.

From: Chang, Chloe
Subject: RE: Sachon to Sachon
Thursday, 10:01 PM

That's the thing. What if the surgery doesn't go well? What if I missed my one chance to make this official?

Hey, I know it's late, but would it be okay if I came over tonight? I just don't feel like being alone in this big house.

# CHAPTER 27

I don't wait for Jin Young to respond to my text before asking Mr. Kim to take me to his house. He must've been in a deep text conversation, as I startle him by walking down the stairs. He fumbles with his phone and pockets it before bowing to me.

"Can you take me to Jin Young's apartment?"

"At this hour?" He wipes his brow.

"Yeah, I told him I was going to stop by."

Mr. Kim hesitates, but eventually concedes. When we're leaving, I think I see someone lurking around the corner, but when I get closer to check, there's no one there. I can't tell whether someone was there or if I'm just being paranoid after Miso's stalker sighting from earlier today. In the car ride, I'm silent and don't even notice until we're close to Jin Young's apartment that Mr. Kim has been watching me through the rearview mirror.

"Everything okay?"

"No, but . . . you wouldn't understand." When his brows knit together, I know I've offended him. "I mean, it's not that I don't think you wouldn't be understanding. It's just that this is something only I can do for myself," I say, fidgeting with the hem of my shirt.

"If you ever need to talk about this with anyone, you know you can talk to me." His expression softens and it tugs at my heart just how much he cares. Still, as much as I know Mr. Kim is trying to help me, it's not him I want answers from.

"That means a lot to me."

The car comes to a stop at a red light and I notice his eyes disappear in the rearview mirror. He's typing on his phone.

"This really is more than a full-time job, huh?" I say to him. He doesn't respond, suddenly distracted by a text. It must be important because for the rest of the ride, he frequently checks his phone.

At his apartment, Jin Young opens the door wearing slacks and a fitted button-down shirt. He's surprised to see me. "How did you—"

"There wasn't any traffic, so I got here faster than usual."

Puzzled, he checks his phone. A look of understanding replaces the look of confusion when he sees my last message.

"I guess it's good Mr. Kim got me here so quickly, because . . . are you going somewhere?" I ask, confused. I wouldn't have come in my leggings if I'd known he was planning to go out.

"Yeah, some of the guys are headed out." He gives me a polite smile. The mood is different; it's as if something has cooled between us.

"Oh, I just thought—I mean, I was wondering if we could talk."

"What, now?" he asks, checking his watch. He must not have read my last message yet, then.

"It won't take long," I find myself saying, desperate to stay.

"Okay, sure." He opens the door and lets me in.

After slipping off my shoes, I take my time walking to the waterfall island in his kitchen. I can't help admiring how everything is so perfect in his apartment. The vase with the eucalyptus leaves placed so elegantly on the kitchen table, the figurines made out of pottery by the windowsills, the tissue box with the perfectly folded tissue peeking through the opening. None of these items, I realize, were chosen by him. They were chosen *for* him. Now I'm wondering if Jin Young even has any authority over what I'm about to ask him.

Before I can regret coming here, Jin Young asks, "What is it you wanted to talk about?" He's still standing by the door.

"About what we were talking about earlier in the messages . . . Do you really think I should wait until after the surgery to ask Halmoni?" I stare at my leggings, picking off imaginary lint.

When I peer up, he's looking at his reflection and adjusting his hair. "Uh, yeah. Sure," he says noncommittally.

I'm starting to regret coming here. It's obvious he's too preoccupied thinking about going out tonight to listen to me. I should've just continued this conversation online. It's too late now. I'm here. So I forge on.

"Only because it's a stressful time and not because of anything else, right?" I can't even bring myself to utter the words that would suggest they're using me for my liver.

"Yes, of course this is a stressful time for Halmoni," he says impatiently. "Is Mr. Kim still waiting for you

317

downstairs or do you need me to call him back for you?" Jin Young pulls out his suit jacket from the closet by the front door.

"He's downstairs." I slowly pick myself up, walk over to where he is, and by the time I reach him, I muster up the courage to ask. "Hey. Can I come with you?"

"Sorry, I don't think so. Not this time."

"I'll get ready in a flash, it won't take me too long. I promise." I don't know what I'm thinking, I don't even like going clubbing. But there's a small part of me that still hopes that if we spend more time together, we can be close, like a real family.

"No, it's not that. It's just that now that you might be a liver donor for Samchon, you can't have a drop of alcohol, or that eliminates you as a viable candidate. Even if you don't, if Halmoni or anyone else *thinks* you've had a drop of alcohol, it'll be both of us on the line. Besides, Bum Soo is going to be there, which may lead to trouble. It's better if you stay home tonight."

"Okay, but Bum Soo is your cousin, like me. I don't know why you don't just tell him who I am, or what to do, like you do with me."

His arm is partway through the jacket sleeve when he stops. After staring at me for a long moment, he slips on the rest of the jacket and says, "You don't know what you're talking about."

I sense irritation in his voice, but somehow, I can't stop myself from going on. "Then help me understand. You say I'm part of the family, but there's still a lot of stuff I don't know. Don't you think I have a right to know more?"

He shuts the door to the hallway closet so hard it makes a loud popping sound and I jump. "Look, there are just some things that are too complicated to explain. My dad is dead. Do you think whoever steps into his shoes is ever going to fill that void for Halmoni? Every day Bum Soo and his dad come to the store, Halmoni is reminded that her son isn't here. Bum Soo acts that the way he does because he gets treated like he's never good enough almost every day of his life, so I give him a pass, okay? Is that explanation good enough for you?"

I flinch at his biting tone. I only asked a simple question. Feeling the tears rising, I nod curtly, then walk past him. But he grabs my arm, stopping me from opening the door.

"Hey. I'm sorry. I didn't mean it to come out that way, but it's the truth. I didn't mean to hurt you."

"It's okay," I lie, looking down at my feet. I'm barely keeping it together.

"Just go home, Chloe. It's what Halmoni wants."

"Yeah, okay. You're right."

By the time I get to the guesthouse, I'm thankful it's pitch-black outside so Mr. Kim can't see I've been crying. I bow good night to him and go straight into the house. He doesn't leave right away, but I don't wait to see him off. I feel emotionally and physically tired and I need to lie down. As soon as I'm about to head upstairs to my room, I hear someone in the living room.

"Mrs. Na?" I call out.

"You're home?" Halmoni says, sitting on a sofa with the lights turned off.

Startled, I jump. "How did you—"

"Mrs. Na let me in."

"Oh," I say. Of course Mrs. Na let her in. That answers how Halmoni knows I was out late tonight.

Halmoni stands up and slowly makes her way to me. When she steps into the hallway light, her face becomes clearer. There's concern in her eyes. "When I heard you were out late, I began to worry."

It strikes me as odd. She never really cared where I went and who I saw before today. Regardless, I'm touched by her attentiveness. "Sorry you were worried. I was just at Jin Young's."

"Are you okay?" She cups my face with her hands, staring deep into my pupils.

Maybe it's because I'm insecure and emotional after my conversation with Jin Young; maybe it's the concerned lines that sweep across Halmoni's forehead right now; or maybe it's because I'm on my own for the first time and I'm feeling vulnerable, but I start to cry.

"Oh, Halmoni. Every day I'm at the doctor's office and I haven't really spent much time with anyone else. I guess I just feel all alone."

"Eun Young-ah." Hearing my Korean name throws me off at first, but the intensity of her gaze and tone makes my eyes meet hers. "Tell me one thing . . ."

There's this big dramatic pause—like this is *it*. This is the defining moment I've been waiting for. The one that will squelch my insecurities about my position in this family for good.

"Have you been drinking?"

*"What?"*

"You know you cannot have any alcohol, not even one drop. Otherwise, you will jeopardize everything we've been working toward."

Instead of the heart-to-heart I'd been hoping for, I spend the next ten minutes convincing Halmoni I haven't had a drop of alcohol. Instead of taking my word, she insists I breathe into her face. When she's satisfied with her analysis of my breath, she leaves.

Back in my room, I look around. Ornate furniture, crystal chandeliers, and clothes that I'm used to seeing in magazines and not hanging in my closet. And as picture-perfect as everything is, none of it feels real. The dream of meeting my family is wearing off and reality is taking over.

)(

In the morning, I'm barely awake coming down the stairs when I notice someone standing by the front door.

"Mr. Kim?" I startle. "I wasn't expecting you this early."

"Your halmoni decided early this morning that she wanted to see you."

"Oh, okay. Sure. Let me get ready."

I change in a flash and leave right away with Mr. Kim. In the car, I watch the familiar scenes on the streets. Toddlers playing in neighborhood parks, schoolkids in uniforms waiting for buses along with adults in suits and dresses. It's business as usual for everyone. Then suddenly, it becomes residential again. Quiet streets with one or two people walking to or from the main street.

"Mr. Kim, this isn't the way to the store."

"I am told to bring you to the Noh family residence."

"Oh. Is the construction finished?" I ask. Mr. Kim doesn't answer. Instead, he turns the corner and waits in front of a large metal gate. It's so tall no one would be able to see beyond it. A private security guard comes around from the booth, waves to Mr. Kim, who waves back, then opens the gate for us to enter.

Along the winding driveway there are security cameras set up in various places. Gardeners are pruning the lawn; tall, dense trees stick up even above the wall, as if the family wanted to ensure no one would be able to see into their property.

Finally, the car arrives at a stone driveway and Mr. Kim parks. The door to the house is made of metal, with an electronic keypad that Mr. Kim punches the code into. When we enter the house, it's not quite what I'd expected. It's vast, that's for sure, our footsteps echoing as we enter the foyer, but it's decorated very differently than the guesthouse I'm staying in. Like an old European villa, the furniture is overly ornate to the point of gaudy, with filigree and lattice-shaped designs embroidered on the fabrics of the sofas and chairs. The drapery along the windows hangs in sweeping U-shaped bunches, with tasseled ropes holding them open. Even though everything looks and feels expensive, nothing looks new. I wonder what kind of construction was done on this house. I don't see anything obvious.

"Good, you're here," Halmoni says, appearing from

the hallway. Despite being awake before the sun, she's dressed from head to toe in a pale blue pantsuit, with full makeup and coiffed hair.

"Come to my office." She motions me to follow her down a long hallway. At the end is a room with a desk that's shiny, black, and covered with an intricate mother-of-pearl design. As soon as I get in the room, I see we're not alone.

"Oh." I jump back, then bow. "Annyeonghaseyo." When I look the stranger in her eyes, something about her look triggers my memory. "Lady Cha?" I say, slow and drawn out.

Her eyes widen; she appears to be impressed by my recollection of her. She's wearing another cardigan set, this time in red and paired with a black skirt. She's just as conservative and unassuming as before, but now that I know what she is, the hair sticks up on my neck.

"You seemed nervous yesterday. I want to ease some of your apprehensions, so I thought maybe if you meet Lady Cha, she could help you to understand her prediction for you. It is the exact reason why she is an important part of our family. We have so many things to worry about. Family, the business, our reputation. Without Lady Cha, we would not be able to manage everything."

"Ohhh-kay." I shift my stance. If Halmoni wanted to ease my nerves, putting me face-to-face with Lady Cha is doing the exact opposite of that.

"Why don't you start by telling her what you are afraid of exactly." Halmoni motions for me to sit down next to Lady Cha. I look at the empty chair, but don't sit in it right away. It takes my brain a minute to convince my body to move. When it finally does, I sit down on the edge of the chair, as far away from Lady Cha as possible.

Lady Cha stares deep into me. Sweat forms in my armpits, knee-pits, elbow-pits—all the pits—as I think of what to say. After a minute, I clear my throat. "Even if I'm a match for Samchon, what if the procedure doesn't work?" I gulp. "What if . . . what if I die?" I whisper the last part.

Halmoni shifts in her seat. This is the first time she's hearing my fears out loud, too. After a thoughtful second, she translates for Lady Cha. Lady Cha nods, seeming to understand my fears. She asks Halmoni a question, and Halmoni responds. They go back and forth a few times, but she never translates any of it for me. After Lady Cha speaks for a long time, Halmoni's expression changes and she gasps. At first, it seems like bad news, but a second later, she smiles wide, almost beaming.

"What did she say?" I finally ask, looking back and forth from Lady Cha on my right to Halmoni sitting in front of me.

"She said that you're right to be worried; it's a complicated procedure. It won't be easy, especially the recovery. But rest assured, you will recover." She stops to smile at me, reassuringly. "Not only will you recover, but you will also be successful in your career, which we already know." She stops again, smiling even wider. The news of success brings a small smile to my lips, then quickly I snap myself out of it. I'm simultaneously amazed and disappointed with myself at how fast I fell under Lady Cha's spell.

"Halmoni, how does she know this just by looking at me?"

"She asked me questions about your relationship with your mother. I told her about when she barged into my office. How you don't see eye-to-eye about your future, how she lied to you."

I look down at my hands, not because what Halmoni is saying about my mom isn't true, but because it is. I'm still reeling with guilt over the way I left things with Mom.

"She puts the information she already knows about you, your time of birth, location, and your father."

"What about my father?" I ask, sitting at the edge of my seat.

"Not important," Halmoni's quick to say.

Funny, because that's all that's ever been important to me. The fuzzy, blurry image I had of my dad, the one that had become clearer by coming here, is once again fading to something unrecognizable. We talked about the curse and the meaning of his death, but we haven't really talked about *Dad*.

"The important thing is your future," Halmoni continues. "And how to make you not worry so much. You are doing a great thing, and like Lady Cha said, you will not only be saving your uncle's life, you will save yours as well. You will find success in your career, you will have many sons, she said. A big family and a big career, all because you are bringing an end to the curse with your liver."

"She said I'll have a big family?" I say in disbelief.

"Yes, she did." Halmoni is grinning so wide, as if these predictions are supposed to come true tomorrow.

Lady Cha nods approvingly, and together, they look at

me with gleeful expressions, as if I've won some sort of genetic lottery.

"See? I told you. Everything is going to be fine," Halmoni says.

When Lady Cha tells me all my dreams are going to come true, of course I want to believe her. Why is it, then, that I'm still not convinced?

# 23andme.com

**MESSAGES**

From: Chang, Chloe
Subject: Lady Cha
Friday, 8:03 AM

I met Lady Cha. Finally. She is a very compelling person and, at first, she said many things that made me want to believe her. But the longer I thought about it, instead of feeling better about the situation, I felt worse. Originally, I was worried I wouldn't be able to fulfill her prediction of ending the curse. Now, after meeting her, I'm worried that that's all I am to Halmoni: an end to a curse.

From: Noh, Jin Young
Subject: RE: Lady Cha
Friday, 8:49 AM

Halmoni has been the chairwoman of Sam Won
Group for almost twenty years now. This is the way
she's used to doing things. If she seems calculating,
it's only because she is good at her job. More than
anything, I hope you know I don't feel that way
about you. I know you are more than an end to the
curse to us. Although it may not always appear as
such, we are here for you.

# CHAPTER 28

Later in the afternoon, I'm at the hospital, sitting in the waiting room of the VIP ward. Now that she knows I passed the initial tests, Halmoni insists on coming with me to every appointment.

A nurse comes out to show us to the doctor's office.

"You go ahead." Halmoni motions for me to go on without her. "I need to speak to my son's doctor about his progress." She follows a different doctor to a room across the hallway. I watch as they walk in together. The doctor is tall and strikes me as familiar. Before I realize it, I'm following him into his office to get a better look when the nurse taps me on the shoulder.

"Your room, this way," she says politely.

"Oh, right."

I get shown into the doctor's office and sit in a chair directly facing him.

His eyes scan the image on his computer. "Your results show that you are a great match for the liver donation. Your liver is quite large." He holds out his hands to show me about a foot in length. "Your samchon's liver is about the same size. We run the tests and you are very healthy. A prime candidate to be a donor."

"Oh." I sit there, stunned. It's not like I didn't know what I was signing up for, but there was a part of me that didn't think it would ever happen. Not only is it happening, it's happening at lightning speed. It was only a few days ago my mom was warning me against this. Now I'm being told I'm a perfect match. There are so many thoughts running circles in my head right now.

"Aigo, you're stunned. We are, too. It was such a long process to find a solution to this problem."

"Long?" I ask, confused. We just found out a week ago, didn't we?

"The chairwoman was the only one who was a match for her son out of everyone in the family, but she is simply too old. Now here you are, so young and so perfect, it's like miracle."

"Miracle. Huh." An unsettling feeling begins growing in the pit of my stomach.

He goes on, saying how wonderful it is that the DNA match came at the most opportune time. I agree with him. The timing is almost too coincidental. Just as he's about to show me out of his office, I can't keep it in any longer.

"When did the family know that my samchon needed a liver transplant?"

He sits back down at his desk and checks the chart. He flips back a few pages. Then he flips back a few more pages. My heartbeat intensifies, anticipating the answer.

"It looks like we found out the news in April." He turns the page over to continue. "In May, Jin Young came back from the US and he and Soo Young take the test and no one was a match. In June . . ." He licks his finger, turns the page again. "No, May 15 is when we find out that Chairwoman Lee is the only match."

My heart sinks at the news. It takes thirty days to find out the results of your 23andMe test. Jin Young's results came in on June 15, exactly one month after they found out they had no other matches. The very night he found out his results, he contacted me. Coincidence? Maybe. But I don't know whether I can take it if our chance encounter wasn't by chance at all. So instead of asking a follow-up question, I thank the doctor for his time and leave.

"Eun Young-ah!" Halmoni is beaming at me as soon as I step out of the doctor's office.

I look around and when there's no one else but me, I realize she's calling me by the Korean name she picked out for me.

"I just heard the news. That you are a perfect match for Samchon!" She clasps her hands together, practically radiating.

"You did?"

"See? Lady Cha is right. She said everything would work out, but I still couldn't believe it when I heard the news. Let's go home and get ready."

"Get ready? For what?" My pulse quickens. Surely she doesn't expect the surgery to happen right now, does she?

"Dinner. The whole family will be there. Now let's go."

On our way out, I turn to Halmoni. "Who did you hear the news from? About me being a perfect liver match?" I ask out of curiosity.

"Dr. Seo. He is the best liver transplant doctor in Korea.

We made sure he was in charge of everything from the beginning."

"That's whose office you were in?"

She nods. "Why, is something the matter?" She adjusts her glasses as we're about to get into the car.

I try to put my finger on what it is about that doctor that troubles me, but I can't. So I shake my head and say, "No. I'm just having a déjà vu moment."

"Déjà what?" Halmoni asks.

"Never mind." I smile at her.

※

Right before dinner, there's a knock on my door. When I open it, Halmoni is standing there holding a box. She hands it to me and urges me to open it.

"I had the store wrap this up for you." I open the box and unwrap the tissue paper, which reveals a soft white silk cloth. When I pick it up, the fabric unravels into a pantsuit.

"It's the color of angel wings. Because that is what you are. An angel, sent from heaven. Your father must've sent you to us."

Emotions slow me down as I try to put the pants on, one leg at a time. What would my dad think of me right now? Would he be proud of me for stepping in when his family needed me the most? Would he be ashamed of the way I turned my back on my mom? I'm surrounded by family but feel so much more alone than I ever have in my entire life.

I somehow manage to get changed and even put makeup on. Mostly to cover up the bags under my eyes, but also to avoid any comments about my health and how I need to take better care of myself now that I'm a walking lifeline.

Standing in the foyer, Halmoni beams at me as I walk down the stairs. She's dressed in a gold St. John woven dress with a jacket and giant pearl earrings and necklace set, and clutching a Prada handbag—the epitome of wealth and fashion.

"You look perfect." She eyes me up and down. "Like a Noh." As we walk through the garden of the guesthouse, she turns and says, "We're going to the Seoul Palace Hotel restaurant. They have a top-rated American restaurant and a nice private room. Soo Young and Jin Young will be there with their mother, who will be coming back from temple to see you."

"When do you think I'll be able to meet Samchon?"

She jerks her head back. "No, no, no. He's resting."

"Shouldn't I at least meet him? After everything we're going through together?"

"You will, one day. We don't want to bother him now."

"Okay," I say calmly, but inside I'm screaming. Why is it such a bother to meet the person who's going to be saving your life? Not only that, I'm not a complete stranger; I'm his blood relative. It would be more acceptable to me if I didn't know precisely what stage of illness he's at with his liver failure, but I know he found out the news three months ago. He should be well enough to meet me.

"Besides, Lady Cha says meeting him after will be better for his health."

333

"You believe that?" I can't help saying as we get into the back seat of the car. Lady Cha dictating the family is getting too much for me to keep quiet about anymore.

Halmoni doesn't answer me right away, but as soon as Mr. Kim starts driving, she says in a low voice, "She was right about you." She glances sidelong at me. "I know what you did for Jin Young, that night of the car accident."

"You do? How did you—?"

"I sacrificed my life building this business and I'm not about to throw that away for some reckless adolescent behavior. Jin Young is young and stupid; he makes many mistakes. It's not his fault. He doesn't have a father to show him the way, so I must watch over him. Soo Young, too. She is too silly, too boy crazy for her own good. After all, Jin Young will one day be head of Sam Won Group and Soo Young will oversee Sam Won Beauty. So you see, everyone in the family is not just in the business. They *are* my business."

I understand how the business and the family are intertwined and the value of their importance to Halmoni. That's not what bothers me. Halmoni mentioned Jin Young and Soo Young don't have a father, but neither do I. Surely she cares about me as much as she cares about them?

We pull into the hotel and the attendants fawn over Halmoni just like they do at any other restaurant, building, or hospital. They treat her like she's a god. I carefully watch her through the corner of my eye. She's so used to the attention, she barely acknowledges the attendants swarming around her, opening doors, bowing, and making way for her. When we get to the top-floor restaurant, much of the hotel staff shows us to the private room.

The room has a long rectangular table with Halmoni at the head, Soo Young and her mom on one side, and Jin Young on the other. Jin Young motions for me to sit in the chair next to him.

"Hey," he says with a smile. "I heard the good news."

"Yeah," I say with a little less enthusiasm.

Halmoni clinks her champagne glass. "We are here because of Eun Young. *Eun* means *grace* and she is definitely that, bringing us just what we need during our time of desperation. Let's drink to Noh Eun Young." She raises her glass.

Everyone raises their glass of champagne without hesitation, even Soo Young's mom. She even gives me a slight smile before she takes a sip, which is the warmest reception I've received from her since I've met her. I raise my own glass and take a sip cautiously. It's water. Of course.

Without taking our order, the waiters bring in a tray of food and immediately begin serving us. An appetizer salad to start, except mine looks different than everyone else's. I look over at Jin Young, who is taking in a forkful of lettuce slathered in some creamy dressing, then look back down at my own salad with a light sheen of oil and vinegar. Without asking, I know what this is about. My liver.

"When's the operation?" Jin Young asks me.

"Next week," Halmoni says.

We both look over at her. "I didn't know that," I blurt out.

"I arranged it with the doctor today," Halmoni says coolly.

"Ohh-kay." I'm trying not to come off as entitled, but

shouldn't I be informed about when the operation is happening? Since it's my liver we're talking about.

I somehow manage to eat the entire salad, despite it tasting like lawn. Then the main dish arrives, and I see the others get served chicken braised in a brown butter sauce with a heaping spoonful of cheesy polenta and grilled vegetables. My dish is a plain grilled chicken breast with no sauce and a stack of raw carrot sticks.

What I wouldn't give for a bowl of Shin Ramyun right now. I miss coughing up the spicy soup base with Hazel and watching K-dramas on her laptop. I miss showing Seb my latest creations and geeking out over the latest apps with him. I even miss waiting for my mom to come home from a late-night shift at the hospital. Suddenly, it dawns on me that what I'm really craving right now isn't a bowl of instant noodles. It's being around the people who love me most.

I put a piece of the chicken in my mouth and chew so forcefully, my jaw is sore, and the dryness of the meat scrapes my throat on its way down. I cough, almost choking.

"Slow down, Eun Young-ah." Halmoni waves a concerned hand at me. "It would be a shame if you choked now. My son is depending on your liver."

I'm able to swallow the lump of meat with some effort, but it sits like a brick in my stomach. Did she just say what I think she said?

"Tomorrow morning, Mrs. Na can help you pack for the hospital. She can get you the things you need, silk pajamas, neck pillows, magazines—anything you want while you convalesce."

"That's not necessary, I can get those things by myself."

"Nonsense. You are our guest. That's what Mrs. Na is there for," Halmoni says, raising her glass up at me.

Watching them eating their high-fat, cholesterol-filled food, talking at me like I'm not even there, makes me snap.

"But I'm not your guest, am I?" I say. All of a sudden, the movement in the room comes to a screeching halt. Jin Young and Soo Young stare cautiously at Halmoni. Soo Young's mom narrows her eyes at me.

"Now that I'm going through with the surgery, I'll be here for a while. Shouldn't I move out of the guesthouse and into the main house with everyone else?"

"The main house is—" Soo Young's mom begins to say.

"Not under construction. I saw it for myself yesterday when I met with Lady Cha."

Stunned, Soo Young's mom tries to respond before she gives up and shuts her mouth for good.

"You are right. You're not a guest anymore." Halmoni is cool and calm, smiling so wide there's a glare off her gold-capped molar. "However, once you are recovered, you will be going to New York for fashion school, remember?" She pauses, raising an eyebrow up at me. "We shouldn't move you too much. It would only be a nuisance."

Why am I getting the feeling that *I'm* the nuisance? It needles me until I say what's been on my mind the entire evening. The thing that could satisfy my insecurities once and for all. "I was thinking about the family registry."

Jin Young's hand is suspended in midair, holding a spoon. Soo Young has a mouthful of ice cream but isn't swallowing. Their mom's mouth hangs open and Halmoni is a statue.

I urge myself to continue despite their apparent touchiness on the subject. I've already brought up the topic. There's no turning back now.

"A friend here told me that it's a very simple process. I just need to provide my birth certificate and DNA test, which I already have. The only thing I need is someone in the family to come with me to the city registry office." Out of the corner of my eye, I glance at Jin Young to the right of me. He slowly drops his spoon and stares into his lap, avoiding eye contact at all costs.

"Why do you want this, suddenly?" Soo Young's mom asks, her eyes narrowed into slits. For once, Halmoni doesn't admonish her. Instead, she stares at me for an answer along with the rest of them.

"I just thought, now with the surgery scheduled, that we could make it official. I'm family, all but on paper." This way, it'll prove to my mom, *to me*, that I'm a part of this family just as much as they are. Besides, it's just a piece of paper. It shouldn't be a big deal to them.

Halmoni finally clears her throat. "People know my son died, but they don't know he had any children. If they find out about you, they will think you are a child he had out of wedlock. They'll make it a public spectacle, with questions surrounding why it was a secret marriage. It will be a big mess. Better to do this quietly."

"There was nothing improper about it and you can't just wipe people out of your lives just because they marry people you don't approve of." In this moment, I'm thinking not only about myself, but my dad. Because she did erase him, didn't she? And that's not how families are supposed to work.

Halmoni's face hardens. "People like us, we have to be careful about the way we lead our lives. We are chaebol, high society. There's a public side and a private one. *This* is private."

"I'm not trying to cause trouble. I just want to make things right. I have a right to be on the registry, just like any of you." I can't help myself from pressing on. She may not know she's doing it, but Halmoni is prioritizing their lives over mine.

"Chloe." Halmoni's tone shifts as she changes from calling me by my Korean name back to my English name. "Your mom would be thrust into the spotlight. They will make her a circus act in this show. Surely you wouldn't want that for her. Would you?"

My face radiates with heat. Using my mom as an emotional plea is a low blow.

"The tabloids live for this kind of information. We don't need this kind of negative publicity, not now or ever." Halmoni picks up her spoon, signaling she's done with the conversation. But I'm not. I'm nowhere near done.

"Couldn't you just pay the tabloids to keep them silent?" I press on.

There's a collective gasp from Soo Young and her mom. Even Jin Young's eyes bulge from their sockets.

"Isn't that what you did with Jin Young and Soo Young's dad? I know he didn't die of a heart attack. How is this different?"

Soo Young's mom says something to Halmoni in Korean. Halmoni stares holes at me.

"My friend said it was common here—"

"The same friend that told you about the registry?" Soo Young's mom sneers.

"The one who came over to the guesthouse?" Soo Young says.

Jin Young says nothing but shifts uncomfortably in his seat.

"What?" I draw back my head. They've been spying on me?

"Tell me," Halmoni says instead of answering, "are you in a relationship with this friend? Dan Miso?" She raises an eyebrow at me.

A protective rage bubbles up in me, hearing them drag Miso into this family affair, and my hands clench into fists. "You have no right—" My tirade gets cut off before I start.

"I knew it!" Soo Young points an accusing finger at me. "It was always about the money."

"What? No! How can you say that about me?" This is literally the first time I have brought up money with them. Tuition, the clothes, everything was offered to me by Halmoni. I never once made any demands before today.

I look to Jin Young with pleading eyes. He knows me better than anyone at this table. Maybe he'll stick up for me like he did with Bum Soo. He knows I'm not about the money. He *has* to know. But no matter how much I will him to speak up, he just sits there with his head bowed down, as if he wishes he could be anywhere else but here.

"Jin Young oppa said she couldn't even go to FIT without the money from our family." Soo Young points an accusing finger at me.

My jaw drops open, still facing Jin Young. How could

he tell them that? I opened myself to him; I've even taken the blame for him crashing his car and *this* is how he repays me?

Jin Young has the audacity to stare back at me, unwaveringly, and shrug. "What? It's true, isn't it?"

My face radiates with heat. He knew I didn't mean it like that, he had to have known.

"If you knew your mother couldn't pay for you to attend FIT, how come you didn't tell the school your answer right away? I don't think it's a coincidence you take this DNA test right before you have to tell them your answer." Soo Young's mom smirks at me.

"I'm not the one who reached out, it was Jin Young—"

"See, Omonim. I always told you she is like her mother. Always sneaky, trying to take something from you. If you're not careful, she will try to take your fortune away from you, just like her mother tried to," Soo Young's mom says to Halmoni. "Maybe it is her mother who sends her here today, to try to finish the job she couldn't do all those years ago."

It destroys me to know they've been talking about me behind my back. They think I'm the one with ulterior motives? I'm the one keeping their secrets, giving up my liver, jeopardizing my health for them. I'm the one who's giving up *everything* to be a part of this family.

"It was never about the money. Never," I repeat over and over, but no one seems to be listening. The tears are streaming down my face now.

"Then how come you want to be added to the registry so badly? It's obvious you're here because you feel entitled to the lion's share of the inheritance." Soo Young raises her eyebrows up at me.

"What?! I swear, I didn't even know about that! The only type of inheritance I was interested in is the inherited genes I got from my father, you have to believe me!" I knew this wasn't going to be an easy conversation, but I never imagined this. My head is spinning as accusations are being hurled at me, one after another. *This can't be happening*, I think over and over to myself. *This can't be happening to me.*

"Enough!" Halmoni slams a hand down on the table, finally putting an end to the clamor. An eerie silence descends in the room so suddenly, my ears are ringing.

"Lady Cha said you would be good luck." Halmoni pauses, then angles her head, staring at me through the corners of her eyes. "But only if you follow obediently. There is no place for someone who wants only to cause disruption. We are accustomed to a certain way of living. You are an outsider to our ways. Why do you think you can dictate how we do things?"

Even if I'd always known it, hearing that I'm an outsider in this family breaks me and I am sobbing silently as the four of them bore their eyes into me.

"This is what we are going to do." Halmoni zeroes in on me. "We will go ahead with the surgery. I will pay for your tuition at FIT. You will have a job, like I promised, in our fashion design department at Sam Won Department Store. However, you will not be added to the registry. Jin Young will still be the heir of Sam Won Group and your mother will never see any money you receive from us. In fact, you must cut your ties with her, the way she did to us all these years. That is my final word. You will have money, protection, security—more than you ever had before in your old life with your mom." Halmoni says all this as if it's a good deal and I should take it.

Ever since I got here, I've given myself up to these people in pieces. Hiding Soo Young's secret, covering for Jin Young, potentially giving up my liver for Samchon. It's only now I realize that nothing I do will ever be good enough.

Mom was right. They'll *never* accept me as one of them.

A quiet sob takes over my body at this new revelation, while everyone stares at me, cold and stoic.

"Why don't you sleep on it," Halmoni eventually says. As if she's repulsed by the show of emotions. "All of these tears are not good for your health. I'll have Mr. Kim take you home. You can get some rest and we'll talk tomorrow when you're thinking more clearly."

Before I can muster up enough energy to say another word, Halmoni pushes a button on the table and instantly the doors to our private room fly open. Next thing I know, I'm being escorted out to Mr. Kim, who is waiting to take me home.

# CHAPTER 29

I follow the staff member robotically out of the restaurant and to the car out in front. When Mr. Kim starts driving, I mindlessly stare out the window as we weave in and out of traffic. The streetlights streak my vision and everything is a blur—the streets, the people, the entire night.

The light ahead of us turns red and the car slows to a stop. The images become clear outside in the busy intersection. It's Saturday night and the streets are filled with young people. I see a group of teenagers walking down the street. There's a guy with dyed blond hair with two girls on each side of him. He has his arms around both of them, and one of the girls has her hand around his waist. Suddenly they burst into laughter about something and they almost keel over. The sight is so enviable, I'm crying again. I should be hanging out with my friends, living each moment together before they head off to college. I should be laughing about inside jokes and making memories, not being taken back to an empty house.

Was any of this trip about me? Or was it just about my liver? Halmoni said Dr. Seo had been hired by them months ago, but I only arrived last—

Then it hits me.

I *have* met Dr. Seo before.

Not as *Dr. Seo*, Samchon's doctor. But as *Mr. Seo*, the personal trainer.

I couldn't place it before, but it's starting to make sense to me. Why he seemed so familiar, why he hooked up the monitors to me the day we met. He wasn't *training* me. He was *assessing* me.

And the nurse. *Of course.* The one who seemed to recognize me during my initial testing. She was the aesthetician who drew my blood for the facial. No wonder my results came back so quickly. By the time I went to the hospital for the initial tests, *they already knew.*

Suddenly I can't breathe. I begin gasping for air.

"Are you okay?" Mr. Kim asks.

"No. I'm. Not." I struggle to get words out.

"Bend your body down and breathe in and out slowly," he instructs me while his eyes dart nervously in the rearview mirror.

I do what he says and after a minute I feel marginally better. At least I'm not hyperventilating anymore.

"Better?" he asks.

I barely nod, still catching my breath.

"I am so sorry I haven't been there for you more, Chloe. I've been under strict instruction not to speak to you."

"Is that so?" I respond dryly. Mr. Kim is the only one I can talk to, but Halmoni has control over him, too.

He nods. "But I might as well tell you, since my position with the family will be changing soon. After Jin Young goes back to school in the fall, I'll be released from my role as his assistant. Your halmoni made it clear to me that I'll have a different set of responsibilities, ones that would allow for us to have a more personal relationship." His eyes pinch in the corners, revealing that he's smiling.

I wish I could celebrate with him, but Mr. Kim doesn't know that nothing could distract me from learning that my own family has been deceiving me since before I even knew about them.

In my silence, Mr. Kim's eyes stay focused on me through the rearview mirror. "Is everything okay?" His eyes become increasingly concerned.

"No. It's not," I answer plainly.

"What happened tonight?" he asks hesitantly.

"I did something I shouldn't have. I asked to be put on the family registry."

Mr. Kim sighs, shaking his head. As if he knew just how badly that conversation would go.

"I don't regret saying what I said, but it was a mistake to bring it up tonight in front of everybody. I should have waited to speak with Halmoni alone." I bury my hands in my face.

"Right," Mr. Kim says in a less than sympathetic tone. "I told you, you should have waited until after surgery. Your halmoni is under a lot of stress right now."

"I know, but you should've heard the way they—" I start to defend myself, then stop when something clicks. Mr. Kim has been my one constant in my experience with the Nohs. He's nice and kind and really cares about me. The way he always asks about my day, always makes sure I understand what the family really means. Things with Mr. Kim are so familiar, it's like I've known him for much longer than the daily car rides these past few weeks. Now I know why it feels familiar. It's because we've been talking for much longer than I realized.

"It was you, wasn't it?" I only told Jin Young I wanted to ask Halmoni to be added to the registry. Not anyone else.

Mr. Kim's eyes dart back to the road. He doesn't respond, but it doesn't matter. I already have my answer.

"The messages on 23andMe. They were all from you, weren't they?" My heart shatters into a pile of shards along with any notion that I truly belong here. I wipe away the tears only for them to be replaced with fresh ones.

"It's not how it looks," Mr. Kim manages to say.

"You mean, you didn't pretend to be Jin Young for the past few weeks, luring me to Korea to be an organ donor?" It sounds more ridiculous saying it out loud.

Mr. Kim is back to being silent while my world is crumbling right before me. No explanation, no apology. Instead, his hands grip the steering wheel tightly; he's probably trying to figure out a way out of this betrayal. Job or not, there's no explanation that could warrant what he did. Mr. Kim was paid to find me and make the connection so the family could get what they want. The kindness and closeness I felt with the family wasn't genuine. It was manufactured by a stranger, orchestrated by the family to gain my trust. It is the ultimate deception. I can see how far the Nohs will go to get what they want.

If I stay here, not only will I never be a part of the Noh family, I'd be like Bum Soo—close enough to be useful, but never fully accepted in the family. I would be like that unlucky number on their twelve-story building that

347

they pretend doesn't exist just because they gave it a new name. They can't just give me a new name, cut my mom out of my life, and expect me to be who they want me to be. That's not how family works. Mom was right all along. If I stay here, my life will never be my own.

Suddenly it's as if the spell is lifted and I've come to my senses.

What am I doing here?

I can just leave any time I want to.

I *chose* to stay here when I thought I was a part of the family.

Now that I know I'll never be a part of this family, I can choose to leave.

The light on the other side of the intersection turns yellow. If I want to leave, this is my only chance.

So I take it.

# CHAPTER 30

I hop out of the car, slamming the door behind me. The cars behind **Mr. Kim** honk furiously as he attempts to roll down the windows. He calls out for me to come back, but his voice, along with his message, get drowned out by the white noise of the night. Mr. Kim has no choice but to drive on. I watch the car move to the right lane and turn the corner.

I waste no time **and start running down the alley**, weaving through couples holding hands and groups of people huddled in clusters. Even though the air feels heavier than it's been since I got here, thick with humidity, I feel lighter than I have these past few days.

That is, until I get to the end **of a dark** and isolated alley. There are a couple of big guys pacing around the back entrance of a building and I realize I'm alone in a foreign country. Where am I supposed to go now?

Sitting on the stoop of a closed storefront, I pull out my phone to call my mom. It goes straight to voice mail. She's probably working. In fact, she's probably at the hospital on **a double shift**, trying to pay for the airfare from when she visited me. The guilt mixed in with the homesickness becomes too much for me and the tears pour out uncontrollably as I stare at my phone.

A message alert pops up in KakaoTalk, startling me. I hesitate to click on it. It's probably Halmoni checking up on me, worried that I'm putting her son's life in jeopardy. Against my better judgment, I click on the app and a series of messages and photos floods my inbox. They're not from Halmoni, or anyone else in the Noh family. They're from Hazel and Seb.

Stranded with nowhere to go, I scroll through the photos of them in front of iconic landmarks—London Bridge, Cinque Terre, the Parthenon. When I look closer at the photos, I notice that beside them is a picture of my head cut out, as if they brought me along with them. Every caption, every message, ends with: "Wish you were here." In the last photo, Seb is holding an umbrella for Hazel in front of the Eiffel Tower and Hazel has her arms wrapped around him. A smile somehow finds its way to my lips. They found their way back to each other. They even managed to bring me with them.

Then it occurs to me.

I have a family.

And I need to find my way back to them.

Adrenaline courses through my veins, urging me to run. When I get to the next block, I catch sight of Mr. Kim and fall back and lean against the wall of a building. With my head peeking down the alley, I see Mr. Kim racing down the street, peering into the buildings while periodically checking his phone. How did he find me in this busy neighborhood? I pull out my phone to search Maps, when it hits me.

My phone. It must have a tracking device.

Immediately, I toss the phone in the trash bin at the corner and run in the opposite direction of him, hopeful that'll throw him off my trail. I'm running hard, weaving in and out of people, crossing the intersections, and narrowly missing cars. The only thing I care about right now is getting home. It isn't until I get to the enormous intersection that I realize I'm completely lost. Mr. Kim is the one who drove me around. Without him or my phone, I have no idea where I'm going.

Droplets begin to fall on my head. Slowly at first, then it quickly turns into a downpour. Of course, when I'm stranded and alone, rain finally comes.

It's strange not having my mom with me at a time like this. She may miss a lot of moments in my life, but she's always there for the big ones. And this is huge. What am I supposed to do now? Before I know it, I'm crying again.

I stand there at the crosswalk, sobbing, while the light changes and people bump into me. I don't even care that the rain is coming down hard now, pelting me in the head. I'm already soaked through. At this point, it's hard to tell what're raindrops and what're tears. I know I should go, have my meltdown in a private corner somewhere, but I can't seem to move.

Suddenly the rain stops, and I look up. Someone's shielding me with an umbrella. When I look over, I almost jump out of my skin.

# CHAPTER 31

"Mom!" I leap into her arms. "What are you doing here?! How did you find me? I thought you left."

"You didn't think I'd really leave you here by yourself, did you?" She dabs me with a handkerchief, tears streaming down her own face. "I've been following you from a distance. I just couldn't leave you, not without knowing you'd be safe."

I take her in—the baggy black clothes, the black baseball hat. "You're my stalker?"

"What?" she asks, confused.

I can't explain to Mom that her version of incognito is the spitting image of a K-drama stalker, because I immediately start bawling from the overwhelming swell of emotions. I'm sad and happy and remorseful at once. "Oh, Mom. I'm so sorry," I say, muffled, my face buried in her shoulder. The sweet familiar scent of her skin soothes me with every inhale. Mom always shows up when it counts. I can't believe I ever doubted her.

"Chloe-yah." She hugs me tight, rocking me back and forth. "I'm sorry, too."

We stand there for a while, sobbing. People are staring, but we don't care. I feel safe and loved and I know

I'm going to be okay now that my mom is here.

She hails a cab and tells the taxi to take us to her motel. It's a run-down establishment with blinking lights and a single twin-sized bed. As soon as the door closes behind us, Mom starts apologizing.

"I'm sorry about this place, but I just didn't know how long I was going to be here, and it was all I could—"

"Mom. It's perfect." I stop her and hug her tightly. "Oh, Mom. I'm so sorry for not listening to you." I cry into her shoulder.

"It's okay," she whispers over and over in my ear, rocking me from side to side.

After a while, I look up at her and smile through my tears. "I'm so glad you're here."

"Me too."

Then suddenly, I pull away from her. "What about work? What did you tell them?"

"I told them someone very important needs me." She tucks a strand of hair behind my ear. "Also, that I haven't taken a vacation in over ten years, which is roughly one year of vacation days that I'm owed. So . . ." We laugh. Then Mom gets sad again. "If you want to go to fashion school, I can figure something out. I can get a loan—two loans—"

"No, Mom," I cut her off. "I don't want you to do that."

She frowns. "Does that mean you've given up on fashion design?"

"I don't know," I say honestly. "I realized something, though. The Nohs, they depended so much on Lady Cha to tell them what the future would look like and that didn't make things any easier for them. I know now that I don't need to have a crystal ball to know if I'll be happy." I grab Mom's hand and squeeze it tightly.

She smiles back at me, her eyes scrunching together like she's trying to hold back tears. "You make me so proud to be your mom. I love you so much." She squeezes my hand back. "Which is why I'm going to insist we come up with a plan to get you to FIT—"

"But—"

"No buts. I'm not going to let you give up on your dreams, just because of our—my—situation." She winces.

"Oh, Mom. I said some hateful things. I wish I could take it back, every last word. I was just so desperate for family, I didn't realize I had it all along."

"I realized something on this trip, too. I spent so much of my time at the hospital so that we could have a better life. Now I'm not sure it was entirely worth it." She grimaces. "So here's what we're going to do when we get back home. We're going to come up with a plan, together, to go to the FIT. Then we're going to watch more K-dramas together."

My eyes light up. "Really?"

She nods. "Your father, he really did love K-dramas. I didn't realize how much like your father you are until now."

"I don't know, Mom. I have a lot of you in me, too," I say.

She hugs me, and her chest heaves as she silently cries.

X

We have an extra day in Seoul since our return flight isn't until the following day. Mom surprises me by taking me to the N Seoul Tower.

"I've seen this in so many K-dramas, I can't believe I'm actually standing here." I walk around Namsan Park at the base of the tall tower with my mouth hanging open.

Mom chuckles, staring at me. "I haven't been here for so many years, it's like being here for the first time, too." She buys two tickets for the observation deck and we take the elevator up to the top. As soon as the elevator doors open, I gasp. Three-sixty-degree, panoramic views of the entire city.

"Whoa," I whisper, rushing over to the nearest window. Clusters of buildings and dark green trees go for miles and miles. Mom joins me and we stare in silence at the beautiful landscape. When I turn to Mom, her lips are curved downward.

"What is it?" I ask her.

"My first time back in over eighteen years and not much has changed." The far-off look in her eyes tells me she's not talking about the scenery.

"Mom, I need to show you something." I pull out the Polaroid that now has a permanent crease in the corner. It's time we were honest with each other.

Her brows knit. "How did you—"

"I found it in your closet the day I got the first 23andMe message." She takes the photo from me and tears instantly well in her eyes. "What happened between you and Dad?" Up until yesterday, I wasn't sure I could believe anything she told me about him. But after everything we've been through, I know she's the only one who can answer this question for me.

"You may know this already, but your father and I met while I was working at the department store."

"Was it love at first sight?" I can't help myself from asking.

She nods. "For him." We both laugh. Once the laughing subsides, she adds in a quiet voice, "For me, too." It sends a sharp pain to my chest.

"But his family didn't approve?"

She shakes her head. "They warned him I was after his money and forbid him to marry me."

"Is that why you left Korea?"

"That's more complicated." Her posture tenses, but she remains unguarded. "Before I met him, he had struggled to fit in with his own family."

"He did?" My heart twists into a knot. "Even Dad felt that way?"

She nods. "He wanted to study fashion design. Your halmoni was adamantly against it. She was grooming him to take over the company, but he had no interest. It was the source of many, many arguments. In fact, by the time he met me, he was already planning on cutting ties with the family and the business."

"You mean, you didn't convince him to leave?"

"Of course not. I would never ask someone to do that for me." She sniffs, handing me back the photo. "That day, in the photo, your father applied to be disinherited by his family. It would mean he would renounce his claim to any family inheritance he was entitled to."

"He did that for you?" I whisper.

"I begged him not to, thinking one day he'd regret it. He did it anyway, thinking that by renouncing his claim to the inheritance, his family would accept me. They did not. It wasn't enough for your halmoni. She was convinced I had ulterior motives. Still, he told me he had no regrets. That he never had so little in his life, but that he had never been so happy either. I'll never forget that day," she recalls, staring fondly at the photo. "We were so, *so* happy." Tears stream steadily down her cheeks.

"Oh," I say. At least there's some comfort knowing that Halmoni wasn't capable of just cutting people out of the family. It seemed too evil, too unbelievable, even for her.

"You have to believe me, I didn't want their money. I only wanted to be happy with your father," she pleads with me, just the way I pleaded with the Nohs last night.

"You don't have to convince me. I believe you. I don't want their money now, just like you didn't want their money then."

Mom's face crumples. "My Chloe-yah. I can't imagine what it was like for you. You posed a much bigger threat than I ever did."

"Me?" I put a hand up to my chest. "How?"

She dabs her eyes. "You're the eldest Noh grandchild. You're the heir."

"*What?*" My mouth hangs open in shock. "Isn't Jin Young the eldest? He's a grade older than me. *He's* the heir."

"For Koreans, when they are born, they are already one year old. It may seem like he's older than you, but if

357

you adjust your age to match the Korean custom, you are the eldest. Which means, if they put you on the family registry, then it will change everything. For Jin Young, for Sam Won Group. For you."

"This whole time, they were worried . . . about that?"

Her forehead divots in the middle. "Oh, Chloe-yah. I'm so sorry for keeping them from you, for the disappointment I've caused you."

Tears begin flooding my own eyes thinking about how much I contributed to my mom's sadness. "Mom, you could never be a disappointment. In fact, you're the best family anyone could ask for. I just wish I knew what I had in you without having to go through all this heartache and drama. I regret ever coming here."

"I don't," she says, surprising me. "When your dad died, we were so young and foolishly in love. We didn't want you to live under the family's restraints like he had. After your father died, I held on so tightly to his beliefs, keeping them from you, but I didn't realize then that I was keeping them a secret from you. That wasn't part of the deal." She sighs, sitting down on the nearby bench, bringing me with her. "I wasn't honest with you, and you had every right to be upset with me."

"I'm not upset with you. I know you were doing what you thought was best for me. I just wanted a connection to Dad so badly, I didn't care what got in my way, including you." Fresh tears stream down my cheeks, thinking about the mean things I said to her.

"Oh, Chloe." She sighs. "You are more your father's daughter than you know."

"Really?" A single tear escapes and slides down my cheek.

She nods, wiping her cheeks and nose with the back of her hand. "Twenty years ago, your dad was in the same position as you. Your father had to choose between a prominent position at the head of the Noh family or starting over in a new country with nothing but me. I couldn't offer him any of the luxuries of life he was used to, but he didn't want to be controlled by his family forever. He knew that with me, we could start a life together that would be ours. Today, when you were faced with a similar decision, you made the same choice. Just like your father."

I wipe my eyes with my palms. For the first time in my life, I feel a closeness to my mom *and* dad. There's so much I want to say to my mom, about feeling sorry, about loving her unconditionally . . . but the emotions are so overwhelming, and for a while, we sit there in silence.

Then, suddenly, she says, "I have an idea." She grabs me by the hand and leads me to the elevator. A few minutes later, we're on the second-floor terrace of the N Seoul Tower.

"Hold out your hand," she tells me.

When I do, she places something on it. It's cold and heavy. When I recognize it as a padlock, I know instantly what it's for.

The padlocks of love are a phenomenon spanning the globe and the N Seoul Tower is one of the locations. People from around the world come here to write messages of love on padlocks and lock them to the railing around the terrace. They're featured in so many K-dramas, I can't believe it didn't click until now. Though, to be fair, my mind has been preoccupied these days with a Korean drama of my own.

"The locks of love weren't here when I was last in Korea, and I thought of doing one for your father. Now that I'm here with you, I think we should do one together. As a family."

I smile through the tears. "I love that idea."

Mom hands me a Sharpie and I write my message on one side: *To the father I never knew, but always loved. You will forever be stitched in my heart. Saranghae.*

Mom writes her own message to Dad on the other side in Korean. When we finish, we find a spot to lock our padlock on the railing. Truthfully, we don't need the padlock to know our love will last forever, but it's befitting to end our trip on a dramatic note.

The next day, we're on the plane to go back home. Getting last-minute international plane tickets, as you might imagine, isn't exactly cheap. As a result, we're sitting in the two middle seats of the middle of the last row of the plane. After wedging my way past the large gentleman in the aisle seat, who so unhelpfully did not get up from his seat to let us in, I attempt to recline the chair, which hardly moves.

"Sorry, the seats only partially recline. They were the only ones I could get." Mom looks as if she's going to tear up.

"It's fine, Mom. I don't mind."

"Are you sure you're not going to regret not getting your things from their house? All those fancy clothes? It'll

360

probably be a while before you ever get anything nice like that again."

"None of those things were mine. Besides, I have everything I need right here." I put my hand on hers. She smiles and blinks back tears.

"Mom, I am worried about one thing."

"What's that?"

"I feel bad about Samchon. Family or not, I could have saved his life."

"He's not going to die," Mom says with a level of certainty that takes me by surprise.

"How do you know that?"

"People like the Nohs, they won't accept defeat like that. Not if they can help it."

"But the law—"

"Money. That's how they solve everything. Don't you know? They'll find a way; they always do."

A week ago, I would've said she was wrong. Now, after everything I've experienced, everything I've witnessed, I know she's right. Money is the way they solve their problems, not love.

# 23andme.com

**MESSAGES**

From: Noh, Jin Young
Subject: Apologies
Sunday, 5:29 PM

> Dear Chloe. I am so sorry for hurting you. I accepted this job knowing I would have to do anything that the Noh family asked of me. As time went on, I started to have feelings for you. I'm sure you felt it, too. If I could have done anything differently, believe me, I would have. But your halmoni is very powerful and leaving this job could ruin any chances my family has to get out of debt. I wish you didn't find out this way, but I hope you can see that I had no choice in the matter. I know I don't have any right to ask, but is there any way we can start over now that you know everything?
> —Bong Suk

From: Chang, Chloe

Subject: RE: Apologies

Sunday, 5:55 PM

Bong Suk—You definitely had a choice. You chose the job over doing what's right. Now you have to live with your choice. Goodbye.

*Dear Halmoni,*

*By the time you receive my letter, I'll have left Seoul. You mentioned my mother ran away almost twenty years ago, taking your son, my father, with her. I didn't want to give you the same impression, so I am writing you a letter to explain my sudden departure.*

*All I wanted—all I ever wanted—was to know more about my dad and to be closer to everyone, like a real family. If you had just asked me to be a liver donor, this outcome could have been very different. It's the deception that hurt me the most.*

*As for Samchon, I offer myself to be a donor to him. Not because I am the only match. Not because of a curse. But because I am family. My only condition is to be treated as such. I realize there is no quantitative measure to define acceptance in one's family. It will have to be an agreement entirely based on trust. I will have to trust that you will accept me as a member of the family, and you will have to trust that I have no interest in gaining control over Sam Won Group. Those are my conditions for being a donor.*

364

*So you see, I have not run away. I am returning home. This is where I belong. Should you want a relationship with me, a real one, I will always remain open to it. After all, you are my paternal grandmother, bound by blood, and no amount of money can change that.*

*Your granddaughter,*

*Chloe*

# CHAPTER 32

I deleted the 23andMe app promptly after I sent the message to Bong Suk, and I send the letter as soon as we get home. For weeks I had no response from Halmoni, or anyone else in Korea. Then one day, a month and a half later, a large box arrives on the front step of our apartment. I open it up carefully, unsure of what I'll find. As soon as I see the familiar zebra-print fabric of Miso's Hammer pants sticking out of the top, I know it's my things I'd left at the Noh family guesthouse.

After taking inventory, every last item of mine is accounted for, minus the clothes from the department store shopping spree. It's not the clothes that I'm sad about. I don't find a note, a response—*anything* from the family that suggests any kind of acknowledgment of my letter. Then again, what did I expect?

Trying not to dwell in the past, Mom and I look ahead to the future. We decide, together, to defer FIT for one year. To our surprise, the school even agrees to transfer the partial scholarship until then as well.

For my year off, I decide to work two jobs—but this is not like some K-drama sob story. They are dream jobs, as far as jobs go, for a recent high school grad with an eye for fashion design. I work during the week at Sew Fantastic, where I have easy access to the latest sewing pattern books that I happen to catch glimpses of while replenishing stock. Plus, there's a 20 percent employee discount to sweeten the gig. On the weekends, I work at Second Time Around, where I have first dibs on any item that gets dropped off in our donation bin. Suffice it to say, between the new sewing patterns from Sew Fantastic and the fabrics from Second Time Around, I'm never at a loss for design projects. By the time I'm off to FIT in the fall, I'll have a whole new wardrobe to take with me.

True to their word, Hazel and Seb call me weekly, keeping me up to date on college life in real time. The adjustment to living out of state isn't as easy as they imagined and Hazel claims that our calls are what keep her sane. Seb agrees wholeheartedly.

Since the European trip where Seb binged *Crash Landing on You*, his first K-drama series, he has become a convert. Now we have standing K-drama viewing parties every Thursday night (and let's be real, sometimes every night of the week), and my dramas are back to being the ones on-screen and not in real life.

Even though things have been put on hold, I don't let that stop me from living my life. I can't change the past and I can't control the future, but at least I know I have people around me who I love and who love me back unconditionally. And that makes all the difference.

# EPILOGUE

## ONE YEAR LATER

My latest assignment at school is a modern-day hanbok made of different types of fabrics. Like a quilt, I patch together meaningful pieces of fabric; sky blue for my dad, deep red for my mom, even leopard print for Miso. When I secure the last stitch, my phone rings. It's Mom.

"Hi, Mom."

"Chloe-yah, it's the night before Thanksgiving. Why are you in the studio by yourself? I knew I should've found a way to go there. Or better yet, to have you come home for the holidays. It's not right that you're by yourself on Thanks—"

"It's okay, Mom." I'm quick to stop her from spiraling. Some things will never change. "I'm not going to be alone, I'm going to visit Miso, and Hazel and Seb are flying in tomorrow to meet me there." Miso has her own studio apartment off-campus and when she'd heard I'd be spending Thanksgiving by myself, she invited me over. Then when Hazel and Seb heard I'd be visiting Miso, they invited themselves over. I'm really looking forward to it.

"Oh, that's right. I forgot. I just worry about you."

I smile. "I'm going to be okay, Mom. If I wasn't, trust me—you'd be the first one I'd go to."

"That means a lot to me . . ."

"Mom? What are you not telling me?" During my gap year, not only did Mom and I work on saving up for FIT, we also spent a *lot* of quality time together. K-dramas are typically thirteen hours of bingeable material—and that's just one K-drama. Suffice it to say, we got even closer than ever before. So much so that I can *really* tell when something's not right.

"Well, I don't want to reopen old wounds, but I heard your samchon got the liver surgery. It turns out they found another long-lost 'relative' who happened to be a match."

I'm silent. There are just too many questions taking up brain space to construct an actual question.

"Are you okay? Chloe-yah, did I do the right thing by telling you?"

"Yes, I'm glad I know. Thanks for telling me. It's just . . ." I sigh deeply into the receiver. "Do you think the person was an actual blood relative of theirs?"

"I don't know. Would that information change anything for you?"

I think about her question a minute before I respond. "No, it doesn't change anything for me," I finally say. "I'm just glad he didn't die."

"I love you, Chloe-yah."

"I love you, too."

After I promise to call her as soon as I get to Miso's, we say goodbye. I flip off the lights and grab my overstuffed backpack, slinging it onto my shoulder with a grunt. As soon as I open the doors to leave the building, the crisp air hits me.

"Burning the midnight oil again?" A voice catches me off-guard.

"Oh. Ethan. I didn't realize you were still here, too." Between my assignments and the commute, I hardly have time to notice anyone in class, but I recognize Ethan instantly. His familiar medium-brown hair gets tussled in the wind.

"Wow, I've been in the room with you this whole time. I guess that tells me what kind of an impression I've left on you." He rubs the back of his head with a lopsided smile.

"Don't read too much into that. I tend to have tunnel vision when I'm working on a piece. Ask my roommates, all three of them."

"I know, I've seen you in the studio," he says with a stretched-out smile and flushed cheeks.

"Um, yeah, I . . . I've seen you, too." I want to roll my eyes at myself. Is that the best I can come up with?

"Are you going somewhere? Or is it your plan to spend the night in the studio? I mean, I can't say I haven't thought about that before. You said you have three roommates? I've got four."

"Wow, that's a lot." I chuckle. "I'm actually going to see my friend in Philly for Thanksgiving."

"Oh. A *friend*?" His expression shifts.

"Yeah. Miso. She's a family friend who's become, well, more like family, really. In fact, she gave me the material to make this headscarf." I point to the leopard-print fabric taming my wild, crazy hair. (Mom and I may have found the means to make FIT work, but fancy salons with hair-straightening treatments are a luxury I won't be revisiting for a while.)

"Oh." His mood brightens.

"Well, when you get back, we should get together and swap stitching patterns." Now we're both kimchi red, but all smiles.

"Yeah, I'd like that."

"Cool, cool, cool. Okay, better not keep you up, then." He waves, flustered.

"See you when I get back." I return the wave.

As soon as he leaves, I stand there, smiling stupidly at the back of him. Then I'm reminded of the last time I'd felt the buzzing excitement of the beginnings of a crush, and soon my smile fades.

Having some time away to reflect, I now understand better Mr. Kim's struggle between his family obligations and me—a girl he'd just met and barely knew. But no matter which angle I view it from, I still can't get behind the deception. I do, however, believe that his feelings for me—our feelings for each other—were genuine. To know that we could have been happy together had things unfolded differently makes it all the more bittersweet. Mom says it's for the best that we learned about our differences before the relationship went any further. I can't say I'm fully there yet, but knowing Mom, I'm sure she's right.

Staring at the busy Manhattan street, I take in how far I've come. Taxis whiz by, buses hiss as they open and close their doors, and people walk in endless streams, block after block. Sometimes I still can't believe I'm really here.

I check the time on my phone and realize it's getting late. I'm about to go down the stairs to the subway terminal when I get that eerie feeling that someone's staring. I turn around, expecting to see Ethan waving once more, but no one's there.

Then, out of the corner of my eye, I spot a car on the opposite side of the street, double-parked with its windows rolled down. It's dusk, so the sun is barely still peeking through the sky, and the tall buildings shadow any remaining natural light. I catch myself from lunging right into oncoming traffic. The eyes from the car window sparkle through the dark. I blink and blink again. Is that . . . Halmoni?

## THE END

# ACKNOWLEDGMENTS

I'm going to make a prediction that this is easily going to be the most heavily revised page of this book. (Update: It was.) I talk a lot about the importance of family in this book, and the truth is, I couldn't have written this book without my family (both born and chosen). I'm going to attempt to make this sound as least like an awards acceptance speech as possible, but I make no promises.

First, this book wouldn't be a book if it weren't for my agent, Andrea Morrison. Thank you for hand-holding me through my first everything in publishing (you probably didn't know what a nutcase you bargained for with me!). With you, finding the perfect home for this book has been a dream, complete with our very own dramatic pause. I can't wait for what comes next.

To my brilliant editor and real-life Hazel, Zareen Jaffery. You took this novel to a place I could never have imagined, and I absolutely loved getting carried away in K-dramas with you. When I first met you four years earlier at a writing conference, I never dreamed that I would one day be working with you. Some days I'm convinced that I must have made it all up, then an email pops into my inbox from you and I realize it's not a dream and freak out all over again! Thank you for loving this book as much as I do. Sending you a million finger hearts.

So much gratitude to Rini and Kristin Boyle for their vision of this sparkling cover (the neon sign wrecked me in the best possible way). It truly has all the K-drama vibes this book deserves, and more. Thank you to Mary Pender and everyone at Penguin Teen and Kokila for all the book love and support.

I would not have been able to write this book had it not been for the encouragement and inspiration of the inimitable Jesse Q. Sutanto. This is how much power and influence you have, to get someone who just shelved manuscript #4 and with three children at home doing the virtual school thing during the height of a global pandemic to write a brand-new manuscript in three months. You are a real-life superhero, and I am eternally grateful to you!

To Jessica Kim, who, for the longest time, was my first and only CP. I know you're a real friend because you read all my crappy chapters when I first started my writing journey and stuck around to keep reading more. Considering where we started together, it's surreal that we are now both #TeamKokila. If this were a text message, I would insert the sobbing emoji here.

Writing can be a solitary occupation, but thanks to my writing family, I never feel alone. To my #kimchingoos, Graci Kim, Sarah Suk, Susan Lee, and Jessica Kim— you're all an inspiration to me, both personally and professionally, and I am so blessed to have you in my life. Nude putchears and mochi donuts for life. To Jesse Q. Sutanto and Kate Dylan and the club that we belong to that shall not be named—thank you for the laughs and for the space that we share where we can talk about our insecurities without judgment. Last but not least, thank you Nicole Lesperance, Marley Teter, and Margot Harrison for your constant excitement and support.

To Dr. Jennifer Chang, who I've asked for ungodly amounts of medical facts that seem to always get cut from my novels—thanks for your friendship and for listening to the highs and lows of publishing. And thank you to the entire Delos Reyes clan for your encouragement and for keeping me so well-fed.

To Lee Min Ho, whom I've never met but am nevertheless grateful for—thank you for your contribution to K-dramas and your eternal agelessness. Maybe one day I'll be lucky enough to ask you about your skincare regime.

To the ones I share DNA with—being born into a family is such a crap shoot, but with you all, I feel as if I've hit the jackpot. To my mom for her strength, determination, and love of K-dramas I'll never be able to match and to my dad for his kindness, spirit of adventure, and love of books—your unfailing love and support gave me the courage to pursue my dreams. To David, who is the golden child of our family (remember when Mom said she was proud of you when we were talking about my book deal? Lol, I can't even.). I'm not even the slightest bit resentful because you're so stinking nice and supportive and the best funcle to my kids. Special shout-out to my sister, Sue, for encouraging me to write this story and for reading early versions of it even though you don't read for pleasure. I'll never forget how after reading my first draft, you told me "it's actually not that bad" lol. To my nieces, Alison and Natalie—you both have hearts of gold and my kids are lucky to have you as cousins.

To Jin—thank you for believing in me when you had no reason to. It means something when an extreme pragmatist goes out and buys a brand new laptop for his wife because she one day wakes up and says she wants to write novels. Tyler, Troy, and Kate—I love you more than words. Thank you for being my number-one fans. I don't deserve you. PS: Sorry for ignoring you when I was on a deadline.

To J.H. and J.H.—meeting you has changed my life. Thank you for opening your hearts to us and for our continued relationship.

Though this book is my debut novel, it is not the first manuscript I've written. In fact, many of my friends and family learned I was pursuing writing when I announced this book deal. The truth is, I didn't think that I, a Korean American from Tulsa, Oklahoma, could ever become a published author. So if you're wondering if it's possible, it's possible. Keep breaking that bamboo ceiling.

21982320401874